changed

T.S. MURPHY

Made in the U.S.A.
KDP ISBN: 978-1-983155-60-4

Book Cover Design by Cover Me, Darling
Editing by Victory Editing

Dedication

·······⸙·······

To all MRKH warriors.
Love is possible. It is not improbable.
·······⸙·······

"Imperfections define perfection."

- COLLEEN HOOVER, *SLAMMED*

Chapter 1

Wilmington, North Carolina

"WHAT DO YOU MEAN, SHE'S never had a period?" Kate flinched at the sound of her gran's voice carrying across the kitchen. She glanced up as she seasoned the green beans, trying to catch her mom's eye, but Meredith McGuire was too busy shushing her own mother. Sitting across the counter, her fourteen-year-old sister Miranda was snickering as she played on her phone. They were having their traditional Sunday-before-Christmas dinner, and with Christmas four days away, tonight was only the beginning. This year she was doing it all on her own, though her gran had forced Miranda to wash dishes and help wherever needed. Tomorrow she would start making cookies and Christmas candy until she was sick of it, but she knew she wouldn't get any complaints out of the rest of the house.

"Keep your voice down. She doesn't want anyone to know," her mom whispered.

"But it doesn't make sense. She's eighteen," her gran said. "Are you sure?"

"Yes, I'm sure. Do you think I'd be this worried if I wasn't sure?"

"Well, what did the doctor say?"

Her mom sighed. "They have no idea what's going on. Every appointment we make is two months apart at least because they're all specialists at this point."

"I don't get it. How did you not know she'd never had her period? She's your daughter, Meredith."

"She lied."

Kate heard her gran make a sound of disbelief. "Who lies about getting their period? Maybe it's her birth control." Her gran glared at her from across the room, as if the words *birth control* tasted foul. "I don't know why you put her on that stuff. In my day—"

"Kate's not on birth control. She said she quit taking it because she didn't need it," her mom said, cutting her gran off. "She said she's not doing anything that would… require it."

"Can we not talk about this right now?" Kate finally asked, exasperated. "You both suck at whispering, by the way."

She was relieved to hear silence from the other side of the kitchen. The last thing she needed was one of the men coming through the door and hearing the details about her missing period or speculation on why she was or wasn't taking birth control.

"You just going to keep seasoning them, huh?" her sister asked.

"What?" Kate glanced down at the pile of salt that was covering the green beans. "Shit."

"Quinn's going to gag when he eats them," Miranda said, her eyes practically filling with glee. "So much for impressing him. Or is it Andrew?"

"I'm not trying to impress anyone. Go away." She scooped the top layer of beans into the trash and hoped that it was good enough, then glared at her sister as the whiff of burning bread caught her attention. "You forgot to set the timer!"

Kate whirled around to the oven to check on the rolls, then burned her fingers trying to use a dish towel to get the pan out. She groaned at how dark they looked. The meal was slowly turning into a disaster. It was twenty minutes past time to eat, and for the life of her she couldn't remember why this had been a good idea.

"They'll be fine," Meredith reassured her as she came around the island to lend a hand. "It all looks wonderful."

"It does. I'm proud of you," her gran added, shuffling forward. "You're a natural in the kitchen, my girl. Even if you don't become a world-famous chef, you'll always be my special little kitchen helper."

"Your special helper is tired," Kate replied with a sigh. Her feet ached as she finished transferring the last of the food into her mother's Christmas-themed serving dishes. She put another tray of rolls into the oven and carefully set the timer. "Bertie loved your black-pepper biscuits, Gran. He's thinking about adding them to the menu."

"Don't give my recipes out," her gran scolded. "Someday you'll need those, and Bertie Cameron will be cooking for you."

She laughed. "I'll keep the best ones. Promise. But you have to come get me next summer and take me to the farm. I want to learn how to preserve tomatoes."

"You'll need a green thumb first," her mother replied wryly. "Killed every one of my hydrangeas."

"I watered them every day," Kate protested, earning a howl of laughter from both her gran and her mother.

"Even I know you aren't supposed to water them *every* day," Miranda said, scraping furiously at the bottom of a burned roll.

"Yeah, well at least I know how to turn a timer on," she

replied, watching as her sister threw her a discreet middle finger, although not discreet enough since her mother reached across the counter and flicked her ear.

"Miranda, go get the boys. They can at least carry the food to the dining room," Meredith McGuire ordered.

Her sister flew out of the room, red hair streaming behind her, and immediately started yelling for everyone to go to the kitchen. Kate glanced up as the door opened and her brother Jon came in, eyeing the food eagerly, followed by his best friend, Quinn Haley, and her boyfriend, Andrew Whitman.

"Jesus, you did all this yourself?" Jon asked, hefting the turkey up off the counter.

"Language, Jon McGuire," Gran said. "I won't have you sassing Jesus."

"Sorry, Gran." He winked at her even as she leveled a grandmotherly glare his way. He backed out of the room, acting like he was going to drop the turkey as Kate scowled at him.

Kate felt a presence on her other side and turned her head to find a pair of wide shoulders blocking her view of everything else. She was barely aware of her brother returning and grabbing up more food to carry into the dining room.

There wasn't any other guy in the world who could make her as brainless as Quinn Haley. His thick chestnut hair had gotten long... long enough to begin the adorable curls that she had always wanted to touch. His years on the weight lifting team in high school had helped him develop some very nice muscles, and every one of them looked good on his over-six-foot frame. Andrew, standing slightly behind him, seemed short in comparison though they were actually about the same height. At five three, Kate barely came up to Quinn's chest. She looked up into a familiar face that shouldn't give her insides the squiggles after having the world's biggest worst-secret-ever crush on him for so long, but he was standing close enough for his arm to brush against hers, and she felt heat that had nothing to do with the oven flood her face.

She had been up for hours and barely had time to shower and fix her hair or put on makeup, so she knew she looked a mess. In a dark green sweater that matched his eyes and faded blue jeans, he looked as handsome as ever.

"Got anything for me, McGuire?" Quinn asked, his eyes dancing with laughter. "I pinky swear I won't drop anything."

"You'd better not," she replied, tucking two pot holders around the bowl of potatoes and handing it to him. Her heart fluttered as his hands covered hers for a moment, and she almost let go before he had a good grip. "Careful, it's hot. Has Roxie made it yet?"

"She just got here," he replied. His expression softened a bit. "Thank you for inviting her. Inviting us."

"You're family," Kate replied simply, ignoring the little pang in her stomach at the thought of sitting through dinner with his girlfriend.

"I'm just going to wash my hands real quick," he said, setting the potatoes back down. He gave her a lopsided smile as he turned toward the sink. "Everything looks good. I've been bragging on you all week to Roxie."

"Well, it might be a disaster. Miranda burned the rolls, and the green beans were probably salted enough to cure a ham."

"It's going to be great." He was still smiling at her, and she realized that she was smiling at him, and it suddenly felt awkward since everyone was watching them smile at each other like idiots.

She turned away quickly, passing the green beans to Andrew and giving *him* a big smile so maybe all the smiling would seem less weird. "Hey, handsome… I'm sorry I've been trapped in here all day. I haven't even had a chance to sit down. Who's winning?"

"Not us," Andrew replied dejectedly. "We're down by three touchdowns."

"Maybe it will pick up after halftime."

"Not likely." Quinn snorted as he dried his hands. He grabbed the potatoes, then began backing out of the room. "Not with our defense this year."

Kate watched Andrew's blue eyes narrow after Quinn left, and it wasn't the first time she had noticed him get riled over anything Quinn related. Andrew had reacted with disbelief when he had found out that her brother's best friend lived with them during the summer and on the weekends they came home.

"Why is he here again? Doesn't he have his own family?"

Her mother and Gran exchanged a look, then both grabbed a dish and left the room quickly.

"He's here because he belongs here," Kate said, turning to pull the last batch of rolls from the oven. She piled them high into a bread basket. "Be nice. Quinn is part of our family. I told you, there's nothing to worry about. He thinks of me like a little sister. I mean, he brought his girlfriend with him. His *live-in* girlfriend."

"Sorry," Andrew said, giving her a quick smile. "I didn't mean to sound jealous."

"Uh-huh." Kate leaned over and gave him a kiss. "That didn't sound jealous at all. You don't have anything to worry about. He's only got eyes for Roxie Rogers."

"Sounds like a stripper name."

"How would you know what a stripper name sounds like?" Kate replied, arching her brow at him. "Now go, before it gets cold."

Kate grabbed the rolls and followed Andrew into the dining room, where her family was already seated and arguing over football at one end and politics at the other.

Kate set the bread down on the table and took a seat between Andrew and Quinn's girlfriend. Roxie Rogers, Kate thought glumly, would probably make a fantastic stripper. She was tall with endless legs and a tan that she could probably get after a day in the sun and the kind of Gibson-girl figure Kate had seen in her gran's old pictures. She had curly blond hair that was always styled perfectly and expressive brown eyes enhanced by dark makeup that looked ridiculous on Kate but perfect on Roxie. Her hand was clenched tightly around Quinn's, and she probably felt out of place in her distressed band T-shirt and jeans, but Kate thought she looked edgy and beautiful. A little silver stud winked in the crease of her pert nose, and part of a tattoo peeked out from her sleeve. It looked like a tattered butterfly.

"Hey, Roxie. Have you met my boyfriend Andrew?" Kate gave him a little nudge when his gaze lingered on Roxie a beat too long. "Andrew, this is Roxie."

Roxie greeted him with a little wave, then turned her attention back to her empty plate.

Since Quinn hardly ever talked about her, Roxie was a mystery to most of them. Jon complained about her frequently after she moved in the apartment he shared with Quinn at Duke, but Kate mostly ignored him since he complained about everything.

"Thank you for inviting me," Roxie murmured, sounding a little embarrassed. "This house is amazing. Now I know why Quinn likes it here so much."

"He only comes here for the food," Kate whispered, grinning at Quinn. "Mom threatened to put a padlock on the refrigerator after Thanksgiving. Our leftovers only lasted a day."

"He does like to eat. A lot."

"Thanks," Quinn said dryly.

"No sense in denying it, Haley," Kate replied. She

grinned at Roxie. "So are you taking classes at Duke too?"

"No." Roxie fidgeted. "I got a job waitressing. I never was very good at school."

"Me either. I'm working at Cam's. Some nights I still waitress, but most of the time I help his line chef." She leaned forward to look at Quinn. "Eight months until law school. Are you ready?"

"Not even close, but I did get promised a summer job at a firm here in Wilmington," he answered, his expression full of eagerness. "It will probably be less than I make working at the mechanic shop, but I'll get my foot in the door."

"That's all that matters, right?"

"Yep." He helped himself to some potatoes that had made their way down the table. "I can't believe you did all this by yourself. Everything looks amazing."

"Except for the rolls," Kate replied, shooting a glare at her sister.

"I bet they'll taste good anyway," he replied, smiling at her. He glanced at Roxie. "Kate makes the best pecan pie in the whole world. You've got to get that recipe and make it for me."

Roxie's face barely moved, but Kate saw something in her gaze shift, like a warning. Quinn must have noticed, because he shut up and turned around and started talking to her gran on his other side.

"It's my gran's recipe," Kate said, trying to smooth away any awkwardness. Did the gorgeous Roxie not know how to cook? "It's really easy to make. I can give it to you if you want."

"Sure." Roxie gave her a bland smile. "That sounds good."

Kate thought she might have been making Roxie feel nervous instead of welcome, so she directed her conversation to Andrew beside her and Jon across the table, but she could hear Roxie speaking to Quinn shyly. He caught her looking at them a couple of times, and she couldn't look away fast enough, hoping her face didn't reflect any emotions she was feeling. She'd only hero-worshipped him since the first time Jon brought him home—a wide-eyed, skinny kid covered in bruises and wearing clothes that didn't fit, who had been afraid to touch anything in the house for fear of breaking something and being punished or sent away. Her mother always ensured that he left with a full belly, new clothes, and a trim to his always-shaggy hair. Hero worship slowly devolved into what had to be the worst case of unrequited love on the face of the earth.

Handsome, sweet, gentle Quinn Haley, who was completely unavailable and had never seen her as anything more than his best friend's little sister.

There was a mountain of dishes to wash, and everyone had gone back to the family room after the meal to watch the game, or in her dad and granddad's case, to shout at the television. Kate had stayed for a little while, but the sight of Roxie holding Quinn's hand on the couch and his arm around her was distracting. She tried to focus on Andrew, who was sitting beside her, but he was more interested in the game, joining her family in voicing their complaints about how much their team was screwing up. There were times, like this, when she realized they didn't really meld at all.

Andrew was a jock. He liked sports, he had perfect grades, and was always talking about all the expensive things his parents owned. Kate was a bit of a movie nerd, and her grades had never been stellar. She had been working in an upscale steakhouse for the past couple of years and had finally worked her way up from waitress to kitchen assistant. Her parents did buy her stuff, but she had chores, and she always had to throw some of her own money in for things like her cell phone or car insurance. That was one thing she had always admired about Quinn. He worked for everything he had because his parents had never been around to give him anything, though she knew his dad had been trying to be more involved in his life. Sometimes it seemed like Andrew didn't care about anything but football or going to parties, and he had no responsibilities at home. Though he was sweet, she just didn't feel the way she knew that she ought to feel about a boyfriend, and part of the reason was sitting across the living room.

When she saw Quinn steal a kiss, she was so full of envy that it was a wonder she wasn't green. Then he glanced over, saw her looking, and winked.

As soon as she'd been able to leave without it being noticeable, she'd gone to her refuge. She'd rather wash a hundred dirty dishes than watch them cuddle and kiss. Roxie seemed like a nice girl, but there was a threshold to how much Kate was willing to endure... though on her tenth plate, she was seriously considering going upstairs and just going to sleep. The dishwasher was already full, so she was washing the rest by hand, but after being up for hours on end, she was exhausted.

"Do you need help?"

Kate jumped at the voice behind her, then gave Quinn a cautious smile. She peered behind him, but he was alone. "Hey, creeper. You scared me. Where's your sidekick?"

"She's still watching the game." He glanced around the kitchen, wincing a little at the aftermath. "You cooked all this. You shouldn't have to clean up."

"It's all right, Haley. I don't want Gran in here trying to tackle it, and she will, if it sits here long enough."

He plucked the sponge from her, gave her a towel to dry her hands, and then nudged her out of the way with his hip.

"Go sit down, McGuire. You look tired."

"Oh gee, thanks. How have you had a girlfriend this long and don't know it's not okay to tell a girl she looks tired?" Kate demanded with a laugh, taking a seat on the other side of the island. "You might as well tell me to put a bag over my head."

"It's pretty bad," he said, his eyes teasing from over his shoulder. "But not that bad. You fishing for compliments?"

"No." Her face flushed. "Not from you."

"You know you don't need them," he said after a moment, pausing at his task but not looking at her. "Sorry if I insulted you."

"I can take it." She relaxed on the barstool, watching him work. She'd missed him. Since Roxie moved in with him, he hadn't been coming around as much, and when he did come home, she had been finding an excuse not to be around. "So what have you been up to? Besides school?"

"Work and school. That's me."

"All work and no play makes Quinn a dull boy," she teased, using a line from *The Shining*. He hated scary movies as much as she loved them.

He gave her a look. "Don't start quoting horror movies, or I'll leave you in here with this mess."

"Fine, wuss. Jon staying out of trouble?"

"Ha. Not really. What about you? We didn't really get to hang out this summer, and I barely saw you at Thanksgiving." He turned partially around, studying her, and she tried not to move her face at all. "What was that other guy's name? The one you were seeing this summer?"

She cleared her throat, pushing a wave of regret away. "Jacob."

"Didn't work out?"

"No. He turned out to be an asshole," Kate replied, her gaze sliding to the counter. She frowned, then cleared her throat when she looked up to find him still watching her. Her face turned scarlet. "What?"

"Nothing. You just don't cuss very much." He grinned suddenly. "If he made you cuss, it must have been bad."

He had no idea. Just thinking about Jacob made her want to punch something or cry, or both. She must not have been very good at hiding her thoughts, because he turned around and dried his hands, then reached across the counter and touched her arm briefly, looking concerned. Kate felt her heart leap at his touch and tried to remember that they were both seeing someone and he didn't mean anything romantic by it. Quinn had always been really sweet to her, but he'd never treated her as anything other than a friend.

"You okay?"

"Yeah." Kate shook her head slightly. "I just wish I'd known he was such a jerk. I wouldn't have gone out with him."

"You know all you have to do is ask, and no one would ever find the body," he said quietly, looking at her intently. "You shouldn't be worried about boys right now anyway. Have you decided on a college yet?"

"Now you sound like Mom," Kate said with a snort. "She wants me to go to school here."

"There's nothing wrong with staying here… but what do you want to do?"

"Well…" She gestured around the kitchen. "What did you think of dinner?"

"It was amazing. So you're going to do it? Go to culinary school?" he asked, grinning. "Jon is really, really excited about having a chef in the family."

"Jon is a pig," Kate said, rolling her eyes. "I'm thinking about it though. I applied to the Art Institute of Atlanta."

"You're going to be a great chef, Kate." His eyes lit with mischief suddenly, and he pulled his phone out, coming around the counter to stand beside her. "I have something to show you, but you can't tell Jon. I'm waiting for the perfect moment to blackmail him."

Kate grinned up at him. "You know he'll get you back. You remember what happened when we went swimming at Tahoe. You had to wear my gym shorts back to camp because he stole your clothes. They so did not fit."

He blushed. "Thought we weren't going to mention that… ever."

"It's a good thing they weren't Daisy Dukes," she said, snorting. "But pink's a good color on you, Haley."

"Shut up. You weren't even supposed to be out there with us. You about gave me a heart attack when you jumped in."

"Your fault for going commando that day." Kate poked him in the side. "Come on, show me. Hurry up, Haley."

"Give me a minute, brat." He took a swipe at her, mussing her hair, then pulled up a picture on his phone of Jon passed out with his head completely shaved except for several patchy spots along the top of his scalp.

She burst out laughing. "Did you do that?"

"No." He grinned. "This is what he gets for crashing at random people's houses. I tried to tell him you can't trust anyone."

Kate found herself looking up at him, studying his features that she had admired for years and trying to push away the wistfulness she suddenly felt. She had a thousand memories of him, of a friendship that had often outshone friendship with kids her own age. When Jon would complain about her tagging along all the time, Quinn was the one who would tell him to leave her alone. He'd never made her feel like she was just Jon's little sister. At least not in a rejective way. He turned his head suddenly, their faces close. The smile faded from his face, and she realized she'd been looking at him in a way that friends weren't supposed to. She'd probably been looking at him like she was curious what kind of cologne he was wearing, because he smelled really nice, and it was making her want to invade his personal space to breathe it in. Realizing he'd caught her leering, Kate jerked her lips into a smile and took a step back.

"You're going to be so dead when he sees it," she said, glancing back at his phone.

"Sees what?"

They both turned to find Roxie standing behind them, her eyes narrowed a little. Quinn held out the picture of Jon with a semishaved head.

"Oh." Roxie crossed her arms and raised her brows at him. "I hope I don't get caught in the cross fire of your pranks again."

Quinn looked a bit chagrined. "Jon set up a trap for me in the closet. That nun thing off *The Conjuring*. Scared Roxie half to death."

"That was a good one. I'll have to remember that." She touched Roxie on the arm, laughing. "Sorry. Jon and I used to do that to Quinn after we made him watch scary movies. That's why he hates them so much. But he always got us back."

"Yeah?" Roxie slipped her hand around Quinn's waist. "What did he do to you?"

"He always put fake snakes in my sleeping bag when we were camping. I *hate* snakes. One Halloween he dressed up as Michael Myers and sat on the porch for two hours. I thought he was a *decoration*. He waited until I was passing out candy and scared the crap out of all of us including some poor little boy who peed his pants. *I* almost peed *my* pants. The worst was when he got Miranda to crawl under my bed and grab my feet when I was about to go to sleep. Mom and Dad did not appreciate that much."

"No," Quinn agreed, wincing. "Miranda didn't even snitch on me, and she got grounded for a week."

"Sounds like you guys have a lot of fun together," Roxie said, a strange look on her face. Almost like she was…

jealous. Kate didn't understand why she would be jealous though. It was obvious that Quinn really loved her.

"Yeah," Kate agreed quickly. "He's like the brother I never wanted. Oh wait… I already have one of those."

"You know you like me better than Jon," Quinn said, oblivious to the look Roxie was giving them.

"Yeah, but that's only because you don't fart as much. You guys can go back to the game. I'll finish up in here," Kate said, starting to get off her stool.

"Nope." He set his hand on her shoulder and pushed her back down. "I said I'd help."

Roxie pulled up a seat next to her at the island, and they both watched as he returned to the sink and started washing dishes again.

"Believe it or not, he does this at home," Roxie said after a few moments. "He likes things neat. Your brother is a slob. No offense."

"None taken. If Mom wasn't such a clean freak, Jon's room here would look like a frat house. When he still lived at home, Jon and I used to take turns mowing, and Miranda and I cleaned the house." Kate leaned close to Roxie. "But I know half the time, Quinn did his chores for him. Sometimes he'd mow for me. It takes me all day because Dad won't let me use the riding mower after I crashed into the side of the house. He can do the whole yard in half the time it takes me just to do the front."

"That's because you're a wimp," Quinn said over his shoulder.

She flung a towel at him, catching him in the back of the head.

"Dorkasaurus."

"Brat."

Roxie shook her head, looking at them both like they were crazy, and Kate felt a pang of self-consciousness. What the hell was she doing? Flirting? With Quinn?

"I'm going to see what Andrew's up to," she said, sliding off the barstool. "Thanks for the help, Haley."

"You deserve it." He turned and gave her a thumbs-up. "You got my vote for Atlanta."

Chapter 2

"**S**O THIS IS IT," QUINN announced, pushing open his bedroom door. "Home sweet home."The McGuire house had intimidated him the first time he'd seen it... red brick on the bottom, with what he'd heard Meredith call Tudor-style gables. It didn't really look like a house that belonged anywhere in the South. It looked more like an oversized English cottage. Built in the early twentieth century, the inside was all hardwood floors and thick wood crown molding, the walls painted in warm, neutral colors. Meredith was a bit of a neat fiend and made a fuss every time she found a pillow out of place in the living room or a wet towel left on the floor in the guest bath. Quinn didn't mind and in truth envied the McGuire kids for having a mom who took pride in her house. He was always extracareful with where he left things after he became accustomed to her rigorous housecleaning standards. She even somehow made Jon keep his room clean... under the bed and in the closet... there was nowhere for junk to accumulate. If he mismanaged something, it would come up missing, and he may or may not ever have it returned to him. His mom was devious like that.

"I thought you were joking when you said you had your own room," Roxie commented, going to his bedroom window to gaze over the McGuire's immaculate yard. "This is a lot better than Vickie's dump."

Quinn leaned against the sturdy cherrywood dresser, keeping his distance from her and leaving the door open. He still remembered the first time Meredith had called it Quinn's room, as if it actually were his own… as if he was a permanent part of the McGuire family.

She had ferreted out his favorite color—blue—and the room had been painted a soft creamy white, with navy accent rugs covering the hardwood floors, along with tartan plaid drapes in a deep blue. They'd let him hang posters on the wall the way that their own children had done, and beside a poster of his favorite football team were posters of all the places he wanted to travel one day. Argentina. India. New Zealand. Going on vacations with the McGuires the past few years, he'd been to almost every state in America, but he wanted to see the rest of the world. Hopefully one day, after he had saved up some more money, he would be able to.

Roxie's attention moved over to a sketch that Kate had drawn of his motorcycle, an older Harley Dyna he had scraped money together for when he turned seventeen. Kate hadn't meant for him to see it, but he'd asked to keep it and she'd reluctantly handed the small sketch over. He had it framed on the wall next to another drawing she had done of the huge five-hundred-year-old Oak in Airlie Gardens. Roxie frowned, leaning down to inspect the signature at the bottom, which was Kate's initials.

"Have you thought anymore about taking classes?" Quinn asked, pulling her gaze away from the sketches. They had talked about it before, but Roxie always put him off. Chances were, she wouldn't get into a school like Duke, but there were plenty of other options available, like the technical college. Every time he brought it up, she became defensive. He knew that she was afraid that their status was changing… he was going to law school after he finished his business admin degree, and she still didn't know what she wanted to do. Roxie seemed to think the fact that he was going to law school meant he was trying to climb the social ladder. He wasn't. He just didn't want to be poor the rest of his life. "I wish you would reconsider coming back with me this summer while I'm doing my internship here. I'm letting the apartment go after we graduate. I can't afford it without Jon's part of the rent."

"I told you, I want to stay in Durham. My friend Crystal said I could stay with her until you came back, and they aren't going to hold my job for me. You know I hated school," she replied, cutting him with a look.

"I'd just like to see you do something, Rox. You're a great artist. You could do something with that or get a job in a salon. You're really good at cutting hair. You don't want to waitress forever, do you?"

"So what if I do?" She turned back around to face the window, only giving him her profile. "I need to go. My mom will bitch if I don't show up and she cooked something."

He heard the edge in her voice and recognized the stubborn set of her jaw. She hadn't wanted to come back to Wilmington for the holidays. They had come home for Thanksgiving and only stayed a day before heading back to Durham. He had done everything in his power to make sure she was safe when she went back to her mom's, but anytime Roxie spent time with her mother was enough to depress her for weeks on end. He felt the weight of sadness inside her as if it were his own, along with all the anger she tried so hard to keep at bay.

"We can drive back tonight," he offered gently. "You don't have to go over there."

"I'll be fine."

"What about—"

"I said I'm fine," she replied. "Don't make a big deal out of it. I don't care if you stay here. I just don't want to be around these people. I don't know them, and I'm around Jon enough at the apartment."

Her voice was so sharp he nearly flinched. Sometimes it felt like she was pushing him away, and sometimes it felt like she was clinging so tight he couldn't breathe. It had been a relief when Kate had insisted, through Jon, that Roxie come. He had hoped that bringing her here might make things easier. He'd introduced her to his father, but his relationship with William Knight was inconsequential. His real home was with the McGuires, but Roxie wanted nothing to do with them. She barely tolerated Jon, and the feeling was mutual. Jon didn't understand what he saw in her, but Roxie was the only one in the world who had ever needed *him*. They had broken up three times this year, twice when Quinn had come back to Wilmington, so he invited Roxie to come to Duke to stay for a couple of weeks. That had been almost six months ago, and the distance between them had somehow gotten greater instead of closer. There were times where he felt like he hadn't even scratched the surface of turmoil inside her.

"I'm sorry," he said, coming up to stand behind her and resting his hands on her arms. "Next time we'll save up and get a motel or something. We still can if you want to."

Guilt pricked him, but he knew Roxie wouldn't let him go to her mom's with her, and he couldn't ask the McGuires to let her stay. Usually they crashed with friends on the rare weekends they came home, but during the holidays, it was harder to find a spare couch to sleep on with everyone visiting family. Cash was tight… they both only had part-time jobs, but that was his own fault. William had offered him money when he had first gone to college, and he'd refused to take it. He briefly thought of his dad's beach house on Figure Eight, a private island about half an hour from Wilmington, but immediately discarded the idea. When he was sixteen, he used to sneak out there after finding it on his sister's social media page. She posted tons of photos of the place, a beautiful solitary paradise, and apparently his father only used it twice a year. He hadn't been there in a long time, and it wasn't like he could ask his dad out of the blue about a house he shouldn't even know about.

"It's all right," she replied, resting her head backward against his shoulder. "I just don't see how you can stand it here. They're so... perfect."

"They're not," he murmured with a laugh. "They argue, just like everyone else."

"Not like everyone else," Roxie said, her voice soft. "I bet Kate's never been slapped a day in her life. She's like a little princess here, isn't she? Her sister too."

"Rox—"

"I should go." She interrupted him. "Mom's probably burned her frozen pizza by now."

He sighed, not wanting to argue with her. "Call me if you need anything, okay?"

"You can come over after Mom's asleep if you want," she said, turning in his arms and running her hands under his shirt. She peeked up at him from beneath her lashes, pouting a little, becoming a seductive, mercurial sylph all at once. "I'll make it worth your while."

"I'm about to enter the turkey-coma phase," he replied ruefully. "I doubt I could work up the energy for that. Kate did a good job today."

"Yeah?" Roxie murmured, her hand slipping down and cupping him through the front of his jeans. "I bet little Miss Perfect wants to sneak in here later and give you another kind of job, but I bet that's one thing I'm better at than she is. Want to find out real quick?"

"Behave," Quinn said, stepping out of her reach. "It's not like that."

"No?" Roxie crossed her arms over her chest and stared at him for a moment. "You really don't see it? She has a huge crush on you. All that fake nice chitchat she made with me was really an excuse to talk to you. I could tell she was jealous of us last summer. Every time I kissed you, she looked like she wanted to cut me. And don't even get me started on your threatening her boyfriend for kissing her."

"She was seventeen, and he untied her top on a public beach." Quinn growled, his blood boiling at the memory.

"She didn't look like she was complaining," Roxie replied with a shrug. "It doesn't look like she had any problems moving on to Andrew. As long as she keeps her hands off you... but she really needs to work on her poker face."

He wanted to defend Kate, because there wasn't anything fake about her, least of all her friendliness, but he knew that would make it worse. As far as the crush, he knew. Of course he knew. Whatever Kate was thinking or feeling reflected in her eyes, and she'd been looking at him like that for a long time. Two or three years ago, it had been sweet. Now it was sometimes distracting, but she had never tried to be obvious about it. If anything, she tried too hard to hide it. Kate had turned into a very beautiful young woman, and he could understand why Roxie was jealous. He was friends with Kate as much as he was with Jon. They used to be much closer, but in the past year or so, they had both pulled away. Kate had begun dating, and Quinn had been focused on getting his degree, and he had thought she lost interest. Maybe she had. Andrew seemed like a spoiled, rich dick, but Kate had smiled at him in a saccharine sort of way, like she was in love. It surprised him that the thought of her with Andrew was irritating. Then again, he hadn't liked Jacob either.

"She's Jon's little sister," Quinn replied quietly. "I wouldn't do that to you or to her."

"She's prettier than me."

"Don't do this, Roxie. Don't compare yourself to someone else. You know you're beautiful."

"Probably still a virgin," she added bitterly. "Though I bet you could take care of that."

"Stop."

She finally broke off, caught off guard by the force of his tone. Finally having the grace to look ashamed, her eyes grew bright and she looked away, whispering an apology.

It hurt that she still didn't trust him after all that he'd done, but he knew how hard it was to trust someone. How hard it especially was for her, ever since the night her mom's boyfriend had snuck into her bedroom while her mom was passed out drunk. She was fourteen years old the first time it happened, though from the little Roxie had said, he'd been doing it long before that. Her mom kicked him out for a month before she'd taken him back, saying she no longer believed Roxie. That her precious Curtis would never do *that* to her daughter. Afraid she would end up in foster care if she kept insisting that he did, Roxie had caved and told the social worker and police that she had made everything up. Having to bottle it up again and pretend it never happened had broken something inside her that he didn't know how to fix. Curtis was long gone, but the scars he'd left behind were scored permanently on her heart.

"I'm sorry, Quinn."

He pulled her back into his arms and wrapped his arms tightly around her.

"I'm doing this… all of this… for us," he whispered. "Just hold on a little longer for me, Rox. Please."

"Okay."

"Okay?" Quinn leaned back so he could see her face. "I

love you."

"I know you do."

Her arms tightened around him, but he still noticed she didn't say it back.

The McGuire house at night was one of his favorite things, especially during the holidays. In the hours before bedtime, there were always movies or games. Sometimes Frank built a fire on the back patio, or they gathered around the kitchen table and Meredith's father would teach them how to play poker. Tonight it was movie night. Jon's parents and grandparents had the big family room at the front of the house to themselves and had relegated the rest of them to the smaller sunroom. The cushioned wicker furniture wasn't exactly comfortable, especially given his height, but Quinn lay back enough so that the hard wicker supported his head. His legs crossed at the ankles, taking up more floor space than Jon, who mimicked his pose from the little matching chair on the other side. Miranda was lying on the floor, more absorbed in her phone than in the movie they were watching, and Kate was beside him on the couch on the opposite side. She stuck a foot out toward her brother and waved it in front of him, repeating an earlier demand she had made for a massage.

"Please?"

He batted her foot away, shooting her an annoyed look. "I don't do feet. That's disgusting."

"Jon," she complained, drawing his name out into several syllables. "I've been up since four this morning. I was up all night last night making pies. Rub my feet."

"Get Quinn to do it." Jon shot his friend a quick look. "He don't mind."

"I don't?" Quinn drawled. He threw Kate a smile. "I really don't. Come on."

He patted his knee and saw Kate hesitate. She poked

Miranda in the back of the thigh with her toe.

"Miranda?"

"Ew, no. I'm with Jon. Those things stink."

"They do not stink." Kate looked mortified.

"They probably do," Quinn teased, and he leaned over and grabbed her by the ankles, swinging her feet over into his lap. "But since you did such a good job today, I'll just make sure I use extra soap when I wash my hands."

"You don't have to… That's… oh." Her eyes slid closed as he pressed his thumbs into her arches. She relaxed and let out a little sigh. "Thank you."

"Welcome." He focused his attention on the movie, trying not to think about Kate's soft, delicate feet in his lap. About her pink toenails or the fact that his arm brushed against her bare shin as he twisted and ground her feet, stretching and rubbing. He tried not to think at all, especially about the prickle of guilt that he felt, knowing Roxie would be hurt even by this innocent touch, but things had always been easy around Kate. She was so confident and happy, so beautiful and full of life that he doubted she would ever really understand him or need him, and that was something he craved.

"I hope Roxie had a good time," she whispered.

He glanced over to find her watching him. For a moment he was distracted by her slim legs, and his hands tightened over her feet when she started to pull away. He jerked his gaze back up to hers and shook off a sudden curiosity of how soft the rest of her skin might be. She had always been really pretty, but… damn. He was startled by a rush of awareness of her. The shape of her face, free of makeup and still beautiful. Her full lips and large blue eyes. She had some of the darkest blue eyes he'd ever seen, and he had noticed earlier that there was a tinge of green in the left one but not the right. She still had freckles across the bridge of her nose and upper cheeks, though most of them had faded. Miranda's freckle situation, on the other hand, was completely out of control.

"She did," he lied. Roxie had hated it and hadn't been able to leave quickly enough. "Thank you again for inviting her."

"Are you going to marry her?" Miranda asked without looking up from her phone.

"Maybe, squirt," Quinn replied. "Why, you want to be a flower girl?"

Miranda threw him a look over her shoulder, her red braid swinging around and hitting her in the other cheek. "Yeah, right."

"Better get her under control before you marry her," Jon muttered. "Psycho."

"Jon!" Kate reached across the arm of the couch and slapped her brother. Her foot ungently dug into Quinn's rib as she grappled for purchase. "That was mean. She's really nice. I like her."

"Thanks," he replied, shooting Jon a glare. He rubbed his rib cage, thinking he would probably have a bruise.

"Marriage is a big step," Kate said, settling back onto the couch. She noticed him rubbing his side. "Sorry, did I kick you?"

"With these little things?" he teased, tickling her toes. "Couldn't hurt a fly."

"Jerk." She smiled at him, her blue eyes sparkling, but removed her feet from his lap quickly and faced the television. "Thanks, Haley."

"Anytime," he murmured.

Her long auburn-brown hair hid most of her expression, but he watched her hands, noticed her twisting the fabric of her jeans the way she did when she was nervous or upset. Had it been Miranda's comment about him marrying Roxie? Or had his touch affected her the same way that it had him? She would be graduating high school the same time that he and Jon would be graduating college. He thought of Andrew, a pretty boy who lived close to the country club, who probably wouldn't need a scholarship to go to school since his parents would make enough to pay for him to go anywhere in the world. He'd scurried home right after the game, probably to wash his car, get stoned with his friends, and stare at other girls.

"How long have you and Andrew been dating?" he asked suddenly.

"Hmm?" She glanced at him, her mind obviously elsewhere. She looked at him strangely, as if wondering how his relationship with Roxie could possibly make him wonder about her own personal life. She had looked stricken when he had asked about Jacob earlier. "Andrew? About two months."

"He seems nice."

"He is." Kate smiled. "He's going to be valedictorian if he keeps his grades up. He's actually headed to Duke this fall. Maybe you guys can hang out sometime."

Behind her Jon made a gagging motion, and Quinn did his best not to smile. The chances of his hanging out with Andrew Whitman were less than zero.

"What about you?"

"Me? My grades suck," she said with a laugh. "The only thing I'm good at is cooking. Miranda has better grades than I do."

"They can't be that bad."

"She got an F in science," Miranda commented. "Dad took her car away."

"Shut up." Kate poked her sister with her foot again. "I just forgot about a test. It's all these stupid doctor appointments Mom has me going to."

"What?" Jon asked.

"What doctor appointments?" Quinn demanded.

They spoke at the same time, and Kate shook her head,

her hair cascading down to hide her face.

"It's nothing. I don't know why she's making such a big deal out of it."

Miranda turned on her hip to look at her sister, and they battled silently for a few moments until Miranda rolled her eyes and turned back around.

"Are you sick?" Jon asked, actually sounding concerned.

"No. Just forget it," Kate muttered. "It's stuff you don't want to know about."

"Seriously." Jon studied her. "Are you sick? You do look kind of pale."

"I'm fine." Her face started turning red, and her hands turned into fists in her lap.

"Girl stuff," Miranda clarified, looking at Jon meaningfully. "Lady business."

"Okay, okay," Jon replied, holding his hands up in surrender. "I *definitely* don't want to know about it. Geez. Can we just watch the movie please?"

"Yes, please," Kate said quickly. She pulled a pillow up around her stomach, her arms tightening around it.

Quinn watched her for a few moments, wondering if everything was all right, but he was only slightly more willing to talk about it than Jon was. He didn't know anything about *lady business* other than what Roxie overshared or the few times he'd had to go get her tampons. As far as he was concerned, the mechanics were a welcomed mystery, only to be explored for the purposes of sex. He wore a condom, every time, because he didn't know if he would ever be ready to be a father, but he damn sure wasn't going to do it until he had a steady job and didn't have to depend on anyone for a handout. He pushed the thought of Kate's problems away. He couldn't help her.

If his heart wanted to reach across the couch and pull her into his arms, that was his heart's problem. He certainly had no intention of listening to it.

Chapter 3

·····◦℘◦·····

W HEN SHE GOT HOME FROM Cam's the next day, Quinn and Roxie were out to dinner with Quinn's father. She knew, deep down, that their time together was coming to an end, but the thought was depressing. She would be going off to college soon, and he would be consumed by law school… and probably end up married to Roxie before finishing. He had a determination about him that most guys his age lacked. He was definitely more responsible. He'd confessed once that he had a plan, and like dominoes falling, she had watched him achieve every last checkpoint. Top honors in high school, then a full scholarship to Duke. He'd been accepted into law school. She knew that was where his father had gone to school. Jon had told her once, right before they'd graduated from high school, that the father Quinn barely knew was a local Wilmington attorney who had a wife and daughter who knew nothing about him.

In the past few years, his father had become more involved in his life, though she didn't think the relationship was very strong. She had heard Quinn joke once that his dad only ever called him *kid*, like he might not know what his name was, and she knew that they always met in places it was unlikely William Knight would be recognized talking to a young man who strongly resembled him.

Climbing the stairs, she dropped her bag just inside her bedroom door and walked to the end of the hallway to Quinn's room. She didn't come in here often. It was his sanctuary, and she would die if he found out how she felt about him. Miranda knew. She was pretty sure her parents knew because her mom was like a ninja, sneaking into rooms when no one was paying attention just to check up on them. She pushed the door open and walked over to the desk near the window, switching on the lamp. Jon's car was gone, and she knew her parents and grandparents had gone to do last-minute Christmas shopping. She had no idea where Miranda was. Probably in her room, stalking her classmates online like usual. Kate sat down at his desk, studying the framed photograph he had of Roxie.

In the image, Roxie was looking down and sunlight shone from behind her, making her golden curls look a bit like a halo. There was a smile on her face, as if she'd just been caught laughing but the camera was seconds too late to capture the exact moment. There really wasn't much left of Quinn in this room other than a few clothes that probably didn't fit anymore. He'd taken most of his things to Duke to the apartment he shared with Roxie.

Kate switched off the lamp, swallowing against a lump of emotions crowding her throat. She should really give Andrew a chance. She hadn't dated much in high school, always holding out hope. Looking back. Looking forward. Never at what was in front of her, because what she wanted wasn't there.

"Hello?" Miranda's voice called out nervously from the hall. "Quinn?"

"It's me," Kate replied.

"You scared me." Miranda pushed the door open, then

flicked the overhead light on. "Why are you sitting in the dark? In here?"

"Just thinking."

Miranda, who was nosy enough to have routinely searched both her room and Jon's, had probably not left Quinn's room undisturbed. Her sister gave her a look that only a sister could.

"You should tell him that you love him."

"He's in love with someone else," Kate said quietly. "And anyway, I don't know if I do or not. It's stupid."

"I know it's stupid. You should just tell him and get it over with. You're way prettier than Roxie."

"Pretty doesn't have anything to do with it, Rand," she murmured. "They've been together a long time. They *live* together. And it would be weird if I told him and he didn't feel the same way."

Miranda was silent, as if the thought of him turning her down had never occurred to her.

"So are you going to do it with Andrew?"

Kate rolled her eyes. "I am not having that conversation with you. No way."

"Well? I know you've never… you know." Her sister made a motion with her hand. "It's kind of weird, actually. Some of the girls in my class have already done it."

"Well they shouldn't be," Kate replied, her face heating. "I don't want to talk about it."

Miranda looked embarrassed suddenly, and Kate reached for her sister's arm.

"Don't let some guy talk you into it, Rand," she said forcefully. "You're too young to even think about that kind of stuff. And just because the girls in your class are doing it, doesn't mean you should. Half the girls in my class had sex by the time they made it to ninth grade. Don't give in to the first guy who makes you feel… like that. I'm eighteen, and

I still don't know if I'm ready."

She didn't tell her sister the truth. That she'd already tried—and failed—to lose her virginity. That awful experience was what prompted her to tell her mother that she'd never had her period. Her mother had looked at her with the strangest expression for a moment, as if she'd meant that she *missed* a period. Kate had to emphasize the *ever* part through a series of awkward confessions until her mom understood. She'd never… ever… gotten her period. For years she had been lying about it because it was easier than answering her mom's embarrassing questions that started when she turned twelve. She accepted the pads her mom bought her until she had so many boxes in her closet she started throwing them away.

By the time she turned sixteen, she started to wonder why she hadn't had her period yet, so she asked her doctor while her mom was out of the room. He'd looked a little perplexed but assured her that it would come whenever it was time. After her confession a few months ago, her mom had taken her straight to a gynecologist who did a brief exam then referred her to another doctor. Her next appointment date was coming up, and she dreaded it, because there would be another physical examination. She knew and had known for a while that something was wrong with her. She just didn't know what, and the longer it went on, the worse her anxiety was becoming. Especially after what had happened with Jacob.

"I didn't hear your car pull up," Miranda said, going to look out the window.

"It wouldn't start. One of the waitresses gave me a ride home." Kate sighed. "I'm tired. It's been a long day."

"I was going down to get some ice cream… Want some?"

"Yeah." Kate reached over and tugged on the end of her braid. "Let's get out of here, brat."

The sound of Quinn's voice pulled her out of the movie she was watching, and she pressed mute so she could hear what he was saying. His voice was quiet, but it was deep and carried through the slightly open door. He sounded upset, mainly because he was sighing loudly, cursing, and apologizing all in the same breath. When he cursed in the house, he always corrected himself at the last possible second, using "shoot" instead of "shit" or "dang" instead of "damn." He didn't appear to have a substitute for the *F* word, and after it slipped out, he said shit dammit, then apologized.

"Look, just wait for me. Please? I'll be downstairs in a minute. Okay? Fine."

Kate walked to her bedroom door, then down the hallway and knocked on his door. He was throwing clothes into a duffel bag.

"Is everything okay?"

He froze, his gaze snapping up to hers. "Are your parents here?"

"No." She glanced at the clock. "Mom said they would be back around ten, so they should be here soon. Are you leaving?"

"Yeah." He sounded angry. "Roxie had a fight with her mom. We're going to go back to Durham."

"Tonight?"

He lifted a shoulder, snatching things off his dresser. "We don't have anywhere else to go."

"So stay here." When he just kept throwing things into his bag, Kate walked up to him and stopped him. "Quinn, you'll stay here. I'll talk to Mom."

He shook his head. "I can't ask your parents to let my girlfriend stay here. They've already done enough."

"We have five bedrooms. Gran and Granddad are

staying in the attic room." She grabbed the bag from him and threw it across the room. "You don't have to ask them anything, and you should know they wouldn't care."

He groaned, tilting his head back to look at the ceiling. "Look, Roxie is really upset right now. She wants to be alone, and I don't think she would feel comfortable staying here. I appreciate it, Kate. I really do."

"You are not driving back to Durham and spending Christmas somewhere else." She licked her lips, nervous, and tried not to sound as desperate as she felt. "This could be your last Christmas with us. Please don't go. Miranda and I got you a gift. And so did Mom and Dad. They'll be disappointed if you leave. Just let me call her. Please?"

He blew out a breath, his expression torn. "God, this night has sucked. First my dad and then this. Fine. You can ask your mom, but convincing Roxie is another story."

"Just give me two minutes." She ran back to her room and talked to her mom, who sounded like she'd had several glasses of wine, so Kate could have asked her if she'd get her a tattoo and it would have been the best idea ever. Then she snuck outside and knocked on the window to Roxie's old car.

Roxie rolled down her window, then glanced at the house. Her eyes were red from crying and the skin beneath them streaked with black mascara. It looked like she had a handprint on one of her cheeks, and Kate's heart broke for her. What kind of mother would do this?

"Hey. Is he not coming?" Roxie asked, her voice slightly hoarse.

"*You* are coming with *me*." Kate opened the door and grabbed her by the hand. "Do you have a bag or something?"

"What?" Roxie pulled free, a frown forming on her lips. "What are you talking about? We're about to leave."

"No, you're about to stay. Come on. I've already asked

my mom, and she's fine with it. You can stay with us this Christmas."

She heard the front door open and Quinn's footsteps as he jogged down to them. He glanced between the two of them, looking nervous.

"Quinn?" Roxie's voice was laced with anger. "What is going on?"

He closed his eyes, another sigh rumbling out of him. "I told you this was a bad idea."

"It's not a bad idea," Kate insisted. "Would you stop being stubborn? It's late. If you want to leave in the morning, fine, but tonight you stay. Roxie can have your room, and you can sleep on Jon's futon."

"Separate rooms?" Roxie echoed.

"Well, yeah," Kate replied awkwardly. "My gran is conservative. But if you stay, you can help me make Christmas cookies, and I can tell you all kinds of embarrassing stories about Quinn, like this time at a ranch in Wyoming—"

"Hey. Uh-uh." Quinn narrowed his gaze at her. "That's not fair."

"And in Colorado his horse had lain down in the creek with him and got all his gear soaked," she teased, laughing at him. "We take a lot of camping trips west. My dad likes to pretend he's a cowboy once a year, and he drags us out to guest ranches. Quinn doesn't seem to have a cowboy gene. At all."

"The horses hate me," he muttered.

"He gets left behind a lot. He always seems to get a horse that likes to eat, even though they tell us not to let them stop on the trails. And he whines *so much* about his butt hurting."

"I changed my mind. We're going back to Durham," he said, but he was laughing. He glanced at Roxie. "What do you say? One night and we can decide in the morning?"

Kate squeezed her hand. "I would really like it if you stayed. So would my parents. Please?"

"Yeah, okay." Roxie sighed, then reached in and grabbed her keys out of the ignition. "One night. But you have to tell me about Wyoming. And Colorado."

Kate slipped her arm through Roxie's and steered her toward the house, throwing Quinn a victorious look as he grabbed Roxie's things out of the car. She couldn't exactly read his expression, but he looked somewhere between amused and terrified.

<hr />

By the time her parents and grandparents came home, her mom was stumbling and giggling a little and her dad was sneaking a kiss in the upstairs hallway. Her parents had long grossed them all out with their public displays of affection, but Kate had always secretly thought it was sweet that her parents were still in love. She poked her head out of her bedroom and cleared her throat, earning a slow blink from both her parents.

"Uh, hi, Katy-did," her dad said. "How's it going?"

"Good." She leaned against her door, giving them both an amused look. "Mom, did you have fun tonight?"

"Yes," her mom replied, sounding like a snake. "I had fun. I bought you a present. It's a bracelet."

"Meredith." Her dad laughed. "You weren't supposed to tell her."

"It's blue," she added, pronouncing her words carefully. "Are your friends still staying tomorrow night?"

"Is that okay?"

"It's going to be a bit crowded… but I guess it will be. Just tell Brittany to tone it down a bit."

"I'll try," Kate murmured. Telling Brittany to tone anything down was like waving a red flag in front of her face.

"Where are Quinn and Roxie?" her mom asked.

Kate pointed to Jon's door and mouthed Quinn, then at Quinn's door and mouthed Roxie's name, but her mom had stopped listening and was nuzzling her dad on the neck. Kate looked away, a wave of embarrassment forming.

"I'll go look at your car tomorrow," her dad said, his voice sounding strained.

"Thanks, Daddy."

"Anything else?"

"Uh, no. Good night." Kate slipped back in her room and closed the door. She was just climbing into bed when her phone went off, and her heart gave a funny little kick when she saw a text from Quinn.

> **Quinn:** Your parents are so cute it's sick.
>
> **Kate:** I KNOW.
>
> **Quinn:** Your gran just snuck in here and told me I had better behave.
>
> **Kate:** OMG. I'm so sorry. Did you pinky swear that you'd be a good boy?
>
> **Quinn:** Ha. Ha.
>
> **Quinn:** Thank you for helping me tonight.
>
> **Kate:** No problem.
>
> **Quinn:** No, really. THANK YOU. It's hard for her to be around people she doesn't know, and tonight was really rough on her.
>
> **Kate:** I'm glad I talked you in to staying. Both of you.
>
> **Quinn:** Did I hear you tell Roxie you were making cookies tomorrow?
>
> **Kate:** Seriously? You're thinking about cookies at midnight?
>
> **Quinn:** I always think about cookies.

She laughed against her pillow, then turned her FaceTime on. He was laughing when he answered.

"I made some cookies earlier today. I was trying a new recipe," she whispered. "They're in that little tin by the microwave."

"What kind?" His eyes lit up.

"They're snickerdoodles."

"You're my favorite short person," he whispered back. "Thank you."

"Good night, Haley."

"Night, McGuire. By the way, your brother farts in his sleep. I need a gas mask."

"Would you two shut up?" Jon mumbled. "I'm trying to sleep. Bring me cookies."

"No one said anything about cookies, you asshat. We're talking about Wookiees," Quinn retorted. He glanced back at his screen. "I have to go. See you in the morning."

She sighed after she had hung up, feeling a load of guilt and pleasure that she couldn't fathom trying to straighten out in her mind. It was the best thing in the world to talk to him, to text him.

The best and the worst, because she knew that she had three more days until Christmas, and she had to stop staring and drooling and fantasizing about him because she had all but coerced his girlfriend into staying with them just so she could see him for a little longer.

After a morning cooking marathon the next day, Kate went into the sunroom where Jon was just putting on a movie. She had let her mom handle Roxie's multiple protests about staying, and after bribes, threats, and outright manipulation, the poor girl had finally given in. Quinn had moved his things into Jon's room, and Roxie had settled into Quinn's. With her friends coming over in a few hours, the house was about to be packed, but her parents had never minded having a full house, especially during the holidays. Kate watched the opening credits of the movie Jon had put in and rolled her eyes. She was not in the mood for *Die Hard* even if she did think it was a Christmas movie.

"Miranda, do you want to watch a movie in my room? We've already seen this a million times."

"It's a classic," Jon protested but didn't offer to change it.

Miranda glanced at Roxie, then gave her a quick smile. "Sure. Roxie, do you want to come?"

Roxie lifted her head off Quinn's chest, and though Kate was sure she wanted to say no, she agreed, following them up the stairs.

It felt weird having Roxie in her room, but she did her best to ignore her as she put on a romantic comedy. She sensed, more than saw, Roxie studying the things on her dresser, then on her vanity.

"Where was this taken?" Roxie asked.

Kate glanced over, her heart skipping when she saw a picture of her brother and sister, Quinn, and her, taken together. There were other photos from that trip, and the ones of her and Quinn alone were tucked away out of sight, thank goodness.

"Two years ago... that was at the Grand Canyon."

"Your mom and dad didn't mind him going on family vacations?" Roxie asked.

"No, of course not."

"I don't suppose his mom or deadbeat father ever coughed up any money for your parents either. They probably spent a fortune on him, as much as he eats."

"He paid for his own food, and my parents never cared about that," Kate replied softly. "As far as I know, he hasn't spoken to his mom in a few years. I don't know much about his dad."

"Vickie isn't that bad," Roxie murmured. "He could have had worse."

"I think it was her boyfriends that were mean. He wouldn't ever say. I just assumed." Kate plucked at the ruffles on her pillow. "Vickie used to show up here sometimes, drunk off her ass if he stayed over here longer than she thought he should. My parents put a stop to that eventually. I know it embarrassed him."

"He never cried on your shoulder?" Roxie asked, a biting, mocking edge to her tone. "I bet he wanted to."

She exchanged a glance with Miranda, who was looking at Roxie with wide eyes.

"Uh, no. I've never even seen him cry," Kate said, letting out a laugh that sounded strange even to her own ears. She pushed the buttons on the remote, bringing up the movie quickly, then settling back beside Miranda on the bed. "Come on up." She patted the mattress beside her.

"I'll just lie here," Roxie said, kicking off her shoes and stretching out in front of them.

Kate tried not to compare herself to Roxie, but the differences between them were so vast. Roxie... blond, tall, tanned. Herself... reddish brown, petite, pale. She knew a lot of guys thought she was pretty or cute, but she had never been called sexy. She noticed another tattoo on Roxie's ankle, a delicate, broken chain. She wondered if Quinn had any. With the summers they spent at the beach, she'd seen most of his body. It wasn't hard to look at, with all those muscles and tanned skin.

"I'm going to get some cookies. You guys want anything?" Miranda asked.

"Sure, I'll take a couple," Roxie said.

"Ugh. I don't even want to smell cookies right now," Kate replied, making a face.

"This movie have any love scenes?" Roxie asked once

Miranda was gone.

"I… I'm not sure," Kate replied.

"Staying in this house is going to kill me," she said, giving Kate a wicked, knowing look over her shoulder. "Quinn's going to be a prude, I can already tell. I tried to get him to come to his room last night, but he chickened out. You should have seen his face. He looked like a teenager who was about to get busted by his parents."

"Really?" Kate blushed. "We're not like, religious or anything… Well, my gran is. She actually had a talk with him last night. She can be kind of scary when she wants to be."

"So he never tried anything with you?"

"Quinn?" Kate stared at her, shocked.

"Well yeah. That's kind of every bad boy's dream isn't it? The best friend's little sister." Roxie raised her brows. "And Quinn is definitely a bad boy. Y'all think he's this perfect little college boy. You don't know him at all, do you? He's a dirty fighter and even dirtier in bed. Just between us girls, sometimes he likes it a little too rough. Like Christian Grey on steroids… spanking, handcuffs… the whole deal. Last week we almost got caught in the bathroom at a bar off campus. It was superhot. He loves that kind of kinky shit."

Kate didn't know what to say. Heat flooded her, and she tried to block out sensual images of Quinn Haley doing dirty things, but they etched themselves into her heart. She glanced up and saw Miranda standing in the doorway, a look of shock on her face, and her sister was giving Roxie a look that she knew all too well. Miranda might be a brat, but she was a loyal brat. Roxie was in danger of being shoved off the bed.

"Maybe he loves it because you're a sl—"

Kate's hands flew up to stop her, but the word bounced through the room, followed by Roxie's laughter, hard and bitter.

"That's right, little girl," Roxie murmured. "And he's my little slut too."

"Miranda!" Kate turned around to look at Roxie's smug expression. There was a challenge there, unspoken but clear. "Don't talk like that in front of my sister. She's only fourteen. Would you both apologize, please?"

"Sorry," Miranda mumbled insincerely, and Roxie turned back around to face the television, clearly not sorry.

"I have a big surprise planned for him New Years. We'll have to make up for lost time when we get back home. He likes it when I dress up for him."

Miranda slid a glance at Kate, and she could practically see her baring her teeth. "Yeah, he really liked Kate's Catwoman outfit at Halloween. He gave it a heart emoji."

Kate squeezed her arm in warning. "Shut up, Rand."

"A heart emoji, huh?" Roxie gave Kate a smile that was the equivalent of a pat on the head. "That's supersweet. We're talking about getting matching tattoos. Maybe we'll get matching heart emojis."

Her face heated in embarrassment along with a healthy dose of jealousy. "That sounds permanent."

"Oh, it's permanent," Roxie agreed. "Everything about *us* is permanent. As soon as Jon moves out, we're going to talk about making it official. Of course, Quinn won't be able to stay here anymore once we start a family. I know he'll miss you guys though."

Miranda began to speak, but Kate elbowed her. She sensed Roxie's jealousy and considered herself warned, but it wasn't fair for her to cut him off from everyone who cared about him. She honestly couldn't blame her because if Quinn was hers, she would guard him with a pitchfork, but this girl was so damned beautiful and Kate didn't understand where the animosity was coming from. Quinn had tunnel vision, and in three years, it had never strayed.

"Quinn will always have a home here," Kate said, trying to keep her voice even. "He thinks of Miranda and me like sisters. Jon is his brother in every way that matters."

But Roxie wasn't listening anymore. She'd slid off the bed and was staring at Kate with what looked like outright hatred.

"You just make sure he keeps thinking that. Because I don't share."

Then she turned around and walked out, leaving Kate and Miranda staring after her in shock.

"Wow," Miranda said after a few moments. "Jon's right. She is psycho."

"What is wrong with you? Heart emoji? *Really*?" Kate asked in exasperation. "Yeah, it sounds like he's totally ready to commit to me because he hearted a picture I was in with four other girls. Maybe he hearted one of them."

"Why did you invite her here anyway?"

"Because Quinn cares about her, and we care about him. That's what you do when you love someone. You suck it up and deal with it."

Miranda wiggled down into the blankets and got comfortable. "Yeah, well good luck dealing with that the next two days."

Chapter 4

·····⁕·····

QUINN'S STOMACH RUMBLED FOR THE tenth time, and he finally gave up trying to sleep and climbed off Jon's uncomfortable futon. It was Kate's fault. The house smelled like Christmas, and there were Christmas cookies downstairs that needed to be eaten. Everyone was in bed except for her and her friends who were still downstairs watching television. Roxie had gone to bed early saying she had a headache, and she really had looked a little sick. He moved silently toward the stairs, heading to the kitchen. Quinn could hear the girls laughing as he made it to the landing, Brittany's high-pitched giggle grating on his nerves.

Her other friend Lindsay wasn't so bad. She was kind of quiet and pretty in a girl-next-door kind of way. Brittany was gorgeous but extremely obnoxious. She was always flirting with him and touching him, no matter who was present. He really didn't know why Kate was still friends with her.

"So are you ever going to hit that?" Brittany asked someone. "God, I just want to take a bite out of his ass. If I were you, I'd handcuff him to the bed, and he wouldn't have a choice."

"That's because you're a ho." That was Lindsay. "He is pretty hot though. I mean… Mitch is amazing, but… damn."

They were talking about Andrew, he thought. Quinn stilled completely, waiting for Kate's reply. He felt irritation billow through him. Andrew had been over every day, stuck to her side like a burr. Meredith didn't let him go upstairs, but that didn't stop him from cornering her every time the adults left the room and shoving his tongue down her throat. It actually looked like she had been trying to avoid being alone with him.

He heard Kate mumble something but couldn't make it out. Whatever she said, both girls started laughing.

"Come on, Kate. You're telling me he's not in your spank bank?"

"Brittany!" Kate hissed. "Keep your voice down."

"God, you are such a prude. No wonder Jacob gave you that nickname."

"Shut up." Hurt colored Kate's voice. "If you're going to bring that up, you can leave."

"Sorry." Brittany didn't really sound sorry. "All I'm saying, if I had someone that damn fine living in my house, neither one of us would be able to walk for a week."

Heat flooded Quinn's face. They weren't talking about Andrew. They were talking about *him*. He froze, not sure if he should go back upstairs or make a bunch of noise coming the rest of the way downstairs. He really did want some cookies… and there was a sudden burst of curiousness inside him. Did Kate really think about him that way?

"I like my face just fine the way it is," Kate said, her voice tight. "His girlfriend would claw my eyes out. She basically told me she would. And not that it's any of your business, but he doesn't like me like that."

Roxie had threatened Kate? He wouldn't put it past her, but… Kate? It surprised him how protective he felt of her. He didn't know what had happened between them, but it might explain why Roxie had taken refuge in his room the entire day. Maybe he could get Miranda to tell him what was going on.

"Girl, he wouldn't have a choice," Lindsay said with a snort. "He's got eyes in his head, don't he?"

"It's probably her little titties holding him back," Brittany added. "Some guys just prefer something to hold on to, and that girl has a nice rack."

"Would you two just shut up?" Kate again, sounding exasperated. "I have a boyfriend, in case you forgot."

"You haven't hit that yet either, so it doesn't count," Brittany replied.

"We've only been together for a couple of months, and once again, would you shut up?" Kate's voice was hard now, full of anger. "I'm sorry if I don't sleep with every guy that looks at me longer than two seconds. Jesus, Britt. I just bought you a pregnancy test. I think you're the one who needs to give the vag a break for a while."

Quinn turned and went back up the stairs quickly before one of the girls stormed out of the family room and found him eavesdropping. When he finally closed the bedroom door, he damn well couldn't think and it felt like his ears were on fire. He pressed the heels of his hands into his eyes and groaned, trying to scrub his brain of mental imagery… specifically the idea of Kate having a spank bank and whether or not her breasts were *little titties*.

Were they small? He didn't really consider them small. They looked more like they were hand-sized, which was all you really needed…

And what the hell was he doing thinking about her breasts? Her breasts were none of his business. He had breasts… Roxie's breasts, and they definitely weren't little.

Jon's sister… Jon's sister… Jon's sister.

He groaned, then cursed, but he couldn't stop thinking.

"What are you doing?" Jon mumbled, pulling his earbuds free and blinking up at him.

"Shh." Quinn dropped his head back against the door. "Brittany."

Jon rolled his eyes and then buried his face in the pillow. "Good luck with that."

It could have been five minutes or ten before he heard the girls whispering as they finally went into Kate's bedroom and closed the door. Knowing he wouldn't be able to sleep, he headed back toward the kitchen. He was about to step off the last stair when someone came out of the family room, their arms full of blankets and pillows. They plowed right in to him, and he reached out to steady them before they hit the floor. The person squeaked, and there was only one person in the world who made that noise.

"You okay?" he whispered.

"What are you doing up?" Kate whispered back.

"I want your cookies. *Cookies.* I. Want. Cookies." He was turning into an imbecile. Quinn realized he was still holding her arms and let her go. "You headed to bed?"

"Yeah." She looked uncomfortable for a moment. "I'm hoping Brittany falls asleep before I make it up there. She's being annoying."

"Isn't that kind of her thing?" Quinn murmured, doing his best to forget what he'd heard. "You can hide out with me for a couple of minutes, if you want."

Kate glanced up the stairs, looking torn. Quinn pulled the blankets out of her arms and dropped them on the floor, then pushed her toward the kitchen. She smiled at him over her shoulder but didn't resist. Wearing a pair of pink sweatpants, fuzzy pink socks, and an oversized T-shirt, she looked adorable and tempting. Since she pretty much always looked that way, he didn't hesitate to follow.

"Is Roxie feeling any better?" she asked, going to the refrigerator and grabbing them both a bottle of water.

"I checked on her before I went to bed. She was sound asleep." No longer in the mood for cookies, he rooted around in the pantry and pulled out a bag of popcorn. "Want some?"

"Sure." Kate slid up onto a barstool and pushed one of the bottles toward him. "So what did you get her for Christmas?"

"A necklace," he answered. "She was looking at it one day in the mall. At least I hope it's the same one."

"Not a ring?" she asked, her voice light.

Quinn turned and frowned at her. "No. Why?"

"Nothing." She shrugged. "Just thinking about what Miranda asked you."

"I said maybe." He raised an eyebrow. "When I'm thirty. Or forty. Trying to marry me off, McGuire?"

"Well, we might lose the farm if you don't," she said, her voice teasing, but she didn't really look him in the eye when she said it.

He faced the microwave, silence and awkwardness between them suddenly. Frank and Meredith had been pretty overprotective of her the past two or three years whenever he was staying with them. Always popping downstairs to check on them. Sleeping with their bedroom door open. Sometimes he would hear Meredith get up in the middle of the night, and more than once she'd checked his room to make sure he was where he was supposed to be. He'd started leaving his door open so she didn't have to be so paranoid, but maybe it wasn't that she didn't trust him. He wondered if, maybe, it was Kate that she didn't trust.

He was relieved when the microwave was finally done, and he pulled the steaming bag of popcorn out and set it on the counter, then dumped it into a bowl.

"There's some seasoning in the cabinet," Kate said. "Second shelf. I'd get it, but I'd have to get the stepstool."

"Stay where you are, Shorty," Quinn replied.

"Thanks, Jolly Green."

He relaxed, their familiar teasing putting him at ease. He found the seasoning and sprinkled it over the hot popcorn, then they dived in. His mind kept replaying the conversation he had overheard, and he shoved popcorn in his mouth, trying to think of something safe to discuss.

"You're feeding me after midnight," he said suddenly, thinking of *Gremlins*, one of their favorite movies to watch together. "Isn't there a rule about that?"

"Oh no." Her eyes widened dramatically. "I forgot. Maybe you'll just get fat this time."

He started laughing, then almost choked on popcorn. "The way I eat when I come home, I don't doubt it. If I put in an order of cookies every week, would you ship them to me?"

"Roxie doesn't make cookies for you?"

"Yeah. She will if we bug her enough. Jon's a pig though, and she gets mad when she makes them and they don't last longer than a day."

"Guess you need to learn how to bake your own cookies, Haley," she teased.

He grinned, pushing the bowl toward her. "So, what does a restaurant owned by Kate McGuire look like? You going to make it one of those fancy ones I'd need a tie for?"

"No." She made a face. "Look at me. I'm pretty low maintenance. I mean, I don't wear makeup and dresses. I don't have a Gordon Ramsey personality. A lot of chefs are drama queens, and I'm more awkward antisocial. I still say 'you're welcome' when people wish me happy birthday or something equally dumb like, 'you too.' I feel sorry for my future kids. Their mom is going to be so weird."

changed

He looked at her. Short and pretty, with straight cinnamon-colored hair and big blue eyes and full pink lips. He didn't know if her skin was peaches and cream or milk and honey, but he knew it was flawless and looked incredibly soft. She didn't wear a lot of makeup, usually just mascara and lip gloss, but she didn't need more than that.

"Nah. You'll probably be pretty awesome at raising a bunch of little booger eaters," he said, grinning. "Probably bake them cookies all the time and shit."

"That's me," Kate replied with a laugh. "Mom of the year because I bake cookies and shit. Your mom didn't ever do that?"

"Vickie?" Quinn scoffed. "I'm pretty sure she made some meth in the bathtub, so that's a no. The closest she ever came to cooking was opening a can of something."

She winced, her expression sobering instantly. "I'm sorry."

Quinn wished he could take the words back as soon as he spoke them. He knew that Frank and Meredith had kept a lot of his history from Kate and Miranda. Jon had been the one who told his parents, and Quinn had been angry with him for a while, the shame he felt something so intensely private… he hadn't wanted anyone to know.

He turned away, that old embarrassment creeping across his skin. He hadn't seen his mother in three years. Not a word from her or to her. She could be in jail for all he knew. She might be dead.

"So, uh, you're thinking a barbecue joint?" he asked gruffly. "Old-fashioned diner?"

"Gran used to have one of those. A little grill that made these great hamburgers, and she had the best ice cream. It burned down when I was little."

"You're still pretty little, McGuire," he teased.

"Jerk." She showed him her middle finger, laughing at him. "I don't know what I want. I don't even know if I'd want my own place. I like so many different things and want to try everything. I'd like to go to Paris and Italy. Barcelona. I want to eat all the things," she said, grinning.

"You gonna try weird stuff?"

"Like what?"

"I don't know. Fried bat wings? Some of that fish that will kill you? Snails?"

She shrugged. "I'd try it. I mean, I've already eaten balls, so it can't get much worse."

Quinn blinked. "Uh, what?"

"Mountain oysters?" she said, perfectly serious.

"Oh." He stared at her, confused. "I ate those when we were in Wyoming. What's weird about that?"

"Quinn." She started laughing. "Mountain. Oysters. You didn't know what those were?"

"No," he replied slowly. "Do I want to know?"

"I just told you." She wheezed, doubling over on the counter. "They're balls. Calf fries."

"Jon told me they were beef nuggets." She exploded then, and he reached over the counter and put his hand on her mouth to shut her up, but she kept right on laughing until there were tears coming out of her eyes. "I'm going to kill your brother," he said, feeling faintly ill.

She put her hand over his and moved it out of the way, her eyes sparkling.

"You went back for seconds," she reminded him.

"Ugh." He shuddered, closing his eyes. "I'm really, really going to kill him."

"They tasted like chicken, didn't they?"

"Shut up, McGuire. I'm really going to puke."

Balls. He'd eaten balls.

"Do you want to get him back?" Kate asked.

He realized his hand was still touching her face, and her hand was curled around his wrist, and she must have realized it at the same time because she sat back on the barstool, blushing and looking flustered. He remembered suddenly where he was. Who he was with. That he had a girlfriend asleep upstairs, along with Kate's parents, siblings, and grandparents. Here he was, having a little intimate chat with her alone, after midnight. It wasn't the first time they had been alone in the kitchen at night. But it was the first time they had been alone when she was old enough for him to be aware of her as more than a friend. The first time he was aware that Kate's crush might have actual feelings behind it. That she might want more, and he... he'd always thought she was about the prettiest girl he'd ever seen, but she was way too good for him.

"I, uh... I should get back upstairs," he said, feeling a sting of guilt. He didn't want to give Roxie any reason to doubt him. Not once in the time they had been together had he ever looked at another girl. He also didn't want to ruin things with Kate by giving her hope that this meant anything.

It didn't mean anything... just two friends sharing a midnight snack.

Right?

"Yeah. You go ahead. I'll clean up our mess."

"You sure?"

"Go on, Haley, I got it." She raised a brow at him. "Just think about this... mayonnaise-filled chocolate cupcakes, made just for Jon."

"I ate balls, Kate. *Balls.*" Quinn shook his head. "No. It's best you stay out of this one. We're talking head shaved while he's sleeping, blow-up dolls in his backpack, and naked grandmas duct-taped to his ceiling where he can't reach them."

"Quinn." She started laughing again. "Are you really going to Google naked grandma pics just to get back at him?"

"Yep. A guy's gotta do what a guy's gotta do." He waggled his brows at her. "Even Googling naked grandmas."

Christmas Eve morning, Kate yawned into the cup of coffee her mom set in front of her as she listened to her gran complain about her insurance company and doctor. Roxie looked like she was still a little under the weather, and Kate wasn't feeling all that chipper herself. She had slept poorly after her midnight encounter with Quinn. The memory of his hand against hers had sent endless flutterings through her every time she closed her eyes, and not only that, Brittany kept sticking her feet in Kate's face. She'd lain awake for a long time, remembering the way it felt when Quinn touched her. Like electricity had skated across her skin. She'd had dozens of little moments like that with him… awareness and breathlessness. Last night had been different. He'd noticed her reaction and had withdrawn immediately, as he should have. She'd finally given up and crawled on the floor beside Lindsay and let Brittany have the bed to herself. When she had left her friends, they were both still sound asleep.

This morning he'd greeted her like nothing had ever happened, his sole attention on Roxie until her dad announced he was going to work on her car. Meanwhile, Kate felt horrible, wanting another girl's boyfriend while she had one of her own. Maybe it was time to admit that things weren't going to work out with Andrew. He had been hinting around for a while that he wanted to take things to the next level, and Kate knew she wasn't ready for that.

"Roxie, are you feeling better?" Kate's mom asked as she set a platter of pancakes down on the table.

"A little." She patted her stomach, giving them a shy smile. "I think it was too many Christmas cookies. I don't usually eat sweets, but those were delicious."

Roxie had not spoken to her since her warning. She had barely left Quinn's bedroom except during meals.

"Thank you for helping with them."

"You're welcome, Mrs. McGuire."

"You sound like Quinn. As I've told him a hundred times, you can call me Meredith. More coffee, Kate?"

Wordlessly Kate held up her coffee cup for a refill. Normally she didn't drink more than half a cup, but she was tired and it was cold in the house. Her mom handed her the hazelnut creamer, and Kate poured it liberally into the strong black coffee that her gran preferred.

"Me too," her gran said with a yawn as she held out her cup for a refill. She ran her fingers through her fluffy white hair, then turned to study Roxie for a moment. "So, Roxie. Is that short for Roxanne?"

"No. Just Roxie."

"Where are your folks from again? Are they still living?"

Roxie's expression went from neutral to tense. "My dad died when I was three. My mom isn't really... well... I guess if you know how Quinn's mom is, you can pretty much say the same thing about her. She's an addict and a drunk."

"Ah." Her gran looked contrite for prying. She reached over and patted Roxie on the hand. "I'm sorry, dear. You've found you a good one then. Quinn's a sweetheart."

"Yeah." Roxie blushed prettily. "He is. He's so romantic. We're talking about maybe a summer wedding."

"Oh, those are beautiful. My Dale was a romantic," Gran said with a wink. "Flowers and chocolates. He slipped notes in my locker at school and wrote me poetry. Took me to Asheville for our honeymoon. It was magical."

"Granddad wrote poetry?" Kate asked, doing her best to ignore Roxie's taunt. She wondered if Quinn would be surprised to hear that he was getting married soon.

"Really?"

"It was bad poetry, but it was sweet," Gran replied. "Your Andrew doesn't romance you?"

If groping counted, then yes. "He takes me on a lot of dates. We're going out tonight, actually, after I get off work… Mom, if that's okay. He's giving me a ride to work and bringing me home since my car is messing up."

"Midnight," her mom said, giving her a look. "Go and wake those girls up for breakfast. I'm not dealing with Brittany after you leave for work."

"Yes, ma'am."

"And make sure she's wearing pants this time," her mom called after her.

Chapter 5

·····ↄ❧ↄ·····

AFTER WORK, ANDREW TOOK HER to Coopers, a little late-night diner that served greasy hamburgers and milkshakes. He was nearly equal to Jon in his appreciation for food. It was a miracle neither of them had an ounce of flab on them, but they didn't. And Quinn, God help her, looked like every girl's dream with a six-pack, complete with that little V that guys got. When he wasn't wearing a shirt, her brain completely shut down. Thank heavens it was winter.

"How was work?" Andrew asked as they slid into a booth.

"Exhausting," Kate said. "I really need to get some better shoes. These are killing me."

"Why don't you get an office job or something? My dad's firm is always looking for girls to answer the phones… and you're only a half-day student."

"I like what I do." Kate leaned over and kissed his cheek. "It's the only thing I'm good at."

"Well, have you tried anything else? I mean, being a cook isn't really what most girls your age dream of doing."

"Andrew." She tamped down a flare of impatience in her voice. "I *want* to be a chef. Not a cook. You know I've applied to culinary school."

"Yeah, but I thought that was just for fun." He looked at her strangely. "Are you serious? You're going to school to learn how to cook? For a living?"

"Yes. Haven't you been listening to me talk about going?"

"So are you going to run a restaurant? Or… what?" He was frowning a little, like he disapproved.

"I don't know." She'd just had this conversation with Quinn. He'd been supportive, and Andrew sounded like she would be an embarrassment to him. Kate cleared those thoughts from her head. She always got in trouble when she started comparing guys to Quinn. "Maybe I'll go on one of those cooking competitions and become world famous and have my own show."

"Huh." He looked down at the menu for a moment. "Yeah, I guess that would be cool."

Fat chance, Kate thought. Anytime she got in front of a group of people, her tongue started moving and saying words, but they usually didn't complete any semblance of a sentence. They were just words, and there was no telling what they might be.

The waitress came over, and Kate ordered some fries and a Coke, and Andrew ordered about six different things, and she watched him eat pretty much all of it. After they left the diner, he took her hand and pulled her toward the Riverwalk, which was decked out with lights and Christmas decorations. They walked to the railing along the river and looked out over the water toward the USS *North Carolina* battleship. Andrew slipped his arm around her waist and kissed her on the side of the neck.

"Sorry if I was being a jerk. You do make some pretty awesome stuff," Andrew murmured against her ear. "I guess I can see you doing something like that. Maybe a hot pastry chef."

"Well thanks," Kate replied, giving him a little eye roll. "That's what I was going for."

"If you're going to be a chef, you're going to be hot, Katie," he replied, perfectly serious.

"Is that your way of saying I'm pretty?"

"You're beautiful and you know it."

"I wouldn't make you put a sack over your head either," she said, teasing him. He was really good-looking with thick, dark blond hair that was always styled, sharp cheekbones, and a defined jaw. Lindsay called him Captain America, and he did look a little like Chris Evans. His eyes were blue like hers, but they were several shades lighter. More Caribbean than Pacific. He was always clean-shaven, well dressed, and smelled like heaven. She didn't know what cologne he wore, but it was very manly. His nose and cheeks were red, because it was freaking cold out, and she realized that her uniform wasn't very good insulation from the wind coming off the water. "I should have brought my coat. It's freezing. Are you cold?"

"Yeah," he admitted, pulling her in close and cupping her face with both hands. "But I don't want to take you home just yet. We still have an hour… and my parents aren't home."

"Oh." Kate felt her face flood with heat. "I, uh… not tonight. I'm sorry."

He sighed, wrapping his arms around her. "That's okay. We're headed to Martinique in a few days. I just wanted to spend some time with you before I left. That reminds me… Mom wants you to come over Christmas Day."

"Really?"

"You are Andrew's Mom-Approved." He grinned at her. "She thinks you're a good influence on me. She told me that if I messed this up, she'd kick my butt."

"What about your dad?"

"Oh, he totally hates you. Said you were ugly and if I stayed with you, we'd have a bunch of ugly kids."

She made a sound of outrage but couldn't help but laugh. "You're such an idiot."

With a sigh, he grabbed her hand and tugged her toward the direction of his car. "Come on, Cinderella. Better get you home before midnight. But one day, Kate McGuire, you're going to have to stop running away from me."

"Who said I was running?"

He just smiled at her. "You're so adorable when you don't want to have sex with me."

"Andrew…"

"I'm kidding." He stopped abruptly, then gave her a quick kiss. His gaze warmed as it skated over her face. "You're always adorable. It's kind of your thing."

The garage door was open when Andrew pulled up in the driveway, and Kate could see the hood of her car was raised. It was a hand-me-down from her mom, about ten years old, but other than a couple of dents that she had put in it, the car was in good condition. Her dad, granddad, and Jon were standing around the engine talking. On the concrete floor under the vehicle she saw a pair of long legs sticking out clad in shorts and a pair of sneakers. Quinn was always doing this… he worked on all their cars. He changed the oil, spark plugs, air filters. Sometimes he did it in the garage, and sometimes he drove them down to the little mechanic shop where he had worked in high school.

"What's he doing? I could have fixed it if your parents can't afford to take it to a shop," Andrew said as he killed the ignition.

"Do you know how to fix cars?" she asked.

"No, but I could figure it out." He frowned, his

expression showing annoyance. "When are they going back to Duke?"

Kate shrugged. "I guess they'll leave after Christmas. I doubt Quinn's boss is going to let him have the rest of the year off."

He made some kind of grunting noise, then reached across the car and pulled her close. He kissed her, his tongue and teeth taking possession of her mouth a little roughly. She tried to lean back, conscious of her family standing just a few feet away, but he just kept kissing and kissing until she finally managed to twist her head to the side.

"Andrew," she protested. "My dad is right there."

He glanced at the garage, then his eyes widened and he moved back to his seat quickly. Kate looked up to see all four men staring at the car, all four of them frowning. Her face burned with embarrassment as she leaned over and gave him a peck on the cheek, then scooted out the car.

"I'll text you later. Good night," she said, then closed the door and hurried past them into the garage. She heard the roar of Andrew's engine as he backed out of the driveway, then pulled away.

"Kate," her dad called.

"Yeah?" She turned reluctantly, a half step from making it to the kitchen door. Her dad was still frowning, and Quinn was practically scowling. She noticed he wasn't wearing a shirt and pulled her gaze away from his chest before it grew roots. As cold as it was outside, it felt pleasantly warm inside the garage from her dad's heater, but she imagined the concrete hadn't been at all comfortable this late in December.

"I want to have a talk with Andrew before you leave this house with him again."

She wanted to argue. She really did, but four pairs of eyes were watching her, and only her grandfather was smiling.

She just nodded.

"What'd that boy have for lunch?" her granddad asked.

Kate squinted at her grandfather, noting a glint of mischief in his dark eyes. "What's that?"

"Just wondering if you were trying to taste what he had for lunch." Her granddad gave her a wink. "Relax, Frank. She's young and in love. Let her enjoy it while he still has all his hair."

"If she's in love with that douchecicle, I'm leaving the family," Jon announced, wincing as their granddad slapped him on the back of the head.

"Watch your damned mouth, boy. At least the kid's got a decent family, unlike that shithead she was dating this summer."

Her eyes flew to Quinn as he was putting her dad's tools back, and she saw him pause, glancing at them all from over his shoulder. He caught her gaze and turned away quickly.

"Dale." Her dad nudged her granddad. "It's getting late. Will you check on Miranda? She should be asleep by now, and if she's not, tell her she's grounded."

Her granddad left, grumbling a little as he went, and Jon followed him into the house. Hoping her dad wasn't about to lecture her, Kate walked over to Quinn and sat down at her dad's workbench.

"Thanks for working on my car. Is it fixed?"

Quinn nodded. "Just needed a new starter. I gave it a tune-up while I was at it."

He moved to the sink and started washing up, and Kate felt a rush of warmth and heaviness in her stomach as she fought the urge to stare at his bare torso. He was covered in grease from hand to elbow, some of it smeared across his stomach and back, along with his hair and clothes.

"You didn't have any work clothes that fit, did you?"

He smiled, his gaze flickering over to her. "No. I had an

old Dickies suit in the closet, but I couldn't raise my arms in it."

"Is Roxie already in bed?"

"Yeah." His smile faded, and he flexed his jaw. "She said she wasn't feeling well today. She's been asleep since just after lunch... or pretending like she was. Did something happen that I should know about?"

She was saved from answering as she heard her father come up beside her, and she turned to give him a sheepish look. He gazed back at her, his gaze full of irritation, but he didn't say anything... just stepped up to the sink once Quinn got out of his way and began washing up. Kate slipped off the stool and headed into the house, hoping her dad would be in a better mood by morning. She spotted an envelope on the kitchen counter with her name on it from the Art Institute of Atlanta and grabbed it up, her heart giving a little kick against her ribs. She glanced up at Quinn as he came into the kitchen behind her.

"What's that?"

She held the envelope up and showed him, her hands shaking a little. "I've been waiting on this to come in."

He blinked at her. "Well, what are you waiting for?"

Kate pressed the envelope to her chest, closing her eyes. The thought of moving so far away excited her and terrified her at the same time. "I'm going to cry if I don't get in. Just fair warning."

"Should I get a snot rag ready?"

She cracked one eye open. "Thanks for the reassurance, Haley."

"Open it." He crossed his arms over his chest, not even having had the decency to put a shirt on. "You know you got it."

Her hands ripped into the envelope, and she pulled the letter out. Then she started jumping up and down.

"You got it?"

She couldn't even speak, just nodded frantically, smiling and laughing all at once. "I got in!"

"That's awesome." He smiled, then leaned forward and scooped her up into a hug. All that skin coming into contact with hers was like throwing gasoline on a fire. She didn't know if she should hug him back or push him away or just give in to the boneless sensation that thrummed through her.

His arms were wrapped around her, her face pressed against his chest so tightly that it was all but squished against his skin. He smelled like grease and male sweat and whatever cologne that he'd been wearing that had faded. She didn't think she had ever... *ever* been this close to him. She'd rarely been this close to Andrew and never when he wasn't wearing a shirt. His skin was cold and felt slightly gritty beneath her cheek. After tensing for a moment, she relaxed enough to lift her hands to hug him back, but the moment she came into contact with his skin, he seemed to realize what he was doing.

"I can't breathe, Haley," she mumbled against his chest.

"Sorry." He took a step back but didn't immediately drop his hands, so she didn't drop hers either. "I'm glad you got in. You deserve it."

"Thank you."

The words were barely a whisper above the chaotic voices in her head. The ones that were screaming at her to kiss him before it was too late. Surely a friend wouldn't still be holding her like this? He was looking at her strangely, his gaze moving over her face with an almost regretful expression as little spikes of euphoria danced across her skin. She didn't think about Andrew or Roxie, because in that moment there was no room for anyone else but Quinn. She could feel guilty about it later. She could blame herself for making it harder on herself to get over these feelings instead of trying to move on. But right now all she wanted to do was move back into his arms because once this Christmas was over and summer came, it would truly be the last time… the last chance she would ever have to see if the feelings she felt were real or just some holdover infatuation.

Be brave.

Just kiss him.

You'll never know unless you do it.

"Did he hurt you?"

Kate swallowed against a spasm in her throat. He was frowning now, his gaze on her mouth.

"What?" Her heart began to pound in her ears so loud she imagined he could hear it.

"Your lips are bruised," he murmured, his expression darkening. He moved one hand and touched them with his thumb. "What the hell did he do? Bite you?"

Understanding dawned at once, and with it the cold reality of how he saw her.

Friend.

Innocent.

And why would he see her any other way? He was a man in love with a beautiful girl, confident in her own sexuality. A dull ache bloomed through her chest, eviscerating the feelings that had been aroused by his proximity and her own foolish hopes.

Never again.

"There's nothing wrong with the way Andrew kisses me," she said, her face growing hot. Her voice came out sharper than she meant it to, and she knew he heard it because his expression turned hard. "And it's none of your business."

"He shouldn't be leaving marks on you," he snapped back. "Guys that do that kind of crap turn out to be controlling assholes."

They stared at each other for a moment, Kate absorbing

fresh wounds at his words. She batted his hand away from her face and stooped down to pick up the acceptance letter she'd dropped when he hugged her. She felt the formation of tears, her eyes burning and throat tightening as she refolded the paper and pushed it back into the envelope. When she was certain she wasn't going to actually cry in front of him, she stood back up and met his gaze.

"Maybe he isn't perfect," Kate replied, her voice warbling slightly. "But I find it strange that you of all people would object to a man passionately kissing the woman he cares for. Even if he was a little *rough*."

"What the hell does that mean?"

"It means I'm old enough to decide who I want to kiss and how I want to be kissed, and you don't have any say in it because you ain't my daddy."

A throat cleared from behind her, and she glanced over her shoulder to see her actual father staring at them both with raised eyebrows. His red hair and red face was a combination she usually only saw on her sister, but she knew her own face probably looked about the same.

"Kate—" her father began.

"I'm going to bed," she announced. "Would either of you like to tuck me in and read me a bedtime story? No? Then good night."

She brushed past Quinn without looking at him, a volcanic churn of feelings close to spewing over. She felt like such an idiot. No wonder Roxie had given her a warning. It took a sledgehammer to finally break the blinders off her eyes. Quinn was never, *ever* going to see her as anything other than a friend. And if she couldn't accept that, then she needed to stay away from him, because it was obvious she couldn't control her emotions where he was concerned. Once she was in her room, she pressed the envelope from the Art Institute against her chest and willed herself not to give in to tears. She would be in Atlanta in a few months. Maybe then she would be able to move on.

Her phone chimed in her back pocket, and she immediately knew it was from Quinn. She ignored it, grabbing it and placing it on the bed facedown while she got ready for bed. Her gaze lingered for a moment on a small bruise below her bottom lip, and she glared at it, annoyed that Andrew had done it, that Quinn had pointed it out, and with herself for losing her temper. She stalked over to the bed and grabbed her phone when it chimed two more times.

> **Quinn:** I'm sorry.
>
> **Quinn:** You were right. It's none of my business. But you matter to me. He doesn't deserve you.
>
> **Quinn:** I don't want to see you get hurt.

Slowly Kate typed out the words: You hurt me every time you look at me. Every time you look through me.

Then she deleted them and turned her phone off, hoping that whatever it was she felt for him might be burned up forever in the fury of her broken heart.

The silence of his phone kept him awake long into the night. Quinn lay on the futon in Jon's room, listening to him snore and wishing that he'd handled things differently with Kate. He had crossed a line, and he knew there was no going back. Something had shifted inside him in those quiet moments he'd held her, and it was as if his mind suddenly expanded, his memories of her reshaping themselves… the perception he had of her one way, now another. He saw her at fifteen, ignoring the warning of their trail guide in Wyoming as she raced her horse across a field, hair whipping behind her. He remembered smiling just because she made you feel like you were part of her happiness, and he'd never been around someone so free with their kindness.

At seventeen on one of their camping trips she slipped away from Frank and Meredith and followed him and Jon to one of the more secluded lakes and leaped off a rock after them, not knowing he had left his swimming trunks behind. He'd been too embarrassed to say anything, and he wouldn't have... if Jon hadn't stolen his clothes and left him there—alone—with her. Kate had laughed and laughed, so much that he hadn't worried much about anything other than covering what he could with the pink shorts she lent him. By the time they'd made it back to Jon who was waiting a few feet up the trail, he was laughing too.

That was just Kate. She held a joy within herself that obliterated everything in its path. She had always been a force of good in his heart, but now... at eighteen... he recognized that what he felt for her was as confusing as anything he had ever felt. He didn't want to ruin their friendship. He didn't want to let Roxie down... but at the same time, he knew that his feelings for Kate weren't just of friendship anymore. Things had been changing between them for at least a year, when Kate had started pulling away. When it was obvious that she was trying to stop having feelings for him, and he was a bastard for realizing suddenly that he didn't want her to stop. If he was completely honest, he had always liked the fact that Kate had a crush on him. He had basked in her innocent adoration, because what guy didn't want to be admired by a pretty girl? His regard for her had always been wholesome, and he had never wanted to change that. Kate was his one, perfect thing... and now? Now she was everything. Yet what right did he have to do anything about it now? She was still in high school, and it was obvious that she had at least some feelings for Andrew too. Feelings she wouldn't have to fight, because Andrew wasn't blind and he wasn't an idiot, and in reality, he would probably mature into a decent guy one day. The thought didn't give him any comfort.

Now his conscience was riddled with sharp feelings and regret, because he knew he'd screwed up... badly. He had made promises he shouldn't have to Roxie, and he kept them for all the wrong reasons. Not because he didn't love her... he did love her but in a way that had nothing to do with romantic love and everything to do with duty and guilt, with trying to prove to himself that he wasn't the kind of man that his father was. That he wouldn't choose a woman like Amelia Knight over an underdog like Vickie Haley. He'd seen his relationship with Roxie as a mirror of the one his father had with his mother, even though he knew less than nothing about it. All that he knew was William had chosen Amelia over him, and he had built his relationship with Roxie on the foundation of sheer, self-inflicted stubbornness. He did feel protective of her. He felt a desperate need to save her.

He'd never before considered the disservice he was doing to Roxie and to himself, and now it slapped him in the face like a wave of cold ocean water. Yet even knowing all these things and being swamped by the newfound feelings that had begun for Kate, he didn't know if he could shirk the responsibility he felt toward Roxie in lieu of what he thought might be the most important person in his entire life.

Chapter 6

......ෙ⁓......

"WAKE UP, SLEEPYHEAD," QUINN MURMURED, sitting on the edge of the bed to wake Roxie up. "It's Christmas."

"Mmm." She blinked up at him sleepily. "What time is it?"

"Early. Miranda doesn't like to wait to open her presents. Come on. They're all waiting." He gave her a nudge, chuckling when she groaned. Roxie had never been an early riser.

"Be down in a minute," she mumbled. "Go on. You don't have to wait on me."

"Nope." He pulled the covers off her and threw them onto the floor. "Come on. Out of bed."

"Quinn," Roxie complained.

He leaned over and gave her a kiss on the forehead. "You have presents too, Rox. Get dressed, bunnykins."

She gave him a look. "*Bunnykins?* No."

"Sugar pie?"

"One more and I'll punch you," she warned, only half teasing.

"Come on peach face, out of bed."

She threw a pillow at him, smacking him in the head.

"You guys coming?" Jon asked, knocking tentatively at the door. "Miranda's about to have a meltdown."

"Yep. If I have to carry her," Quinn replied with a grin.

"Try it," Roxie grumbled, finally moving to a sitting position.

They had barely made it downstairs when Miranda started ripping open paper like she was a Chihuahua on crack. Frank passed out gifts to everyone, and he was happy to see that the McGuires had gotten Roxie something too.

"Quinn said you liked to draw," Meredith said after Roxie had opened her gift—a fancy set of illustration markers. "I hope they're all right."

"Yeah, um, thanks." Roxie jabbed him in the side. "I didn't get them anything."

"It's okay. I put both our names on theirs," he whispered. "It's a candle set."

Frank and Meredith had gotten him some clothes, and his present from Kate and Miranda was a new leather messenger bag. Her gran made him a quilt, so that would make this his third or fourth from her. He never exchanged gifts with Jon by mutual, manly agreement.

"Here, young lady, I think this is yours," Frank said, passing Roxie the gift he'd placed under the tree for her.

"Thank you," she murmured. Her brown eyes lit up a little when she saw who it was from. "You didn't have to get me anything."

"Like I was going to skip my sweet pea." Quinn put his arm around her and squeezed, watching as Roxie opened her gift. It was a delicate gold chain with two linked hearts connected in the center.

"Oh, baby, it's beautiful," she whispered. "I love it."

She turned and pressed her lips to his, and he tried to push away the guilt he had been feeling. Kate had never replied to his texts. He decided that for now, he wasn't going to do anything. He wanted Roxie to have a good Christmas. Once they got back to Duke and things settled down, he was going to be honest with her about his feelings for her and hope that she could forgive him. Maybe by the time they got back, he could even figure out what his feelings were, other than conflicted.

"Kate, this is yours," Frank said. "It's from Quinn."

Roxie stiffened instantly.

"From both of us," he added, wincing when he realized he hadn't added Roxie's name to her present or to Miranda's. "It's nothing special."

"It's a Julia Child cookbook," Kate exclaimed after she opened it, beaming at him. The sight of her smile made the shitty feeling he had been carrying around disappear. "I've been wanting to get one of these."

She opened the book on French cuisine, and her expression softened.

"Aw," Miranda said, reading over her shoulder. She grabbed the book out of Kate's hands and stood up, reading the inscription he'd scribbled in. "He wrote 'To the greatest chef in Wilmington and the greatest in wherever else life takes you. Your biggest fan.' That's so sweet. Isn't it sweet, Kate?"

Quinn felt his face turn red all over, and Miranda gave him a little grin over the top of the book, then flicked a glance over at Roxie that had *screw you* written all over it.

"Yeah, it was sweet." Kate's face was as red as his own. She grabbed the book out of Miranda's hand and frogged her sister in the leg. "Thanks, Haley."

"Welcome," he replied, his voice gruff from embarrassment.

What in the hell had possessed him to write that? He tried to take Roxie's hand, but she brushed him off, her glare cold enough to bring a snowstorm.

"Just friends, huh?" she seethed softly. "Like a *sister*?"

"Roxie." He tried to touch her again, and she gave him a look that indicated he'd lose his hand if he did.

She leaned in close. "You're a bad fucking liar, you know that?"

Then she got up and left the room, leaving everyone staring after her in surprise.

Quinn gave her a few moments to cool down, then slipped upstairs as the McGuires resumed their Christmas. As he had expected, she was throwing everything she could into her duffel bag. He sat on the end of the bed and waited for her to look at him, but she refused. The framed drawings that Kate had given him were smashed on the floor, and his fingers twitched with the urge to put them back in their place.

"Are you screwing her?" she finally asked, her voice breaking.

"No." Quinn met her gaze. He knew then that no matter what he did, he was going to hurt someone. "I've always been faithful to you."

"But you don't love me." Her eyes filled with tears as she stared at him. "Do you?"

For the first time, he hesitated. "I do love you, Roxie. After everything we've been through—"

"Just stop." Roxie's hands tightened over the shirt she had been haphazardly folding. "Do you think this house is so big that I haven't noticed? Sneaking down to the kitchen at night? You working on her car all day… the little spat the two of you are having now?"

"Nothing happened. I swear."

She threw the shirt at him, hitting him in the chest. "You think that makes this okay?"

"We're just friends."

They both looked at the open door to see Kate hesitating before she stepped into the room. Her gaze slid over Quinn for a moment before fixing on Roxie. Her face was pale but determined.

"Kate, you don't have to—"

"No, let her talk," Roxie said, interrupting him. "This should be good."

Quinn clenched his hands over his knees, wishing the ground would swallow him whole. He didn't want to do this here. He certainly didn't want to do it today of all days. Not after he'd insisted on her coming to Wilmington with him instead of staying behind in Durham for the holidays. He hadn't figured things out yet in his own mind, and he wasn't ready to let Roxie go… They had been together for a long time. He did love her, and it was going to break him if he hurt her. She had been through so much in her life, and he was the only person she had ever allowed herself to rely on. On top of that, Kate looked scared to death… like she was on the verge of throwing up. Whatever she was about to say, he knew he didn't want to hear it. He didn't want Roxie to hear it either.

"Quinn has never… ever been interested in me that way. At all. I am really sorry for anything I've done to make you think otherwise." He watched her hands begin to shake until she stuffed them into her pockets and her shoulders went up, as if trying to make herself smaller. He wanted to stop her from saying anything else, but all he could do was sit there and watch as she did what she must have thought would push him out of her life for good. She took a deep breath, her gaze landing on the floor at Roxie's feet, who he realized was watching his reaction carefully. "I've always been a brat to him, under his feet… bothering him… bothering Jon. I can't tell you how many times they told me to go away so they could do boy stuff, but I never listened. Nothing happened… nothing's ever going to happen. He really has always seen me like a little sister, just like he does Miranda. And he loves you. I just… I just wanted to tell you I was sorry. It's Christmas, and I don't want you to leave like this. Please stay. I'm… I'm going to be gone until tomorrow anyway. Andrew's picking me up to spend the day with him, and I asked Lindsay if I could stay with her tonight."

There was a world of things she didn't say about her own feelings while she put words in his mouth. She had never been a brat to him. Jon had always been the one telling her to go away… and he definitely didn't see her like a sister.

"So why are you fighting?" Roxie asked, lifting her chin.

"Because of me," Quinn said before Kate could speak. "I thought Andrew was being too rough with her. I stuck my nose where it didn't belong."

"Yes, you did," Kate replied, finally looking at him. The pain in her eyes nearly did him in. She was devastated. Humiliated. Heat crawled across his skin as he felt the same acute devastation swamping him. Kate McGuire had steel that he'd never seen before in her gaze, but right now her heart was broken. And she was never going to forgive him. "If you'll excuse me, I've got to get ready."

She was gone before he could apologize. Before he could tell her that she was wrong about everything that she had said. It felt like he'd swallowed a torque wrench, incapacitated as he sat there and listened to her door closing, imagining her crying on the other side. It was Roxie's scoff that finally pulled him out of it. He looked over to find that she'd resumed packing.

"Do you think I didn't see this coming? I thought if I went to Durham with you that things would change. *You* have changed, but not me. I'm always going to be poor, mistreated Roxie to you." She stopped packing, wiping angrily at her tears. "Not everyone sees me that way."

"I never meant to make you feel like that," he said,

getting to his feet and crossing over to where she stood beside his dresser. "I don't see you like that. I think you're strong after what you've been through."

Her jaw set, and she glared at him. "I don't need you to see me as strong. I wish I had never told you at *all,* because now it's all you see about me. Every time I get upset or mad, that's what you blame it on. Every time I drink a little too much, you act like I've committed a crime. Do you know how exhausting it is watching you wait for me to turn into her? I'm not Vickie."

It felt like he'd taken a punch directly to his heart. He reached out and cupped her cheeks, but the finality in her gaze stayed the words that he wanted to say. "I know."

"You're not entirely wrong about me. I do bad things. I make stupid choices." Her eyes closed. "I cheated on you."

For a moment he wasn't sure what she had said. It took a while for the words to register, but he felt certain he misunderstood. "You what?"

Roxie tilted her head back and looked up at him, her eyes full of tears. "I cheated on you for almost two months, Quinn. I didn't try to hide it… and you didn't even notice."

Jon found him sitting on his bed after Roxie had packed up the rest of her things and left. He didn't want to go downstairs and face Frank and Meredith or Meredith's parents. He could only imagine what they thought of the very loud argument he had with Roxie before she left or the fact that their daughter was hiding at a friend's house. He looked at Jon when he walked into his room but didn't really see him. He felt numb inside, thinking about the three years he had spent with Roxie and realizing that everything she had said to him was right. He saw her as broken… damaged, and he saw those broken parts in his mother… but he didn't think that he had loved her any less for it.

"So what's going on with you and Kate?" Jon asked,

because his friend had absolutely no filter.

"Nothing." Quinn glared at him. "If your parents are worried, then tell them there's nothing going on."

Jon held his hands up defensively. "Just asking. Miranda has been pestering me all day after the dick move she made. But in her defense, you did write that in Kate's book."

"Did she bring guys to the apartment?"

"What?" Jon frowned. "Roxie? I saw some guy drop her off a couple of times. I figured they worked together or something."

Quinn scoffed. "Yeah. Or something."

Jon sank down on the floor in front of his closet and picked up a tennis ball, then began tossing it into the air. "I take it this isn't one of your usual breakups?"

"She said she's been cheating on me since the beginning of November… and she got mad at me for not noticing. How the hell am I supposed to notice something like that? It's not like she was dropping clues all over the place." Quinn raked his hair back, his fingertips digging into the base of his skull. "I'm not a mind reader."

"Uh…"

Quinn glanced over at Jon, finding his expression ill at ease. His friend was beginning to blush. "What?"

Jon cleared his throat, his gaze straight ahead. "Roxie tried to uh… the bathroom door. I thought at first I didn't lock it or that she didn't realize I was in there. But then she tried to climb in the shower with me, and it got so awkward. I swear I didn't do anything. I can't say I didn't touch her because… well… her boobs are huge and it was an accident because I was trying not to look."

Quinn blinked at his friend. "When?"

"A few weeks ago." Jon got to his feet quickly and began to pace. "Look, man, it was finals. I didn't want you failing a test this close to graduation, and I figured she was going to tell you… at first. Then she started messing with me…

like walking around the apartment in her bra and underwear when you weren't there or how she started eating bananas like a porn star. I don't even think she liked me. I think she was just trying to come between us. So before you punch me in the face, I want you to know that I'd never do that to you, even though she has amazing breasts and her pot brownies are fantastic."

"She made pot brownies?" Quinn raised a brow. "Oh, you mean when you put pot in the brownies she was making me, and I didn't get any of them?"

"If that's how you remember it." Jon grinned for a moment, then tossed the tennis ball at him. "Are you going to be okay? Do I need to bring up a pint of Cherry Garcia and *The Princess Bride?* You know, Gran makes the best hot chocolate in the world."

"Too soon for jokes, dickwad," Quinn muttered, throwing the ball back as hard as he could and catching Jon in the stomach but not his cods, which was where he'd been aiming.

"I know." Jon wheezed. "Just promise me one thing. If you start going out with my sister and we're still roommates—"

Quinn followed up on the tennis ball by throwing a pillow at him, but he couldn't help but laugh. Jon couldn't be serious about anything... ever... but Quinn knew he used humor to make people more comfortable.

"Get out of my room," he replied without heat. He let out a deep breath, trying to stop his mind from spinning in so many directions. What Jon just told him had pissed him off more than the fact that Roxie had been cheating on him, because he knew Jon was right. She had been trying to come between them. She'd been doing it for as long as they had been dating. If he was even five minutes late coming home, she grilled him, especially if Jon was with him, because she knew Jon had a fondness for strip clubs and she assumed that meant he'd been spending his afternoon getting a lap dance. He felt like his anchor had been yanked away, only Roxie hadn't been the anchor. He always thought *he* had been the anchor. "So Kate is staying with Lindsay?"

"Yeah. Why?"

"I need to straighten things out with her before I leave. She would barely look at me."

"What about Roxie?" Jon asked, studying him. "Are you going to forgive her?"

"She didn't apologize. But if you're asking if I'm taking her back... no. She asked me to stay away from the apartment for a few days until she could get her things out. We probably won't have a TV when we get back."

"Shit," Jon drawled. "We probably won't get our deposit back by the time she gets done with the place."

Someone tapped gently on the door, and Jon opened it to reveal a sheepish-looking Miranda standing on the other side, her face so red it almost blended with her freckles. Jon glanced at Quinn. Quinn glanced at Jon, knowing she had probably been standing outside the entire time listening to them talk. Jon swore sometimes that she had figured out how to bug their rooms, because she knew more about what was going down than anyone else in the house.

"I just wanted to say I was sorry for earlier," she said so meekly that it was hard not to crack a smile. "I'm not sorry that you guys broke up. Roxie was a beotch. But I'm sorry I put you and Kate on the spot like that. She's not talking to me right now."

Quinn crossed his arms over his chest and leaned back on the headboard. "Well, I guess we have that in common. She's not talking to me either."

Jon laughed. "So wait... I'm the only one she's talking to? That's a first."

"Don't get used to it. You'll find a way to piss her off before you leave." Miranda punched Jon in the arm. "Mom grounded me."

"So that's why you're lurking. She made you apologize, so you thought you'd listen through the door so you can tell Kate what we've been talking about?" Jon asked.

"Does that sound like something I would do?" she replied, all innocent smiles and mischievous gazes. Then she looked back at Quinn, and her expression sobered. "I am sorry, Haley. I didn't think she'd get that mad at you."

Though he really should be thanking her, he supposed, Quinn just nodded. Miranda being a little snot was something he should have factored in when he'd brought Roxie around in the first place.

"I doubt your mom will unground you, but I forgive you," Quinn said, barely having time to prepare himself before Miranda launched herself across the room and hugged him. For a little thing, she had surprisingly strong arms, but her bony chin cut into his shoulder.

"Well one of my sisters still likes you," Jon said with a laugh.

"If you need directions to Lindsay's house, you know where to find me," she whispered, then let him go and bounded off toward the door.

"Hey, aren't you forgetting something?"

She glanced at Jon, looking confused. "Like what?"

"Like promising you're not going to tell Kate or anyone else what you heard in this room?" Jon glared at her meaningfully.

"You mean the pot? I already knew you smoked. You smell like it every time you go behind the garage after dinner." Miranda cocked her head at her brother. "I am curious about something though."

"No, I'm not giving you pot," Jon replied, still glaring.

"Oh, I tried it. It didn't really do anything for me. I just wanted to know... how *do* porn stars eat bananas?"

Chapter 7

"I'M SO STUPID," KATE GROANED as she sat through one of Lindsay's coerced makeovers that she liked posting to YouTube. At the moment, all Kate wanted to do was crawl under her friend's covers and go to sleep, and hopefully when she woke up, this day would be over. "I'm *so stupid*."

"Hold still. I'm going to mess this up." Lindsay squinted at her, trying to draw on her eyeliner. "Yeah. I mean, if it had been Mitch, I would have probably slammed your head in the door or something, but that's just me."

"So you think I did something wrong?" Even as she said it, she knew that it was true. She hadn't flirted with Quinn outright, but she had definitely been too free with the longing gazes.

"Maybe. You guys have always been weirdly close. You can't tell me he's never given off any vibes like that."

Kate shrugged. "Maybe a little? But then... no. He wasn't giving off vibes. I was just wishing he was giving a vibe, and now I probably ruined our friendship for good."

"I think he likes you. I saw him glare at Andrew a few

times when we were at your house, and if I remember right, he glared at Jacob this summer every time you two were playing tonsil hockey." Lindsay tilted her head to the side and studied her handiwork, then looked through her makeup for something else to torture her with. "If you want him, go for him. Brittany already has her eye on Andrew though, just so you know."

"I know." Kate sighed. Andrew had been really sweet to her after he picked her up. For Christmas he'd given her a beautiful pendant necklace, and his present from her had been a Duke sweater since that was where he was going to college. Around his parents, he was a completely different person than when they were alone together, and his mom seemed to really enjoy her company. Her emotions were all jumbled, knowing that she didn't have a chance with Quinn, and being around Andrew just made her feel… guilty. "That girl is not subtle."

Lindsay tossed her long blond hair over her shoulder and stepped back so that Kate could see herself in the mirror. The makeup sessions might be tortuous and pointless since she usually washed her face off when it was over, but her friend was really good. She looked older and so glamorous that Kate touched her face, wishing she could put Lindsay in her pocket and take her everywhere. She had fixed her hair first, doing some intricate side braid that looked easy on YouTube but just made her arms tired before she gave up. Whenever she tried to do her own makeup, she never could make her eyes pop like that or her cheekbones look so perfect… and trying to do her own eyebrows? That had resulted in Miranda actually collapsing on the floor because she was laughing so hard.

"No, I mean, she's got more than her eye on Andrew, Kate," Lindsay said, grabbing Kate's chin and coming at her with lip liner. "She already tried to sleep with him, and he said no."

"What?"

"Ugh. I said hold still." Lindsay grabbed a tissue and wiped at the smudge on Kate's lip. "She showed up at his house the other night. Mitch was there. She brought over a bottle of tequila and asked him if he wanted to party. Andrew told her to leave."

"What night?" Kate asked, trying to imitate a ventriloquist.

"I don't know. The night after we stayed at your house."

The same night Kate had told him no when he asked if she wanted to come back to his house, he'd turned Brittany down. The same night she'd been in the kitchen with Quinn, happily in his arms, he'd been turning down sex with one of her friends. Andrew had asked her out for a solid year before she said yes. She always put him off, because he was a player and because he was surrounded by a lot of girls *all* the time. She'd even gone out with Jacob instead, believing that he would be more mature. For all the things Andrew had pulled… he liked to drink, and he liked to smoke and liked trying to touch her boobs. He hadn't really pressured her into anything, even though he was always trying to get her alone.

She felt something shift in her heart, along with another sting of guilt. Quinn and Roxie had been together for three years, and thanks to her stupid, pointless crush, they had broken up. She had never been fair to Andrew, and he deserved someone who loved him. She should probably just be alone for a while until she figured out what she really felt for him. In a few months they would be going separate ways. He'd be going to Durham, and she would be in Atlanta. She didn't think their relationship would survive that kind of distance. Maybe that was part of the reason she was holding back… because she always thought that once Andrew went to college, he would be unable to remain faithful.

"So are you going to do anything about Brittany?"

Kate shook her head. "There's no point."

"Kate, she tried to sleep with your boyfriend." Lindsay frowned at her. "You don't care? Not even a little?"

"Of course I care. I just… It's not like I can get mad at her. I know how she is. I'm actually a little happy that it happened."

"You're going to have to explain that one to me."

"Andrew's been with a lot of girls," Kate replied. "At least four that I know of, and those are just the ones we go to school with. You saw the Snaps of him last year, partying in Mexico. Girls were all over him, and he was loving every minute of it. He knows if he stays with me, it's not going to be like that. He did the right thing. But still, he's really experienced. And I um… I've never…"

"You're still a virgin?"

Kate nodded, feeling her face heat. "I've got some stuff going on right now that I haven't told you guys about. I've lied about two big things in my life, and both have come back to bite me in the ass. I lied about losing my v-card because of Jacob and that stupid Super-Virgin nickname, because Brittany wouldn't shut up about it."

"O…kay," Lindsay said, sitting down on the floor in front of her. "What was the other thing?"

"I've never had a period," Kate mumbled.

"What? Like, ever?"

"Never ever." She sighed, embarrassed. "My mom is making a huge deal about it, and honestly it's starting to worry me too. Most girls start getting theirs after they turn thirteen. Some sooner. Miranda did."

Lindsay scoffed. "Well, I think you're lucky. Not having to deal with bleeding body parts once a month or more would be frigging awesome."

"Not having a doctor stab you with his fingers would be

even better," she muttered. "The last time they did an exam, it hurt really bad. I started crying so hard that they stopped. Mom got me a prescription for anxiety so I can take one the next time, but unless they plan on knocking me out, then they can forget it. I'm not doing that shit again."

"So do they know what's wrong?"

"Nope." Kate lifted her shoulders. "Guess I'm just a weirdo."

"I know." Her friend jumped to her feet and gave her a hug. "It's okay, weirdo. I don't want my period anymore. You can borrow it anytime."

They were both laughing when Kate's phone went off, indicating she had a text. She glanced down at it, and immediately all the air in her lungs left.

"Oh my God."

"What?" Lindsay looked at her phone, then let out a squeal "He's here!"

> **Quinn:** Meet me outside.
>
> **Quinn:** I'm not leaving until you talk to me, Kate.

The words taunted her from her screen, and she tiptoed over to Lindsay's bedroom window and peeked outside.

"Is he out there?" Lindsay whispered, pulling her curtain back.

"Yes," Kate groaned, spotting the gleam of chrome from Jon's car parked along the street. "I don't want to go down there."

"I don't blame you." Lindsay patted her arm sympathetically. "At least you stopped crying and you have *awesome* makeup on, thanks to me. You looked like crap."

"Thanks," Kate replied dryly.

"Well? Are you going to go talk to him? Or are we just going to stare at him all night?"

They both jumped as the car door opened and the interior light came on, illuminating a tall, male figure that she knew wasn't her brother. She felt the beginnings of panic, hoping he wasn't about to knock on Lindsay's front door this late. It was past midnight, and both her parents had to work the next day.

Quinn: Come outside. Please.

She glared at her phone screen.

Kate: I don't want to talk to you right now.

After she sent the words, she regretted them. She didn't want to be a coward, but she wasn't ready to face him either. Not after everything Miranda had told her about his fight with Roxie and how she had left in tears. She definitely didn't want to have the conversation with Quinn where she had to acknowledge, in any way, the feelings she had been trying to stop having or the fact that said feelings had caused the end of his three-year relationship.

Something struck the window, making them jump again. Kate moved the curtain aside just in time to see him rearing back to throw something at the house. It hit the house this time instead of the window, making a loud thump. Then he pulled his phone out of his pocket and started typing.

"He's going to wake my dad up," Lindsay hissed. "Do something!"

Her phone chimed, and she glanced at the screen.

Quinn: Next one is coming through the window. Five minutes.

Kate showed it to Lindsay, who grabbed her hand and hurried her downstairs, through the kitchen, and out the side door next to the detached garage. She all but pushed her toward the front yard, then closed the door behind her with a quiet snick that was superloud in the dead of night.

"Took you long enough," Quinn whispered as he jogged across the yard to her side. He grabbed her hand and—once again—she was forced to go along. His fingers held hers firmly, giving her no chance to escape, and she didn't want to protest in case Lindsay's parents heard something. He didn't stop jogging until they reached Jon's car, and while she was out of breath, he didn't even look winded. "Get in."

She did but only because it was freezing and she was wearing thin cotton yoga pants and a T-shirt, not to mention Lindsay's flip-flops. Her teeth began to chatter, so as soon as he got in the car and turned it on, she cranked the heater all the way up. She'd expected him to just let the car idle, but he put it in drive and pulled away.

"Did you really just kidnap me?" Kate glared at him. "Take me back."

"No. Not until we're done talking." The lights from the dashboard and the silent radio highlighted his features, making him look angry.

"Can we please, please not do this right now? Look, I'm really sorry. I am really, really sorry, Quinn. I don't even know what to say to you right now except for how sorry I am. I… God, I didn't mean for anything like this to happen. I like Roxie. I feel like shit, and I understand if you never want to speak to me again. So just take me back. Please." Her voice went soft at the end as it became harder to speak, because he wasn't looking at her, and she didn't know what he was thinking other than he must be mad at her.

Since he didn't say anything else, she turned to look out the window, doing her best not to cry. She didn't comment as he drove, making his way toward Wrightsville Beach but turning off at the last moment and backtracking until they were on a stretch of road with no houses, just water on one side of them where she could see the lights of a marina in the distance and a row of hedges on the other. He pulled onto the shoulder and killed the lights, leaving the engine running. He yanked his seat belt off and pressed his fingers against his closed eyes.

"How could you think I'd never want to speak to you

again?" His voice startled her, the roughness of it sounding almost pained. "You haven't answered any of my texts in the past two days. How do you think it makes me feel when you won't talk to me? When you won't even look at me?"

She couldn't answer him, because every mile they passed had driven a spike of anxiety deep in her stomach, making it almost impossible to breathe. Kate clenched her hands tightly in her lap, feeling the confines of the car all around her and the press of December on the outside making it impractical to flee.

"If you won't talk to me, just listen," Quinn said, his voice gentling. "I'm not mad at you, Kate. Not even a little."

Reluctantly she turned to face him, but it took forever for her gaze to move from his shoulders to his eyes. "You're not?"

"No. I'm the one who should be apologizing to you." He let out a sigh. "I put you in that position. In hindsight, knowing how Roxie felt about my being around you, I shouldn't have written that inscription. I shouldn't have brought her to the house. I know she said something to you. I overheard you telling Lindsay and Brittany about it. Was she mean to you?"

Instead of making her feel better, his words made her feel smaller. So, it was official. He knew... and apparently they had discussed her having a crush on him. The conversation she'd had with her friends came back to her. Unable to withstand him reading the humiliation in her gaze, she looked back out the window.

"Take me back to Lindsay's. Please."

"Not until we fix this."

"All this is doing is making it worse. You're making it worse. I don't want to talk about anything with you right now."

"Why are you so mad at me? Have I done something? Because I don't get it. I really don't. I'm sorry for sticking my nose in your business with Andrew, but if that's the reason, you're overreacting."

"Yes. Yes I am mad at you, because you kidnapped me in the middle of the night, and I'm cold, and I'm tired, and it's Christmas, and all I've done today is ruin your life, and you want me to sit here talking about it like everything's okay! Well it's not okay, Quinn. You shouldn't even be here with me. You should be getting ready for your *summer wedding*, so you can start a *family* with her after you graduate. Why aren't you trying to win her back?"

"Miranda didn't tell you?"

"Tell me what?"

He peeled his jacket off, jerking it over his head from the back, then off his arms, and he draped it across her front. Kate stilled at the gentleness in his hands, the proximity of him as he turned toward her, the only thing separating them was the console between the bucket seats. He didn't remove his hands, and she clocked the places he touched her with them… one on her shoulder, the other settling against her neck, his long fingers tracing a steady circle on her skin.

"Roxie cheated on me. She has been for a while apparently. And she tried to sleep with Jon." He moved just his thumb, stroking the softness of her cheek. "I've been feeling like something was off for a while, but I figured she was just getting ready for some time apart. She does that sometimes. Breaks up with me when we start fighting too much, but I never thought she'd be unfaithful. Not after…" His voice trailed off, shaking his head. "I can't tell you what all she's gone through. You have no idea how lucky you were to have parents like Frank and Meredith. Roxie and I were raised by monsters. She had it so much worse than me though."

There was regret in his voice and so much pain. He rarely ever talked about this stuff, and it was usually in the form of a joke… never anything intentional. She understood now why he didn't talk about Roxie much. She could imagine what it would have been like to a girl trapped in a cycle of poverty and abuse, and Roxie had said it herself… her mother was like Quinn's mother. An addict and a drunk, who was probably never sober enough to protect her child from a predator, doling out her affection with fists and invective.

"I'm sorry that you had to go through that. I'm sorry that Roxie had to… that anyone would. And I'm sorry that she hurt you. You don't deserve that." She slipped her hand out from the bottom of his coat and squeezed the hand that was at her shoulder. "I know you love her. You'll figure things out."

"We never talked about a summer wedding, Kate. Or starting a family. Whatever she said to you, it was because she's always been jealous of my friendship with you. Even when you were still in braces. She has broken up with me eleven times in three years. It's always over something dumb, but I realized today that more than half the times she's dumped me has been because it had something to do with Jon or you or your family. Every time I went on vacation with you guys? Dumped. When I came home for the holidays, but I stayed with Jon? Dumped. Last summer, she broke up with me because we had a fight about you."

"What did I do?"

"Nothing. It's something that I did. And until she brought it up, I didn't even realize I was doing it."

Kate raised her eyebrows. "Okay. What did you do?"

"I was complaining about your boyfriend—Jacob—too much. I thought he was being disrespectful. Untying your bathing suit in front of everyone, and he couldn't keep his hands off you. When you went to the bathroom, Jon told him to knock it off. He just ignored him, so I… I might have told him if he didn't stop I was going to break his freaking hands. I don't like seeing guys treat you that way,

Kate. You deserve so much more."

She remembered that day. They all spent a day at the beach together. It was the first time she really spent time with Roxie, and she'd been extremely standoffish even though Kate had tried to talk to her. Jacob, who she had been dating for a few months, was all over her, just like Roxie was all over Quinn. She didn't even think he noticed them. She remembered coming back from the bathroom and Jacob wanting to leave. He took her to his house, asked her if she wanted to have sex, and she said yes. It had been the worst experience imaginable.

She wished Quinn had broken his freaking hands. And kicked him in the nuts for good measure.

"I don't know where we go from here, Kate. I just want you to know that I care about you." He gripped her fingers in his hand, then lifted it and pressed a kiss to her knuckles. She felt like screaming at him to do it again, and she knew her breathing was out of control because it was audible over the motor of the car. He turned to look at her, his gaze intense. "I don't think of you like a sister. You've never been a brat to me. I'm not telling you this for any reason other than I want us… *need* us… to keep being friends. I know you're with Andrew and I might not like him, but I'll respect your decision if that's what you want. If I'm being honest, I don't think there's anyone out there good enough for you Kate, and that includes me."

There were so many thoughts and emotions eddying in her mind that it was hard to pick one. "I'm so confused."

"So am I," he admitted quietly. "Don't break up with Andrew because of me. I'm about to start law school. You're going to Atlanta in a few months. You're going to meet new people. Experience so many new things. And I know you're going to be great at everything you do, because I know *you*. And I know that I can't… I won't… hold you back. If you want to know the truth, I think that you're beautiful. Really, really beautiful. Outside. Inside. You have the best heart in the entire world."

And it's yours. It's yours. Just take it.

She swallowed back all the words she wanted to let out. That she loved him. That he meant everything in the world to her and he always had... but he needed to sort through whatever mess he had going on with Roxie, because she didn't think that he was over her, and she thought it would be a long time before that happened. But his words made her cautiously hopeful, because they knocked down all the other barriers that had been standing in her way. The age barrier, because she was eighteen now. The friend zone, because it seemed as if she'd finally breached it. Everything else could be overcome.

Then she remembered what Lindsay had just told her about Andrew. That he'd been loyal to her when Brittany tried to seduce him, and she felt horrible, even though she hadn't done anything wrong. Her feelings were engaged with someone who couldn't return them right now. Maybe ever. But she was planning to break up with a good guy so she could wait for Quinn, and that wasn't fair. She had turned so many guys down because she'd been waiting... until she turned eighteen... waiting until he noticed her... waiting... waiting... waiting.

She couldn't wait for him the rest of her life. He might go back to Durham, forgive Roxie, and six months would go by before she saw him again. Or he might find someone new. Her heart couldn't take any more disappointment. Yet she knew she was about to do the girl thing and lie to him, because the thought of being honest was crippling.

"I understand. You don't owe me anything."

"Don't do that. If you have something you want to say, say it." In the darkness she could see him glaring a little, and she felt like a coward.

"I don't *want* to say anything."

"So you're just going to let me tell you how beautiful you are and that I care about you, and you don't have anything you want to say to me?"

"Quinn, you just gave me a list of reasons why you don't want me. I don't know what you expect me to say. Do you not understand how girls work? We don't like to tell guys who just rejected us how hot we think they are. I'm sure you and Jon are going to have a blast this semester trying to pin anything that holds still long enough, but if you want your ego or anything else stroked, you're going to have to wait until you get back to college."

A quick smile crossed his lips, but he ran a hand down his face to cover it up. "I didn't reject you. I just don't think now is a good time… for either of us. And I don't need you to tell me how hot I am. I mean, have you even been looking at me? I'm totally hot."

"You're a jerk." Her cheeks went red, and she had to hide her own smile.

"But you still think I'm adorable." He reached over and mussed her hair. "I think you're adorable too, McGuire."

Kate rolled her eyes. Everyone thought she was adorable. Kittens were adorable. Babies were adorable. She didn't want to be adorable. "I wish everyone would stop telling me that," she muttered.

"Telling you what?"

"I'm not a kitten!"

"Uh… okay. You're not a kitten." He gave her a look like he thought she'd lost it.

"Unless you mean it like a sex kitten, stop telling me I'm adorable. I'm not adorable."

He shifted toward her, bringing one of his hands behind her neck, then he pulled her toward him. She felt his lips press against her forehead, then he kissed her cheek twice, his lips trailing toward her ear. Kate reached for him, touching his face, his hair… doing everything in her power not to drag his mouth to hers. Stardust shattered inside her, creating an entire new being that had no fear in worshipping him. Somehow she had ended up halfway in his lap, because she was twisted sideways across the console. She wanted to kiss him so badly, but she didn't want him to think she was the kind of person who would do that when she was committed to someone else. Especially not after what had happened to him today... but it was hard not to with his arms around her like this and his cheek pressed against hers. She settled for relaxing into him, burying her face against his throat and fulfilling a long-held wish of being able to smell him without it being overly weird.

"I can't kiss you," she whispered.

"I know." His arms tightened around her even more. "I want to kiss you too."

She couldn't help the tremor that went through her suddenly... a spasm that originated from her heart and made its way down to her curling toes. She slid her hand back into his hair and stifled about a dozen noises that were trying to emerge from her throat, because her reaction to him was nearly overwhelming. If she didn't get back in her seat, she couldn't be responsible for what was about to happen.

"Haley?"

"Yeah, kitten?"

She almost swallowed her tongue, because the way he'd just said kitten was sexy as fuck. Like a sexy kitten. Not an actual sexy kitten... but a sex kitten. His voice was deep and rumbly... so perfect for saying things like that.

Focus. You have a boyfriend. You need to stop this.

"The gear shifter thing is trying to go in my ass."

"What?" She felt his hand cup her ass, and he moved her slightly. "Sorry."

Well. That wasn't better. Now she was actually in his lap *and* his hand was on her ass. "Haley, we have to stop, or it's about to get weird."

"This isn't weird. What's weird about my stealing Jon's car, kidnapping you, and forcing you to hug it out with me at midnight where neither of us know where the hell we are?"

She started laughing. "This isn't a hug, stupid. This is an embrace."

He sighed. "Well that did it. You made it weird. Get back in your seat. And stop stroking my hair. It's kinda my jam."

Yeah, along with spankings, handcuffs, and exhibitionism.

After a few misplaced knees and elbows, she managed to make it back into her seat. He drove her back to Lindsay's, and she sent her friend a text to let her know she would be coming inside in a few minutes. Lindsay messaged her back immediately and let her know she had left the side door unlocked.

"Thank you for…"

"Kidnapping you?"

"Yes." She sighed. "And for everything else. When are you leaving?"

He glanced at the clock. It was almost two in the morning. "In about twelve hours. Jon's worried that Roxie is going to take half the apartment with her."

"I won't see you before you leave." Kate glanced at him, then looked away. "Andrew is leaving town for a vacation with his family. I'm going to spend some time with him tomorrow."

"Are you going to tell him about this?"

"No." She knew it wasn't going to work out with Andrew. Not after tonight. But she wasn't going to break up with him before he went on vacation. And she wasn't going to tell Quinn anything either. "I need to get in. Lindsay is waiting on me. Drive safe tomorrow. And make sure you delete your search history after looking up those naked grandmas when you get revenge on Jon. I don't want to have to explain that to anyone if something happens to you."

"You're so sweet. Always thinking of me." He grinned. "Come here. One last embrace, and you can go get your beauty rest. I don't know what happened to your face, but you look *so* tired."

She launched herself across the car and threw her arms around his neck, hugging him as tightly as she could.

"Dorkasaurus," she whispered.

"Sexy kitten," he murmured back, grunting when she pinched him on the side. His whiskers burned her skin as he moved his lips to her cheek and kissed her. "I'll make you a deal."

"What's that?" Hope bounced around in her heart.

"We can have this totally weird conversation again… after you graduate… if neither of us are in a relationship."

Yes. Yes. Yes. She wanted to yell it at him. She wanted to scream. Her hands automatically went to his hair, and she petted him, then slid her fingers into the thick mass and closed the distance between them. His gaze met hers in the light from the dash, then dropped to her lips. He glanced back up at her.

"It's a deal, Haley." Kate pressed her lips to his once, softly, then got out of the car. She leaned down to look at him before she closed the door and was satisfied to see that he looked a little dazed. "And now it's sealed."

Chapter 8

KATE KNOCKED ON THE DOOR to Andrew's house the next morning, feeling nervous and guilty. After she had made it back to Lindsay's room, she had collapsed to the floor in a catatonic girl fit. She felt like she'd ingested some sort of narcotic, but eventually that feeling of euphoria left her when she realized what she was going to have to do—break things off with Andrew. He wasn't going to see it coming, and she thought that might be the worst thing of all.

"Katherine." Delia, Andrew's mom, practically sang as she opened the door. She was perpetually cheerful and energetic and always smiling. And she always called her Katherine. "Andrew's just getting his bags packed. Why don't you go up and help him? Tell him I said to make sure he has everything on the list. He's old enough to start doing things himself."

"Yes, ma'am," Kate replied with a laugh. "I'll tell him."

She made her way upstairs, following the sound of loud music to his room.

And found him dancing.

In his boxers.

It wasn't so much a dance as a wiggle, but it was definitely hilarious.

Kate clapped a hand over her mouth to stop the laugh that erupted, but she couldn't help it. He was so ridiculously good-looking, but right now he looked a little ridiculous, because he had absolutely no moves.

"Kate!" He didn't look embarrassed at all as he caught sight of her. He padded across the room to her and pulled her into his arms. "I wasn't expecting you this early."

"Obviously." She bypassed the kiss he tried to give her and hugged him. "Go put some pants on. You're as bad as Brittany. She's always running around in her underwear."

She didn't know why she invoked Brittany's name, but Andrew looked down at her with a bemused expression.

"Please don't compare me to her." He let her go and walked over to his bed and grabbed a pair of jogging pants, shoving his legs into them. "She's not your friend, Kate."

"Why didn't you tell me she came over here the other night?"

He jerked the pants up over his hips, then sat down on his bed. "I don't want to mess this up. I was going to tell you. I just thought Christmas would be a suck-ass time to do it. I assume Mitch ran his mouth to Lindsay?"

"I doubt either of those two know how to keep a secret." She could have used this as an excuse to break things off with him, but she didn't like dishonesty. She felt guilty enough without adding another lie. Kate leaned back against the wall next to his door. "Your mom said something about a list?"

He rolled his eyes. "She's obsessed with lists."

"So where is it?"

"You're not mad at me?" Andrew asked.

"I'm not mad at you. I'm not happy with Brittany."

"I know what you think of me, Kate." He crossed the room and put his arms around her, lifting her up slightly. "I know you think I'm a man-slut, but I promise, I'm trying to be better. For you."

Kate wiggled, trying to get loose, but he just tightened his arms and lowered his mouth to hers. He'd apologized for how he had kissed her the night he dropped her off, and he had been gentle with her ever since. She felt *something* for him… she wasn't dead, and Andrew was a good kisser. But he didn't make her feel even close to what she felt for Quinn. They had never done more than kiss, and Kate had always stopped him when he'd gotten carried away. Not once had he ever really pushed things too far. It was her own horrible pressure that made her abandon ship every time he touched a boob.

She finally pulled her mouth free from his, and he let her slide to the ground. He reached down and lifted the pendant that he'd given her for Christmas.

"It looks good on you."

"If you put your sweater on, I could tell you the same thing." Kate took a step away from him. She should have just told him she would see him when he got back from his trip. She didn't want to break up with him before he left and ruin his vacation, but letting him kiss her and touch her like everything was okay made her feel awful.

"You sure you're not mad at me?" Andrew asked quietly.

"I'm not mad at you," Kate replied gently. "I promise."

"You don't trust me." He peered down at her, searching her expression. "It's okay. I can tell you don't trust me."

"It's not that. It's not just about you." Maybe she could at least give him something to think about, and when he got back, he'd make the decision for her. She took a deep breath. "Okay, here's the thing. I'm not like the other girls you've… dated. I know it shouldn't bother me because all that stuff happened before you asked me out, but it does."

"Are you waiting until you get married or something?" He raised his brows at her.

"No. I... *personally*... don't think anyone should be that casual about sex. I did something stupid earlier this year, and I've regretted it every day since then. It made me realize that I'm never going to be one of those girls who needs to sleep with a lot of guys to make sure they have the right one. I'm not going off to college in September with plans of sleeping around with every guy I meet. There's nothing wrong with it. More power to girls who want to do that. But *I* don't. What happened to me... that should never happen to another girl. Especially not their first time. The first time should be with someone you love. That's just how I feel now. I wish I had been smart enough to feel that way then." She sat down on the edge of his bed and dropped her gaze to the floor. She didn't know why she was telling Andrew this when she was planning on ending things with him, but telling Lindsay the night before had made her realize that locking it all up was making her feel worse. And it was part of the reason why she knew things weren't going to work out with him. It wasn't just that she didn't trust him. She just knew, in her heart, that he wasn't the one.

"Who was it?"

The anger in his gaze made her tense. "Does it matter?"

"Was it Quinn? Is that why you act weird around him?"

"What? No." She felt her face go red. "It was *Jacob*. He hurt me."

"Because of the nickname? Super-Virgin?"

"That too, but no. I mean, he hurt me."

His eyes narrowed. "Did he force you?"

"No." It felt like lava was creeping across every inch of her skin and inside her heart. "It just hurt. A lot. And it didn't... work."

"Oh."

He looked uncomfortable, and Kate looked away,

feeling ashamed. Every time she thought about Jacob, all she felt was mortification. "I just thought you should know, because I don't plan on doing that again anytime soon. I'm not waiting until marriage... but I'm not going there again until I'm sure. Anyway... I should let you get packed. I want to see my grandparents before they leave."

"Wait." Andrew walked over to her and knelt down in front of the bed. "I'm sorry. You just surprised me, that's all. Brittany said something to me, and I should have known better than to listen to anything that comes out of her mouth."

Kate narrowed her eyes at him. "What did she say?"

"It doesn't matter." He slid his hands behind her knees and pulled her forward. The worshipful look in his eyes filled her with panic because she was afraid he was about to say something that she wasn't ready to hear. That she could not let him say, because it would make everything so much harder when he came back. "The important thing is, I'm okay with waiting until you're ready. Don't let that one time, with one asshole, ruin everything for you. I'd never do anything to hurt you, Kate."

"Andrew, if your bags aren't packed in the next twenty minutes, you're going to stay with your aunt Karen!"

"Oh shit." Kate giggled, relieved that his mom had interrupted what was becoming a way-too-serious moment. "Who is Aunt Karen?"

"My mom's sister. Total cat lady." He got to his feet and grabbed her hand. "Help me. I have no idea what I'm doing."

"List?" He dragged her over to his nightstand and handed her the list. She scanned it quickly. "How much of this have you packed?"

"None of it. I don't even know where my suitcase is."

"Maybe if you spent less time dancing in your underwear, you could have been looking for it." She laughed. It was impossible to not be charmed by his immaturity. He was like a little kid sometimes but a really cute one. "Go see if she has a spare suitcase or something. Where are your shirts?"

He waved a hand toward his closet, and Kate walked into a room that was the size of her bathroom at home. She grabbed a few of the T-shirts she recognized and a few button-down shirts, then some pants. Hopefully they fit. If they didn't, maybe he would learn to pack his own clothes. She folded everything neatly on the bed, grabbed things from his bathroom haphazardly, then went back to his closet for his blazer, which he would probably be required to wear for dinner at the resort his parents were staying at.

"Katherine?"

"In here, Mrs. Whitman," she called.

"You shouldn't be doing that for him." Delia sighed as she stepped into the closet. "Oh. Before I forget, we have a dinner reservation at the country club when we get back. I'd like you to meet Andrew's godfather. He's flying in from New York."

What was she supposed to do? Tell her no? Kate swallowed a groan. "Sure. Just let me know when so I can make sure I request that night off."

"I wish you could go with us. It would be nice for Andrew to have someone to hang around with. We invited Mitch, but I guess his girlfriend wouldn't let him go."

"That sounds like Lindsay." She smiled. "It's okay. I have a doctor's appointment in Raleigh the day before you're flying in that I can't miss."

"Everything okay?"

Kate shrugged. "I hope so."

"Me too." His mom started moving things around until she found the suitcase hiding behind a stack of extra bedding on the top shelf of the closet. "Aha. I told him it should be here."

"Here, let me get that," Kate offered since his mom was holding back a mound of pillows and comforters. Honestly, how many blankets did an eighteen-year-old boy need?

She pulled the suitcase free but tripped over a pair of his shoes, sending the suitcase—which was open—flying in the other direction, then she heard his mom gasp.

Then she gasped. There had to have been fifty condoms covering his closet floor. She was pretty sure she had never seen so many condoms in her entire life, and it was the most awkward moment of her life to be standing in her boyfriend's closet, with his mom, surrounded by *all the condoms.*

"Mom, did you find it?"

A giggle bubbled out of her, and she slapped her hand over her mouth, carefully avoiding his mom's gaze.

"Yes," Delia replied, though it sounded more like a hiss.

Andrew stopped at the closet door, his eyes going as big as plates when he saw what they were looking at. Then he looked at Kate. "I can explain."

Kate held her hands up. "I… uh… no. Please don't. I know what they're for."

"Kate, I haven't used my *suitcase* since spring break." He glanced at his mom. "Can you give us a minute?"

"There's no need. We can talk about this later. You guys are going to miss your flight. Okay? Bye." She ducked under his arm and tried to make it out of his bedroom, but he grabbed her and spun her around.

"I know what it looks like, but everything I said to you was the truth," he said, his words in a near shout. "You have to believe me."

"Andrew, calm down. Please." Kate touched his cheek. "We'll talk when you get back. I promise."

She would have said anything to get out of that house, because his mom emerged behind him and looked like she was about to breathe dragon fire.

"Thank you. I'll see you in a couple of weeks." Looking upset, he kissed her on the forehead, and she ran down the stairs as fast as she could manage without breaking her neck. The sound of Mrs. Whitman's voice cracked through the house just as she reached the front door.

"Andrew James Whitman, you are so grounded!"

"Anything missing?" Quinn asked, poking his head into Jon's room. The complete opposite of his room at home, this one always looked like it had been hit by a tornado. "Not that you could tell with all this crap on your floor."

Jon threw a shirt at him and smacked him in the face with it. "That's yours. It's dirty."

"Gross." Quinn tossed it across the hall into his own room's laundry basket. "Why do you even have my clothes? My shirts look like nightgowns on you."

"I have something else for you." Jon made a production out of giving him the finger, then threw himself on his bed. "So... she just left and didn't steal anything or break anything. That's not like her."

"I know you think she's evil incarnate, but Roxie is a good person. She just does dumb stuff sometimes."

"She tried to do dumb stuff," Jon replied, sticking his index finger to his chest. "Dumb stuff said no."

"I think you mean stupid shit." Quinn grinned, then wandered back to his room. The apartment felt empty without Roxie there. No more scented candles that he complained about but actually liked... no more makeup covering every available counter space in the bathroom. He had expected anger when she left, but it felt more like she had been waiting for things to end, and once it was over, she wasn't even pissed enough to steal his television.

Of course, she didn't know about Kate kissing him, which he had been trying not to think about. He shouldn't have made that deal with her, but he didn't regret it. Not really. He had promised himself he was going to let her down easy. She was too young, and they were about to live almost six hours apart instead of two when she moved to Atlanta in the fall, but that went out the window when he pulled her across the seat and into his arms. He had a moment of fear that if he let her slip through his fingers, she would be gone for good. He'd watched her heart break right in front of him too many times to count. The first time Jon had casually mentioned his new girlfriend... the look on her face when he didn't come home because he'd spent the night with Roxie. The way she didn't look at him when he told her that Roxie was moving to Durham with him and the utter silence from her in the months after that. She'd always been there, in the back of his mind, and he had always attributed that to his sensitivity about her feelings for him. Apparently it had been more than that. He'd just been too stubborn to see it. Now he was free, and she had a boyfriend.

A boyfriend whom she would see at school every day for the next five months... who liked grabbing her ass and shoving his tongue down her throat. He hadn't hit another person in well over a year... the last one had been some drunk guy who'd cornered Roxie in a bar and tried to stick his hand up her shirt... but he wanted to punch Andrew Whitman in the face.

He also wanted to text Kate and tell her he'd changed his mind. That he wanted her to dump Andrew. That he'd be coming home every weekend until she graduated so he could see her. He wanted to turn back time and give her a proper kiss instead of that half-second kiss she had given him in the car.

Yet he knew he needed time. His breakup with Roxie had not even begun to sink in. He knew he'd made the right decision in ending things with her. He was hurt and angry with himself, but more than anything else he felt relief and guilt for feeling relief. What Roxie had said about comparing her to his mom had struck a nerve. He'd always seen just a little of Vickie in her. Not in looks. They were both blond. Both pretty. Both tragic. It was the diffidence, beneath the surface, that meekness turned to anger in a flash because they knew no other way to express themselves. They were both hard because the world had made them hard. It was something he saw in himself, that he had tried to soften, because he hated the way violence and ignorance made him feel. Roxie had the power to break the cycle, but every time he tried to help her, she resisted to the point where it escalated into a fight with him, and it felt like instead of freeing her from that life, she was pulling him back into it.

Thinking about a life with Kate… about kissing Kate, making love to her for the first time. The next time. Quinn lay on his bed and closed his eyes, and knew that everything about it was right.

And he knew he couldn't wait until graduation to ask her.

A month.

He'd give them both a month, and then whether or not she was with Andrew, he was going to call her and ask her to be his.

Chapter 9

HER DOCTOR'S APPOINTMENT WAS NEARLY two hours away in Raleigh, but she had slept almost the entire way there. The closer she got to Raleigh, the closer she was to Quinn. It was all she could do not to beg her mom to drive thirty more minutes northwest to Durham. She was practically bouncing in her seat when they made the turnoff into Raleigh to the medical offices. She even craned her neck longingly toward the exit that would have carried them to Jon and Quinn's apartment, then she heard her mom laugh.

"What?" Kate fought a blush. "I thought I saw something."

"Was it six three with green eyes?" Her mom slid a glance her way. "I take it you two made up or something?"

"Or something," she mumbled.

She heard her mom sigh. "I know you don't like my being nosy, but don't you think you're being unfair to Andrew?"

"I'm going to break up with him." Kate fidgeted nervously. "Only, I kind of told his mom I'd go to dinner with them when they got back. I need a dress for it, by the way. Mrs. Whitman said something conservative. I guess I'll do it after the dinner."

"I think I have a dress in the back of my closet that will fit you. It was a size too small. Don't worry. It's not an old-lady dress."

"Come on, Mom. You don't dress like an old lady." It was true. Her mom wore skinny jeans and trendy tops or formfitting dresses with killer heels. She worked out four nights a week, and even though Kate cooked the nights she was home, she usually only ate a salad or an extremely small portion. "I must have got my fashion sense from Dad. I look ridiculous in that kind of stuff."

"You do not. You're just too self-conscious." Her mom reached over and tugged at her hair. "So what happened with Quinn the other day?"

"Promise you won't get mad?"

Her mom gave her a look. "Is this an off-the-record conversation?"

"One hundred percent."

"I'll *try* not to get mad."

Her mom never got mad at her. Not for anything off the record, so she told her mom everything. Almost everything. She told her about Quinn picking her up... about him throwing rocks at Lindsay's window and about them talking and everything he'd said. Then she told her about the deal he'd made... omitting the kiss, her new nickname, and that she'd mauled his hair and it was softer than she'd ever dreamed.

And she told her about Andrew's exploding suitcase of condoms, and her mom almost hit another car because she was laughing so hard.

An hour later, neither one of them were laughing. She was sitting on an exam table with a doctor she had never met before peering between her legs. Her mother stood behind her, examining the ceiling tiles. Tears of humiliation leaked out of the corner of her eyes as the doctor's fingers stabbed at her insides. She flinched, snatched her legs closed, and glared at him.

"Was that painful?" Dr. Schmidt asked.

Her throat was closing as she swallowed a cry, and she couldn't force any words through. She finally managed a small nod.

"Let's try something else." He stood and disposed of the gloves, and she was surprised they were not covered in blood after what he had done to her. "You can put your legs down now. I want to do a sonogram. I promise, this won't hurt."

Relaxing a little, she locked her legs together tight and glanced up at her mother. She felt her throat tighten further at the unshed tears in her mother's eyes. Taking as deep a breath as she could, she swore that she would not be a crybaby. She had rarely seen her mother cry, and the thought was almost as terrifying as the doctor resuming his exam. She hated it when her mom cried. A nurse stepped forward and adjusted her clothing, then squirted a clear substance on her stomach.

"Could she…" Her mother paused, her gaze becoming unfocused. "You think she might be *pregnant?*"

"Mom!" Kate exclaimed.

"That's not likely," Dr. Schmidt replied absently. "I just want to take a look. There seems to be an anomaly with Kate's reproductive system."

Exchanging looks with her mother, she saw a worried expression grow on her face. Kate's gaze flickered to the doctor, then to the black-and-white image that suddenly appeared on the screen. Unable to make sense of what she was looking at but unable to look away, Kate tuned out the rest of the conversation. She could only remember trying to lose her virginity and the excruciating pain that had followed.

The cold, smooth press of the instrument crossed and crisscrossed her stomach. They all looked at the screen, but it still didn't make much sense to Kate, and Dr. Schmidt was frowning. After taking several pictures, the doctor turned the machine off, and the nurse stepped forward to wipe the goo from her stomach.

"Go ahead and get dressed," he said quietly, then looked at her mother. "Mrs. McGuire, if you'll both come to my office when you are done."

With trembling hands, she managed to find her underwear and put them back on, then the rest of her clothes. Her mother had taken a seat on the doctor's stool and was staring at the ultrasound machine, as if it held the answer to the mystery of the universe.

"It'll be all right, Katie," she said softly. "Don't worry. It'll be fine."

Unable to think of anything to say, she shrugged. "As long as he doesn't have to exam me again, it will."

Her mom smiled, dragging her gaze from the machine. "I know, honey. I'm so sorry. I've went through it too many times to count now. It never gets easier."

She held out her arms, and Kate went into them. For a long moment they just held each other, then her mother finally stood and smoothed her hair back.

"It'll be fine," she repeated. "Come on then. The doctor is waiting."

Kate followed her down the hall lined with white doors, all except for one. Dr. Schmidt's door was a dark grained wood with black hardware, more ornamented than the others. The door was slightly ajar, and the doctor was already sitting behind his desk, reading from a thick medical book. A dozen depictions of the female reproductive system adorned the walls, along with some very official-looking diplomas.

For at least two minutes they sat there, watching him read. He turned one page, then another, before her mother not so subtly crossed her legs and kicked the wooden desk. The doctor pulled off his glasses and rubbed his eyes, then leaned back in his chair.

"I think," he said slowly, "what we are looking at is a condition called vaginal agenesis."

Kate squirmed uncomfortably at the term, her ears burning. It felt as if her tongue were stuck to the roof of her mouth.

"What?" her mother asked.

"The medical term is MRKH, or Mayer-Rokitansky-Küster-Hauser Syndrome. Roughly one in five thousand girls are born with this condition. Kate's reproductive system is not fully developed, and it never will be." He turned the book to face them both and pointed to a photograph of a reproductive chart. "I've read through the other doctor's notes, and it seems to be pretty clear. I would like to have an MRI done to be sure, but it looks as if the uterus, ovaries, fallopian tubes, cervix, and one of the kidneys is missing."

"Her kidney is missing? What the hell does that mean, missing?" her mother demanded, her voice rising. "She has never had surgery."

"No, this is a congenital birth defect. Kate was born this way." He glanced at Kate. "This is the reason you have not menstruated yet. You do not have the proper... ah... equipment. That's why it hurt when I tried to perform the exam. Instead of a vaginal opening, you have a small indentation. A dimple, if you will... which means that you will need to have surgery before you can have sexual intercourse. All signs indicate this is MRKH, but there could be another explanation."

"Like *what?*" Kate asked, finally finding her voice.

"Turner syndrome. Girls born with Turner's are usually

short with visible physical anomalies as well as kidney abnormalities. You appear perfectly normal in your outward appearance for a girl your age, and your mother is petite as well. We'll need to do a DNA test to make sure you have normal chromosomes, then I want you to come back in for the MRI. If this is MRKH, which I believe it is, we will discuss the options for fixing it so that you may have a normal sex life." He withdrew a pen from his coat and reached for a yellow legal pad. "Have you attempted to have sex before?"

"No," Kate replied automatically, her gaze shooting down to her hands. She felt a sudden urge to pick up the book and slam it into the doctor's head. Her entire body tensed, very aware of her mother watching her lie.

"If this is MRKH, you will need to prepare yourself for what comes next. The most efficient corrective procedure is major reconstructive surgery. We take a portion of your lower intestine out and create a vaginal canal. It does come with some risks, but I believe the benefits will outweigh any of those. You will be able to live a normal life."

"What about her kidney? Is she… is Kate going to be okay?" her mother asked, her voice trembling.

"She'll be just fine," he replied. "A person can live with one and have a perfectly normal life. I would caution against any rough contact sports… definitely no motorcycle riding, and she should start monitoring her diet to avoid high blood pressure later on. It's best to start healthy eating habits early."

"Can she have children?"

The doctor leaned back in his chair once more. "If this is indeed MRKH, then Kate will never be able to carry a child or get pregnant. There have been successful clinical trials done with uterine transplants at Baylor University, but as far as I know, those trials concluded in only one live birth and it is an extremely rare and expensive procedure. With the advancements in medicine, if we are able to find a functioning ovary, then she would be able to have a surrogate carry the child. However, there is a possibility that this trait could be passed on to any children or grandchildren that might result. The truth is, there is not enough research to know for sure."

"So it's genetic… This… this isn't something that I did?" Her mom reached for her hand and squeezed it tight. "It's not because I might have had wine before I knew I was pregnant or took some medication that caused this?"

"Honestly, Mrs. McGuire, not enough is known about this condition to prove one way or another. There are studies that have been done, and they are still being done. I encourage you, if you have access to a computer, to go out and do your own research. It will help you… both of you… come to terms with this diagnosis."

"Do our own research?" her mother repeated. She let go of Kate's hand and crossed her arms. "You're serious?"

"I am. Unfortunately, I don't have any brochures or anything like that to give you, and I'm honestly not sure if any exist. But"—he reached for a pen and began jotting something down on a sheet of paper—"this website could help. It's to Boston Children's Hospital. They have some programs for girls with this condition."

Her mom took the paper from him and studied it for a moment. "And this surgery? Kate has school. She starts college this fall."

"There will be an adjustment, to be sure. But we could schedule the surgery for early summer, and she will have plenty of time to recover, or she could delay her fall term. If it's all right with you, I would like to have my medical resident examine Kate. He just graduated from Duke, and this would be an excellent opportunity for him to see this kind of condition. Many of my colleagues would likely find it interesting, to say the least."

"No," Kate whispered, glaring at him. "No, it is not *all right* with me."

Her mother pulled a face, a mulish expression that Kate knew well.

"I don't like this. I don't want my baby having surgery. Not right now."

"Mrs. McGuire—"

"How many of these surgeries have you done?"

The doctor looked fairly uncomfortable. "None. But I—"

"You've never performed it? And you think you'll railroad us into letting you do this without a second opinion while you bring in some kid fresh out of medical school to examine my eighteen-year-old daughter as if she's some kind of exhibit?" Her mother rose abruptly, her chair almost toppling backward. "Like hell you will. There must be another doctor that knows more about this."

"The Children's Hospital in Boston is probably the most prominent facility that deals with this condition, or Atlanta. I can get you a referral, if that's what you want."

Her mother stood and placed her hand on Kate's shoulder, tugging at her shirt to get her to rise.

"If that's where she needs to go for this, then we'll find a way. I want someone who knows what they are doing, and you're sitting there practically rubbing your hands in glee that my daughter *might* have a condition that you've never seen before and apparently have barely heard of. There is no way in hell that you're treating her. Get me a referral, and while you're at it, figure out a better way to tell the next poor girl who comes in here that she has this condition. This is my daughter, and she deserves better."

·····ↄ♀ↄ·····

The ride home was painfully silent, with no sound at all except for her mother trying to muffle the sound of crying.

Kate lay down in the back seat of her mom's car and felt nothing but emptiness. No babies. No sex. She felt cold inside and numb. She thought about Brittany and how just months ago she had bought a pregnancy test for her because she had unprotected sex and had suddenly started feeling sick. It had been a false alarm, and Kate remembered how Brittany had cried in relief and declared she never wanted to have kids.

Kids, Kate decided, she could deal without for now. She didn't want to think about it yet anyway. Didn't want to imagine it, because it felt as though if she let herself think about it, she would start crying and wouldn't be able to stop.

She thought about Andrew instead. He was a long way from being a virgin, and he'd been so crazy for her for making him wait, and she had been trying to prepare a speech for why they shouldn't be together. She could tell him this, and he'd be more than happy to end things with her. She tried to *picture* telling him, and the words that came in her mind sounded stupid and wrong. Like she was some kind of freak. She would tell him, and he would look at her in disgust, then tell all their friends what a freak she was… just like Jacob had done. And Quinn. She thought of Quinn, and it felt like her heart was going to split in half.

Her mom pulled the car up into the garage, and they both sat there. Neither making a move to get out and go inside.

"Mom?"

"Hmm," her mother replied, her voice slightly strangled.

"Please don't tell anyone."

"Oh, Kate. Your dad needs to know. We need to make plans."

Kate bit her lip. Tried to imagine sitting there while her mom explained it to her father. How her female parts were not fully formed. How they never would be. His face would turn red, and he'd all but beg her mom not to say anything else about it. She pictured her father walking her down the aisle and giving her away, but couldn't see it. Not anymore. Being there for the birth of his grandchildren. He would never be there for hers. Jon and Miranda's but not hers.

"I don't want to be there when you tell Dad. And I... I don't want to talk about it anymore."

"It's going to be all right Katie," her mom said softly. She turned around to face the back seat. "Promise me that you'll just put this from your mind. At least for a little while. You have all the time in the world to think about this. Don't worry about it for now. Just finish school, and we'll deal with everything this summer."

"Okay," Kate whispered, her voice small and throat closed. More than anything in the world she wanted to forget it. To put it from her mind and pretend that she was still a normal eighteen-year-old girl and not some kind of freak.

Her mom reached into the back seat and held out her hand. After a moment Kate extended her own and let her mom squeeze it tightly. For a long time both of them just sat there. Not saying a word. And not able to let go.

Chapter 10

K ATE CRIED.
And she cried.

For nearly two days she did nothing but cry, unable to stop no matter how many times her mom hugged and kissed her or her dad hugged her and told her that he loved her. There was a wound so deep inside her heart she knew that it was never going to heal. Thinking it would help, her mom invited Lindsay over, but she couldn't bring herself to tell her friend anything, even though she kept asking her what was wrong. She knew Lindsay would tell Mitch, and then he would tell Andrew, and she didn't want anyone to know. The thought of people at school finding out caused her to have her first panic attack. Her mom rushed her to the emergency room, and they sent her home and told her to see her regular doctor, who promptly wrote her a prescription for an antidepressant and increased the antianxiety medication she was already on. She tried forgetting about it, but it was impossible not to feel *wrong*. As if people could look at her now and tell that she was different.

The night that she was supposed to go to dinner with Andrew's family, she nearly canceled half a dozen times. Oddly enough the thought of seeing him was calming, and she needed something to distract her from the tsunami of emotions she was experiencing. Reluctantly she let her mom style her hair, carefully curling it into beach-style waves, then gathering it to one side so that it draped down her neck in a sort of messy ponytail. She pinned the sides, then finished it off with a dusting of hair spray. Her mom had loaned her a formfitting black dress that had a little flare near the knee. It looked like she was getting ready for a funeral, and that was what it felt like too.

"You look perfect, honey."

"Thanks, Mom." The words felt wooden on her tongue.

"Got your necklace?"

Kate opened her jewelry case and pulled out the pendant necklace Andrew had given her for Christmas, then waited as her mom secured it to her neck. The sound of knocking from downstairs startled them both, and Kate glanced up at her mom through the reflection of the mirror. It was one of those picturesque mother-daughter moments, and her chest hurt, then her throat hurt as she realized that she would never do this with her own daughter. She'd done her best to suppress the thought of her infertility, but nothing seemed to help. The feelings would catch her off guard and had become increasingly distressing. Combined with the frequent crying bouts her mother seemed unable to control, the last forty-eight hours had been excruciating, especially since Jon had shown up for the weekend. More than anything, she didn't want her siblings to know what was going on. Quinn hadn't come home this trip, and for once, Kate was grateful.

"Sounds like Andrew's here." Her mom squeezed her shoulders tight for a moment, then let go. "Kate…"

"Yeah, Mom?" Kate started stuffing makeup in the

clutch that went with the dress. Hearing the hesitancy in her mom's voice, she sensed a sermon coming.

"I know that... what the doctor said, if it's true, it doesn't mean you... I just don't want you to..." Her mom stopped, an expression of discomfort on her face. As if she had waded into this conversation with no real idea of what she wanted to say and now could find no easy way out of it.

"Don't want me to what?" Kate asked. "Have unprotected sex? Get knocked up and have to drop out of school?"

"That's not what I meant." Sorrow flashed across her mom's expression, and she stepped forward, looking up at her. "I don't want you to get hurt. And just because... just because you can't get pregnant, doesn't mean you don't have to be careful. Do you understand what I'm saying?"

It felt as if her head were about to catch on fire. She nodded, embarrassed beyond belief to be talking about venereal diseases with her mom. Their first "talk," when Kate was thirteen, had been just as mortifying.

It suddenly felt as if she couldn't breathe. Just days ago she had found out that she couldn't have sex or children, now she was expected to go interact with Andrew's family as if they were going to have a future together someday. She had already felt bad about misleading him while he had been gone, and now she felt even worse. She was a fraud... a fake girlfriend, and a fake *girl*.

"I don't want this," she asked, her eyes filling with tears. "Why is this happening to me? Andrew isn't going to understand."

"Oh, Katie. Don't cry. You'll ruin your makeup," her mom whispered, grabbing a tissue from her vanity and dabbing at her eyes. "You don't have to tell Andrew anything unless you want to. Aren't you forgetting something?"

"No." She knew what her mom was going to say. That

she had planned on breaking up with Andrew and that she was going to wait for Quinn. The loss of any future with him was overwhelming and unbearably painful, which was why she had deliberately stopped thinking about him. After years of unrequited love, it was remarkably easy to do. "I'm not forgetting anything."

Her mom's gaze filled with sadness. "Don't push him away, Kate. This doesn't change the fact that you have feelings for each other. I think Quinn was right to give you both time to—"

"I don't have feelings for him. Not anymore." Kate clenched her jaw and looked away. She had thought, maybe, he might at least text her, but she hadn't heard anything from him. He was probably back with Roxie by now. "No one will want me like this. Especially not Quinn."

"That's not true. Honey, it is *not true*." Her mom started to cry again, which made her feel terrible. "You can't give up like this. Not on Quinn and not on yourself. You are so beautiful and courageous and wonderful. We're going to get through this Kate. I promise."

She had never experienced such emotional pain in her entire life, and she didn't know how to deal with it. She couldn't imagine anyone accepting her or loving her, and she wanted to lock her heart up tight so no one could hurt it. If they kept talking about it, she was going to lose control of her emotions, and she didn't have a handle on them very well to begin with.

"I need to go. Andrew's waiting on me."

"Okay." Her mom blinked quickly, trying to put on a brave face. "If you want to come home early, call, and your dad or I will come get you. I've been reading up on MRKH and… in some cases there is no surgery needed at all. There is a nonsurgical option available, and the procedure the doctor mentioned, that isn't even the only one. It's actually not even the most common one anymore. I have an appointment scheduled for you in Atlanta, after you graduate. And I found a support group online. They gave me all sorts of good information. There are other girls out there with this condition, all over the world. Some of them in third-world countries with no access to the kind of doctors that we have here in America. You're going to be fine. I promise."

Her dad tapped on the door and poked his head in, thankfully. The anxiety pill she had taken earlier was beginning to work, but she still felt the vestiges of panic that had been coursing through her since her appointment.

"You look pretty, honey." Her dad shifted his gaze to her mom, looking worried. "Are you sure you're up for this? If you don't want to go, I'll tell Andrew you're not feeling well."

"I'm going." She had to get out of the house. Her parents were hovering, and she couldn't bear seeing the worry in their eyes. She forced herself to smile. "I'll be fine."

Her dad didn't look happy about it, but he gave her a quick hug. She left her parents standing in her room, whispering to each other. The look on Andrew's face as she made her way downstairs was almost enough to make her feel better. He smiled, his gaze moving up and down as he let out a soft whistle.

"Kate. Wow." He met her at the end of the stairs, so they were almost the same height. "Holy shit, you look incredible."

"Thank you." She sensed his surprise when she wrapped her arms around his neck and hugged him, and because he was familiar and safe, she let him kiss her.

"I missed you too," he murmured, leaning back to look into her eyes. "Don't cry, babe. I was only gone two weeks."

"Is that what you've been squalling about?" Her brother's voice came from behind Andrew. His gaze was narrowed slightly. "Jesus, I thought you were dying or something."

"Shut up, Jon." Kate felt her face heat. She looked back at Andrew. "Get me out of here. Please."

"Anything for you, babe."

Andrew laced his fingers with hers and pulled her out the door. She lifted her middle finger at Jon as she walked past him, leaving him gaping after her.

"Your dad was kind of intense tonight," Andrew said as he pulled out of her driveway. "I guess he's still pissed about that kiss."

Kate shrugged. "He never said anything to me." Which was true. He hadn't said anything. He just started grumbling whenever Andrew's name was mentioned. She couldn't think of anything to talk about and felt awkward trying to come up with something to say. Andrew glanced at her, giving her a slow smile as his gaze moved up and down the dress with appreciation in his gaze. He was about to tell her how beautiful she looked, and the last thing she felt was beautiful. "How was your vacation?"

Those were the magical words, because Andrew launched into every detail of his trip. One of his cousins had been able to fly in the day after he arrived, so he had spent most of his time with them. His mom, he said, ripped him a new one about what had happened right before they left.

"I just wanted to say I'm sorry you had to see that. I felt like crap right after you told me all that stuff, and then you see my past literally everywhere." He reached over and placed his hand on her knee, looking into her eyes. "But I swear, all that's behind me. I know you want to take it slow, and that's okay. But you have to answer one question for me."

"Okay," she said, distracted by his hand inching up. She put her hand on top of his, stopping him from going farther.

"What color are they?"

Kate blinked at him. "What color are what?"

He waited until he was stopped at a red light, then turned toward her. "What color are your panties?"

"Black," she replied, struggling to keep her voice even. "Why?"

"Lace?"

"Yes."

"Can I have them?" A smile settled easily over his handsome face as drew a lazy circle on her knee. "At the end of the night, take them off and give them to me. Bonus points if you slip them in my pocket in the restaurant. We can take it slow, but it doesn't mean we can't have a little fun. Right?"

The shame was crushing. She pasted a fake smile on her face while beneath her calm façade panic was beginning to set in. She started thinking about Jacob. How he had suggested maybe her hymen was too tough and wanted to try again, so she let him touch her *there* with his fingers, and even that had hurt. He'd tried to force it, more than once, and she'd screamed in pain. He said she felt different from his last girlfriend, though at the time she didn't know what he meant. Kate had panicked and broke up with him. A few days later, she found out that he'd told his friends she was some kind of super virgin. The nickname had stuck for months, with even Brittany and Lindsay teasing her about it until she lied and said that Jacob was the one who couldn't get it up and she wasn't even a virgin.

Reaching into her purse, she grabbed an anxiety pill and shoved it into her mouth, hoping it would take effect quickly. She didn't want to feel anything, ever again.

"What was that?" Andrew asked.

"Nothing," she mumbled.

"Are you okay?" He pulled into a parking spot at the

country club and killed the engine, taking his seat belt off so he could turn and look at her. "You've barely said five words to me tonight. I'm sorry about the underwear thing. I wasn't really joking, but I'm sorry if I made you mad. And if it's about the condoms, I already know how dumb I was back then. I hope you can forgive—"

"Take me somewhere else," she blurted out. "Please."

Andrew frowned. "Right now? My parents are in there waiting on us."

"I can't do this." Her voice wavered, and she felt the sting of unshed tears building. "I can't go in there."

"Talk to me. What's wrong?" He leaned across the console and put his hands on her cheeks, his blue eyes studying her. "Are you mad at me? Is this about the suitcase?"

She shook her head, tears falling across her cheeks. "Just get me out of here. I can't f-fucking do this."

"Okay. There's a house party on the beach if you want to go."

"Yes, just drive. Please."

Without another word he put the car in reverse and backed them out of the parking spot. Within seconds they were flying down the streets of Wilmington. Feeling beneath the seat, Kate found a fifth of whiskey and turned it up. Andrew looked at her curiously but didn't comment. By the time they made it past Wrightsville Beach, Kate already had a buzz. She was almost finished before he took it away from her.

"Are you sure you're okay?" he asked, sounding concerned. "I've never seen you drink before, and you're guzzling it like a beast."

"I'm fine." Kate rolled the window down and stuck her head out, letting the ocean air clear her head a bit. Tears trailed across her cheeks, but the wind blew them away. If she couldn't have sex, she *could* do other stuff with Andrew, but she didn't want that either. She wanted Quinn. She wanted that night back when he'd held her in his arms... when the secret she had been carrying for so long was out in the open, and he had made her a *deal*. The sweetness of it seemed less now. If he felt even a fraction of what she felt, he wouldn't have been able to stay away... and now it was too late.

She wondered if she could get so drunk she wouldn't be able to remember her own name, and part of her was scared that she'd lose control and pass out. She pushed the fear away. What could happen? Someone rape her?

The thought was enough to make her snort with laughter.

Beside her she could feel Andrew's worried gaze on her. Ignoring it, she grabbed the bottle between his legs and finished it off.

Chapter 11

·······⟋⟍·······

S UNLIGHT BLAZED ACROSS HER EYES, coming in from a row of windows facing the ocean. The world was an upside-down kaleidoscope of colors that was tilting back and forth. Why were her bedroom windows open? And when had she moved to the beach? With a groan she pushed herself onto her back and found her gaze locking onto a pair of familiar blue eyes.

"So… you're finally awake."

Andrew's voice whirred in her head, vibrating against the walls of her brain. It felt like she'd been kicked or trampled on. With another deep groan and nausea threatening to send her scrambling for the nearest bathroom, Kate tried to focus on her surroundings.

She was on the floor of an enclosed porch, wrapped up in a pile of sandy blankets, with Andrew. He was shirtless. Upon further inspection, it appeared he was pant-less as well. Taking in the state of her own dress, she realized that she was probably the culprit for his lack of clothing. She was wearing his dress clothes, even the blazer.

"What the hell…?"

He grinned at her as he brushed her hair out of her face. "Let's just say you owe me one. By the way, half the class saw most of you naked last night."

"What?"

"Apparently when Kate McGuire gets drunk, she's a streaker."

"Oh, Jesus. Please tell me I didn't." She fell back against the blankets, and the world began throbbing anew. Exploring beneath Andrew's shirt, she found the strapless bra and hoped that at least she'd left that on. "My parents are going to kill me."

"Your parents think you are spending the night at Lindsay's. I had her cover for you."

"What happened last night?"

"You drank a lot of whiskey, then some tequila. At some point Lindsay took you to the bathroom, and the next thing I knew you were running through the house without any clothes."

"Any?" she repeated, sitting back up.

"Well, at least I got to finally see your underwear," he teased. "So did everyone else, I bet. I couldn't find your dress, but I covered you up the best I could. Had to put my clothes on you at least three or four times, because you insisted that you were hot. I took care of you. Made sure none of those pervs tried anything. In case you're worried, nothing happened."

"Thanks," she replied weakly. "I'm really sorry."

"Sorry?" he snorted. "It was kind of fun, seeing you let go. I've never seen you drunk before. But I am worried about you though."

"Why?"

"Do you remember what we talked about last night?" he asked, sounding cautious. He took her hand and squeezed. "About… about your doctor?"

Kate bolted back up to a sitting position, panic spearing her right in the gut. "What? What did I tell you?"

"I'm not sure. You didn't make a lot of sense," he said gently. "You can talk to me, Kate. You know that, right?"

She gathered her knees to her chest and stared out at the water, rocking back and forth, remembering a haze of tears. Of Andrew holding her and whispering that it would be all right. Of laughing madly while dancing around the fire and everyone looking at her and laughing too. And Quinn. Why did she remember Quinn?

Andrew put his arms around her and held her tight. As much as her chest and throat hurt from the pressure, she couldn't cry. She was too filled with fear that she might have told someone. That she might have told Andrew and well before she was ready to talk about it at all.

"What did I say?" she whispered.

"Something about going to the doctor," he said softly. He pressed a kiss to the top of her head. "You said that you can't... you can't have kids. That you might have to have surgery. You just kept telling me you were sorry, over and over again. I couldn't make much out after that. You should have said something. I would have told my parents you weren't up for their stupid get-together."

"They're going to be mad at you. At both of us. I'm sorry... I just didn't think I could make it through with all this stuff going through my head." She had a birth defect that had been hiding in her body for eighteen years. Some people were born with an extra finger or a cleft palate. Things you could easily identify. Instead, she was missing the upper half of her vaginal canal and her reproductive organs, along with a kidney. She didn't even know where to begin trying to accept that she was deformed, and she felt ashamed of feeling that way because she knew there were other far more serious medical conditions.

"Are you ready to go? I'm starving," he rumbled. "I told

my parents that you needed me last night because of some personal stuff. They were less mad than I imagined, but I have to be home early."

"I'm sorry. So sorry for everything." She felt his hand stroke the back of her head. "I can't see you anymore. I'm sorry, but I can't. It's not you. There's something wrong with me."

"That's what you told me last night. You said it was over."

Kate froze, looking up at him. "I did?"

He nodded. "Is that still what you want?"

"I don't know. I don't know." Her chest rose and fell quickly, tension in her chest and limbs making her tremble. "If you knew everything, you'd understand, but I can't tell you. I'm sorry."

"Stop apologizing." His voice was gentle but confused.

She didn't want to cry, but she couldn't hold back any longer. Couldn't stop the keening wail that began bellowing through her insides until it came out in a near shriek. His arms came around her, crushing her air. It felt wonderful to let it go, and she suddenly couldn't stop as the walls she had erected came crashing down around her.

The sun was a bit higher in the sky by the time she had calmed down enough to wipe her face on his shirt, but she couldn't do anything about the copious amount of snot that was trying to escape.

"I like you, Andrew," Kate whispered. "I really do. But I can't be with you. I can't be with anyone."

He was silent for a long time, and she knew that she must have said something about not being able to have sex. The night was a blur, but she remembered the panic on Andrew's face when she'd started getting hysterical. She hated that she was using her diagnosis to break things off with him instead of being honest, but she was too mentally exhausted for the truth. There was no point in the truth anymore. She just wanted to be alone.

"I don't know what you're going through right now," Andrew said quietly. "But I care about you. I want to be there for you."

Kate shook her head, feeling raw inside. "We can be friends. But I can't... I just can't be anything else to you. Do you hate me?"

"No." He leaned back, his expression filled with hurt. "I don't hate you. I just wish you didn't have to get drunk to tell me how you felt about me."

"What else did I do?" she whispered. There was something he wasn't telling her. She could tell that something was bothering him. "Did I say anything else?"

He stared at her for a moment, then looked out at the ocean, shrugging slightly. "No. Nothing."

"Andrew, please. Did I say anything about... about my doctor? Or s-surgery?"

"No." One dark blond eyebrow raised a bit. "Why? Are you going to be all right?"

"Yeah." Kate let out a breath of relief. She was never drinking again. Ever. "Yeah, of course. It's just a minor surgery. No big deal. I may not even have it."

"Good. You had me worried."

The morning sun reflected in his eyes made them more brilliant than ever, turning them almost aquamarine. They were really beautiful eyes, she thought suddenly. How had she never noticed before? He'd teased her once about them having ugly children, but she could see a little boy with Andrew's eyes and a little girl with long blond hair. She could see Delia being a doting grandmother, and Andrew was going to be a good husband and father.

"One day you'll thank me for letting you go," Kate whispered, pressing a kiss to his lips. "Trust me."

He scoffed. "Is that supposed to make me feel better?"

"No. But it's the truth."

"The truth?" he replied, his tone bitter. "Do you even know what the truth is anymore, Kate? You didn't break up with me because of whatever the doctor told you. You told me you were in love with Quinn. Like I didn't already know."

"Are you sure you don't want me to drop you at Lindsay's?" Andrew asked as he turned onto her street. "Your parents are going to be pissed if they see us like this."

"I just want to go home." Kate wrapped his blazer around her tightly. "I'll have this dry-cleaned and bring it to you at school."

"Keep it."

"Andrew—"

"Please don't apologize again. You were drunk. I shouldn't have said anything." He reached over and squeezed her hand. "It's going to be okay, you know. Quinn's a lucky guy."

Kate shook her head. "I don't think you understand. I can't... I can't *be* with anyone."

"But it's not permanent." Andrew looked at her. "Right?"

"I don't know." She stared out the window, trying to stop thinking about it. "Please don't tell anyone."

"I'd never do that. I promise."

"Did I..." Kate felt tears course over her cheeks. "Did I say anything in front of anyone else?"

"Nothing that would make sense to them. Lindsay's probably going to have a lot of questions though."

Jon was in the driveway washing his car when they pulled up to the house. He did a double take when he saw her get out of the car wearing Andrew's clothes and Andrew wearing nothing but his boxers and a dirty gym shirt he'd found in the trunk. Throwing his sponge back into the bucket, he crossed the yard, his expression set into a scowl.

"You're a dead motherfucker," Jon snarled, looking straight at Andrew.

"Stay out of this," Kate ground out. "Leave him alone."

"You seriously slept with this asshole?"

"Jon!" She cringed, wishing she had accepted Andrew's offer to take her to Lindsay's. "This is none of your business."

"It's all right." Andrew set his hand at the small of her back. "Go inside."

Kate looked between the two of them uncertainly. "Are you sure?"

"I'm sure."

"She's not going anywhere." Jon glared at her. "Weren't you staying at *Lindsay's* last night?"

Andrew glanced at her. "He doesn't know?"

Kate shook her head, silently pleading with him. "You promised."

He stepped forward and wrapped his arms around her. "I promised," he repeated. "I'm here if you need me."

"Thank you."

"What is going on? Kate?" The anger had left Jon's voice, and now it was full of concern. "Is this about that doctor you went to see?"

Without answering, Kate turned and left them both standing there. Jon caught up with her just outside her room, breathless and looking worried.

"Hey. Are you okay?"

"I'm fine," she snapped. "I swear, if you repeat anything he told you to anyone I'll never speak to you again."

Jon drew back, obviously startled at the harshness of her tone. He blinked at her.

"Okay."

"What did he say to you?" she demanded.

"Nothing."

Miranda poked her head out of her room, her eyes wide. Kate glared at her. "Mind your own business, you brat."

Her sister gasped, her eyes filling with tears. She disappeared from view, slamming her door loudly.

"Geez, Kate, what the hell is your problem?" Jon said angrily. "That was uncalled for."

"Go away," Kate said, her voice cold. "Go on and tell Mom and Dad. I don't care."

Jon stared at her, looking bewildered and hurt. She felt like an utter bitch, but her heart was broken. Anger that had been building rapidly since her appointment burned up everything else: depression, anxiety, hopelessness, fear, insecurity. Rage, such an unfamiliar thing, was twinging in her veins. She was jealous of her siblings for all that they would have that she never could. They would have marriage and happiness and children and normalcy. Images of everything she would miss hit her squarely in the chest so hard it felt like she couldn't breathe. She would be alone until the end of time. She suddenly understood why Roxie lashed out the way she did. It was a way of protecting yourself from feeling overwhelming sadness, and that was how she felt. Overwhelmed... by all of it.

"I'm not going to rat you out, Kate," Jon said, an edge to his voice. "Just tell me what's going on."

He would tell Quinn, Kate thought desperately. Even if she didn't care about that, she knew she couldn't tell Jon. She wasn't discussing lady business with her brother, and Miranda was so nosy she'd probably find out on her own, but she had begged her mom not to tell them anything.

"It's none of your business."

"It is if I need to drive over to the Whitmans' and drag Andrew out by his blond hair and beat the shit out of him." He studied her, his dark blue eyes angry. "Did he hurt you?"

"No. Oh my God, Jon. Really?" Kate glared at him. "No. He was a gentleman."

"Then why are you wearing his clothes?"

"Because it's not your business, that's why." Kate opened her door and glanced back at her brother. "You won't tell anyone?"

"What am I going to tell them? I don't know anything. Besides, you have way more ammunition against me." He offered her a tentative smile. "Am I right?"

Kate gave a small nod, some of the tension easing from her. "I'm sorry."

"It's all right. I'm used to all the fighting from when Roxie lived with us. It's just strange to see you acting like a drama queen."

His words caught her attention. "They didn't get back together?"

"No." He shifted his weight uncomfortably. "I thought that you guys were... you know... talking."

"I haven't heard from him." Kate swallowed against a wave of hurt. She couldn't forget Roxie's words about Quinn's sexual preferences. As someone who was officially not capable of dirty or rough sex, well, that excluded her from the running for a place in his bed. "How is he doing?"

"He's Quinn." Jon shrugged. "Studying like he's possessed. Got another part-time job. I barely see him anymore."

"Another girlfriend?"

"Nope." Jon crossed his arms over his chest. He gave her a knowing look, and Kate felt her cheeks heat. "So what's the deal? I figured you'd be jumping for joy. Jolly Green is on the market."

She held her features in place carefully, amazed that she could be so calm outwardly, when a storm raged anew.

"And I'm not," she said, measuring her words carefully. It wasn't technically a lie. She wasn't available. A wave of nausea hit her suddenly, and she tried swallowing and breathing to stop it from happening.

Jon shrugged. "Just thought you should know. So are you going to tell me what happened with Whitman last night?"

"No. I'm going to go puke now." Kate pressed a hand over her mouth and ran to her bathroom, where she puked up what felt like a lung, her stomach, and possibly the one and only kidney she had. She groaned as she sank to the floor. A cool washcloth bathed her face, and she looked up to see Jon hovering over her.

"How much did you drink?"

"How much is a lot?"

"I won't say anything this time," Jon said quietly. "But don't make a habit of it."

"You drink all the time."

"I'm twenty-three, and it's different. You're a girl."

"You've been drinking since you were sixteen," Kate tossed back. "And trust me, if I never drink again, it will be too soon."

"Good." Jon shoved his fingers through his hair. "You should go apologize to Rand. She acts tough, but she gets her feelings hurt easy. You know that."

"I know." She sighed, lowering her face to the cool bathroom tile. "I will. But I need sleep right now."

"You can't sleep here." Jon hauled her to her feet and helped her stumble to her bed. "Do you want to change? You have vomit on your clothes."

"Just go," she mumbled. "Tell Mom I have the flu or something."

"I'm not lying for you." He pulled the covers up to her chin and grinned down at her. "And if you know what's good for you, that apology to Miranda will be sooner, rather than later."

Chapter 12

......⚬⅋⚬......

"HEY, KID, YOU FINISH THIS Camry up, I got another one for you," his boss said from above the mechanic's pit, his boots eye level with Quinn. "Computer glitch on a Honda."

"About ten more minutes," he called.

"Well hurry up," Greg complained. "I'd like to get out of here by five tonight."

"Yes, sir." Quinn was eager to get out of the pit as fast as possible. He preferred working in Luther's shop in Wilmington. At least Luther used a lift. Greg's was a smaller garage, and the old man was grouchy on his best day. Luther didn't care if he worked till midnight. Greg was a strict nine to fiver, the pay was shit, and Quinn mostly did oil changes instead of what he liked to do—motor rebuilds. "What's the problem with the Honda?"

"Hell I don't know," Greg grumbled. "Damn computers. And it's Eddie's day off."

Eddie was the only full-time mechanic in the shop besides Greg, and the old man hated anything to do with technology. One of the most chronic complainers that

Quinn had ever met, the only way to get through a day of work was to keep his head down and agree with everything the old man said.

"I'll take a look." Quinn finished up the Camry's oil change, then went over to look at the Honda. The owner, an older lady with white hair, was fiddling with her phone. "Ma'am, you're having trouble with your car?"

"Yes." She held her phone up to him, frustrated. "I can't get my Bluetooth to work. My grandson drove it yesterday, and now nothing works."

He smiled. "May I see your phone?"

She handed it over, and Quinn took it over to the car, punched in the settings on the car, and synced the phone within a matter of minutes.

"Do you use it for music or your navigation?"

"Both."

"Try it now." He handed her phone back, and she turned her music on, the strains of Stevie Nicks pumping through the garage. "Great band."

"Oh, thank you!" She beamed at him. "I can't believe you already fixed it."

"That'll be fifty dollars," Greg barked.

Quinn shot him a look, but the woman was already reaching in her purse. She stuffed the money into Quinn's hands, and he handed it off to Greg. It was just like the old grouch to cheat someone, even a sweet little old grandmother.

"Thank you again." She patted Quinn on the arm, then got in her vehicle and backed out.

"I'll clean up, then we can go."

Greg waved him off. "Go on, I'll get it. Your girlfriend's been out there waiting for an hour."

"I don't have a girlfriend," Quinn replied. He glanced at his phone, seeing he had a voice mail from Roxie, and wondered what she wanted. He hadn't seen or heard from her since she walked out, and honestly, he hadn't missed the drama.

"Whatever. I'll see you tomorrow."

Quinn grabbed his things from the office and ducked out as Greg was closing the garage doors. Roxie's car was parked beside his motorcycle, the windows up and car running. When they were dating, she would hang around the garage, waiting for him to get off work, which annoyed Greg to no end. This time she wasn't alone. As he approached, she rolled down her window and killed the engine.

"Hey." She greeted him with a smile. "Got a minute?"

"Sure." He set his messenger bag down against his bike and leaned down to peer into the car. Her passenger, the guy she had moved in with, glared at him. "What do you want?"

"How have you been?" Roxie asked softly.

He hadn't seen her in a month, and now she showed up with her boyfriend, wanting to know how he was? Quinn thought of several interesting things to say but decided he wasn't in the mood for games.

"I'm fine. What do you want, Rox?"

"The car." She bit her lip, her dark eyes flashing with hurt. "You said I could have it, right?"

"Yes."

"I need to have it put in Glen's name. Can you meet him sometime and do that?"

"I said *you* could have it. Why would I put it in his name?" Quinn asked, raising a brow.

"Because I'm asking. Isn't that good enough?" Her voice had an edge to it. "Will you do it or not?"

"Fine. Next time a phone call or text is *good enough*." He cut his gaze over to Glen. "When do you want to do this?"

"Friday afternoon," Roxie said. "You don't have class. He can meet you before your shift here."

"Can't it speak?" he murmured.

"Be nice." She smiled at him slowly and began giving him one of her signature, sultry looks.

Quinn narrowed his gaze at her, not sure if she was screwing with him or with the guy next to her. Or both. "Friday is fine. Bring his insurance and license. I'm not doing it twice. And he pays."

"I miss you, Quinn," Roxie whispered, running her fingers over the back of his hand. "I really do. Are you seeing someone?"

It was a fresh reminder of what she had done... or tried to do... with Jon. The time they had been apart had been a combination of regret and relief. Regret because he'd really thought he could make a difference in her life and giving up on someone he cared about stuck so hard in his craw it sometimes felt he'd choke on it... but relief because he was able to see and think clearly for the first time in years.

"Hey, man," he said, tapping the side of the car. "Good luck with whatever this is. I'll see you Friday. Bye, Rox."

She looked genuinely upset as he turned around and got on his bike, putting the messenger bag in his saddle.

"Quinn, wait! Please."

"I have nothing to say to you, Roxie. I wish you the best, but I'm done," he said shortly.

"I'm moving to New York."

Quinn turned to look at her, surprised, then he glanced at the car. "With him?"

Her heart suddenly in her eyes, Roxie nodded. "Please... can we just talk for a minute?"

"Rox—"

"I need you to tell me I'm doing the right thing. That I'm not making a huge mistake," Roxie said, her voice shaking as she walked toward him. "You're the smartest person that I know."

He jerked his head toward the car. "And what does he

think about your being here, asking me these questions? If you're this unsure, maybe you already have your answer. Why do you want my opinion?"

"Because you always have everything figured out." She gave him a tentative smile, but it slid from her face when he didn't return it.

"I *had* everything figured out," Quinn returned impatiently.

Roxie shook her head at him. "No. You were hiding. We both were."

"Yeah? Were you hiding when you tried to sleep with Jon?" he asked.

She flinched. "I told you I do stupid stuff sometimes. I just… I wanted you to see *me*. I felt like you saw this pathetic girl who needed a guard dog. That's not me." Her eyes closed. "Sometimes it is me, and sometimes it isn't. I don't want to be sheltered anymore. You were everything to me… but you never looked at me the way you look at her. I saw it last summer, but seeing you with her for the holidays, I knew. You never laugh with me. We never had fun together. Did you realize that? You're always planning or thinking with me. But with her? You're happy."

Quinn swallowed a load of hurt, not wanting to part with her on bad terms. She deserved to be happy, and he did bear some responsibility for their breakup. In all honesty… most of his hurt came from her infidelity and the way she had used Jon. He still feared for her though. Because Roxie admittedly made bad decisions, and now that she had pointed it out to him, he did see the same outlook of aggression and resentment of the world at large that his mother embraced. He saw a beautiful girl who could easily be ruined by the temptation of oblivion that drugs offered, and he realized at once that he had to let go of that fear. He had to let go of her, because the only person who could save Roxie… was Roxie.

"If it's safe… if he's not an asshole and he treats you like you deserve to be… and it's what *you* want to do, then you should go. Just don't get tied down in something you can't get out of. You don't need me to tell you what to do, Rox. You have to decide this on your own. Okay?"

"Thank you, Quinn," she whispered.

"Is he good to you?"

She nodded. "Yes."

"Then I'm happy for you."

Roxie rushed toward him and threw her arms around his neck. "I'm sorry if I hurt you."

His gaze flickering to the car, where Glen was standing behind the hood now and staring at them both, Quinn hugged her back. "I'm sorry too, Rox. Take care of yourself."

Quinn let her go and tugged his helmet on, then kicked the bike off and drove away. Amazingly, he didn't hurt anymore. The guilt was still there. He'd never wanted to help someone as badly as he'd wanted to help Roxie, but he was done looking backward.

When he got home, he sent Kate a text.

> **Quinn:** I'm thinking about coming home this weekend.

It was a few hours later when he got a reply.

> **Kate:** I won't be here. Going to spend some time with Gran.

> **Quinn:** OK. I was hoping we could talk soon.

He stared at the blinking ellipses on his phone for nearly ten minutes before they disappeared. He waited a week before he sent her anything else, but just like she'd done at Christmas, she ignored him.

⁓⁓⁓

The medication the doctor prescribed went a long way

to numbing some of the stronger emotions that were continually deluging her, but they couldn't drown them out completely. She could tell her family was worried about her. She woke up in the middle of the night sometimes to find Miranda in bed with her, her sister sometimes just lying there watching her with a worried expression. Sometimes it was her mom. The hole inside her was so deep it felt like nothing would ever fill it. After school started back, it was really hard to focus in class. The medicine either made her sleepy or completely numb, and her shifts at Cam's in the evenings were on complete automation. She showed up, she put on her uniform, but the buzz of the kitchen that once thrilled her seemed to revolve around her in a blur.

Bertie Cameron, who owned the steakhouse and was involved in the day to day at the restaurant, called a team meeting to go over their Valentine's Day menu, which was only a few days away. It was something he did every year, and since Kate had never had a boyfriend during that particular holiday, she'd never had a reason to request that night off. She was going to do it this year. Valentine's dinner at Cam's Steakhouse was a huge event for the restaurant, and she didn't want to see couples in love. She didn't want to see the romantic gazes on people's stupid faces while they ate their meal, then went home to do things normal people in love did.

Love was making her couples averse. She had stopped hanging out with Lindsay at school, because seeing her and Mitch together had always been nauseating, and now it was downright revolting. Brittany had finally given up on pursuing Andrew, but she wouldn't stop talking about sex with her new boyfriend... not until Kate had snapped at her in front of everyone at school that no one wanted to hear about her sex life. They currently were not speaking, and Kate had no intention of apologizing. Not after she had gone behind her back and tried to sleep with Andrew. She didn't need that kind of person in her life.

But then Bertie made an announcement as he put his arm around his girlfriend Beth, who had been working at Cam's for almost as long as Kate.

"We're pregnant!" he announced happily.

She didn't remember leaving the restaurant. Or arriving home. The next thing she recalled was cleaning her bedroom and then her mom coming in and pulling the blankets off her face.

"Kate?"

"Yeah?"

"What are you doing home so early?"

"I think I quit my job."

Her mom crawled onto the bed beside her and lay down. "Did something happen?"

"Bertie's girlfriend is pregnant. They're about to do their Valentine's event, and I just don't feel like being there right now."

"And this?" Her mom opened her hand and set a beautiful diamond-and-onyx art-deco ring on her pillow. "Your gran gave this to you. Why is everything your gran ever gave you in my room?"

Kate closed her eyes. "She gave me all that stuff, and it was always so I could pass it down to someone. That's not going to happen now. They're *family* heirlooms. You can give it all to Miranda and Jon or their kids. I don't want it."

Her mom sucked in a breath and was quiet for several moments. When she spoke again, her voice was hushed and full of emotion. "I'm going to put everything in the attic, and you can get it back when you're ready, because your gran wanted *you* to have it. She has other things set aside for Jon and Miranda. You just happen to be the only one responsible enough that she trusted to give them to now. You are still part of this *family*, Kate. That hasn't changed. And I know it hurts, but it's not always going to be like this.

You can't close yourself off from life. We love you so much. I don't like you giving away your things. You aren't thinking about hurting yourself are you?"

Kate looked at her. "No," she lied.

Her mom reached over and squeezed her hand. "You're going to start therapy tomorrow."

"I don't want to talk about it."

"It's not open for discussion," her mom replied firmly. "Call Bertie. You at least owe him an explanation for walking out. He's been good to you, Kate. He wrote you the recommendation to the school in Atlanta. I think it's probably best if you take some time off work. Just focus on school. Sound good?"

"Yeah." She managed a smile. "I'll call Bertie tomorrow."

"Did you look at the information I printed out for you about MRKH? About the dilation process?"

"Some of it." It sounded about as fun as a root canal. She had read a news article online about women born with the condition having reconstructive surgery so they could have a normal sex life and without thinking had gone down to the comments section.

"Disgusting. A waste of money doing a surgery like this. There are other things more important!"

"They still have an asshole and a mouth, right?"

"Even if they do build-a-vag, it's just a hole with no sensation. Neither one of you could feel anything."

"So do they look like Barbie dolls down there? I'm confused."

"So is it a boy or a girl?"

The last one had her throwing her phone across the room in fury.

"How do they pee?"

Seriously, how in the hell did people not know that a woman had a urethra, and it was completely separate from a birth canal? It wasn't just men who posted those horrible things. It was women. Some of them mothers of small children who, in their utter ignorance, wanted to know why MRKH wasn't usually detected until girls were teenagers.

Kate had changed more than a few diapers when she'd been younger, during a few babysitting gigs, and it did not comprise any sort of in-depth physical examination, unless you were a pervert or had a medical reason for doing so. There was no way to tell from outward appearances. Unless you were trying to put something in there, *you had no way of knowing*.

"You shouldn't sleep all day, honey. Why don't you come downstairs and show me how to make your gran's banoffee pie? I never could figure out how to make the caramel without burning it. I know it's your favorite."

"That sounds good." It didn't sound good at all. Food, which she used to both enjoy eating and preparing, was just a reminder that Atlanta might not happen if she had to have surgery. She didn't want banoffee pie or any other kind of pie. She just wanted to wake up from this nightmare.

"Come on." Her mom tugged her hand until she crawled out of bed. "You're probably going to have to hold my hand so I don't screw it up. Your dad told me this morning that he misses your cooking."

"He did?"

"He's been really upset, you know. This isn't just affecting you, Kate. It's been really hard on us too, and Miranda is scared. She doesn't understand what's going on. Jon is worried. I know how embarrassing this is, but you have nothing to be ashamed of."

That was exactly how she felt. Ashamed. That was why she couldn't answer Quinn. She couldn't bear for him to see her differently. But she knew that ignoring him was only going to make things worse.

One day he was going to come home and she would have to face him.

Chapter 13

THE SECOND JOB WAS GOING to kill him, he eventually realized as he rode his bike through darkened streets on his way home. Getting in after midnight was for guys like Jon, who made it through school without really studying or paying attention to anything besides the test and passing it without even trying. Nothing had ever come easy for Quinn. He'd studied his ass off every year of high school and barely squeaked by with a scholarship, even though Frank liked to brag and say he'd done it with flying colors.

His last couple of years of high school, his father had started giving him money here and there. Lunch money. Money for clothes. Money for blowing, he guessed. He'd taken it until he graduated, but then it didn't feel right just to take money from someone who didn't give a shit about you. After ending his relationship with Roxie, he started working at an electronics store at night, doing inventory until two in the morning. By the time he made it home, he could barely keep his eyes open, but he had managed to build up a safety net that would get drained again when he went back to Wilmington. The pay at the law firm he was going to intern at wasn't very good, and he'd already considered working for Luther in the evenings, as much as he hated to do it.

Jon was usually still awake when he got home, but he was kind of dozing on the couch when Quinn opened the front door and slipped inside, trying to be quiet because one of their neighbors was a light sleeper.

"Hey," Jon mumbled sleepily. "How was work?"

"Slow. Thought I was going to fall asleep before, during, and after." Quinn yawned, then grinned as Jon followed suit. "What's up?"

"My mom called me earlier. She wanted me to tell you that she expects you to come home the next weekend you have off."

"Are you serious?" Quinn sank down on the other end of the couch. "Did she say why?"

"I'm also supposed to tell you that Kate and Andrew broke up." Jon, who always laughed whenever he teased him about Kate, wasn't smiling. "I think she needs you right now. She's going through something. Ever since she…"

Quinn waited, but Jon didn't finish his sentence. "Ever since what?"

"Nothing." Jon shook his head. "Never mind."

"Dude, what?"

"I don't know." Jon groaned, running his hands through his hair. "I'm not supposed to tell you this. When I went back a few weeks ago, she went out with Andrew and he brought her home with a hangover the next morning. I was ready to take his head off, because she was wearing his clothes and he only had on his boxers and a T-shirt, but after she went upstairs, he told me that nothing happened. That I needed to go check on her, because she didn't need to be alone. Miranda said she's been acting weird ever since she got back from her doctor's appointment in Raleigh."

Quinn shifted to look at Jon square on. "What the hell do you mean, acting weird?"

"She made *Miranda* cry. You know how hard it is to do that?" Jon shrugged. "She about took my head off. Anyway... she just hasn't been herself. Like she's... depressed."

Kate? Depressed? The girl with the always-ready smile, able to see the good in every single person she ever met? He felt a surge of guilt. He should have tried harder to communicate with her. He should have gone back to Wilmington after Christmas.

"Is she sick?" Quinn asked, his heart squeezing in his chest.

"No. I asked dad, and he said she's not sick, but something is wrong. When I went home that weekend, it was like someone had died. Mom was crying nonstop, and so was Kate. I thought at first they'd had some kind of fight. I don't know what's going on, but if you are serious about her, you'd better get your ass back to Wilmington. That's why my mom called. She said if you didn't care about her like that, it might be best if you stayed away for now." Jon looked uncomfortable. "So, are you going to come home with me?"

"I'll call Kate tomorrow." He felt his stomach begin to churn, wondering what was wrong and what he would say to her. "Maybe I can get her to talk to me."

Jon gave him a doubtful look. "Yeah... good luck with that."

·····◦◦◦·····

She had just made it home from school and climbed into bed when her cell phone rang. Her mom had been calling to check on her every day after school, so she answered automatically, knowing if she didn't answer, her mom would close the shop down and drive home.

"Hello?"

"Hey, Kate."

changed

Kate sat up in bed, her heart jackhammering despite the sluggishness the medicine was making her feel. "Quinn?"

"How are you?"

He sounded cautious, his voice exceedingly gentle. Fear spiked through her for a moment. Had someone told him? Her parents? She could feel a ball of anxiety building low in her stomach, though not as strong as usual. She felt too tired to care, really. After a moment she allowed the dullness to wash through her, relieving her of caring about anything.

"Why?" she murmured, burrowing back under the sheets where it was safe.

"Jon… Jon told me you broke up with Andrew. I just wanted to make sure you were okay."

"I'm fine. Did you need anything else?"

"Kate." He paused a moment, sounding hurt, which was the last thing she wanted. She'd already hurt Andrew. She could barely look at him at school even though he'd been nice to her since their breakup. He even offered to still take her to prom if she wanted to go, but she told him she wasn't interested in going. Quinn sighed. "You haven't answered any of my texts. Talk to me. Please. Did something happen?"

A bubble of laughter escaped her, and she forced it back down, pinching the inside of her arm hard. It was something she had been doing a lot. Her arm. Her leg. Slapping herself for crying all the time. It didn't feel like enough. In the moments she was okay—the moments she forgot what was going on—she realized she was depressed. She could even rationalize it to herself… try to remind herself that it wasn't so bad. That it would pass. That she would be fine in just a few moments. Then something would set her off. Little things, really. Love scenes in movies… movies she had seen a dozen times. A diaper or baby food commercial. Anything to do with mothers and daughters. Fathers and sons. It had been a while since she had even felt like watching television.

"How is school?" she asked instead of answering his question.

"Going," he replied after hesitating a moment. "Exams are coming up."

"I should let you get back to studying then," Kate replied.

"If the United States code is more interesting than talking to a beautiful girl, I better change my major," Quinn returned, his voice teasing.

Kate felt her lips turn up into a smile, but it hurt too. She didn't know what to say to him. All the plans she had been making had turned to dust.

"Are you still there?" he asked after a few moments.

"Yes," Kate whispered. "Still here."

"I'm glad you broke up with him. I don't want to wait until May."

The words hung between them, and the meaning finally hit Kate like an anvil. A sob rose in her throat, escaping before she could stop. She shoved her fist between her teeth and bit down hard enough to draw blood.

"Kate?" His muffled voice echoed from the darkness beneath her blankets.

She brought the phone back to her ear. He said her name again, sounding anxious.

"You're too late," she whispered. "I'm sorry."

"Are you seeing someone else?"

It would have been the easiest thing to lie, but she couldn't bring herself to do it.

"No. I wouldn't do that to you. This isn't about you or anything you did. I just can't… I can't. I'm sorry. You have no idea how s-sorry I am."

"Kate." His voice was soft, like a caress. "If something

happened with him, I understand. I don't want you to beat yourself up or feel guilty. That's why I wanted to give you time… give us time. But I knew as soon as I left that I'd made a mistake. I just wanted you to know and—"

"Stop. Please, don't say anything else." Kate wiped frantically at her eyes. "I've changed, Quinn."

He scoffed, his disbelief echoing against her ear. "Since I've last seen you? Kate, I've known you forever."

"It's too late, Quinn. We're too different. You've been through enough with Roxie. Find yourself a nice, normal girl."

"You're the most normal girl I know." His voice was different now. Anger, or frustration. Without seeing his face, she couldn't tell. It didn't matter. None of it mattered.

"I'm not anymore. Bye, Quinn."

She hung up on him before her voice could break further.

Quinn stared at the dead phone in his hand. Kate McGuire had hung up on him. He'd been nervous about making the call but never imagined it would end like that. She sounded tired and sad. Depressed even. He tried to throw himself back into studying, but her voice kept sneaking back into his mind… replaying the conversation until he knew with certainty that something was not right. Unsure of what else to do, he called her dad.

"Hey, kid." Frank greeted him the same way, every single time he called. "How's my favorite attorney-to-be? Hitting the books?"

"Always. Do you have a minute?" He felt nervous suddenly, wondering if he was making a mistake.

"Sure. Got something on your mind?"

"Yes." Quinn prevaricated. "It's… uh… it's about Kate."

"Kate?" Frank sounded surprised. "What about her?"

"I… Is she okay? She just… I was talking to her, and she doesn't seem like herself."

"She's having a tough time right now, Quinn."

"Because of Andrew?" he blurted out.

"It's… girl stuff," Frank said, his voice filled with reluctance. "I can't really get into it with you. I'm sorry."

"I think you should go check on her."

"Now?"

Quinn thought about the way she'd sounded on the phone. His heart tore a little.

"Maybe don't make a big deal out of it, but yeah. I've never heard her like that before. She hung up on me."

Quinn's eyes widened as a loud curse sounded in his ears. He'd rarely heard Frank say anything stronger than *dang*, and when he did, it was usually because of something stupid Jon had done.

"I'm leaving the office now. Let me try to call her."

"Okay." Quinn felt relief course through him but also more worry. "Let me know—"

The line went dead in his ear. He worried he was being ridiculous, but something was telling him he wasn't. Kate was so full of joy. So full of life. He had always been drawn to that vitality and her kindness. It was two hours before Frank called back. Two hours of pacing and staring at his phone, hoping he was paranoid, worried that he was projecting his fears about Roxie onto Kate. He'd always worried about Roxie hurting herself. The thought of Kate doing something like that… it was unimaginable. He could have been in Wilmington in the amount of time he wore a path across the apartment, and if he had to wait another two hours he was going to go crazy. He was about half a second from jumping on his bike and speeding back to Wilmington when the phone rang.

"Quinn?" Frank's voice was gruff. "She's okay."

"God, I feel like an idiot. I'm sorry." He sat down quickly, his knees threatening to give out from under him.

"You did the right thing," Frank said quickly. "Meredith is taking her in to see a doctor."

"Like a shrink?" Quinn blurted out. "This is my fault."

"Why would you think that?"

Quinn closed his eyes. He had never, ever lied to Frank McGuire. The old fear came back… that if he did something wrong, Frank would hate him. Would turn away from him. That he wasn't worthy of them. Any of them… especially Kate.

"I asked her out," Quinn said quietly. "I'm sorry, Frank. It won't happen again."

"Damn." Frank sighed. "I've got to be honest here, your timing is god-awful, but I knew it was going to happen at some point."

"You did?"

"I've got eyes, Quinn. The question is, are you serious about her?"

"Y-yes. Yes, sir," Quinn stammered. He felt like a tongue-tied idiot. He'd never had to talk to a girl's father before. With Roxie it hadn't been an issue. "It doesn't matter. She said no."

"So you'll ask her again, when she's ready," Frank said gently. "Look, we've always been happy to have you here. You know that. We've tried to stay out of things between you two and let you figure it out on your own. But the truth is, Meredith and I were relieved when things seemed to be changing between you at Christmas. It was either make or break, and after you left, that girl was floating on air. She hasn't smiled like that since… well. It's just been a while."

Quinn's eyes closed, and he felt a little twinge in his heart. The McGuires had been so good to him. He couldn't bear to destroy that. But he wanted her. He couldn't believe he had been blind for so long.

"Are you sure?" Quinn whispered.

"I'm a hundred percent sure."

"Jon said she isn't sick. He said she's been like that since her doctor's appointment." Quinn cleared his throat nervously. "Miranda mentioned something at Christmas about some… uh… female issues?"

"I can't tell you anything, and you're not going to guess. It's very… private for her. Be careful with her, Quinn. Kate is still my daughter, and she's only eighteen. I trust you. I really do… but she's a little lost right now. More than anything else, she needs your friendship. Please don't ask her questions about what's going on or say anything to anyone. She'll tell you when she's ready. Promise me you won't push her for answers. She's not ready to talk about it."

"I promise." Quinn gripped the phone tightly in his hand. "I won't do anything that would hurt her. I swear."

"Thanks, kid," Frank replied, his voice gruff. "Hey… I know it's early, but Mere got your graduation cards in. Do you want me to hand deliver any?"

"You mean to William?" Quinn blew out a quick breath. "I doubt he'd come."

"He's still your father, Quinn. I know he's never been there for you, but you have to admit he's been making an effort lately. I just don't want you to regret that you didn't show him your accomplishments. You have a lot to be proud of."

"I won't stop you, Frank, but I don't need him."

"Okay, kid. Thanks for calling me about Kate. And keep my son out of trouble, would you? Remind him I do read those credit card statements every month. They're for emergencies only. *Tassels* doesn't sound like an emergency."

"I'll tell him," Quinn promised, but his mind was elsewhere.

changed

He sent Kate a text as soon as they hung up.

Quinn: If you need anything at all, I'm here for you.

Quinn: I mean that, Kate. You mean so much to me. If I'm too late, you'll never know how sorry I am.

Silence.

Nothing from her, except more silence.

Chapter 14

·····ↂↄ·····

QUINN CHECKED BACK IN WITH Frank every couple of days, making sure that Kate was going to be all right. Frank told him that some medicine that the doctors had put Kate on had been too strong, and they were going to wean her off it. He wanted to go back to Wilmington, but Frank asked that he give her a little more time. She wasn't doing well in school and needed to focus on that first, but he worried about her, especially after he saw that she had deleted all her social media accounts. He sent her a few more messages that she didn't respond to and left her a couple of voice mails. He tried not to pry, but he needed her to know that he was thinking about her. That even if she didn't want anything else from him, they were still friends.

When Valentine's Day rolled around, he sent her a dozen pink roses and received a single thank-you back from her, with no other acknowledgment of his other messages. Worry for her gnawed at him every single day, then spring break finally arrived. He didn't ask permission this time or give Frank a heads-up. When Quinn pulled into the driveway behind Jon just after sundown, he'd talked himself out of coming half a dozen times but knew that he needed to see Kate. He wondered if anyone would think he was crazy for getting homesick for a family that wasn't even his, but off and on through the years, he'd gone through it… maybe not as much as Jon, but pretty close. This time he hadn't been homesick for just anyone. He had missed her. He didn't like leaving things in limbo, and if there was anything he could do to help her, he would.

It looked like every light in the house was on when he pulled his helmet off and looked up, and he hoped that meant that she was home. He followed Jon through the garage, and his mouth began to water at the smell of Italian food. The sounds of silverware clattering and dishes being stacked came from the dining room. They dropped their bags just outside the door and went inside.

"Hey, Mom," Jon said, going to stand behind his mother as she stood at the stove. He kissed her cheek. "When's supper going to be ready?"

"Ten more minutes," she said, glancing back at her son, then turning around when she noticed him. Her eyes widened. "Oh hey, Quinn! Jon didn't tell me you were coming home this weekend. You hungry?"

Was it just him or was she saying that louder than necessary? And why did she look so happy to see him? Did this mean that Meredith was playing matchmaker? Because if it meant getting Kate to at least acknowledge him again, he would cooperate completely.

"I never turn down your food," he replied with a grin.

The sound of something slamming onto the dining room table made Meredith glance that way, but she said nothing to whomever just abused her furniture. The sound of stomping drew his attention, and he turned toward the dining room, expecting to see Miranda in the midst of a tirade. He was surprised to see Kate, looking bitter and angry as she went to the cabinet, snatched out another plate, then returned to the dining room. She slammed the plate down with enough force that Meredith jumped, her lips pursing in anger.

"Is she still in a bad mood?" Jon whispered.

"Leave her be," Meredith replied sharply, glancing at them both. "Not a word to her about it, do you understand?"

"When are you going to tell me what's going on?" his friend asked.

"It's nothing you should worry about," she said, turning back to the stove. "Just don't pester her so much right now, all right?"

"But she's going to be okay?"

His mom glanced back toward the dining room, then nodded her head. Her eyes flickered over to Quinn, then back to her son.

"Don't upset her," Meredith said. "She could use her big brother right now, but don't suffocate her."

Before Jon could say a word, a shriek filled the kitchen. Quinn braced himself just in time for Miranda to launch herself at him, wrapping her gangly arms around him.

"Quinn! Quinn! Quinn!" she squealed. "Are you staying this week?"

Jon pulled her ponytail. "I see how it is. I'm your only brother, and you don't even say hi to me."

Miranda turned around and punched her brother hard as she could in the gut. Jon doubled over, pretending that she'd hurt him, then grabbed her ribs and tickled her until she got mad and kicked his shin, really hurting him.

They started arguing, but Quinn inched toward the dining room and took a seat beside Kate. He studied her for a moment as she stared straight ahead.

"Hey," he said cautiously. She didn't look at him and mumbled something in reply, shrinking down into her oversized sweater. Her face was pale, and it looked like she was holding back tears. He wanted to ask if she was okay, but clearly she wasn't. "Relax. I'm not here to bother you. I just needed to make sure you were okay."

"I'm fine," she whispered.

"So what have you been up to?"

"Sleeping," she muttered.

Well. What could you say to that?

"You excited about graduation?" he asked, trying again.

"Ready to get away from that place," Kate replied, her voice flat. "I'm not really in the mood for small talk, Quinn."

He fell silent as her family piled into the room, bringing food and chaos, everyone talking all at once and it seemed a little too loudly as if trying to compensate for the utter silence from their end of the table. Meredith kept sneaking glances their way, peppering him with questions about school, which he answered without elaborating. His mind was preoccupied with the girl next to him, who looked lost and broken, and he didn't know what to do or what to say to her.

He leaned over a little so only she could hear him. "I got him back."

Kate glanced at him, then away quickly. "What?"

Quinn tilted his head toward Jon. "Naked grandmas," he whispered.

The laugh that erupted from her was brief, but in the split second that her eyes lit up, he was filled with joy at the way she looked at him. The way she'd always looked at him. Frank and Meredith exchanged a glance, then they both smiled.

It didn't last. Before she'd taken a bite of her food, she pushed her chair back from the table and fled the room.

After dinner, he helped Meredith clear the table in

silence, and the lack of sound nearly drove him mad. He was tempted to leave, growing self-conscious of the fact that if his friendship with Kate was over, along with anything else, that he probably wouldn't be welcome at their house anymore. His stomach was in knots, waiting for Frank or Meredith to ask him to leave. If they did, he knew he would never come back. He'd been kicked enough in his life to know when to stay down.

"Quinn honey, would you mind grabbing me that jar of olives out of the pantry? They're on the top shelf," Meredith asked, her voice making him jump.

"Yes, ma'am." He walked into the pantry and turned the light on, searching the shelves. "I don't see them."

He turned around as the door to the pantry closed and found Meredith standing directly behind him with a sheepish look on her face. His heart sank, and he braced himself, doing his best to mask the dismay he felt.

"Hi," she said. She looked embarrassed.

"Uh. Hi."

"I didn't really need any olives. I don't even know if I have them. I just needed to talk to you for a minute," she whispered quickly. "I need a favor."

"Okay," he said, keeping his voice low. He felt a flutter of hope. "Anything."

"I need you to get Kate out of the house. Kidnap her again if you have to. You're going to have to do something drastic. Something crazy. I can't stand seeing her like this anymore. I don't want to know the details. Just don't do anything dangerous or illegal and don't leave the country."

Quinn's felt his brows go up. "What?"

"All I'm saying is if Frank and I hear a noise tonight, we're not going to come investigate. Just get her out of here for a while. No alcohol. No drugs. I'd really appreciate it if Miranda didn't find out. I don't want her trying something like this. She gets enough ideas on her own."

"You want me to take Kate out of *this* house after curfew," Quinn said slowly. "As long as I don't let her drink, rob a bank, or leave the country."

Meredith nodded. "Drive safe. Safer than safe. Seat belts. No speeding. All that good stuff."

Quinn stared at her a moment. "Yeah, okay. Is the shed unlocked?"

"The shed?"

"If I'm going to kidnap her, I'll probably need a ladder. Or did you want me to throw her over my shoulder and walk out the front door?"

"The shed will be unlocked. I'll make sure it's unlocked. Please don't fall off the roof." She chewed her lip, looking worried. "This is probably the dumbest idea I've ever had. In fact, I know it is. But I'm desperate."

"I'll take care of her," he replied, meeting Meredith's gaze. "I'll send you a text if you want, let you know where we are."

Meredith nodded. "Good. That's good. Okay. Thank you so much."

He froze as Meredith wrapped him in a quick hug. She used to hug him all the time. Meredith McGuire was big on hugs, but it was kind of weird to be hugging her in the pantry.

"I'm going to peek and make sure no one is out there. Just wait a couple minutes, then you can come out."

"Sure," he replied, feeling dazed.

"And Quinn?" Meredith gave him a hard look. "I hope you know this isn't my consent for anything else. That girl is precious. Do you hear me?"

He nodded. "Loud and clear."

Getting the ladder and scaling the roof was the easy part. Trying to knock on her window so she could hear it and the rest of the house didn't was another story. Quinn didn't bother sending her a message. If she had a heads-up that he was coming, he knew she would probably leave the house entirely. Her light was on as he walked across the moderately steep pitch to her window. Kate's room was above the sunroom, unlike the other bedrooms in the house that had a higher drop-off. So if they fell, they would probably break something, but hopefully it wouldn't be their necks. The larger concern was the holly bushes that Meredith had planted around the sunroom, which had extremely sharp thorns.

His motorcycle boot caught on the granules of the roof, and he went down on a knee to catch himself, falling against the latticed casement window but thankfully not through it. Kate yanked her curtain open as he was about to knock, her eyes widening when she saw him. He wiggled his fingers at her.

"What are you doing?" she hissed as she pushed the window open. "Are you crazy?"

"Get dressed." His gaze moved over her oversized T-shirt and sleep shorts. "I need your help."

"You need my help," Kate repeated. "At eleven at night?"

"Yup." He cut her off when her mouth opened to argue. "Don't ask questions. Hurry. We don't have much time."

"Quinn, I told you, I can't—"

"Yeah, I got the message. You think I'm ugly. This isn't about that, so get dressed."

She bit her lip, trying to hide a smile. "What do you need help with?"

"I'll explain in the car. Grab your keys, and get your ass out here, McGuire. Hurry up."

The urgency in his tone must have finally convinced her, because she whipped her shirt off as she turned away, giving him a glimpse of her bare back, then the shorts were off as he forced his gaze away. He sank down on the roof, looking out over the yard as he heard her getting dressed behind him.

"Boots," he whispered.

"What?"

He turned around, seeing her halfway into a pair of blue jeans and a purple bra. For a moment his brain quit working, because she was beautiful and half-naked and apparently didn't care if he was looking. He'd seen her wear a bikini before, but the fact remained that it was not a bikini, it was a bra. He'd seen Kate in her bra. Quinn was still staring as she yanked the jeans up and buttoned them, then grabbed the sweater she had been wearing earlier off the floor and put it on. She flapped her arms at her sides.

"Is this good?"

"Wear your boots."

Rolling her eyes, she disappeared into her closet, then came out wearing the requested footwear.

"Can't we use the front door?" she whispered as she climbed up onto her window seat then out onto the roof beside him. "I hate heights."

"I'd rather your dad not shoot me," he murmured, helping her get onto the ladder and guiding her down step by step until they reached the ground. He grabbed the keys out of her hand and led her to her car, putting her in the passenger seat, then adjusting the driver's side to fit his long legs.

Kate had fallen silent but was eyeing him with suspicion as he started the car and backed out of the driveway.

"Okay," he said once they were a couple of blocks from the house. "Full disclosure… this is a kidnapping."

"Quinn!"

"A mom-approved kidnapping," he added.

"Oh my God. My *mother* did this? I'm going to kill her." She buried her face in her hands. "Quinn—"

"Don't tell me to take you back, because it's not happening."

"Where are you taking me?"

"It's a surprise."

She reached in the back seat, noticing the grocery bags he'd placed there before he got the ladder. Grabbing one, she set it in her lap and started pulling food out that he'd stolen from the kitchen.

She looked at it, then looked at him.

"If you're planning on cooking me something with this, please don't."

"You don't think I could make something delicious with apples, bananas, lettuce, and hot dogs?"

"Hot dogs are disgusting."

"But in Quinn's World-Famous Hot Dog Fruit Medley, they are pretty awesome."

She gave him a disgruntled look and put everything back in the bag. "That is revolting, Haley."

"Kind of like my face, huh?"

The only response he got was *her* resting bitch face.

"You know, it's sad when Miranda is the nice one," he mused. "At least she gave me a hug when I got here."

"Maybe you should have kidnapped her."

"Ouch. So grumpy." He pulled the car over and put it in park. "I'll take you back if you really want me to, but I promise I'm not going to ask you anything about whatever is going on, and I'm not going to say anything about the fact that you've been ignoring me, even though it pisses me off. We don't even have to talk at all. Do you trust me?"

It took her a moment to respond, but she finally nodded. "Of course."

"Your mom set up a very strict set of parameters for our excursion tonight. Unfortunately there will be no drinking, no robbing of banks, and no leaving the country. I assume anything else goes."

"And you won't tell me what we're doing?" For the first time a glimmer of excitement and curiosity filled her blue eyes. "Not even a hint?"

"You'll see."

She huffed, but he took that for her assent and pulled back out onto the road. As the lights of Wilmington faded behind them, Quinn grew nervous, wondering if his idea was dumb. When he had called Luther, his former boss had been glad to hear from him, then confused, but he'd said he would have everything ready for him. He lived across the river from Wilmington on a little farm. A proverbial night owl, he was waiting for them on his porch when they pulled up.

"You brought me to your ex-boss's house?" Kate asked. "Quinn, if he needed food, I would have made him something. Not… whatever the hell this is."

He grinned and grabbed the sack from her and opened his door. "It's not for him."

Grumbling, again, Kate followed him up to Luther's porch. The farmhouse wasn't technically Luther's… it belonged to his parents, who were in a nursing home. Luther only visited on the weekends and in the evenings to feed the animals. He was tall and whip lean, his face a map of wrinkles and laugh lines, with dark brown hair streaked with gray that brushed his shoulders. He had a Tom Selleck mustache and a smile underneath it that was welcoming as always.

"Boy, you grow another inch?" Luther asked, shaking his hand.

"Not that I noticed." He set his hand on Kate's back and pushed her forward. "You remember Kate?"

"I sure do. Haven't seen you since you were… what… twelve?"

"Fifteen," Kate mumbled. "I just looked like I was twelve."

"Well, you turned into a beautiful young lady," Luther replied in as gallant a manner as a sixty-year-old ex-biker could. "So, you bring what I asked for?"

"Right here." Quinn held the bag out to him, but his friend held his hands up.

"Nope. You asked for this, you do it. Come on, I'll show you where they are."

Quinn reached back and grabbed Kate's hand, intertwining their fingers. He glanced down to find her looking around at everything. It wasn't a pristine working farm like her grandparents owned or anything at all glamorous like the resort ranches they went to out west. Luther's father had a collection of junk cars and old farm implements lining a fence that led to an old barn. The lights were on, and ahead he could see two or three horses hanging their heads out of the stalls and watching their approach. An old golden retriever loped out of the barn to greet them, and Kate let go of his hand so she could pet him.

"He likes hot dogs," Quinn said, reaching into the bag and handing the package to Kate. "Just one though. Luther said he'll eat the whole pack if you let him. His name is Jeff."

"You brought me out here to feed hot dogs to a dog named Jeff?" Kate asked slowly, breaking it up into pieces to feed the retriever, who patiently waited for her to hand them over.

"And apples to Betty, Blue, and Barbara," he said, pointing toward the horses. "The bananas are for Roger, and the lettuce is for Popeye."

"Roger is…"

"A rabbit. Popeye is a goat. You could probably switch the snacks around. I'm pretty sure Popeye would eat hot dogs too, but that just seems weird."

"Why am I here, Quinn?"

"Because I know how much you love horses, and Luther

is always trying to get me to come ride them."

A slow smile spread across her face. "I get to ride one? Right now? It's midnight."

Quinn looked up at the sky. "The moon is out. There's nothing in the pasture but grass… it's an old row crop field. What do you say, McGuire?"

Poor Jeff and his hot dogs forgotten, Kate leaped up and wrapped her arms around his waist, giving him a hug. Quinn pressed a kiss to her forehead and hugged her back, tension and doubts leaving him. He felt her sniffle against his chest, and it surprised him how delicate she felt. She'd always been slender, but since he had seen her at Christmas, she had lost weight. She was so *tiny*, this girl who had always had a personality big enough to fill an entire room.

"Are you crying, McGuire?"

"No." She wiped her face quickly. "Come on, Haley. I don't want to keep your friend up all night waiting on us."

She stepped out of his arms and walked to the barn, reaching down to pet Jeff a few more times. He kept his distance as Luther introduced her to all the animals, then brought Blue and Betty out of their stalls… neither of the horses with a saddle on.

"You'll have to ride bareback," Luther said apologetically. "My saddle don't fit either of these fatties. Quinn told me you know how to ride?"

"I've been around horses since I was little. My grandparents raise quarter horses, and we go on trail rides all the time out west." Kate glanced at Quinn. "It's him you have to worry about."

"Well, these are good little draft ponies. My nieces and nephews climb all over them. Never thrown, spook, or run away. These two are half Percheron, half Welsh Pony. Might want to let Quinn have Blue. He's got plenty of extra padding so he don't… uh…"

"What about Barbara?" Quinn asked, cutting Luther off

before he could assure Kate that his balls were going to be fine because his horse was fat.

"She's getting too old," he replied, reaching over to scratch the old gray mare on the face. "Full-blood Percheron. My dad loved draft horses. She probably doesn't have too many years left. We'll let her enjoy her rest."

Kate crooned to the mare and breathed in at the base of her neck. She always smelled horses, which he thought was weird until he smelled one. They each had their own unique scent... a sweetness that he might have enjoyed more if he didn't get bit every time he got around one of the so-called gentle creatures.

Luther bridled both of them, and he watched as Kate easily sprang up onto Betty's back while he awkwardly maneuvered himself onto Blue. Flicking the lights on to a small work pen next to the pasture lit up almost half of Luther's little twenty-acre farm. Luther gave them instructions on putting the horses up for the night, then announced he was going to bed.

"Just keep them at a walk," Luther advised before he left them. "Blue running bareback is like trying to hold on to a greased pig. Ain't gonna happen, no matter how long those legs are."

"Thanks for the warning," Quinn said dryly. He patted Blue on the neck, then followed Kate out of the barn. He let her lead, because his sole focus was on not falling off.

For a while they just rode, making a slow trek across the pasture. Once he got used to the rhythm, he brought Blue up close to Betty and let them walk alongside each other. He glanced at Kate a few times, seeing her expression in the moonlight was peaceful. She looked happy, and his heart eased, knowing he'd done something right.

"Why didn't you bring me here before? I miss riding. Dad wanted to get us a horse, but they're so expensive, and Mom won't leave town. She hated living on a farm."

"Luther's only had this place a couple of years. I've only been here a few times. Roxie is…" He stopped, because he hadn't wanted to bring her up.

"She's what?"

"She's allergic to everything out here. Cats. Dogs. Rabbits. Horses. Breaks out in hives any time she's around animals."

"How is she?"

"I don't know. She moved to New York with her new boyfriend." Quinn guided Blue a half step closer to Kate's horse. "I'd rather know how you are."

"I thought we weren't going to talk."

"We don't have to. I'm just worried about you, Kate."

"You don't have to worry about me. I'm not your problem."

"Damn. Sling that arrow a little harder next time."

She jerked around to look at him. "What does that mean?"

When he imagined finally coming home to this girl, he'd never once thought he would have to fight this hard for her. He had assumed, like a giant idiot, Kate was going to be so happy she would jump in his arms and it would be as natural as breathing. Was he really going to have to bare his soul? Roxie had never liked this part… intimacy. He'd learned the hard way not to open himself up to her.

"It means I care about you, and you make it sound like you think I'm heartless. Of course I worry about you. We've been friends for how long?" She didn't answer him, and he berated himself for pushing. He reached out and took her hand, almost sliding off Blue as he lost his balance. "I'm sorry. I just wanted you to know I'm here for you."

He must have squeezed too hard with his legs, because Blue broke out into a trot and Quinn dropped the reins, forgetting that they were the last things you wanted to drop when you were riding, especially bareback. He lunged for them, cursing as his legs grappled for purchase in a losing battle.

Luther hadn't been lying.

Trying to hold on to a running fat horse was impossible, and trying to hang on with his legs only made Blue move from a trot into a lope. The first thing he heard when he was done spitting dirt out of his mouth was Kate, laughing. She was on her knees beside him, both horses standing nearby inspecting him like he was an idiot.

"Are you okay?" she asked, brushing the dirt off his face and shoulders. "That was quite a bronco you got there, cowboy."

Quinn groaned, letting his head fall back to the ground. "I hate horses, you know."

"I know." She leaned over him. "Did you hurt anything besides your pride?"

"Pretty sure my ass hurts, but I'll let you know when the rest of me quits hurting enough."

"On a scale of one to ten, how dumb was this idea, Haley?"

Looking up into her smiling, pretty face, he knew all the aches and pains were worth it.

"Got you to smile, McGuire." Quinn reached up and tucked her hair behind her ear, just wanting an excuse to touch her. "I'd say my work here is done. I think Blue is worn out though. All that running he did was probably more than he's done in a year."

"You know what the best part is?" Her smile seemed to widen in the dark, and he felt a tightness in his chest.

"What's that?" he whispered, rising up on his elbows. He wanted to kiss her. He'd been wanting to kiss her since he left at Christmas.

"I had my camera on you the entire time, because I knew you were going to bust your ass." She grabbed his hand and hauled him to his feet. "Jon is going to love it."

Chapter 15

⸺⸻⸺

THEY WALKED THE HORSES BACK to the barn, and Quinn sat on an overturned bucket and watched while she brushed them out and set the feed pans inside that Luther had prepared for them. The action of grooming the horses soothed her, and she retrieved the apple she had brought, letting each horse take a bite before tossing the core to the goat. Reluctantly she let Quinn lead her out of the barn, the darkness wrapping around them as he flicked the lights off and they walked back to her car. He kept touching her… placing his hand at the small of her back, brushing her hair away from her face. Little, personal touches that he seemed to do without thinking but drove Kate to distraction. She was trying to hold on to the reservations she had, but he was making it incredibly hard to do.

"You didn't eat anything for supper," Quinn said as they crossed back over the river. "I didn't eat much either. Are you hungry?"

"A little." Kate glanced at the clock. It was just after one in the morning. "Not much is going to be open this late.

There's probably some leftovers in the kitchen."

"Your mom might have known you were gone, but she didn't say anything about your dad." Quinn shook his head. "Coopers is open until two, right?"

Kate shrugged, and Quinn made the turns needed to the little downtown diner. There weren't many customers inside, and the waitress did a double take as she looked at Quinn. At first Kate thought they knew each other, but when she looked at Quinn, she started laughing.

"What?"

"You might want to wash up," Kate whispered. "You are filthy, Haley."

He inspected his hands, then his clothes with a wince. "I'll be right back. Get me a burger or something. You know what I like."

Kate grabbed a booth and ordered for them. She watched the video of him hitting the dirt on her phone while she waited. It was dark, but she could make out enough to see that while he might be athletic in every other way, on a horse he was an uncoordinated klutz, and she couldn't help but smile as she replayed it.

"It's nice to see you smile again," a familiar voice said.

She looked up, her eyes widening when she realized it wasn't Quinn. "Andrew."

He glanced over her quickly, then took a seat next to her. "I saw your car parked outside. I wanted to make sure you weren't having trouble with it again or something. Did you just get off work?"

"No. I… I quit, actually."

"Oh." He glanced around the diner. "You're out kind of late, aren't you?"

"I just…" Kate's gaze darted toward the bathroom. "I…"

Understanding crossed his features, and his jaw

clenched. "You're here with someone?"

"It's not what you think. I was riding horses." She showed him a photo she had snapped with Betty. "See?"

"Who is in the bathroom?"

"Andrew—" He started to get up, but she grabbed his arm and pulled him back down. "Okay," she whispered. "Just please don't be mad, and please don't say anything to him. It's Quinn, but we're not together, together. He was just trying to cheer me up and took me to his friend's farm."

Andrew laughed, sounding bitter. "I take it he doesn't know either. Is that you now? Just shut everyone out so they can't help you?"

"Help?" Kate repeated tightly. "There's nothing anyone can do for me. I'm a freak."

His gaze softened. "Kate, you are not."

Embarrassed, Kate turned away to look out the window. "Can we please not talk about this?"

She felt him press a kiss to her temple and closed her eyes as tears started falling down her cheeks.

"I'm sorry. You should tell him. If he cares about you half as much as I do, it's not going to matter, and the only reason I'm not going in there to punch him in the face is because of you. I've never seen anyone cry as much as you have the past few months. I want you to be happy even if it is with that dickwad."

"Well thanks, Andrew," Quinn said, his voice quiet. Kate looked up to see him glowering down at them both. "I appreciate that."

Kate covered her face with her hands, wishing she had never agreed to leave the house. She avoided Quinn's gaze as he slid into the booth across from her and Andrew.

"What the hell happened to you?" Andrew asked, taking in Quinn's appearance.

"I fell off a fat horse."

"Stop calling him fat. That's mean," Kate said. "He's part draft horse. He can't help it."

"You and Luther keep saying that like it's supposed to mean something to me," Quinn replied.

"Like the Budweiser horses?" Andrew asked. "Is that why they call them draft horses? Because, beer?"

"No, they were work horses," she explained, rolling her eyes. "It's not because of beer."

The waitress brought them their food, and Kate pushed her fries at Andrew. "You sure?" he asked, glancing between them.

"You aren't getting mine," Quinn commented around a mouthful of food. "Better take hers if she's offering."

Andrew stole a couple of her fries, but then he stood. "Nah, I'm going to split. It's too weird. See you after spring break, Kate."

She felt a combination of relief and guilt as he left and avoided Quinn's gaze as she picked at her food. He reached across the table and took her hand after a moment.

"Do you love him?" he asked quietly. "Because if you do, we can forget about what happened at Christmas and we can just be friends."

"I don't love him," Kate replied softly. She met his gaze briefly. "But we have to forget about Christmas anyway. I can't sleep with you, Quinn."

"Wow, just get right to it then." He cracked a smile, but it faded quickly. "I'd never hurt you, Kate."

"No, I'd hurt you, because I'm so mad right now I can barely function. And no, you haven't done anything wrong." Her hands clenched tightly. "It has nothing to do with you. I just can't be in a relationship. Especially not with someone like you."

He reared back. "Someone like me?"

"Someone experienced," she gritted out.

"I've never been with anyone except Roxie," he said quietly, leaning toward her. "Look, I'm sorry about what happened at Christmas. I should have called you after... made sure you were okay. The only reason I didn't was because I was hoping you'd break up with him before—"

"You don't owe me an explanation. It was a mistake."

"Was it?"

"Yes," Kate whispered, but she looked away as she said it.

She had tensed up so much that he could probably see a little vein standing out on her forehead that only made an appearance when she was extremely stressed. For several moments he just stared at her, as if memorizing her face, and she was uncomfortably aware of her attraction to him. His dark hair had grown out and started to get wavy. He had the darkest green eyes she'd ever seen, though they weren't completely green. They had flecks of dark brown inside them, which she knew turned gold in the sunlight. His lashes were extralong and thick on the top and the bottom, his nose proudly aquiline but not too prominent. Her favorite of his features was his jaw, square and strong, with just the slightest cleft to his chin. When he smiled, it melted everything inside her. Even now, with a wall of ice around her heart. She always forgot how handsome he was, and she'd been doing her best not to revert back to pre-MRKH Kate, the one who was oblivious to everything around her but Quinn Haley.

"I promised I wouldn't pry, but it's really hard not to bombard you. I have a million questions, and it's frustrating not being able to ask you anything." He rubbed his eyes, looking tired. "They're about to close. I guess I should get you home."

He went to pay their check, then walked her back to the car and drove her home. Neither of them spoke as he helped her climb back up to her room, and he started to push the window shut behind her.

"What are you doing?"

"I'm closing the window."

She grabbed his hand. "Just get in here. It's late, and you're tired. I don't want you to fall."

"Kate—"

"Get your ass in here Haley," she whispered, pulling his arm until he complied. He crawled over the window seat and stood in front of her, and she felt awareness flood though when she realized that he was in her room with her, alone, in the middle of the night. Kate felt herself sway toward him. "Good night."

"Good night," he repeated, the moonlight casting half his face in shadow. "I hope you had some fun tonight, at least."

She looked at his lips and felt something hot and dark tighten in her stomach. Kate lifted her hand and touched his cheek, rubbing her palm across the coarse shadow of his beard. She hadn't felt anything in so long, but she felt every inch of his skin that was touching her. Her eyes refused to move away from his.

He grew still, his eyes closing. "I'm sorry, Kate. I know you're going through a tough time right now."

She dropped her hand. "So you didn't mean anything you said?"

"What?" Quinn asked, looking surprised. "No, I just meant that I know you need more time, and that's okay—"

"Just forget it, Quinn." Kate rolled her eyes and turned away. "I should have known you were just playing around."

"No!" Quinn grabbed her shoulder, spinning her back around. "I swear that I'm not."

"You want something I can't give you." Her vision blurred sharply, the room careening around her. "Something I can't give to anyone. What do you want

Quinn? A blow job? I can probably handle that. Here, unzip and I'll let you have it right now."

"*Stop it*." He grabbed her arms, gently holding her away from him. He looked shocked and hurt. "I'm not talking about sex. I'm talking about… about us."

She stared up at him, mute and angry. Quinn would never be satisfied with what she could offer, and she wasn't ready to have surgery or do anything else to "fix" her body. Even if he fell in love with her… even then… he would remember the times he had been with Roxie. Roxie, who was a real woman. Roxie, who was sexy and who had apparently been his first and only. The way it should be with someone. He was probably feeling sorry for himself and eventually would realize what he was missing and go back to Duke and find someone else. Someone who had an actual vagina.

"I'm sorry, Quinn, but I can't do this," she heard herself say. "I think you should go to your room now."

"Do you know why I like your family so much?"

His question startled her. She shook her head.

"When I was a kid, my mom never remembered my birthday. Not once. I didn't even think about my birthday until I was probably seven or eight. One day, out of the blue, I asked her when it was, and she couldn't tell me. I bugged her over and over again after that until she finally told me it was the third of May. She had to look it up. And then when the third of May came, and went, I didn't get a present. She didn't even remember to tell me happy birthday." He walked over to her window seat and sank down. Kate stood in front of him as he sat there, and she struggled for something comforting to say. It was like she'd forgotten how to be empathic, because she had been so consumed with her own grief.

"That's horrible," she said softly.

His gaze lifted to hers, his eyes in shadow. He spoke

without emotion, but something between the words said that his secrets weren't easily spilled.

"When Jon brought me home for the second or third time, your mom asked me when my birthday was. I told her. That was at Christmas break. When he brought me back, a week before my birthday, she had made me a huge chocolate cake, and your parents took us all out to dinner. Five months after first meeting me, *your* mom remembered my birthday, when my own mother couldn't do it even once in my life."

Kate felt her eyes sting with tears. She had known that his childhood had been rough but couldn't imagine a mother who ignored her child so much that she couldn't manage to remember their birthday. She'd never thought of him as insecure. He'd always been full of confidence, slightly arrogant, and irresistibly charming.

"I'm sorry, Quinn," Kate said, stepping closer. "I had no idea."

"I didn't tell you this so you'd feel sorry for me," he said roughly. "I told you so that you'd know I would never do anything to hurt you or your family. I wouldn't be here if I was just fucking around, Kate. I want you to smile for me. To laugh. To be happy again. I know we both just got out of a relationship, but I also know that this is right."

She moved closer until she was standing between his knees. "And you think you're really over Roxie? Someone you've been with off and on since you were eighteen? Are you sure you're ready to let go of her?"

He reached out and lifted the palm of her hand to his mouth, kissing her there gently. He tugged her hand until she leaned over and placed her hands on his shoulders. He was muscular and warm and smelled so good. Sensation danced along her skin, and she felt intoxicated, even though she hadn't drunk anything.

"For three years I've been hitting a brick wall, trying with her. To get her to trust me… to love me. I'm a slow learner. I don't like to give up on people the way… the way my parents gave up on me. Letting her go was hard, but it was better for both of us."

"You'd be hitting the same wall with me. I'd just disappoint you." Her voice was shaking. She clenched her hands into his shirt, trying not to tumble into his arms. She had wanted this… wanted him… for so long. Her heart ached so bad it felt like it might extravasate.

"Impossible." His hands lifted to caress her jaw, thumbs sliding up over her cheeks. "You make me feel…"

"What?" she whispered. The muscles of his shoulders tensed, and she could feel his breath harsh against her skin; his gaze was locked on hers with an intensity that made her tingle from head to toe. "Feel what?"

"Good." He caressed her cheek again. "Alive. Free. Come and kiss me, kitten. I know you want to."

Her breath caught on the endearment. She felt alive too. For the first time since she'd gone to the doctor, she felt alive again. Just once, she wanted to know what it felt like with him. She knew it was a mistake, but she closed the distance between them anyway, angling her head so that his lips fit against hers. She felt his hands close around her waist, tight and wonderfully strong. She kissed his top lip, then the bottom. Her tongue stroked the corners of his mouth, and she felt him inhale sharply, and excitement burned through her. He opened his mouth beneath hers, his tongue flicking out to touch her lips. Kate obeyed, letting him in, letting him fully kiss her. She felt her knees weaken, and suddenly she was sitting on one of his legs and his arms were around her, holding her tight.

His hair was soft beneath her fingers, and she hadn't even realized she'd raised her hands to touch it. She took in the sensation of him… taste, scent, texture. Reveled in the feel of him. She knew Quinn, but finding this extra layer of sweetness to him was heart-achingly addicting. His mouth left hers suddenly to feather kisses toward her jaw and brush her ear. His mouth returned to hers, and his tongue thrust inside as a deep, hungry noise came from his chest. One big hand squeezed the top of her thigh, making her gasp in pleasure, though not so mindless that she didn't understand what would happen if she let him continue. She jumped off his lap, trying to catch her breath.

The look in his eyes did nothing to help her find it. She loved kissing. Was fine with kissing. The moment it moved beyond that, she always panicked, knowing that it could lead nowhere. She might as well have been wearing a permanent medieval chastity belt.

"Damn it," she grumbled, flooded with irritation.

"What? Kate?"

"Nothing," she muttered. "You'd better go before my parents catch you."

"Kate, stop," he said, pulling her around to face him. "Was it too much?"

Unwillingly she felt tears start sliding down her face. "It's all too much. Every bit of it. I hate this."

"I'm not asking you to sleep with me," he said, his voice calm. "I'm just asking for a chance, Kate. Can you at least give me that?"

"No." She didn't think her heart could possibly hurt any more than it did in that moment. "What just happened was a mistake. What happened at Christmas was a mistake. We can still be friends. Please… please don't ask me again."

He stroked her cheeks with his thumbs, his gaze lowering to her mouth. "I'm not giving up. I'm going to ask you again. As many times as it takes until you say yes."

He put his arms around her and pulled her close. After a moment she hugged him back, her arms linking behind his back and holding tightly. She felt a surge of tenderness and love so strong it nearly knocked her breathless, but the thought of telling him was like pouring acid on her heart.

"Thank you for tonight. I just don't think—"

"Good night, Kate," he said softly. "Don't think right now. Get some sleep."

He kissed her again, a brief press of his lips against hers, then he walked out of her room and down the hall into his own.

Chapter 16

......⁙......

B EING AROUND QUINN THE NEXT day was awkward. He pretended as if nothing were out of the ordinary. He teased her the way he always had. He winked at her even though she glared in his direction. It was impossible to be mad at him for any length of time, but she held on to her misgivings, knowing it would be better than letting her guard down again.

"Kate, honey, could you go get groceries for me today?" her mom asked, reaching into her purse and pulling out some money and a list. "If I don't keep you guys stocked up, there won't be anything left by the time I get home to start supper."

"Do you want me to cook?" she asked, reaching for the cereal box and finding it empty.

She got up and went to the cabinet to get another box down, and when she turned around, her mom was just standing there, looking surprised. She realized, guiltily, that her mom had been doing all her chores for her and she hadn't cooked in weeks.

"I, uh… I'm sorry I haven't lately."

"No, it's fine. Are you sure you feel up to it?" her mom asked, reaching forward to touch her hair.

"Yeah." Kate managed a smile, aware that Quinn and Miranda were watching. "I want to."

Microexpressions of happiness and hope crossed her mom's face. She hadn't mentioned their midnight excursion, and since Quinn was still alive this morning, she assumed that maybe her father had slept through it… or her mother hadn't told him what was going on.

"Yes. Well," her mom said brightly. "The menu is on the side of the grocery list. If you want to make something different, you go right ahead. You know your father likes your cooking better than mine anyway. Miranda, you have one minute to finish your breakfast, then we're leaving."

"Why do I have to go?" her sister grumbled.

"Because I'm your mother, and I said so." Her mom gave Quinn conspiratorial wink before she left, and he grinned in return. Since her dad always left before anyone in the house was awake, it would just be the two of them alone for a while until Jon managed to get out of bed, which probably wouldn't be before noon.

"So," Quinn said in the silence that fell once the house was empty.

Kate poured her cereal and dug in, hoping he wouldn't mention anything about the night before.

"About last night," he began.

"Quinn," she groaned. "Please, can we just forget it?"

"Is that really what you want?" he asked after a long pause.

"I think if we're going to stay friends, then yeah, we should."

He looked disappointed and maybe a little hurt. After a moment he dropped his gaze to the table, looking uncomfortable. "Fine."

"Hey," Kate said. She reached across the table and touched the back of his hand. "I doubt you'll have a hard time finding someone willing to take Roxie's place."

His hand flipped over quickly and captured hers, drawing a distracting little design on her palm. Her stomach flipped too, and she knew she was going to be in trouble if they kept spending time together.

"I don't think I can, Kate," Quinn whispered. "Forget last night, that is. That kiss… it was amazing. Do you want me to leave? I can go back to Duke."

"No!" The thought of him leaving was even worse than dealing with what might happen if he stayed. "No," she repeated, forcing her voice to be much calmer. "Please don't go. Not because of me. I really appreciate what you did last night. Thank you."

"For kissing you?"

Her face turned fire-engine red. "No, Dorkasaurus. I meant for… kidnapping me. Again."

"You should thank me for the kiss too," he said, his expression as serious as she'd ever seen it. She found herself leaning toward him without realizing. "I thought I nailed it."

"Quinn." She couldn't help it; she started laughing. "You have to stop."

"Kate," he replied, continuing to trace patterns on her hand as his gaze dropped to her mouth, stealing her breath. "I meant everything I said last night."

"I'm sorry, but so did I."

She withdrew her hand, and they finished their breakfast in silence. When he went upstairs to take a shower, she snuck out like a coward and went to buy groceries, taking her time shopping until the trip extended to just under three hours. Jon and Quinn were gone by the time she got back, leaving her to tote in twenty bags of groceries from three different stores into the house by herself. The thought of cooking again was exciting. She hadn't thought about Atlanta or her future in a while or if she was even going to be able to attend school in the fall. Atlanta seemed like a distant dream, but one that she needed to focus on instead of the things she couldn't have.

Two hours later, as she labored over shrimp and grits in a dirty kitchen, she wasn't so sure. It was one of her dad's favorite meals. For dessert she made a creole cheesecake, because her mom loved it and to apologize for how much money she had spent on groceries for one week. By the time her brother and Quinn returned home, she was hot, sweaty, and completely exhausted.

She took one look at Quinn, sunburned and shirtless, and felt herself get even hotter. Even when it was cold outside, they both loved going down to Wrightsville Beach to goof off.

"You get sand anywhere in this house, Mom will kill you."

"We hosed off," Jon said as he came in and sniffed over the pot. "Damn, that smells good. When will it be ready?"

She slapped his hand when he tried to take the spoon off the stove and dip it inside. "That's for dinner. Hands off."

"I'm starving," he complained.

"There's junk food in the freezer and more junk in the cabinets. Help yourself."

Her brother groaned, used to their mom who would have waited on him hand and foot.

"It does smell good," Quinn murmured. "What is it?"

Kate jumped, not realizing he had moved so close. He peered down at her, smiling in a way that made her heart stutter.

"Thanks," she replied, stirring the shrimp and sausage so it wouldn't stick to the bottom. "Shrimp and grits."

"I've never had it. You put grits in it? Really?"

"You put it over them." She laughed at his dubious expression. "It's really good. So what did you guys do all day? Besides lie on the beach and stare at girls in bikinis?"

"You mean we were supposed to do something else?" He winked at her. "You should have come. I wouldn't have minded the view."

"Ahem!" Jon choked, coughed, and laughed all at once. "Jesus, come on, Quinn! We talked about this. You can't hit on my little sister in front of me."

"Jon!" Kate turned the stove off and left the room, mortified. *They had talked about her?* She turned back around with a groan, because she knew she couldn't trust her brother not to eat half of what she had just cooked. Sure enough, he was back at the stove with his big nose right over the whole pot, staring at it like a greedy crackhead. She flicked a glance at Quinn and found him grinning. Her gaze slid away from him. "Don't you dare touch my food. I've been working on this while you two have been lying around in the sun."

"Come on," he groaned. "We're starving."

"Then fix yourself something." She glared at him, hands on hips. "I am not Mom, and I am not going to wait on you hand and foot. Get up and fix it yourself." Behind her, she heard Quinn laughing. She turned to face him, giving him a similar glare but found it hard not to let her gaze stray downward to his muscled chest and taut stomach. "That goes for you too. And… put some clothes on."

"You better watch it." Jon chuckled. "She's getting pissy."

"I don't mind being scolded. Besides, she gets prettier when she's mad." He gazed at her, his expression completely and openly flirtatious. "Gorgeous, really."

Her face had to be the color of a tomato. God, when Quinn flipped the friend switch, he'd lost his mind. She turned the oven on low and put the entire pot inside it to keep it warm until her parents got home from work. "Dream on, Haley. Never gonna happen."

Inside, her heart danced. She did her best to tell it to shut up and sit down.

Saturday, Quinn caught her trying to sneak out of the house, only this time it was midafternoon and she was leaving via the front door instead of her window. Miranda gave him a heads-up that she was going to the movies with Lindsay, and he had every intention of finding a way to tag along. Hearing a commotion of voices at her bedroom door, he looked out and saw a guy taller and broader than him entering her room and closing the door, followed by a yelp of panic. He was across the hall and shoving her door open before he even considered his actions, finding Kate standing in a shirt and her underwear gaping at all of them.

"Does anyone know how to knock?" she demanded, trying to tug the shirt down.

"Sorry," the guy replied, throwing his hand over his eyes.

Spotting Lindsay holding hands with him, Quinn assumed that it was her boyfriend and that he wasn't here to take Kate out. She looked over at him expectantly and held her hand up like she was asking him to cover his eyes, but Quinn just smiled and made himself comfortable on her bed.

"Seriously?" Kate grumbled, grabbing her jeans out of a drawer and tugging them on.

"Not like I haven't seen it before, McGuire," Quinn replied, crossing his legs at the ankles and propping up to look at her.

"Me too," Lindsay chimed in.

"Me three," Mitch said. "At least you have a shirt on this time. Can I open my eyes now?"

Quinn frowned, his gaze shooting back to teenage John

Cena who had moved to sit at the end of the bed. "What?"

"Yes, you can open your eyes," Kate said, ignoring his question.

"You aren't going out with me looking like that," Lindsay announced, inspecting Kate with a critical eye. "Sit down."

"I don't need to wear makeup. That's why movie theaters are dark. So you can be ugly when you're shoving greasy popcorn in your face."

"There's ugly, then there's whatever that is. Sit." Lindsay snapped her fingers, and Kate sat down with a huff. She patted her on the head. "Good girl. If you're nice, you'll get a treat."

For the next ten minutes Quinn watched her get poked and prodded with makeup brushes, and he had to admit, the transformation was remarkable. Lindsay was obviously one of those contour gurus that could wield a makeup palette like a magic wand. The first chance he got, he was going to tell Kate how beautiful she was but that he liked the before option better. The real Kate was beautiful without any needed enhancements. Every time she opened her eyes, her gaze found his, but she kept looking away.

"What is going on between you?" he heard Lindsay whisper.

"Nothing."

"Bullshit, nothing. It's time to grow a pair."

"Hush. He's going to hear you."

Lindsay moved on to her hair, spraying something in it, then braiding down the side, the way her hair had been done the night he had picked her up. "Well if he doesn't stop staring, I'm going to have to take off your blush. Invite him to come with us."

"No... Shh—"

"So, are you two dating or what?" Mitch asked casually. "Isn't this who you were freaking out about the night you broke up with Andrew?"

Kate gaped at him. "Mitch!"

Quinn sat up, suddenly interested in becoming better acquainted with Lindsay's boyfriend. "Now we're getting somewhere. What's he talking about, Kate?"

"Oh God." Kate groaned, burying her face in her hands. At first he thought she was embarrassed, but she suddenly began to tremble, and he was off the bed and kneeling in front of her, watching as her breaths grew shallow and fast.

"Kate," he whispered, worried and shocked.

"Come on. Don't do this again," Lindsay pleaded, patting her on the shoulder. "We were just joking around. I'm so sorry."

"Don't what?" Quinn asked, meeting Lindsay's gaze. "What's wrong with her?"

"I feel dizzy." Kate clawed at her T-shirt, her eyes squeezed shut. "Just need some air. And stop staring at me."

It was on the tip of his tongue to say something flirtatious or teasing, but he stopped himself. He didn't know how to respond to this version of Kate. He wondered if she was having a panic attack or if it was something else. She pressed her nails over her arm, scoring the tender flesh until it looked like it hurt. He wondered maybe if she was diabetic. He remembered having to sit through *Steel Magnolias* one too many times with Roxie.

"Do you want me to get your mom?" Lindsay asked. "Or your medicine?"

She shook her head, tears forming in her eyes. "I'm fine."

"Could you get her some orange juice or something?" Quinn asked Lindsay. "She might need a sugar boost." He placed his hand over Kate's. "Stop clawing yourself. That looks like it hurts."

"That's the point." She huffed.

"Put your head down and take a few deep breaths," Quinn murmured. "It'll make you feel better."

He rubbed her back until the worst of the tremors subsided. He felt a flare of guilt, remembering that he had made promises that he wouldn't push her, yet it was all he had done since showing up. In the back of his mind, he had believed that all Kate needed was him and that whatever she was going through, she would be better if they faced it together. Maybe he was wrong. Or maybe he was just an idiot. Mitch met his gaze, questioning.

What can I do?

Quinn lifted his shoulder slightly.

No idea, man.

"Here," he said gently as Lindsay came back and handed him a glass of juice. "Drink."

She sipped it dutifully, and it did seem like it helped. Her complexion slowly returned to normal, and her breathing evened out, but her hands hadn't stopped shaking and her fingers felt ice-cold to the touch.

"I'm sorry." He took her hands and pressed a kiss to her knuckles. Looking into her haunted gaze was like a knife in his gut. "I'll go so you can get ready."

"Come with us." Kate's hands grasped his as he tried to leave. "Please."

"Are you sure?"

"It's going to be weird if you don't," she replied, her cheeks turning pink again. "We're friends, Quinn. We can go to a movie together. And to eat. I know how much you love that."

He glanced around the room, noting that Lindsay and Mitch were gone.

"Ride with me." Immediately she tensed, and it was obvious she hadn't intended to let them be alone together. "We don't have to call it a date. If you want me to, I'll go back to Duke when it's over."

She smiled, her eyes tearing up. "I hate it when you go back. It's my least favorite place in the world."

"Atlanta is going to be mine," he murmured. "I'm going to miss you."

Her expression shuttered again. "I don't know if I'm going or not."

"You're *going* to culinary school, Kate. What I wrote in that book wasn't a lie, you know."

"Stop," Kate muttered. "I'm not that good."

"Yeah," he said, perfectly serious. "You really are."

"Thanks." She let out a deep breath. "I don't know what I want to do anymore."

"I don't know what is going on. I understand if you don't want to talk about it or tell me anything. But we have known each other a long time. I'm sorry if I messed that up the other night. I don't want things to be weird between us. I just… I just want you to know that if you need me… for anything… I'll always be here."

Some of the tension escaped her, and he felt like an utter ass for teasing her earlier.

"Thanks, Haley." She twirled her fingers idly around the strings she had unraveled on her distressed jeans. "I'm… I'm just not sure where I'm supposed to go now. Who I'm supposed to be. Have you ever had something taken away that you never realized you wanted? One day it's something that's in the back of your mind that might be part of your future. The next day it's gone, and you have no say. None. There's just nothing. No future for you anymore."

He did understand, sort of, though he had no idea what she was talking about. For years he had held on to the idea of his father coming home and fixing things with his mother. Of making her quit drinking and for once, be a mother. Then he had found out about his father's other family and done his best to never think of him again.

"Your future is whatever you want it to be, Kate. You're

only eighteen. Whatever it is you decide to do, I know you'll be great at it." He barely resisted kissing her then, when she'd softened somewhat. "Don't worry so much about yesterday or tomorrow. Worry about today. Will you do something for me?"

"What's that?"

He searched her gaze, trying to find his Kate somewhere. "Think about this… if you stopped caring about me that would be one thing. But if you're afraid of me, or you're afraid that I'm not strong enough to help you or be there for you, you're selling me short. I'm sorry that it took so long for me to realize how I felt about you. I can take it slow. And I will wait for you for as long as it takes."

He looked into her eyes and saw insecurity and fear but also hope and want. Her breaths were hard and fast, a pulse visible in her neck. He worried she was going to have another anxiety spell, so he cupped her cheeks and kissed her once, very softly on the lips, then pressed his forehead against hers and closed his eyes.

"Quinn, there's something I… I…"

"Don't tell me right now," he interjected gently. "I shouldn't have pushed so hard. Whatever it is, it doesn't matter. You can tell me when you're ready."

"And if I'm never ready?"

"I'm a rock, Kate." He took her hand and put it against his chest. "You think I don't have baggage ten miles long? I've been through more than you can imagine."

Her gaze softened. "I know you have. I'm sorry. I'm being selfish."

"You?" He stared at her, amazed. "You're the least selfish person I've ever met. I'm not perfect. I've made mistakes. But I've always been clear about what I wanted, and I'm determined. Say yes. Give me a chance."

"We'd be apart so much." Her eyes closed briefly. "I'm not sure if I'd be very good at that."

"There are law schools in Atlanta. I could take a semester off. Apply wherever."

"But—" She looked shocked. "Quinn!"

"I'm going to tell you something I haven't said to anyone. Not even to Jon." Quinn dropped his gaze to the floor, the words harder than he expected. "I'm having doubts about going to law school. I'm not sure it's right for me. It's something I decided to do when I was fifteen, and it was more or less a way to get my father to pay attention to me. It didn't work how I wanted it to, and now it's like… it's like I'm playing a part I don't want anymore. But everyone is looking at me with these huge hopes… your dad, mine. Your mom. You. I don't want to let anyone down after everything they've done for me. I want to stand on my own. I don't want to rely on William for anything. If we have a relationship, I want it to be because he wants to be in my life. Not because I forced my way in."

"Quinn." Kate pressed her lips to his. "What did you just tell me? Your future is whatever you want it to be. And if he doesn't see how wonderful you are, then you don't need him. You have us. You… you have me. Always."

She put her arms around his neck, and this was the Kate that he knew. The caring, loving Kate, who never took for herself. She was too busy giving to everyone else. He couldn't stand seeing her hurting so much. If plucking open his own wounds distracted her from her own pain, he'd open them all, no matter how much they bled.

Chapter 17

···∘⧬∘···

RUNNING LATE FOR THE MOVIE, they loaded up on snacks at the concession stand. Quinn shared his with her, and at some point during the movie he slipped his fingers through hers. Kate knew it was time to admit that she couldn't fight him anymore. She wasn't going to win against love. It felt natural even if she didn't. She needed to tell him everything before things progressed any further. Let him decide if he wanted in on the new craziness that was her life. Until her doctor's appointment later in the year, she didn't really know what was going to happen, and the uncertainty of her future was scary. Being with Quinn… just being around him seemed to make everything better. Even when he was flirting, although it made a ball of anxiety build in her gut every single time. For years she had built a mental script of all the flirtatious things she wanted to say to him. The few she had tried had seemed to go right over his head, so they must not have been very good. Now the idea of flirting with him made her want to hurl.

Lindsay gave her a thumbs-up as they parted ways outside the theater. Quinn took her hand again and tugged her toward the rest of Mayfaire, an outdoor outlet mall that was designed to look like small-town Main Street, USA.

"What are we doing now?" Kate asked as he hustled them across the parking lot of the movie theater, then into the throngs of people walking around. There were two lingerie stores up ahead, and she felt her heart flip over. "I'm not trying on bras for you."

He grinned down at her. "Why not? I've already seen one. I like purple, but when you wear hot pink... God. I can't quit staring at you sometimes. You should always wear hot pink."

She blushed, her brows rising as they walked past Soma, then Victoria's Secret. Okay. So not trying on bras. Kate squeaked as she felt his hand move to her waist, his fingers brushing the bare skin of her hip, and felt her nerves begin to thrum from the contact of Quinn's hand on her flesh. She wanted to turn toward him and touch him the same way. To know if his abs were as hard as they looked. To explore the dark hair sprinkled on his chest and down his stomach. To touch her tongue to his warm skin and know if he tasted like the sun. How was it possible to feel all these things... all these very normal things... and not be able to act on them? She felt absolutely worthless, wanting him so much and knowing there was no future for her with him. In the worst things she had imagined since being diagnosed, Quinn finding out about her deformity was at the top of the list.

"What was that about, Minnie Mouse?"

"Minnie Mouse?"

"You squeaked like a little mouse." His hand stayed where it was, but his fingers stroked her skin a little. "You always make that noise when you're surprised."

"That isn't very flattering. First I'm a cat, now I'm a mouse," she joked.

"But not an adorable mouse. A sexy mouse," he stressed, his gaze warm as he looked down at her. "What kind of animal am I?"

"A doofus." She laughed at him. "I don't know. Definitely not a horse."

"Damn. I was hoping you thought I was a stud."

"I guess a male donkey is technically a stud, if it's registered and used for breeding." Her stupid heart reminded her that breeding wasn't a subject she wanted to talk about. Not now, not ever. She frowned. "Where are you taking me?"

He pointed. "There."

Across the street was one of her favorite stores in the entire world. Williams-Sonoma. They had an addictively wonderful selection of cookware. She could spend an entire day in the store just caressing pots and pans, drooling over kitchen appliances and cutlery. One of the things her gran had passed down to her was a vintage set of Nordic Ware Bundt pans, and she had planned to have an entire kitchen full of them one day, along with Le Creuset and her gran's beloved cast-iron cookware. She had thought about her mom's advice… putting the things her gran had given her in the attic, but she wasn't ready to get them back and she still wasn't sure if she wanted them. What if she did adopt a child… would it really be hers? Wouldn't Miranda or Jon feel cheated if their flesh and blood didn't get the things that belonged to family? Thinking about it all gave her a headache, so she pushed it all away as Quinn pulled her toward the store. She felt everything fall away from her shoulders as she stepped inside. Even if she didn't go to Atlanta, cooking was the most relaxing thing in the world to her. She needed to get back to that. To find something of what she had lost, before she let all those pieces of her die.

"Thank you," Kate said, suddenly feeling emotional.

"I know you're obsessed with this place." Quinn looked down at her, studying her. "Don't give up on this. I know things are tough for you right now, but you make things that seem impossible to me look so easy. And so... so delicious. I can't even describe how good your pancakes are. And your fried chicken. And gumbo. You've never made anything that I didn't love."

He tucked her hair behind her ear, then pulled her down an aisle, sneaking a quick kiss.

"Dad, what the hell?"

Kate winced as something slammed into her from behind, catching her in the side of the ear. She spun around to see a teenage girl, close to Miranda's age, glaring at her. She was holding a long strapped purse, which had apparently been used to hit Kate and might have contained a dumbbell.

"Ow," Kate said, rubbing the side of her face. "That hurt."

She waited, expecting Quinn to come to her aid, but when she glanced at him, his face was stark white as he looked down at the girl. For a moment she just stared at them, confused.

"Amanda?"

Everyone turned to look at a woman and a man standing just a few feet away. The woman with an expression of utter shock coming over her features and the man with the same look on his face as Quinn's.

The same tall, wide frame.

The same nose.

Same green eyes.

Chestnut hair.

Square jaw.

Equal expressions of horror. William Knight's with regret. Quinn's with pain.

"We have to go," Quinn whispered, wrapping his arm around her shoulder and steering her back to the exit. "Now."

"Who is that, Daddy?" Kate heard the girl ask.

Suddenly it dawned on her. She'd just met Quinn's father.

Along with his sister and the woman who still apparently knew nothing about her husband's illegitimate son.

Quinn's gut clenched as he heard Amanda's voice in person for the first time. He didn't want to hear his father's answer. Didn't want to hear him tell her that he was nobody. He definitely didn't want to see Amelia Knight look at him like he was something to be scraped off her shoe. He'd never met her before, but he'd seen her through Amanda's social media accounts. He'd seen his father and his wife in public a few times but always managed to slip away before he was noticed or at least remain hidden so he could observe them. As an angry teenager, he'd thought more than once about showing up on William Knight's doorstep and causing a scene. A final screw you to the father who left him to rot at the hands of an addict. After they had met, those urges had gone away, replaced by a desire to please him. To prove that he was worthy of them. Eventually those feelings had faded as well, though sometimes that desire still pierced him.

Most of the time, he just thought about telling his father he wasn't interested in having him in his life anymore. That was one of the main reasons he was rethinking law school. He hadn't taken any money from William in years. Once he started law school, it would be like he was indebted to him, and the thought of owing something to a man who didn't care about him didn't sit well.

That decision was most likely made now. William wouldn't thank him for ruining his life. Even if he wanted to go to law school, that dream was probably over.

He didn't breathe until the door of the shop was closed behind him and they had put some distance between them.

"That was your dad, wasn't it?" Kate asked softly. "And your sister?"

"Yeah," he replied tightly. "I'm sorry about that."

"You have nothing to be sorry for." She wrapped an arm around his waist and gave him a side hug as he hustled her back toward the movie theater where they had left her car. He was shaking, so Kate took the keys from him and drove them back to the house, but he just sat there staring out the window. "Quinn?"

"Yeah?" He managed to look over at her.

"We're here." Kate glanced at the house. "Do you want to go in?"

He gave his head a half shake. "Not right now. I'm sorry. I just need... I think I need to go see my mom."

Kate's eyes widened. "Your mom? Why?"

He shrugged. "I haven't seen her in three years. She's my mom." He could feel her questions burning, but she just looked at him. "Can you keep this between us?"

He already knew what Jon would say if he found out.

Your mom who used to beat the crap out of you and almost killed you. Your mom who never gave two shits about you. She brought home crackheads and let them beat you too. Why? Why would you go there?

"Of course. Will it... will you be okay there? Is it... safe?"

"Vickie is the only family I have." His relationship with his mother had always been one-sided. He cared *about* her. He'd tried to take care *of* her. And just like what had happened with Roxie, he'd had to walk away when his heart was getting ripped to shreds because he cared too fucking much. "I'm big enough to defend myself. I can't explain it. I just... I have to see her."

He had been thinking of this for a while... going to see his mother. Sometimes he sent her money for rent, but he never asked how she spent it anymore. He'd started getting money directly from his father not long after Frank had brought them together, and he'd given some to his mom at first for rent and utilities until it was obvious she was never going to actually pay bills with it. Then he'd done it himself, to keep a roof over their head and keep the lights on. He'd started working in Luther's garage when he was sixteen to make extra money, and with money in his pocket, he'd thought he could finally fix things with his mom. She wouldn't be able to party as much. She would finally appreciate that he was becoming a man and straighten up.

Those dreams had been incredibly short-lived.

"Do you want me to come with you?"

"No," Quinn said quickly, inwardly flinching at the very idea. He had no idea what state Vickie would be in. Drunk. Sober. High. But he knew what condition the house would be in, and it could have only gotten worse after three years. The thought of Kate seeing it was acutely repellent. "No, it's not... Your parents wouldn't want you over there, Kate. Trust me."

Her hand covered his, her fingers delicate but strong. "It's already late. Why don't you wait until morning? You're upset."

"I'm not upset."

"Quinn—"

"I have to go. I'm sorry." He leaned over and kissed her cheek without really looking at her, then got out of the car and walked over to his bike. He felt her gaze on him as he put on his gear and started the motorcycle, but he pushed away all his feelings down into the pit of his stomach, then headed out to the last trailer park he'd known Vickie to stay at, finding her old beat-up car in the same spot it had always been. Just looking at the house was depressing, but he parked his bike next to her car and went and knocked on the door.

"Yeah!" A scratchy, smoky female voice called. "Who is it?"

"Vickie, it's me. It's Quinn," he called back.

For a moment he wasn't sure if she'd open the door for him, but the trailer creaked and groaned as she got up and walked to the door. She looked more or less the same, maybe a little heavier in the face and body from all the booze she drank. It probably wasn't because she'd been eating well.

The smell hit him all at once, rotting food and mildew, the memories of childhood.

"Well look who finally decided to come see their mommy," she jeered a little, sounding surprisingly sober. "What do you want?"

"Nothing." He shifted slightly. "I... thought I would come see you. I know it's been a while."

He had almost said wanted but had never been big on lying. She opened the door and let him in, kicking stuff out of the way as she went.

"Why is it so dark in here?" he asked, wondering at first if the electric was off but noticed the television was playing, just on mute.

"Can't reach any of these damn light bulbs."

"You have some? I can change them out."

"Yeah, they're somewhere." She waved him off and groaned as she sank back into her chair. "Did you drop out or something?"

"No." He cleared his throat. "I graduate in May."

"Huh. Imagine that. A Haley going to college," she said, cackling a little. "That jerk-off father of yours still giving you money?"

"No, not since I was eighteen." He sat down on the couch, moving piles of paperwork out of the way. She unmuted her show, and for a while she just sat there watching television, like he wasn't there. Like he hadn't been gone for three years. "How have you been?"

She snorted. "Like you care."

He blinked at her. "I asked, didn't I?"

"I'm getting old, and everything hurts." She grunted. "Every time I drink, my pancreas and liver go to war with each other. I was in the hospital last year for a while."

"You could have called."

"What were you going to do?" Vickie asked, and he could feel her glare from across the room. "Hold my hand?"

Quinn shrugged. "I probably wouldn't have done anything, but you can still let me know if you're sick."

He started to say something else, but her expression was bordering on annoyed, and he really didn't feel like fending her off, even though she wasn't drunk and he was a little big now to slap around. Still, there was a glazed look about her, and he wondered if she was on something else. She wasn't slurring. She just didn't seem *there*.

"You spending the night?"

Spend the night? Here? Quinn would rather gouge out his own eyeballs. So he surprised himself when he asked, "You don't mind? I can pick up a pizza or something."

"As long as you're buying. Get me a six-pack and some cigarettes while you're at it."

"Okay. Mind if I take your car? Hard to carry that on a bike." What was wrong with him? What was he doing?

"If you can get it to start." She handed him her keys. "Don't forget the beer."

At least she wasn't asking for hard liquor. Whiskey made her mean. Anything else just made her dangerous. Beer was usually safe, as long as it wasn't too much.

"I got it. Anything else?"

"Trash stinks," she said absently, turning the volume up on the television. "Take it out."

⚬⚬⚬

His mom was passed out by the time she finished her six-pack, so Quinn took the car down to Luther's garage. It was in serious need of a tune-up. He knew Luther would be there late. He always was. At least a decade older than Vickie, Luther had probably been her longest boyfriend and had definitely been the best. He'd admitted that he'd stuck around as long as he had because he'd liked her kid, way more than he'd cared for her or her shitty attitude.

Luther just put his hands on his hips when he pulled up in her car, shaking his head in resignation. "Jesus, kid, you're a glutton for punishment if I've ever seen one. What the hell are you doing hanging around over there?"

"Just in for a visit. Promise," Quinn said, shaking his hand.

"Didn't get to talk much the other night. You still at Duke?"

"Graduate in a few weeks, then start up again this fall for law school."

"Still want to wear a suit?" Luther grinned, slapping him on the back. "Nothing wrong with getting your hands dirty for a living. Thought I taught you that."

"You taught me a lot of things, Luther." He elbowed him. "Probably a lot of stuff you shouldn't have taught me."

"Don't blame me. I told you thirteen was too young to try whiskey." He walked over to Vickie's car and looked down at it. "Where's your bike?"

"Left it over there. Sounds like she's got a misfire. You mind if I work on it? I stopped and got parts on the way. I'll change out the oil and filters while I'm at it."

"Nah. You're too good for her, you know that?" Luther sighed. "This piece of junk… those dirty filters might be all that's holding it together. Bring her in. We can knock it out together."

"Thanks, Luther."

He pulled the car into the garage and onto the lift and drained the oil quickly, Luther pulling up a stool and handing him what he needed.

"So where's your girl?"

"She's at home."

Quinn felt a tug of guilt. He shouldn't have left Kate like that, but he needed to think things through. Seeing his dad like that had really messed with his head. As much as he wanted William and Vickie to mean nothing to him, the truth was that he still felt like a little kid when he was around his parents… still hoping that one of them would remember his birthday.

"She's a pretty girl."

"Yeah, she is." He glanced at Luther. "Thank you for what you did the other night. She's going through some stuff, and that seemed to help."

"Blue said he misses you. Wants to know when you're coming back over," Luther replied with a twinkle in his eyes.

"Ha ha."

"How in the heck do you do overnight trail rides with them folks when you go on vacation with them? And you actually ride the horse?"

"Yes." Quinn grimaced. "It's not pretty though. But I have this thing called a *saddle* to hang on to."

Finished with the oil, he lowered the car and moved on to spark plugs and wires. The car was older than he was. It was a miracle it was still running.

"So what's wrong?"

Quinn tensed. "What do you mean?"

"You got a pretty girl that thinks you hung the moon, and instead of being with her, you're back over at your mother's. Don't take a genius to figure that one out."

"My dad," Quinn replied quietly. "I guess I should start calling him my sperm donor."

"I thought y'all were getting along."

He shook his head. "No. Just circling each other for the past few years, and I'm done. I saw him with his wife and daughter earlier. Guess the cat's out of the bag now."

"Well it's about time," Luther spat. "Frigging lawyers. I should have married your mom. Better yet, adopted you and gave her the boot."

Quinn glanced at him, giving him an easy smile even though his heart had swollen three sizes, just like the Grinch's. "You'd have been a good stepdad."

Luther guffawed loudly. "Don't know about that. I'd have probably been a good coconspirator though, if you hadn't been such a little shit."

"It's good to see you too, Luther."

They talked as Quinn finished his work, bullshitting each other over cars, the same way they'd done ever since Vickie had brought him home when Quinn was ten. He finished up, said goodbye to Luther, and then drove it back to Vickie's with a full tank of gas. She was still asleep when he got there. He grabbed his jacket off the sofa, noting that it looked like she had gone through it. Probably looking for money. His old room was about the biggest shit hole in the world, but she hadn't got rid of his bed or his ratty mattress. There wasn't a blanket in sight, but he sank down onto the bed, exhausted, without bothering to take a shower. Meredith would have given him serious side-eye for it, but since he was probably cleaner than the rest of the house, he figured it didn't matter.

Grabbing his phone out of his pocket, which had still been on silent from the movies, he saw he'd missed two calls from his dad and a few texts from Kate.

> **Kate:** Are you okay?
>
> **Kate:** Quinn, please… at least let me know you're alive.
>
> **Kate:** I'm really starting to worry.

He sent her back a quick text.

Quinn: Sorry. My phone was still on silent. I fixed my mom's car and spent some time with Luther. Going to stay here tonight. See you tomorrow.

Before his head hit the bare mattress, he was mostly asleep.

He woke the next morning to the sound of the toilet flushing, the only bathroom in the house right next to his room. Vickie opened his door and looked at him with bleary eyes.

"You still here?"

"You need something?"

She closed the door in his face without answering and shuffled back down the hall. Quinn sighed. She wasn't a morning person by any means. She wasn't usually even up until after noon. Vickie was grumbling when he made it to the living room, throwing around piles of clothes and paperwork. In daylight, the place looked even worse, though she had sheets and tinfoil covering most of the windows. The trailer was probably one of her longest residences... maybe seven or eight years. It was a step up from her last place. If they had another hurricane or even a strong storm, this place would be rubble.

"You see my keys?"

"Yeah." Quinn reached into his pocket and handed them to her. "It should run a little better now. I took it over to Luther's and gave it a tune-up."

She didn't look at him as she snatched them out of his hands, and he suddenly realized she was wearing a waitress uniform. Almost as if she was going somewhere. Like... work. His whole childhood, he thought she had maybe five jobs and most of those no longer than a month or two.

"You have a job?"

She grunted at him, mumbling beneath her breath as she headed toward the door. "I'm going to be late. I ain't got time to talk right now."

"You want me to do anything while I'm here?" he asked. "I'm going to be heading out of town again in a few days."

Vickie stopped and looked around. "Clean this shit up if you want, and my toilet isn't working right. Don't throw my paperwork away."

Quinn looked around. There was junk mail and paperwork all over the damned place.

"Go to work, Mom. I'll take care of it."

Vickie just gave him a look, like she was wondering what he wanted, but didn't say anything before leaving. Since he knew there wasn't going to be any food in the house, he went and bought some bread, lunch meat, trash bags, and Lysol. He started in the kitchen and worked his way through the house, trying not to let it bother him that his mom lived like this. Since he'd decided to go to college and do something with his life other than breathe and collect a paycheck, he'd wanted to do something for her. The five-year-old in him still felt guilty that he had ruined her life, and he'd dreamed of doing a grand, life-changing gesture like buying her a house or giving her money to do whatever she wanted, but if he was honest with himself, he knew she didn't deserve it. She didn't want him. She never had.

So he cleaned her house, because though he wasn't completely poor, he knew better than to give her any money when he had precious little to spare. He fixed her toilet and a leak under both the kitchen and bathroom sink, even though the entire house was full of water damage and it was a miracle it hadn't completely collapsed on itself. He organized her paperwork, which he found were mostly collection notices and hospital bills. And he changed her light bulbs, because the idea of her sitting in the dark all the time broke his heart.

Chapter 18

·······ஃ·······

QUINN'S DAD CRASHED THEIR SUNDAY dinner. Frank led him into the kitchen, awkwardly introduced him, and for a moment Kate felt a tiny bit of pity for William Knight. Maybe it was because he looked like Quinn so much or because there was so much sadness in his eyes. The man looked emotionally exhausted. She had started worrying about him... He'd been gone twenty-four hours, and she hadn't heard from him since he had texted her the night before.

Her mom had questioned her about what had happened, but Kate had only given her the basics.

"Sit down, William," her dad said, pulling a chair out for him, then taking his seat at the small kitchen table. "Care for some fajitas? My daughter is the best chef in town."

"No— I-I'm sorry to barge in like this, Frank. Is he here?"

Frank glanced at Kate.

"Quinn didn't come home last night," Kate said quietly.

"But you know where he is?" Familiar green eyes gazed at her desperately. "Please, I just need to talk with him. I tried to call him, but he hasn't answered me."

"He said he'd see me today," she answered carefully. "He didn't say when."

Her dad waggled his fingers at Miranda and Jon. "Finish your dinner in the dining room, kids."

Grumbling, her siblings trudged out of the kitchen.

"Did my daughter do that?" William asked, examining her face.

Kate touched the bruise that had formed on her cheek. "Is that why you're here? Afraid I'm going to sue you?"

"No. I'm worried about… about—"

"Quinn! He has a name," Kate growled. "Quinn Liam Haley."

His dad blinked at her. "I beg your pardon?"

"I don't know what you're doing here, but if it's anything less than being there for your son and not hiding him away for another twentysomething years, then you should leave. His name is Quinn. It's not kid. It's not him or hey you or whatever bullshit excuse you gave your wife and daughter about who he was yesterday."

"Kate," her dad warned.

"It's okay, Frank. I get it." William closed his eyes and finally sat down. "Believe me, after the night I had, I finally get it."

"He's a person," Kate continued, her throat tightening. "You hurt him. You have no idea how wonderful he is. How decent and good, and he is none of those things thanks to you. He's all those things in spite of you and in spite of his mother."

"That's enough," her mom said. "Give the man a chance to speak."

"Thank you, ma'am."

"Oh, don't thank me yet," Meredith said, turning to face him. "I happen to agree with everything she just said. The only reason you haven't received an earful from me before is because my husband wanted to mediate things between you and Quinn peacefully. You knew this was going to blow up in your face one day, and yet you've done nothing but lie and stall and kept that poor boy on a string hoping that you'd acknowledge him. That you would love him. You have no idea—none—of what that woman put him through. I know he was starved. Of food. Of love. Did you know she tried to kill him? She beat him for most of his life, and he hid it, because she frightened him with stories of what happens to kids who end up in the system. Don't you dare give him another ounce of hope unless you plan to love him and show him love like you do your daughter."

It felt like lead had settled in her stomach. His mother had tried to kill him? And she hadn't heard from him…

Kate turned on her heel and went into the dining room, then dialed his number. It went straight to voice mail.

"Everything okay?" Jon asked around a mouthful of food. "What happened yesterday?"

"I'll tell you on the way. I need to you take me over to his mom's."

Jon's eyes bulged. "What the… his *mom's?*"

"Shh. He didn't want anyone to know, but now he isn't answering and I thought he'd be here by now. Just take me over there."

"Can I come too?" Miranda piped up.

"No," they both replied automatically.

"If they ask, just tell them we went to pick him up." Jon reached over and patted her on the head. "You're good at lying. You'll think of something."

Their mom was still giving William the shakedown as they left, her voice sharp with anger and demands. Kate glanced at Jon wide-eyed as Meredith's speech disintegrated into outright name-calling.

"Damn. Mama bear unleashed," Jon said as they got in

the car. "Kinda want to stick around and see what happens."

"Don't worry. Miranda will give us the highlights." Kate tried Quinn's phone again. "Dammit, why isn't he answering?"

The car surged forward as Jon punched it. "I can't believe you let him go over there."

"How was *I* going to stop him?" Kate clenched her hands tightly. "Is it true? His mom tried to kill him?"

"She was high." A muscle in Jon's jaw popped. "Pointed a gun at him… stole all his shit and sold it so she could get high again. That's why he moved in with us… but he gets weird about her sometimes. I guess family is family even if they are shitty. He still pays her rent when he has a little extra. I doubt she even notices."

"We saw his dad yesterday. With his wife and daughter." Kate touched the bruise on her cheek. "Little shit hit me with her purse right in my face."

"So is it official now?" Jon slid a glance her way. "Y'all are a thing?"

"Maybe. I have something I need to tell him. Not sure how that's going to go." She fidgeted. "I'm actually not sure if it's going to work out. It's probably best if it ends now, before… before we both screw everything up."

Jon's expression softened slightly. "Quinn came here for you, Kate. If he goes back to Duke, he's going to find someone else. Or worse, he'll end up with her again."

"He probably should find someone else," she replied, even as the words punched her through the heart.

"I don't get it." Her brother rolled his eyes. "You like him, don't you? Isn't this everything you've ever dreamed of?"

"It's not that simple anymore."

"Don't play these same games with him, Kate," Jon said shortly. "He's been through enough shit with Roxie."

"Is that what he thinks?" she asked, horrified.

"Why wouldn't he? You're hot one minute, cold the next."

"Because I'm a mess, Jon!" Kate cried.

"You really loved him that much? Andrew?"

"What? No. This isn't about him," she whispered.

"He's my best friend. If things don't work out between you, what am I supposed to do?"

She didn't know what to say. If things didn't work out, she didn't have a clue what was going to happen. And it was suddenly imperative that they did work out, because he made her happy, and if there was even the smallest chance that she could make him happy, she was going to take it.

As they passed into the residences behind the big box stores, Kate wondered what she was going to say. Despite being shaken to her core with the MRKH diagnosis, she knew that she was loved. He had been rejected by his father, and his mother had tumbled into the oblivion of alcohol, leaving him to fend for himself. She wondered if he had ever truly felt loved, by anyone except for Roxie.

The entrance into Wilmington Estates was squeezed between a car wash and row of storage buildings that she'd never noticed before. After a few hundred feet, the road looped in a circle, featuring run-down mobile homes on each side of the street, so tightly spaced that it was a wonder there was any room to park. The trees were thick and the streetlamps sparse. If not for the sound of Market Street in the distance, they could have been in the middle of nowhere.

Jon pulled up in front of an older white mobile home with weeds choking the yard. There were a few straggly azaleas, but they did nothing to bring charm to the place. Quinn's motorcycle was parked next to his mom's old car.

changed

The smell of fresh-cut grass greeted her as she opened her door. There was a lawn mower in front of the steps, and it looked like it had been recently used. Jon set his hand on her arm.

"Wait here."

"No way."

"Kate, he's not going to want you to go inside, and there's no telling what kind of mood Vickie will be in. She's not a good person."

"I don't care. If he would have answered his phone, I wouldn't have worried so much. I'm here now."

He closed his eyes, shaking his head. "He's going to be so pissed."

"He can get over it. I'm pissed," she replied.

They climbed a rickety porch that groaned under their collective weight, then Jon knocked on a flimsy metal door with a diamond at the top. A woman yelled from inside the house, which she took to mean to come in since Jon opened it up and stepped inside. A television was blaring a game show loudly, and the house was otherwise dark. His mom sat in a rose-colored recliner wearing a pair of shorts and a too-tight top, a beer in one hand and a cigarette in the other.

"Hi, Vickie. Not sure if you remember me. I'm Jon… Quinn's friend."

"Yeah?" She took a drag from her cigarette. "What do you want?"

"Is he here?" Kate asked. "I'm uh… I'm Kate. Jon's sister."

Mrs. Haley looked her over, then turned her attention back to the show. "He's in his room. End of the hall. Keep it down. My show's on."

"Uh, we will. Thanks." Kate eyed her as she walked by, half afraid that she was going to be assaulted in some way.

She followed her brother down the dark hallway, passing

a bedroom that was so full of clothes and boxes that you couldn't see the bed and then a small bathroom that looked as if the door had been kicked in. It was free of trash, clean to an extent, but nothing could disguise the smell of dampness and mildew or hide the stains on the carpet and ceiling. From somewhere a little dog yapped, but she couldn't even tell if it was inside the house or one of the neighbor's. The paneling was missing in spots or had holes in it, and the floor felt soft in places beneath her feet. Jon knocked on a door at the end of the hall, and Kate wondered if she'd made a mistake. Music played from the door beyond, and she felt a moment of panic.

What if he wasn't alone? What if Roxie was in there with him? Or some random girl?

Jon knocked louder when he didn't answer, and the door finally opened. He was wearing nothing but a pair of shorts, his hair dripping wet. The light was dim inside his room, but she felt a rush of relief when she saw that he was alone.

"What are you doing here?" he asked, his lips turning downward as he looked at them.

"You wouldn't answer my calls," Kate said quietly.

"My phone is dead." He peered down the dark hallway. "Where's Vickie?"

"In her recliner. We wanted to make sure you were okay," Jon said. He glanced between them. "Now that I can see you're alive, I'm going to head home. Next time answer your phone."

When Kate didn't move, Quinn's gaze narrowed at her. "Go home. You shouldn't be here. It's not safe."

Her heart squeezed at the distance in his tone and the dull flush covering his cheeks. She'd embarrassed him by coming here, but surely he knew that she didn't care about that. She loved him. Even if he only thought she cared about him as a friend, he should know that how much money his mom had meant nothing to her.

"I'll leave when you do. Are you going to let me in or not?"

Quinn turned away from her, and she followed him into the room. Jon gave her a glance before she shut the door in his face. His room was painted a dark green, but paint could not disguise the condition of the walls. It was warped and peeling in places. Posters of the Carolina Panthers and a couple of their cheerleaders were the only decoration. She forced her attention to Quinn, but he wouldn't meet her gaze.

"This is who I really am. Poor white trash. Is this what you wanted to see?" He flung himself down on the bed and leaned against the wall. "This is where I belong."

"Quinn you belong with *us*," Kate said, vehemently. "You shouldn't have run off yesterday." He didn't say anything, just stared at the wall. "Please talk to me."

"What do you want me to say, Kate?"

"I want you to talk to me." She sat down on the bed beside him, drawing her knees to her chest. "Your dad came to our house."

He turned to look at her, his gaze zeroing in on her cheek. He reached up and touched the bruise his sister had left. "I didn't see this yesterday. I'm sorry."

"Miranda has done worse." She gave him a tentative smile. "Why didn't you come home? Or answer me?"

He pulled his phone out of his pocket and pressed the power button. Nothing happened. "I don't have a charger on me. It was late when I got done working on her car, and I've been doing stuff around here. I can't stand seeing her live like this."

Kate brushed his hair out of his face. "You just got out of the shower?"

"Nothing gets by you." His lips quirked to one side. "My clothes are in the dryer. I was about to leave."

"That's good. Because I need to tell you something

before you go back to Duke. I can't… I can't tell you everything. I'm not ready for that. It's medical stuff. Stuff I don't want to talk about."

"You're sick?" He shifted so he could look in her eyes, but she refused to look at him.

"No. It's not like I'm dying or anything. I'm not sick at all. It's… complicated. And weird."

"You can tell me anything."

"Not this." She felt frozen inside. She squeezed her eyes shut, the words she wanted to say dying in her mouth. What was the point of falling in love if you couldn't have sex? Couldn't have kids? Everything she had read about the surgery sounded scary. There were no guarantees that she'd ever have sex the normal way, and all she could think about were the comments she had read online, with people telling her to just have anal sex and live with the fact that she didn't have a vaginal opening. She knew she had to tell Quinn something. She would have to tell him everything eventually. Part of her hoped that she could deal with everything without him finding out, but she didn't know how long it was going to take to fix things. What if he didn't wait? What if he found someone else?

He pulled her into his lap so that she was straddling his legs. He caressed her face, looking at her tenderly. "I'm not going anywhere, Kate."

She leaned forward and pressed a kiss to his forehead. "You would be better off running as fast as you can. You have no idea what you would be getting into. I think I'm going crazy, Quinn. There are some days I just want to die. I don't want to be like this anymore."

"Hey." He brought his head back so he could look at her, his expression tight. "Don't. Don't ever think like that."

She felt panic welling inside her again, and the room began to get smaller. She was aware of Quinn wrapping his arms around her. Her mind began spinning in circles, all the *what ifs* and opportunities she would never have, beating against her brain. She would be condemning him as well to a life of no children, no legacy, and very possibly abnormal sex, but she felt her heart reach for his.

"Let's get you home," he whispered. "I don't want to do this here. I need to get my clothes and take the lawn mower back to the neighbor."

He was gone for about five minutes and came back carrying his clothes. She watched him dress, then he held out his hand and led her back down the hallway. She had a vague impression of Vickie complaining about people coming in and out, but he ignored her. It was dark out, well past the hour her parents preferred her to be home, though they hadn't said much of anything to her since her diagnosis. Apparently it had gotten so bad that Quinn keeping her out after midnight was no longer a concern… since they knew nothing could happen between them. She'd been angry more than once and flung words back at them in bitterness about them never having to worry about her getting knocked up or an STD. They walked on eggshells around her now, afraid that one wrong word would send her over the edge. The memory of her darkest moment wasn't something she liked to talk about, no matter how much her parents pressed. Things had gotten so bad that her gran had come to stay and installed herself as Kate's babysitter for two weeks.

"I wouldn't ever hurt myself," Kate said as they walked toward his motorcycle. "For a while I would just… I would just think about it. That it would be easier than feeling like this all the time."

He squeezed her hand hard. "Don't let yourself think about that. Whatever it is, you're strong enough to get through it. Your mom… your dad… Jon and Miranda. Me. We would all be devastated, Kate… completely eviscerated if something happened to you."

"I was on this medicine earlier this year," she mumbled. "It made me groggy, but numb. I think that's worse... to not feel anything. One of the side effects was suicidal thoughts. I'd like to think that's what it was, but I don't really know. I was pretty messed up before I started taking it. Then I got drunk. Broke Andrew's heart. I quit my job. I'm in therapy. *Me.* I started cussing, and honestly it's about the only thing that makes me feel better. Unless someone wants to give me a baseball bat so I can break something. I have no idea what I'm doing, Quinn. I don't know if I can handle anything else happening to me right now. Do you understand?"

His gaze was fierce as he looked down at her. "You're worried about Roxie?"

Kate scoffed. "Her and a million other girls."

"I'm not a cheater."

"I know." Kate blew out a breath, her chest hurting. "I know you're not. It'll make sense when I tell you. Maybe. Maybe not."

Quinn leaned down and kissed her. "You're adorable when you're being mysterious."

"Ha ha."

"You think my sperm donor's gone yet?" He grabbed his helmet and plunked it onto her head, then removed his jacket. "Put these on. It'll protect you in case we wreck."

"My mom was ripping him a new one when I left. Probably long gone." She glanced down at the bike, feeling a little excited. Her parents had never let her ride his bike before, and with the doctor's diagnosis for her to avoid it, she'd probably never get another chance. "Can I drive?"

"Funny, McGuire. Your feet won't even reach the ground." He got on, then grabbed her hand and helped her get her leg over. "Hold on tight. Move when I move. Don't do anything crazy like let go or fall off."

changed

"You're telling me not to fall off? How can you ride this thing but not a horse?" she asked, laughing.

"That's easy." Quinn cranked the bike. "This one does what I tell it to."

Chapter 19

QUINN FELT HIS ANXIETY CREEPING up as he walked into the house with Kate and found Frank waiting for him in the den. He'd been half expecting it. When he had cut things off with his mom, Frank had pushed for it—hard. He'd issued threats. Made promises. Tried to ease things with William. He'd only been partly successful.

"We need to talk," Frank said. "Kate, do you mind giving us a moment?"

"Sure. I'll fix us something to eat." She squeezed his hand then slipped into the kitchen.

"So what's up?" He took a seat across from Frank on the love seat, worry blooming in his chest.

"Where were you last night?" Frank asked, his quiet voice filled with the authority of a parent.

"I went to see Luther," Quinn said quietly. "And I stayed with Vickie."

Frank sighed. "I know she's your mom, Quinn, but you know how she is. She's dangerous. Unpredictable. Was she…?"

"She wasn't high. Drunk, maybe a little." He didn't

mention that he had bought her beer. "She has a job."

"That's good," Frank said, his tone implying otherwise. "She steal from you this time?"

"No." He glanced away. "She said she was in the hospital. I didn't even know about it."

"Last time you saw her, she pulled a gun on you. Don't forget that."

Forget? His breath hitched a little at the reminder, the image of Vickie standing over him with a gun, so high she had been weaving back and forth, her entire body loose limbed and twitching. She had taken every last dime he had on him, plus his phone, to get her next fix. For a while after Meredith had given him the spare bedroom, he had still gone back to Vickie's to stay, every time he had a sudden flash of self-awareness of his situation or suddenly felt like a moocher even though he always helped out on yard cleanup day and helped with any of the chores Jon or the girls had to do. He hadn't given in to that weakness since, until now.

"She's still my mom. The only real family I have. That I can actually claim, I mean." Quinn swallowed. "I know how she is. I'm not blind. If she had been bad, I would have gone somewhere else. I just stayed and fixed some things at the house and took care of her car. I know better than to trust her."

"I don't want Kate or Jon over there," Frank said sternly.

"I know. Jon shouldn't have brought her." He didn't say anything about Jon going over there. Jon had been his little pest sidekick since they'd become friends. He'd seen every side of Vickie there was to see.

"Your dad feels really bad about what happened. He came here to apologize. I'm sorry Quinn. I thought things were going good."

Dad. The word sounded so much more familiar to use than *father*. It was something you would call someone who knew more about you than your name, and even that was questionable. They had barely ever had an actual conversation, though the last time had almost seemed… cordial.

"He texts me sometimes… asks about school, but that's about it. Look, Frank, I appreciate everything you've done. But it's time I accepted things for what they are. There's a reason he never told his family about me."

"He did have a reason," Frank replied. "It doesn't make it any less fair to you, but he did have one. He wants to talk to you. Explain."

"It doesn't matter anymore."

"Do you ever text him?" Frank asked.

"What do you mean?"

Frank smiled at him. "Ever ask *him* how work is going?"

"Uh, no."

"Quinn, believe it or not, he does care. He's always asking me about you."

"He does?" Quinn frowned. "Since when?"

"A lot the past few years. He calls me once a week to see how you are. How your classes are going."

Until Luther… until Frank… there had been times he hadn't even felt human. Just an animal who survived and little else. He was ten years old when Luther taught him the basics of cooking. Eggs and ramen noodles. Between those delicacies and the free school lunches, he'd eaten like a king or at least thought he had until Meredith invited him to dinner. Then there was Kate's cooking. Each step like a graduation to something normal, and glorious.

But for years… *years*… he'd gone Dumpster diving with Vickie after she sold her food stamps, and he'd eaten every kind of canned vegetable or soup from dented cans that the grocery stores threw out. He'd worn not just hand-me-down clothes but clothes that were thrown away, just like he had been. More than once, late for rent, his mom had taken their landlord into her bedroom to work off the rest of it, though it wasn't as if the money hadn't been there. It had. She just blew it on booze and drugs or went to Atlantic City and only came back when she was broke.

So to hear that his *father* was taking a sudden interest in him was unsettling. He didn't know how to feel about it. When he had been younger, there had been anger. Lots of anger. He'd been well on his way to having a serious attitude problem, but with no responsible adult around to shave the rough edges off, all his outbursts had been virtually ignored.

Until Luther. Until Jon and his family. Until Roxie, who had given him someone to love and something to focus on other than himself.

His father had nothing to do with the person he was. All he had ever done for him, his entire life, was throw money at Vickie or at him so he didn't have to be bothered and his precious family didn't have to know about his dirty little secret.

"If he wants to know anything about me, he can ask me," Quinn said evenly. "But I'm done with him otherwise."

"I don't want you to give up on law school. It's too important."

"Is it?" Quinn returned.

"It is if you still want it," Frank replied.

"And if I don't?"

"Then you'll figure something else out. Just let it sit for a while longer. Don't do anything until you're sure." Frank stared at him patiently. "Thank you for coming home. Meredith really wanted you here, but I was afraid it was going to make things worse. With Kate I mean."

"I'm still working on that. She's stubborn."

"Kid, she smiled for the first time in months this week. She *laughed*. You don't know, Quinn… You can't imagine how hard it's been, watching her like that." Frank shook his head. "Anything is an improvement. She quit a job that she loved. She almost failed this semester. School is almost over, and she could still fail if she misses any more school. You mean a lot to her, Quinn. She broke her own heart, inviting your girlfriend here for the holidays, but even then she was still Kate. Still my happy, sweetheart of a daughter. This other stuff going on has messed with her head. I understand that you and Roxie had troubles. That she was a troubled girl. And I understand if you can't handle this and you want someone a little less... complicated, but you need to decide now, before it's too late. Do you trust me?"

He felt the weight of Frank's burden and struggled with it for a moment.

"Always," Quinn replied.

"Don't give up on her. She just needs time to adjust. I told you. She needs your friendship more than anything else right now. You need to *wait*, and be patient. If you can't do that, then just stay friends."

He suddenly remembered Kate's words.

...can't sleep with you... just disappoint you... can't... can't... can't...

"I..." Quinn cleared his throat, suddenly very uncomfortable. "I respect you, Frank. You know that."

Frank just cut his eyes over at him. "I know. I also know you're young. You've had a live-in girlfriend for the better part of a year. I don't think you're a saint, kid. I was the same age as you once. Hell... I was married when I was your age, and Mere was Kate's age. I want Kate to go to college and focus on her education. I also want her to *live*."

"I'll take care of her," he promised. "I won't... I won't push her. On... anything."

"As long as you're sure," Frank said quietly. "I don't want to burden you."

"She's not a burden," Quinn said, anger threaded in his voice. "She's an angel."

"I know." Frank nodded, pinning him with a look. "*My* angel. Don't forget that."

"Quinn?" Kate poked her head in. "I've got us a plate ready. Fajitas. Do you want some, Daddy?"

"No, I'm headed to bed. You kids don't stay up too late."

"Of course, sir."

Quinn felt relief roll through him as Frank got to his feet and kissed Kate on the cheek, but then he paused at the doorway, glancing at them from over his shoulder.

"Make sure my ladder goes back in the shed before you leave tomorrow. The last thing I need is some jackass stealing it. Or worse." Frank raised one eyebrow. "Breaking in."

·······∽♧∾·······

"Well, so much for leftovers," Kate said as she watched Quinn stuff the last fajita in his mouth. They were sitting at the breakfast nook side by side, trying to steal every last second they could. "You cleared us out."

"I was starving," he said after swallowing the last bite, then washing it down with water. "God, these were good. If I could afford it, I'd just hire you as my personal chef. Then you wouldn't have to go to culinary school. You could just cook for me. Every. Single. Day."

Kate rolled her eyes. "Those are called wives."

Quinn put his hand over hers. "And girlfriends."

"Boyfriends can cook too," Kate informed him cheekily, feeling tingles everywhere from her chest to her toes. A week. She had a week left with him until he went back to Durham. Going back to school was going to be hard, but maybe not as bad as it was before. Quinn Haley was her boyfriend. "When are you leaving?"

"Sunday night." He shifted on the bench seat, then pulled her legs across his. "I wish I could stay longer. I'm sorry I bailed on you last night."

"It's okay. You got blindsided."

"No. I came here to see you. Not get caught up in the past or shit I can't change. I need to know you're going to be okay when I'm not here. That you're not going to worry about things that aren't going to happen," Quinn whispered, pressing his forehead against hers. "You have to start living again. Go see your friends. Make plans for Atlanta, because you're going. Take a year off school if that's what you want to do. You don't have to decide right now. Just don't let whatever this is consume the happiness that I know is inside you. You're strong, Kate. It might not seem like it right now, but everything is going to be okay. I promise."

It felt like there were bands of iron around her chest, squeezing her tight. "I'm going to miss you, Haley."

"I'm going to miss you too, kitten."

"Ugh. That name." She burrowed closer to him. "We may have to put a hold on your calling me that."

She felt him laugh. "Why?"

Kate turned her face up and kissed his chest, her mouth moving up to his neck, then his ear. "Because it makes me want to do this." She turned his head, kissing him on the lips. "And this."

They broke apart as the sound of someone coming down the stairs echoed through the house. Kate grabbed up their plates and carried them to the sink, hoping her face wasn't as flushed as it felt.

"You rode his *motorcycle*?"

Kate almost dropped the plates as her mom's voice snapped through the kitchen. She glanced at her. "I had to get home somehow."

"You heard what the doctor said. No motorcycles."

She felt her anger flare up. "He also said no horses. Are you going to ban me from that too? You can't put me in a bubble."

"What's she talking about?" Quinn asked, getting to his feet. "Kate?"

Kate glanced at him, then at her mom. "We can talk about this later."

"We can talk about this part now." Her mom looked at Quinn. "Under no circumstance is my daughter—either of my daughters or my son for that matter—to ride your motorcycle. That's the *only* thing I don't approve of with you, Quinn."

"Mom, he was careful. I swear, he drove slower than Gran. I wore a helmet."

"You can't predict what another driver will do," her mom argued. "Riders get hit all the time from people who don't pay attention to the road."

"Quinn has been riding for years. He's never had an accident."

"You have to take care of yourself. I love you so much, honey."

"I love you too." The words felt wooden in her mouth. "Don't jump all over Quinn. He hasn't done anything wrong."

Her mom sighed. "Please, just stay off of it. Please?"

"Mom…"

"Kate…"

Quinn's gaze ping-ponged back and forth between them, the undercurrent in the conversation not lost on him.

"Ma, chill," Jon said as he walked in. "Quinn really does drive like Gran. He's really careful. He loves that bike. Won't even let me drive it."

Well. That was a lie. She'd seen Jon drive it plenty of times, but she wasn't about to rat him out in front of their mom.

"What's the difference between my riding a horse and

riding Quinn's bike?" Kate asked. "We're going to Colorado this year, aren't we? To the ranch?"

"Those horses are gentle," her mom replied. "They go on those trails all the time, with no problems."

"Don't the instructors always say that horses are unpredictable?" Jon offered helpfully. "And why is it a big deal all of a sudden anyway?"

Her mom glanced at her. Kate shrugged. This part of her condition didn't really bother her. What was a kidney? She wasn't about to tell them about the other stuff.

"I only have one kidney," she said quietly. "The doctors said if I get in an accident, I'd probably die or something."

"What?" Jon looked confused. "I don't get it."

"I was only born with one." She shrugged again. "It's fine, as long as I don't get tackled by a football player or hit by a car... but I mean, whose going to survive that anyway?"

"He specifically said motorcycles," her mom added. "And horses."

Quinn stared at her oddly for a moment, as if trying to figure something out. "Sorry, Kate. I'm going to have to agree with your mom on this one. I'm sorry, Meredith. I didn't know."

"It's okay, honey." Her mom walked over and gave Quinn a hug, then moved to Kate. "I'm sorry. I didn't mean to put you on the spot like this. I probably overreacted. That's what moms do."

"Yeah well, I wouldn't know anything about that since— " She broke off, aware of the audience she had. Kate closed her eyes for a moment. "I'm going to bed."

She walked out of the kitchen and up to her room, going straight into the bathroom where she could turn on the shower and cry in peace, but tears refused to come. She'd cried so much that she was tired of it, so she sat on the side of the bathtub and pinched her arm.

"I told you to stop doing that." Quinn was leaning against the doorframe, watching her. He'd changed into a plain white T-shirt and dark blue pants. "You taking a shower or not?"

"You shouldn't be in here."

"You ain't big enough to throw me out, McGuire." He walked into the bathroom and turned off the water, then grabbed her hand and pulled her into her room. "Get in bed."

"Quinn—"

She stared at him as he sat down on the edge of her bed and removed his shirt. "What do you think you're doing?"

"I'm going to sleep. Come here."

Kate glanced at her door. "But—"

He crooked his finger as he slid down into the sheets. "Come here, kitten. I'll be back in my room by morning. No one's going to know."

Feeling a surge of rebellion… and yes… want… she moved forward. Then she stopped, changed directions, and went to her dresser. "I need to change."

"I don't mind watching." He smiled when she looked at him. "Did I say that out loud?"

"You know you did," Kate muttered.

She saw him looking in the reflection of the mirror as she undressed, the room mostly dark except for the light coming in from the bathroom. She had the only other bedroom in the house with its own, besides her parents. Her eyes met his in the mirror as she flicked off her bra, then she slipped a T-shirt over her head and went into the bathroom to brush her teeth. A sprig of joy had planted itself inside her chest, and he was sitting up against her headboard, patiently waiting as she came out with her face freshly washed and teeth scrubbed clean.

"If anyone catches you in here, you're dead," she whispered as she climbed in beside him.

"Worth it."

She sucked in a breath as he reached for her and jerked her to his side. She felt like she was going to hyperventilate at all the skin that was touching hers. His hand on her upper thigh, drawing her leg over the top of his. His arm sliding beneath her neck and bringing it around to her shoulder. She tentatively set her hand on his bicep, then skated her fingers up to his shoulder and down his chest.

"I don't think I'm going to get much sleep tonight."

"Tell me about your kidney."

Kate shook her head. "Kiss me."

"I'm going to kiss the hell out of you, as soon as you tell me that you're going to be okay." His hand moved beneath the edge of her shirt to her waist, then to her lower back where her kidneys would be. "Why do you only have one?"

"They don't know."

"They? You mean the doctors?"

Kate nodded, emotion quickly clogging her throat and making it hard to speak. Hard to breathe. "I don't know everything. But as far as I know, I'm going to be fine. I'm not sick. I swear. I'm just… Parts of me are missing. And I didn't find out until recently. In January."

"You should have told me," he whispered, sliding down a little so that his mouth was closer to hers. "I don't want to do anything that could hurt you, Kate."

"It's not a big deal. They said I can live with one." She sighed. "That's not the thing that's making me crazy anyway. You don't know what you'd be giving up to be with me." Kate touched his face, a frown beginning to form. She wasn't going to cry again. She was *not* going to cry. "I can't have children. I can't… I can't carry a child. There's other stuff that I'm not getting into right now. But I wanted you to know that, so you could decide."

Quinn pushed her onto her back and placed one hand on the other side of her pillow, leaning down to look at her straight on. "There's nothing to decide. I'm sorry that you can't have kids. I really am. Nothing you say is going to get rid of me. I'm going to wait for you."

"It's going to be a long wait," she whispered.

Tell him. *Tell him.*

"I don't care."

"Quinn I'm not… It's not like I was ready to… you know, start popping them out. I know you probably weren't either. But it's a big deal. It doesn't really hit you right away. And if… if we stay together, it's going to be my fault that you—"

He moved his fingers to her lips briefly. "We'll figure all that out later. The only time I've ever thought about kids was how not to have them. I know it hurts, and I'm sorry. You've buried yourself in grief, and I get that. But you said yourself that the doctors haven't told you everything. There's other ways to be a mother. I know I'm probably not saying the right thing here. I know it's a big deal. For you. Maybe for me. I don't know. I know I can't lose you, and that's all that matters to me."

He lay half on top of her, his hands skimming her side as she processed his words. She pushed away the wall of feelings, focusing instead on his words. She resented the craving she felt to kiss him senseless, knowing it would only end in frustration again. She hadn't had this problem with Andrew—this inability to keep her hands to herself. Even now she wanted to touch and touch and touch until they were skin to skin.

She was, she realized with sudden astonishment, horny. For the first time in her life, she was genuinely, frustratingly, horny, and she couldn't do a single damned thing about it.

She started laughing suddenly, covering her face with both hands.

"Something funny, McGuire?" he asked.

"Hilarious." She wheezed silently, doing her best to

regain control. "I swear, my last name should have been Murphy with the luck I have."

"Crazy person," Quinn said, laughing with her.

She lifted her hands to his jaw, then rose up slightly and bit the underside of his throat. He groaned softly, and the sound was addictive. Everything about him was addictive. The way he tasted. His scent. A battalion of butterflies exploded in her, making her want to do more. She moved his mouth to hers and kissed him. And kissed him until they were nothing more than a tangle of limbs and breathless wonder.

"You trying to kill me, kitten?" he whispered. "Because that's a good way to start."

"Sorry." She felt heat rush over her. "I couldn't help it."

"Don't apologize." He studied her for a moment. "You are so beautiful, Kate. You don't have to… to prove anything to me."

Then suddenly she remembered.

Christian Grey on steroids.

Sex in public.

Spanking.

Handcuffs.

"I should get some sleep," she murmured, the joy she had felt earlier trying to snuff itself out.

"I'll be right here."

He didn't have to persuade her again. Kate slipped back into his arms, a warmth spreading through her when he pressed a kiss to her temple and squeezed her hand tightly. It wasn't long before her eyes drifted closed and she was fast asleep, exactly where she had always wanted to be.

Chapter 20

·····◦◦◦·····

KATE MCGUIRE SNORED IN HER sleep.

That hadn't been a revelation. He'd been camping with her enough to know that she made little noises in her sleep, and sometimes when she was really tired she waved her arms around like one of those inflatable tube men that car dealerships used.

The revelation was the depth of her pain. He lay there for a long time and thought about all the things that she would miss, and he let himself briefly think about how that would affect his life, before deciding it still didn't matter. *Her* depression and pain suddenly made sense, but Quinn felt a release of pressure inside his chest, like a balloon being deflated. The rare moments that he had ever thought about having kids, he'd thought of his mother and known that he would never treat a child the way that she had treated him. The thought of another kid being raised the same way he had was enough to make him want to throw up. Kids were something so far down on the list of things he wanted that it barely made the list at all, but he knew it wasn't about him. It was about her.

And he knew he loved her. All of her. Even the parts that were missing. When she turned onto her side, facing away from him, he curled around her, pressing a kiss to the side of her neck. He wanted to tell her that he loved her, but he was afraid to push things too fast. He had no idea what she needed. A friend? A lover? Something in between? She was going to have to set the pace. Frank had all but warned him against moving too fast with her physically, which made him think about the *Steel Magnolias* movie again.

Kidney issues.

Couldn't have a baby.

He dreamed about that movie off and on the rest of the night, and every time he woke up he was sick of hearing Sally Fields screaming, and a very real fear had taken residence in his stomach. He'd never understood why Roxie liked that movie, and now he hated it.

"The f…?"

"Jon!"

Quinn opened his eyes as Kate squeaked, realizing it was morning. They were in the same position they'd fallen asleep in, though he was pretty sure the morning erection was new.

"Are you kidding me?" Jon's eyes narrowed as he stepped into the room and closed the door behind him. "You better be glad mom sent me up here instead of Miranda."

"Mind your own business," she grumbled.

"It's not like that, Jon," Quinn said quietly.

"You're in my sister's room, in her bed. What am I supposed to think?" he said.

"I'm eighteen. Think whatever you want, but to be honest it's kind of weird if you're thinking about it at all."

"Ugh. Mom wants you and Miranda to help her in the shop today, so hurry up and get ready." He glared at them both. "You need to lock your door."

"Well, that was awkward," Quinn murmured after Jon had left. "I guess I fell asleep. Sorry."

"It's okay. I could get used to this." Kate stretched and yawned, then froze. "Um. Except for that. Really, Haley?"

"Sorry." Quinn shifted his hips backward. "That's not exactly something I can control."

For a moment she held perfectly still, then she shot out of bed and into the bathroom. Quinn pulled on his clothes and went to his own room without encountering anyone. He showered, the cold water waking him up quickly. By the time he made it downstairs, Kate and Miranda were eating breakfast and Meredith and Frank had already left for work.

"Morning." He kissed Kate's cheek as he passed her at the coffeepot, then took a seat beside Miranda, who was grinning at him. "What?"

"No kiss for me?" Miranda batted her eyelashes at him, giving him a shit-eating grin.

"You can kiss my ass," he replied, feeling his cheeks heat. "Mind your own business, twerp."

Jon glowered at the toaster as he waited on it to release his frozen waffle. Quinn was surprised at the way he was acting. For the past year he had been dropping hints that he was rooting for them to get together. And after the skinny-dipping incident at the lake, he hadn't been subtle about it.

"Got to go," Kate said as she finished her coffee. "I'll be back around noon."

She gave him a kiss before she left, both of them ignoring the snickering coming from Miranda and the eye-roll from Jon. "I'll be here," he murmured. Once they were gone, he turned around to look at Jon. "So you gonna punch me in the face, or what?"

"My dad will kill you if he finds out. Are you crazy?"

"I'm pretty sure they both knew."

Jon blinked. "Both knew what?"

"That I've been climbing up to her bedroom window and sneaking in." Quinn sighed. "She's going through some deep shit, Jon. Stuff that isn't... normal. She's really hurting right now."

"What the hell is going on?" Jon's expression darkened.

Quinn shook his head. "I can't tell you. I don't even know all of it. It's like pulling teeth to get anything out of her. We weren't doing what you think we were doing."

"I don't want to think anything." Jon shuddered. "Nope. Let's talk about something else."

"I'm serious." Quinn studied him for a moment. "She's been really depressed, Jon."

Jon's brows drew downward. "What, like suicidal?"

"Yes."

"Then what... why the hell are you trying to start something with her now?" His friend shook his head. "I don't believe it. She'd never do anything like that."

"You never know what someone is going through until you live it with them. I screwed up. I shouldn't have waited. I should have told her at Christmas to break up with Andrew, but I was afraid that if I didn't give her time to spread her wings a little that she'd regret it later on." Quinn glanced at the ceiling, feeling a tightness in his chest. "And now they're clipped, and the only thing I can do is hope she believes that I'm with her because I want to be and not for anything else. She's strong. She just needs to remember that. What your mom said the night we got here... that she needs her big brother. She does. She needs her family right now."

The doorbell rang, interrupting the dark mood that had fallen over the kitchen. Quinn told Jon to finish his waffle and went to answer it, finding William standing on the McGuire's front steps, wearing a suit and tie, holding a briefcase. For a moment Quinn just stared at him, not sure what to say.

"Hey, I hope you don't mind my dropping by." William shifted his feet. "I called you a couple of times, and I came by yesterday."

"What do you want?"

"I just… I was hoping we could… talk."

"Talk." Quinn raised a brow at him. "Okay. About?"

William spread his hands slightly. "Can I come in?"

Quinn stepped aside and let him in, his nerves ratcheting up a million degrees. He struggled for something… anything to say but remained silent, the awkwardness ramping up with every second. He'd stopped waiting a long time ago for his father to notice him, to take responsibility for him. Now he showed up and just wanted to *talk*?

"I'm kind of busy right now," he finally stated, leading William into the living room.

"This won't take long." His father looked him over for a moment, then glanced around the room before his gaze rested back on Quinn. He looked like he was struggling to speak. "I wanted to tell you I was sorry for what happened the other day. When I was your age, I was an all-out asshole. I spent years ignoring you, and I'm sorry for that too. I know that doesn't begin to make up for it, but I hope that things can change. I always planned to tell them about you after we met the first time. I just… I kept putting it off. I don't want to keep making excuses. I just want us to move forward, because I can't change what I did."

"Give me one reason why I should give a damn what you want." Quinn crossed his arms over his chest, remembering the look in Amelia Knight's eyes when she had looked at him. "You had your chance. You blew it."

Quinn could almost count on one hand the number of times they'd seen each other since the day Frank McGuire drove him out to Hugh McRae Park and they had met for the first time beneath the towering pines, and that day had been about as crushingly disappointing as it could possibly be. To this day he didn't know what Frank had done to get William to agree to the meeting... just that he made an appointment with William's secretary, went to the appointment, and came home and told Quinn that he was going to meet his father the next day.

"I was an asshole—"

"So you keep saying. I hope you aren't expecting me to argue with you."

William barked out a laugh. "No. I don't. I suppose your mother had nothing but nice things to say about me?"

"Vickie never talked about you. Ever," Quinn said quietly. "She'd beat the shit out of me and lock me in a trunk if I so much as *looked* like I had a question about you."

"I didn't know, kid." William winced. "She wasn't like that when I... when we knew each other. So how did you find out? About me?"

"My birth certificate." Quinn sat down, resigned to having the conversation. His dad took a seat across from him in Frank's recliner. "And she got a check in the mail one day, in one of your company envelopes. I put it together pretty quickly when I saw your website, with a picture of you."

"You favored my side of the family more than I expected," William admitted, smiling a little. "And you had more guts than I would have, the first time we met. You're nothing like I thought you would be. I was a spoiled little rich kid who was rebelling against my father. I did everything I could to piss him off, including joining a rock band that played dive bars up and down the coast. I dropped out of college. Stayed stoned or high or drunk... took whatever I could snort or smoke or swallow. Amanda doesn't know about my past. I never wanted either of you to know, but I owe you the truth."

"Is that how you met Vickie?" Quinn asked, surprised to hear William admit to being a former addict. "I know she was in a band before she had me. She's always blamed me for ruining that for her."

William nodded. "She was the lead singer's girlfriend, but she had her own gigs. We all used drugs, but it was mostly pot before I joined. I had money. I bought them whatever they wanted. I've had to accept the fact that I enabled their addictions as much as mine, because I hated getting high alone. They kicked me out when I... when I started sleeping with her. I didn't even *like* her. Hell, she didn't like me. And when I say they kicked me out"— William threw a hand through his dark hair—"they kicked the ever-loving shit out of me. Broke a couple of ribs. Broke my nose. After I left the hospital, I went crawling back home to my parents, like a little whipped piece of shit. I finally got sorted out, or maybe they beat some sense into me. Whatever happened... I met Amelia not long after that... and I fell in love with her. Pretty damned hard."

As reluctantly curious as Quinn was to know this story, he was relieved at least that it hadn't been what he'd always thought. The way Vickie always reacted when his dad was mentioned, Quinn had thought she'd been raped. That *he* was a product of rape. Like that was the only possible justification she should have for the way she'd treated him. Ignored him. Starved him. He felt his bowels cramp, hating the way this conversation was making him feel. Perhaps some things were best left in the past. Forget, forgive, and move on. Still... he'd wanted to know ever since the first of Vickie's boyfriends had shoved him to the floor the first time he reached for him, calling him *Daddy*.

"When did you find out about me?"

"A year after I got married." William cleared his throat. He began twisting his wedding ring as he stared down at it. "Amelia saw something in me that no one else did. I changed for her. Turned myself inside out. I stumbled a few times, and she was always there. Her father didn't approve of me, and that just made me more determined to be a better man. Then Vickie Haley showed up wanting money. She never wanted me. She was pretty clear about that. She just wanted money, so I gave it to her. I was so afraid that Amelia would find out. I think you were four, when I saw you the first time. Every few months, she'd call. I'd finally had enough of wondering, so I went to see her. I took one look at you, and I knew. I knew you were mine. You guys weren't living in the best house in the world, but it was clean, and you seemed like a pretty happy kid. She didn't want me to know what she was like, because then I would have stopped giving her money. I swear, if I had known, I would have stepped in. It's the sorriest excuse in the world. I shouldn't have... I shouldn't have trusted her. I should have been... better."

Quinn stared in shock as his father's eyes began to glitter with tears. He'd never really seen William show any kind of emotion. He barely even smiled. But as far as he could remember, he'd never lied to him, and he'd never said anything unless he meant it. He'd just lied to everyone else.

"So what now?" Quinn asked quietly. "Why tell me all this?"

"I've been a coward long enough," William said, wiping at his eyes. "My wife is heartbroken. I've known all along that she would be, and I know I made it worse by keeping you a secret. Amanda isn't speaking to me. I don't... I don't know if they'll forgive me. And I know how that sounds. I'm not giving up on them. I'm not saying that because they hate me right now that it's the reason I'm here. You're family. I want you to be part of everything we do. That's what I've always wanted."

"Frank said you had a reason. Is that it? You were a coward?" He tried not to sound judgmental but knew he failed.

"Pretty much," his father replied. "My wife wanted more

children. She had… difficulties before and after Amanda. Multiple miscarriages, and each one of them completely wrecked her. Those years when I would think about you, I knew it would devastate her if she found out. After I outgrew being this huge, self-centered jerk, that was my main reason for keeping it from her. Honestly, it was. It still hurts but maybe not as much as it would have hurt her ten… fifteen years ago. God, I hope not anyway."

Quinn thought about Kate. How a similar situation would affect her, and it was never more stark in that moment how real her pain would be. "What does your wife think about your wanting to have a relationship with me? Won't that hurt her more?"

William looked vaguely ill. "I'm not saying it would be easy, but Amelia is pretty forgiving. I hope that one day you'll be able to meet her. Would you like that?"

"I don't know. I'd have to think about it," Quinn replied slowly. "I would want her to be okay with it. I don't want to force anything."

"I don't want you to think this is a bribe. I've got something for you." William reached into his pocket and pulled out a set of keys. "Frank has always said you were welcome here, but I know you're getting old enough to want your own place. I think you know there's a beach house on Figure Eight Island that sits empty most of the time."

Quinn tensed. *Shit.* Somehow his dad knew he'd broken in, but that had been a long time ago.

"How long have you known?" Quinn asked. "About my breaking in?"

"The first time the guard asked me where my motorcycle was." William smiled slightly. "He thought I was you. Couldn't see all the way under the helmet, which I'm guessing you counted on."

"I didn't take anything."

"I know. That's why I never said anything. Did you ever break in to the house in Wilmington?"

"No," Quinn said swiftly, feeling embarrassed. "I was just curious about you. And I was kind of a little shit for a while. I… I found Amanda on Facebook a long time ago. That's how I knew about the house."

It was a surreal thought that hit him sometimes… that he had a younger sister he had never met and only knew about through social media. He had vacillated his entire teenage years between wanting to meet her and wishing he had never heard of her.

"I'm not angry," William murmured. "I was never angry. I wasn't even really surprised. That was my parent's place, you know. I had a brother, Jackson. He died of cancer a few years ago. The house was supposed to go to him."

"So your parents…?"

"Gone." His father grimaced. "You're the last of us. After Amelia and Amanda, you're the only family I have left."

He wondered what Frank and Meredith would think of Kate visiting him there. Figure Eight was on the outskirts of Wilmington. It wasn't like she would be going across the country with him. "Why don't you rent it out?"

"My parents loved that house. So did my brother." William shrugged. "I've let friends stay there and sometimes clients. This summer Amelia and I are supposed to be going to Europe for a few weeks. I was wondering if you'd be interested in dog sitting for us. We're just going to set the alarm for the house in Wilmington and have a neighbor keep an eye on things. But our dog, Artemis, gets really nervous if we leave him alone for too long. Starts tearing the house apart."

"I've never had one. Not for long anyway."

"He's got a lot of energy. If you could take him out for a run every now and then, it'll help work some of it off."

William offered him a slow smile. "So you'll do it?"

Quinn's gaze flickered away. This surprise visit had shaken the foundation of his feelings toward William. He wanted to be honest with him, but at the same time, he had always felt loads of pride eating up at him, wanting to prove himself to his father in other ways. Eventually he'd settled for ignoring him. "I've been thinking about renting a place when I come back this summer for the internship. If you're sure it's not a big deal, then yeah."

"Can I ask you something?"

"I guess." He had a feeling he knew what William was going to ask him. He'd been waiting for it for what felt like forever.

"Why do you want to be a lawyer?" When he didn't say anything, William cracked a smile. "I have a pretty good idea. You wanted to stick my nose in it, didn't you?"

"Maybe at first," he replied, feeling his cheeks heat. "I set my mind to it a long time ago. It was a career instead of a job."

"That's debatable," William said with a chuckle. "It's not glamorous. Nothing like I expected. My father didn't want me to go into law. He wanted me to take over his business. Well. My brother and I. Jackson was the businessman. I just liked to argue, so I figured that was a good career choice at the time… but you? You could stop now. Four more years of school… that's a long time. I'm not saying I want you to stop or that I can't pay for it. I actually have a job for you, if you wanted it."

"Did Frank say something to you?" Quinn asked.

"No. Why?"

"Nothing." He shrugged. He wasn't ready to talk about dropping law school yet. Giving up something he'd been planning for this long wasn't something he was going to take lightly. "What kind of job are you talking about?"

"My dad left me his business when he passed away. I've

hired outside help to run it, but it's not the same as family. I don't have time for it, really, and Amanda wants to go law school too." William glanced at him, his gaze turning wary. It must have been as awkward for him to talk about his daughter as it was for Quinn to talk about her as a sister. "Just think about it this summer or even after that. If you change your mind… it's not going anywhere."

"What kind of business?"

"Real estate development. Ever see those ugly condos all along the coast?"

Quinn nodded.

"Knight Developers put a good many of those up. The business has stagnated a bit since dad died, but it's still making a profit. The rents from them alone are still bringing cash flow into the business. They have a property management company handling the day-to-day complaints from tenants, collect rent, that sort of thing. The building side of the business is what needs work."

"Is there even vacant land to build on in Wilmington?"

"Those old condos could come down. New, better ones could come up."

"Evicting the tenants and raising the rent? Isn't that illegal?" Vickie had been evicted constantly when he was growing up. The last thing he wanted to become was a landlord who had to throw people out of their homes when they were already struggling.

"Maybe you should be a lawyer," William said, grinning. "You could build anywhere. Doesn't have to be here. The offer is there if you want to think about it. There's a key to the beach house on your key ring. You can start using it whenever you want."

"Can I have friends over?"

"Sure. Don't do anything crazy or anything to get me sued. I'm sure you've noticed the island is pretty quiet. The neighbors are liable to get cranky if there are any parties."

"It would just be Jon." Quinn cleared his throat. "And maybe my girlfriend."

"I thought you broke up with Roxie."

"I'm seeing Frank's daughter Kate."

"Ah." William looked embarrassed. "She gave me a piece of her mind yesterday. I like her. It's not a problem. Invite whomever you want."

Quinn thought about it for a moment. "Frank and Meredith may want to come at some point."

"Just leave their names at the front gate, and the guard will let them through. I can get you set up at the yacht club for meals if you'd like and get you a copy of the homeowner's rules. Maybe by this summer, Amelia and Amanda will be on speaking terms with me again." William leaned forward, bracing his hands on his knees. "I know I did this all wrong. But is it too late for me to… to do all the things I should have done? Am I too late, Quinn?"

Hearing his father speak his name for the first time ever was so painful, Quinn felt warmth spill across his cheeks before he even realized there were tears in his eyes. He *willed* them to stop, unable to look at him until they did so.

"No," he finally managed to say.

"That's good," his father choked out. He reached out and put a hand on his shoulder… another first. "Thank you. God, thank you."

Quinn clenched his fists, fighting to keep his voice from shaking. "I don't want your money. I never wanted your money."

"I know. You've got a lot of pride. My old man… he was like that. Wouldn't take money unless he earned it." William set the briefcase on the coffee table. "Here's the thing. I like giving you money. All these years, I wasn't buying your silence. It was like taking pressure off a wound for me. After you graduated from high school, you said you didn't want it anymore. I was thinking about how I was at that age. I should have been spending time with my parents. With Jackson. Trying to fix all the damage I'd done. I'll probably never be done cleaning up all the mistakes I made. I can fix this one."

He opened his briefcase and handed him some legal documents.

"What is this?"

"It's Jackson's estate. I told him about you just before he passed away. He was going to leave everything to me. I asked him to put it in your name instead." He shifted some things around. "Some of the things… like the house and Knight Developers… are held in a trust. My parents arranged it that way to ensure future generations would have it. But there's some money you would have access to. You could do whatever you wanted. Travel. Frank said that's always been one of your dreams."

Quinn stared at the numbers on the papers. There were quite a few of them. He could actually feel his heart begin to race, then it began to sour when he thought of everything he'd gone through to get where he was now. Did he really want to sell out? No. He didn't want William's money. He had just wanted *this*.

"Don't say no." William took the papers from him and set them aside. "I know you want to. I can see it in your eyes. Quinn, your sister has had a very privileged upbringing. You have no idea the amount of money a teenage girl costs her father, and my wife loves spending money on her. Amelia has her own money. I'm going to split my estate between you and Amanda equally, and there's nothing you can do to stop me. My brother was dying in front of me and found the strength to tell me what a bastard I was when I told him about you. He signed the papers I gave him without question, so this money isn't from me. It's from your uncle Jackson, and it's been more than ten years since he died. Before Frank contacted me and said that you wanted to meet. Please don't say no. Jackson wanted you to have this. There are stipulations, of course. You wouldn't get the bulk of the estate until you turn twenty-five. Until then you would have a modest monthly allowance. I've never really asked you for anything. Don't fight me on this. It will take a weight off my chest that's been there for years, and I know you wouldn't spend it recklessly. One day you might even understand why I did it, when you have children of your own. And you are my son, in every way. That's all that matters."

Again, a sledgehammer to the soul. If this conversation didn't end soon, he was going to need one of Kate's anxiety pills.

"I don't think you'd approve of what I'd use it for," Quinn said slowly.

"What did you have in mind?"

He met his gaze directly. "I'd get Vickie a house."

William frowned. "Is that the only stipulation?"

Quinn thought about it for a moment. "If it means I could get her out of that trailer, then yeah. It's falling apart around her. She's been sick, and it can't be good for her to live in a house like that. I'm not saying she needs a mansion… but something stable. And you don't have to say it… I know not to give her money." He blew out a breath. "Frank doesn't want me to have any contact with her."

"I can't say that I blame him, but he didn't know her before." His dad's gaze turned sad. "She was really talented. Your relationship with her isn't my business now that you're grown. I won't give you grief about it. I trust you. Come by my office in a couple of hours, and I'll have everything in order."

"Your office?" Quinn stared at him. "Isn't that going to be awkward?"

"Everything is going to be awkward for a while, son. It'll get better." His dad sighed. "It has to."

Chapter 21

⸻❦⸻

K ATE WAS PRACTICALLY SHAKING WITH excitement as she went into the house. It was ridiculous how long the hours had dragged by at her mom's shop, knowing Quinn would be waiting for her at home, but even Miranda teasing her on the way there hadn't wiped the smile off her face. Not even the customers who complained about every little thing from the price to the texture of a certain fabric. Everything in the world was beautiful and awesome, and she couldn't believe what a difference a few days had made.

She had slept with Quinn Haley.

Quinn Haley had slept in her bed.

With her.

In her bed.

"Hey." Kate squeaked as she walked past the living room and Quinn's voice appeared right at her ear. He was standing just out of view, looking down at his phone. He smiled when he glanced up. "What's wrong with you, Squeaker?"

"Why are you lurking?" She pressed a hand over her heart. "Don't do that."

changed

It seemed like all the confidence she'd felt throughout the day dissipated as their eyes met. She felt awkward suddenly, not knowing what to say to him. What did you say to your new boyfriend, whom you slept in the same bed with for the first time, after you woke up with his not-so-insignificant-feeling erection pressed against your butt?

Quinn reached out and tugged her purse off her shoulder, dropping it to the floor, then pulled her into the living room. He closed the pocket doors behind her, then kissed her.

Apparently words weren't needed.

Why did you need to speak, when you could kiss instead?

She could get used to Quinn Haley kissing her. He was good at it. He obviously enjoyed it based on the rough sounds he made and the way he held her. Kate gave herself up to it, wondering if they could just keep kissing until it was time for him to leave. The reminder that he was leaving in a few days made it feel like her heart was getting pinched. He broke away, leaning down to rest his forehead against hers.

"Bout time you got home."

Kate's eyelids fluttered open. "Hey to you too."

"How was your day?" His eyes were gleaming.

"It was fine." Heat washed over her face as he swayed with her side to side.

"Just fine?"

She squinted at him. "Did you get into Jon's Horny Goat Weed?"

Quinn started to choke with laughter. "No. I'm happy to see you. I missed you."

"I missed you too." She sighed. "All day I've been wanting to come home and make you cookies, but now all I want to do is snuggle you."

"Cookies?" He grinned at her. "But they have to be

snickerdoodles. Jon doesn't like them."

"It's a deal, Haley."

"I like your deals, McGuire," Quinn murmured, tugging her toward the couch. "Come here and snuggle me… I have something to tell you."

He planted himself on the couch and pulled her down into his lap. Kate kicked her shoes off and curled against him, sensing a sudden graveness taking over him.

"Is everything okay?"

"My dad showed up after you left," he said quietly. "He apologized. Really apologized… which he's never done before. It's just always been this awkwardness between us, with neither of us knowing how to breach it. I felt so stupid. I don't think I've cried since seventh grade. It was weird, but it was like I didn't have control of anything."

"It wasn't weird, and you aren't stupid," Kate said gently. Her heart squeezed at the vulnerable tone in his voice. "He's your father. I can't imagine how tough it was. You've waited for this for so long. I'm really glad he's trying."

He was silent for a moment, a muscle in his jaw leaping and lips pressed together.

"I have a trust fund now." He didn't look happy about it. "I didn't want anything from him like that, but he made it hard to say no. So now I have a trust fund and a beach house."

"What?" Kate sat up and raised her eyebrows. "You have a beach house?"

"On Figure Eight. The house actually isn't mine, but he said I can use it as long as I want."

"Oh my God. That's fancy." She blinked. "Are you serious?"

"He said he'd open a tab for me at the yacht club. They'll probably take one look at me and throw me out."

"Quinn." She snickered. "No they won't. Have you

taken a look in the mirror?"

"Are you laughing?" His arms tightened around her. "It's not funny."

"No." She tried to stop. "Come on, Quinn. You know you're handsome. Every time you went downtown when they were shooting movies, they asked you to be an extra. *Every* time. That lady from the agency called you for a month to ask you to audition for her."

"I'm pretty sure that was for a porno."

Kate laughed harder, her sides beginning to hurt. "It was not."

"Jon teased me for two months about that."

"It was almost as funny as that time Mom's Roomba goosed you and you screamed like a little girl."

He snorted. "That thing *stalked* me. I felt violated… and we were watching *The Conjuring*, and I knew that demon nun was about to pop out."

"Mom still hasn't forgiven you for kicking it down the stairs." She snickered as he made more grumbly noises.

"Uh-huh. That wasn't me, and we both know it," he complained. "That was your sweet, innocent baby sister. She was on her third strike, and I didn't want to get her in more trouble."

"Miranda needs all the help she can get," Kate agreed.

He cleared his throat, hesitating a moment. "He wants me to dog sit for him this summer, but I can start using the house now if I want. He said I could have friends over. I thought maybe you could talk to your mom, see if you could stay. Not overnight, unless she was cool with it. Jon and Miranda can come too. Figure Eight isn't that far."

"I'll ask her." Kate bit her lip. "We're going to Atlanta right after graduation. We'll only be gone a couple of days though."

"Going to check out schools?"

"No." She squeezed her eyes shut. "I'm going to see another doctor."

He was silent for a long time, and the tightness in her chest increased moment by moment. She should just tell him and be done with it. It was *Quinn*. She had known him forever… but the words wouldn't come.

"I don't have a vagina."

"You can't have sex with me because I've got some weird thing going on down there. No, I don't have a penis."

Or maybe a soft, breathy, *"You're too big, Quinn. I'm afraid you won't fit."*

"I'm sorry. I know you can't tell me anything. I wish there was something I could do," he said softly.

"Just talking to you makes me feel better, Quinn. And this. This right here." She rested her head on his shoulder and closed her eyes. "I hate going."

"Do you want to talk about something else?"

"Please."

"So I found out today how Vickie met him," he said. "I always thought it was weird… my dad this well-known attorney and my mom so far from the other side of the tracks that I think there might have been another set of tracks. I… I used to think that someone had… that she'd been forced or something. I thought that was why she hated me so much. It turns out they were just drunk and she was cheating on her boyfriend."

"Quinn, I know it's not fair of me to ask… I mean, I haven't told you what's going on with me…"

"You can ask me anything you want to know, Kate."

"Was she… your mom… was she the one who left all those bruises on you when you were a kid?" Kate winced, hoping that she wasn't prying into a sore subject. She had never broached the subject with him before, and their parents considered the topic off-limits after Miranda had nosily asked about it one day.

"Sometimes. It was mostly her, but every now and then her boyfriend of the week would knock us both around."

She winced again. "I'm sorry. You never talked about it before, and I was never brave enough to ask."

"She burned our house down one time, when I was in kindergarten. Fell asleep on the couch with a cigarette... passed out drunk is probably more like it. We moved every three months, when she got behind on rent." He drew a breath and let it out. "There was never any food in our house. I think you all probably know based on how much I used to eat when I'd come over. My dad sent her money, and she'd either be gone for days, or she'd go out and get a boyfriend and bring him home, and that lasted as long as she had money. That was when it was always bad... when she was broke. I couldn't ask her any questions about my dad or even about her family. She *hates* me, Kate, and I'll probably never know the real reason why."

"I'm sorry, Quinn. You don't have to tell me any of this stuff."

"I don't mind. Not much bothers me anymore."

"I hope I never see your mom again. I might punch her in the face."

Quinn laughed. "Vickie's pretty scrappy, McGuire. I wouldn't bet against you though."

"I can probably run faster than she can. I didn't say I would stick around. I'd sucker-punch her, and I'd be out of there," Kate explained.

"God, Kate. You're going to make me cry." She could feel him laughing again. "Punching my mom in the face is the sweetest thing anyone's ever offered to do for me."

"Just trying to be a good friend."

"Girlfriend," he corrected. "I don't know if you realize it's official... so you're my girlfriend."

"Yes. Yes I am." Her blush was probably out of control at this point.

"And I'm your boyfriend."

"Stop. You're going to start a fire with this thing," she said, waving in the direction of her face. "You boyfriend. Me girlfriend. Thank you for the mansplanation."

"Just trying to be a good *boy*friend," Quinn replied, before his gaze turned serious. "I told William the only way I would take the money was if I could use it to get Vickie a house."

"Are you sure that's a good idea?"

"You saw what that place is like. I'm the only one she has." He closed his eyes briefly. "And she's sick. I found all kinds of medical records and bills when I was cleaning up over there. I need peace of mind where she's concerned. I've thought about her a lot the past three years, and I know I have to keep my distance. I can't get mixed up in her crazy. But it will make me feel better knowing she's got a decent place to live. William told me that it would be better, for now, just to rent a townhouse or something. See how it goes before I go all in and buy. The monthly allowance isn't all that much anyway after you factor in utilities and everything. I would get full access in two years, but I don't plan on living off of it."

Kate worried for him. Vickie had proved that, more than anything else, she was unstable. A few times when she had come to get Quinn when he stayed with Jon, it caused an uproar in the entire house. Her mom made them go upstairs and into their rooms. Warned them to stay away from the windows. She threatened her parents with violence. She caused scenes that drew their neighbors outside. A few times the police had been called. Other times she would be overly friendly. Casually mentioning that she wasn't sure how her light bill would get paid or how she would be able to afford groceries. Her parents had given her money a few times until it turned in to a once-a-week thing. Now Quinn had access to money, and she didn't want his mom to use him. But she also understood, on some level, what he meant by needing to be at peace with her. He was selfless and honorable, and that was one of the many reasons she loved him.

"I hope everything works out. Have you told her yet?"

He shook his head. "I was hoping you might help me look for houses while I'm here. And I thought about it… I'm going to let the second job go. I can make it without the extra money now. I just liked to have something to fall back on. So I plan on driving back every Friday after I leave the mechanic shop, and I'll go back Sunday night."

"Really?" Kate slipped her arms around his neck and hugged him. "You're going to make me cry, Haley."

"I can't miss our date night," he whispered. "Every Friday, forever?"

"Yesssss." She sighed and relaxed against him as his hands skimmed up and down her back. "You could put me to sleep doing that."

"What every guy wants to hear when their girlfriend is sitting in his lap." He shifted slightly so he could kiss her forehead. "So, are you going to see if Cam's will hire you back?"

"No. I'm taking the summer off. Mom really wanted me to. I promised I'd help her in the shop when she needs it." Kate sighed. She felt like her life was in limbo… a few months ago she had a plan, and now the last thing she could do was make plans. "I'm not going to go into detail, but I might be out of commission for a while this fall. As in stuck in a bed for a few weeks after surgery. She wanted me to just enjoy my summer instead of stressing about work. Cam said he'd hold my job if I ever wanted to come back."

Beneath her, Quinn tensed. "*Surgery?* Every time you talk about this, I feel like I'm going to screw up and say the wrong thing, but I can't… I can't just not worry about you. You don't have to tell me, Kate. Just promise me it's nothing bad."

"It's nothing bad. I said I might. Nothing is certain yet." She shouldn't have used the word surgery. Now he would have more questions that she wasn't ready to answer. "The surgery might be elective. I won't know anything for sure until after my appointment."

He was silent for a long time, then let out a sigh.

"You're going to make your boobs bigger, aren't you? Don't do it, Kate. They're perfect. I promise, I like them fine the way they are. I mean, you don't want to start having backaches, do you?"

It took her a moment to realize he was teasing her, and she started laughing again, the tension easing from the pit of her stomach. "I don't know, Haley. I was really thinking of some double *D*s. I mean, I wouldn't be able to clap or cook with my short arms, but just think of how I'd fill out a bikini."

"God, don't give me that image, K. rex," Quinn said, groaning.

"Did you just call me *K. rex*?" She gasped, outraged.

"You're the one with the short arms."

"Okay, so tonight when you're sleeping, instead of my big boobs, just think about creepy clowns and you'll be fine," she teased.

"I will dump you on the floor," Quinn threatened.

"Maybe I can get Jon to jump out of your closet tonight while you're sleeping." She warmed to the idea.

"What happened to my sweet Kate, and what have you done with her?" he demanded, laughing. "You sound as bloodthirsty as Miranda."

My sweet Kate.

She practically swooned. "No clowns," she relented. "Maybe just one creepy doll in bed with you when you wake up. Doesn't Jon have a mask from *Annabelle*?"

"That's it. First trip to the beach this year, and you're getting dunked. I might hold you under for a few seconds."

"You're the only guy I know that actually hides his face during scary movies, Quinn."

"Yeah, yeah, make fun. I might just hide out in that beach house all summer, all by myself. Private beach. Private pool."

"Okay, Haley, I'll stop teasing you." She shifted so she could meet his gaze, then felt suddenly shy. "I liked waking up with you this morning. I don't think I've slept that good in a long time."

"Well, thanks to you, I'm going to be dreaming about creepy dolls, clowns, and you with ridiculous beach-ball-sized boobs and arms not long enough to go past them. I may never sleep again. God, I can't believe I'm still talking about your boobs."

"Would you feel better if I start making penis jokes?"

"No."

"It might be hard, but I bet I could come up with one or two." She pressed her hand over her mouth to stop a snort, but it came out anyway.

"You really just snorted about your own penis joke."

"I'm crying now. Really." She wiped her eyes. "I think my brain is tired. That was pretty lame."

"My beautiful, lame brain," Quinn whispered. He shifted slightly so that she was lying down and her legs were over his thighs. "Don't ever change. Everything about you is perfect, Kate. And I think your jokes are hilarious. Even the corny ones."

"Come here, Haley." Kate wrapped her arms around him and began to kiss him until they were both breathing hard, eyes locked on each other's faces. He kissed her one final time, then rested his head on her chest and closed his eyes.

Her heart felt full and heavy, but for the first time in a

long time, she knew that things were going to be okay.

Quinn left the McGuires' house at the end of a perfect week with two containers filled with cookies stuffed down in his saddlebags and a picture of Kate on his phone as she made them. The cookies didn't make it long, and he probably lost half a battery life a day, staring at her picture, and the other Facetiming her every night. Even working in the shop with Greg and his grumpy old ass couldn't get him in a bad mood. His classes, which had become tedious after Christmas break, were suddenly the most interesting lectures he had ever attended. He knew he was getting on Jon's nerves when his friend complained about him randomly singing in the apartment. Apparently the neighbors didn't appreciate it either since they yelled at him to shut up at least once. When he went back to Wilmington for their first date, he endured a lot of good-natured teasing from everyone, but it was worth it when she came downstairs, her eyes sparkling with excitement. He took her to Figure Eight once they had dinner, and they walked barefoot along the beach together. The barrier island was unique in that there were no streetlights, so at night the sky was completely amazing.

"It's beautiful," she whispered one night as they lay looking up at the stars. "I never want to leave."

So they came back every Friday. He couldn't bring himself to go inside the house yet. It reminded him of when he had first gone to the McGuires. He felt like he didn't belong. He just kept imagining the disapproval that Amelia Knight and her daughter would feel at the interloper who had suddenly descended on their lives. The hatred they must feel. He'd made a mistake in taking William's money, and it was William's money no matter how he'd tried to spin it as accepting an inheritance from his uncle Jackson. He'd been… lawyered.

Sometimes he would take her out to the farm instead and let her ride Luther's horses. He was usually content to just watch, and she quickly developed an attachment to all three. Luther teased the hell out of him every time they went out there, especially after Kate showed him the video she had taken of him eating dirt.

Kate had helped him find Vickie a small, already-furnished house close to the restaurant where she worked. She hadn't even thanked him… not that he expected her to. There hadn't been much to move, just a few clothes and the gobs of paperwork she insisted she needed. When he asked specifics about the medical bills, she just glared at him. He tried to go see her for a little bit every time he went home, but he kept his visits short, usually on the pretense of bringing her a few groceries. It surprised him that she was mostly sober when he showed up. She hadn't stopped drinking, but it seemed like she was content just to drink herself to sleep instead of getting high. Oddly enough, she didn't ask him for money, which he had expected. She barely even acknowledged it when he showed up, which made him begin capitulating on the edge of giving her cash until something would remind him that lack of funds might be the only thing keeping her from calling up one of her meth-loving friends.

On Sundays he began meeting his dad for lunch, bringing Kate with him to make it less awkward. William told him stories of how he had grown up. About his band… his own time at Duke. They even had some of the same professors. Things eased with him, though Quinn could tell that William was suffering in his personal life, but he didn't pry. He confessed that Amelia had asked him to leave, and that he'd been staying in one of the condos that Knight Developers owned. He'd shaken his head when Quinn suggested that he stay at the house on Figure Eight and insisted that it was Quinn's to use as long as he wanted it.

"I'm going home," he said quietly. "As soon as I can."

Meredith invited him to have a family dinner with them, and it was much easier to see William in a group of people than one-on-one, or even two-on-one.

But Quinn spent most of his time with Kate. He showed up every Friday with flowers, waited awkwardly with Frank in the family room as she got ready upstairs, and said goodbye to her on the porch like it was any other date. Some nights he stayed in his own room. Others, he stole the ladder out of the shed and climbed up to her window, and that more than anything was what made him think about the beach house on Figure Eight. It was ticking closer to graduation, and he had four years' worth of clutter to get out of the apartment in Durham. His room at the McGuires wasn't big enough to fit everything, and Meredith would most likely have a coronary if he moved a bunch of boxes into his room.

Right before summer break, he told Kate that he was going to do it. He was going to move in to the house on Figure Eight, with Jon, and if Frank and Meredith didn't object, he wanted her to stay with him for the summer.

Chapter 22

·······⊙ℓ⊙·······

WHEN SHE FIRST TOLD HER mom that Quinn was going to move in to the house at Figure Eight, she looked intrigued for all of five minutes until she realized what Kate was really asking her.

"He said that Jon and Miranda could stay," Kate wheedled. "Come on, Mom. Figure Eight Island. How many chances do you get to stay on a private island? It's not even half an hour away. And I graduated last week. Remember? And I'm eighteen…"

"I…"

"Mom, please. I don't have to stay every night."

Face tilted heavenward and eyes closed, her mom groaned. "Your grandmother will have a fit if she finds out."

"So we don't have to tell Gran."

"Are you kidding? Where do you think Miranda got her nosiness from?" Meredith complained.

"You're the one who arranged to have me kidnapped," Kate reminded her. "Besides, what do you think we're going to do, have wild sex all summer?"

Her mom gave her a death stare, and Kate was pretty sure her eye twitched a little. "I'll talk to your father about it, but I can already tell you, it's not going to be seven days a week. And don't forget, we're still planning on going to Colorado in July."

"Mom…"

"Kate… We'll see." Her mom took a seat at the kitchen table and watched as she prepared dinner. "Did you look at the information I gave you?"

She felt her face heat. "Yes," she mumbled.

Her mom had given her links to websites again for the fifteenth time, even going so far as to give her access to her personal Facebook page to look at the MRKH support groups online since Kate had deleted her own account. There was a whole community out there of girls and women of all ages who cared about each other, who offered advice and friendship or just a place to feel free to rant or cry or share. One day maybe she would reach out, but she wasn't there yet. She didn't know why, but she just couldn't bring herself to want to share anything about her condition. As if by reaching out, she was accepting that it was happening to her and not someone else.

"I want you to write down any questions you have before we go to Atlanta. I know you must have some. I certainly do. You don't have to ask them if you don't want to. I can do it for you."

"Thanks."

"I don't mean to embarrass you, honey. I just want to make sure we get all the answers we need, and it sounds like dilation is what more doctors are turning to instead of surgery. From the girls I've spoken with online, this is worth exploring."

She bit her lip, hesitating a moment. "I do have one question. For now."

"Sure."

Her face was the color of the marinara sauce she was making. "Can guys... can they tell?"

"You mean... tell a difference?"

Kate nodded, just once, unable to look at her mom.

"No. I asked that question in the group, and they all said that once you're... done with either the surgery or dilation... guys can't tell. I don't want to tell you that surgery is out of the question, Kate. Some girls need it. I hope you don't have to. I really do." Meredith sighed. "That came out wrong. You don't have to do *anything*, Kate. I think you were perfect the way you were born, but I know you're hurting. I just want you to know this is your decision."

Kate closed the lid on the sauce and turned the heat down, then stepped away from the stove. "I can't stay... like this. I'll think of some stuff to ask them. I'm sorry I've been... I'm sorry for everything."

"None of this is your fault, Kate."

"Is this costing you and Dad a lot of money?"

"That's what insurance is for. Jon broke his arm. You needed braces. Miranda is probably going to make me pay for years of personal therapy. Money doesn't matter, Kate. Don't worry about that. And that isn't why I don't want you to have surgery. I don't want you to think that. If you need the surgery, you'll have it. I just want to make sure we have the right doctor. Everyone I've spoken with likes Dr. Anderson."

"Is the doctor a man or woman?"

"A woman. I thought that might be easier."

"I hope so. Will they have to... will there be an examination this time?" She felt cold every time she thought about another exam. It seemed like every time she had an appointment now, the doctors wanted to do one, and they always hurt.

"I don't know. It's going to be okay. You can take an

anxiety pill if you want beforehand."

"No." Kate shook her head. "I can't focus. I'd forget everything she said."

They both quit speaking as the side door opened and Miranda and her dad came through from the garage. Miranda had her usual expression on her face, mutinous teenager with a side of bitchy, and her dad looked vaguely irritated. His eyes lit up when he looked at her, and Kate smiled at him.

"What smells so good?"

"Nothing fancy. Just spaghetti and meatballs."

"'Nothing fancy,' she says." Frank bent down to kiss Meredith on the cheek. "I've gained ten pounds this year, you know."

"I know," Meredith teased, reaching up to pinch his stomach. "I can tell."

"So can I ask him?" Kate pleaded, glancing at her mom.

"Ask me what?" Frank murmured, looking at his wife, then back at Kate.

"Quinn and Jon are moving in to the house on Figure Eight, and he invited us to stay with him anytime we wanted to," Kate said in a rush.

"Are you serious?" Miranda squealed. She started hopping up and down, her crabbiness gone immediately. "Please, Daddy, please!"

"Whoa... slow down," Frank said, laughing. "I don't think so, kiddo. Meredith?"

"I said we'd talk about it," Meredith said patiently. "I didn't make any promises."

"I don't know," he said, looking a little flustered. "I don't really see the point... It's only thirty minutes away. I haven't minded you going over there, but staying overnight is another story."

"It doesn't have to be all the time," Kate offered. "Just

maybe the weekends or something?"

"Please," her little sister added. "I'll be good the rest of the school year."

"I'll think about it. I'm not making any promises. I'll talk to Quinn, and we'll see."

"Thank you," she replied, knowing he would only dig his heels in more if she kept begging. She cut Miranda a look, and it seemed her sister understood not to pester them anymore, but Miranda couldn't resist one last *please*?

Frank pinched Miranda on the chin. "Run upstairs to your room. Let me talk to your sister for a minute."

"Ugh." Miranda rolled her eyes. "Not fair."

Her dad just tilted his head pointedly toward the door. Once she was gone, he sat down beside Meredith. "I'll talk to Quinn about you staying, but there are going to be rules…"

"He can't have parties over there, Dad. No loud music, no cars parked everywhere. You know Quinn doesn't like that sort of thing anyway. You should be more worried about what Jon's doing," she grumbled. "Besides, he wouldn't do anything to mess this up. His dad trusts him."

"I trust him too, but that doesn't mean I'm going to let my teenage daughters spend the night on an island, unsupervised except for two twentysomething boys even if one of them is my son," Frank said wryly. He glanced at his wife. "What do you think, Mere?"

"I think it will be fine for Kate to stay within reason, but Miranda, we'll have to see. I'll have to threaten Jon within an inch of his life."

"If it goes good, I'll keep Miranda when you go to Colorado," Kate offered, hoping her mom would let her go. It sounded like her dad could be persuaded. She'd work on him. "We can stay here at the house. Then you two can go on vacation by yourself for once."

She didn't miss the way her mom's lips moved into a

smile or the way her dad sat up a little straighter.

"Really?" Meredith asked. "You won't want to kill her by the end of the week?"

"I didn't say that," Kate said, laughing. "But I know it's been really... rough around here lately."

"A vacation for just the two of us," Frank mused. "I like the sound of that."

"You'll have to prove you're responsible enough to stay by yourselves," Meredith ordered. "Otherwise you're both going to be stuck with us, and no one will be happy. Your father and I will need gate access to the island. There's no telling when we might drop by to check on you. That's *if* we agree."

"Right now it's still a big if," Frank added. "Miranda is still very young, Kate. I don't want her thinking it's okay for *her* to—"

"Frank," Meredith broke in. "She knows."

Kate felt her face turning red. Of course they would let her go. There was no chance of her getting knocked up or even having sex. Miranda was another story.

"I didn't mean it like that," he said gently.

"It's the truth," Kate said quietly. "And I won't let anything happen to her."

Her dad's fears made sense. She knew that logically. Miranda was already unruly. In a few years, she'd be throwing this back at them every time she wanted to set foot outside the house. Not that they hadn't been strict before... They had. Now they were giving her a wide berth about this topic, but Kate knew how awkward it was for them. If they were too strict with her, she broke down. The truth was, she didn't feel any stronger than she had a month or even two months ago. Talking to Quinn... being with him... it was the only thing that made her feel good.

She would have to tell Miranda the truth, as much as she didn't want to do it... yet who else could she tell? As much as she loved Lindsay, she knew that it was the sort of gossip her best friend wouldn't be able to stop sharing.

"I'm going to talk to Rand," Kate said, double-checking to make sure that dinner was ready. "I'm going to tell her."

"Are you sure?" Meredith asked.

"I'm sure. Miranda mines secrets," she replied with a laugh. "She's pretty good about keeping them."

"We're proud of you, Kate," her mom said, then walked over to her and gave her a hug. "We've always been proud of you... and it's a fine line we've walked the past few months between being overprotective and trying to... let you sort some of this out your own. You're eighteen now. We can't stop you from staying with Quinn, and I want you to know how much we appreciate your asking. You've always been my little rule follower." Her mom lowered her voice so her dad couldn't hear. "It's okay if you break some of them. Just don't break all of them at one time. Hm?"

Her mom let her go, then her dad gave her a hug. "Thank you for cooking tonight."

"Welcome." She hugged him back, kissed him on the cheek, then went upstairs.

Miranda's normally eternally closed door was open, and she was lying on her bed looking at her phone when Kate walked in.

"Hey... got a second?"

"Sure. What's up?" Miranda bounced up to her knees. "Did he say yes? He said yes, didn't he? I can't believe Quinn gets a beach house on Figure Eight."

"That's not what I want to talk about." Kate reached out and tugged on her red braid. It was something she'd always done. A small, sisterly gesture that sometimes annoyed Miranda, yet she couldn't stop doing it. "I want to tell you something, but I don't want you to tell anyone."

"You wouldn't believe the stuff I know," Miranda said with a grin. "I can keep a secret."

She closed her eyes and lay back on the bed, facing the ceiling. "You know how mom has been taking me to all these doctors, and I haven't... I never had a period or sex or any of that stuff? It's... it's because I have this... I'm different." Kate felt tears slide down her temple. "I won't ever have a period. Or have a baby. I don't know if I'll ever have sex. At all. That's why Mom and Dad are letting me off so easy. Why they might let me stay with Quinn. I either have to have surgery or... or this other thing called dilation to have sex, and it's going to be a long time before that happens. Maybe a year. I don't know yet. They're afraid because they're letting me go, that you'll think it's okay to start sleeping around and get knocked up. I mean, they didn't say that, but I can tell that's what they're worried about."

Her sister didn't say anything for a long time, and Kate finally opened her eyes to look at her. Miranda was crying so quietly that Kate hadn't even realized, but she didn't look surprised.

"You knew?"

"I thought you had cancer or something." Miranda bawled suddenly, wrapping her arms around her knees. "You were all acting so weird. I looked at Mom's computer and found it. I swear I haven't told anyone, Kate. I swear that I won't."

"I'm sorry," Kate whispered. "I didn't think about... about how it looked to you."

Miranda lay down beside her and put her head on Kate's shoulder. Her sister sniffled, trying to stop crying. "Does Quinn know?"

"I haven't told anyone," she replied, brushing away tears. "You're the first person I had the guts to tell. About the sex stuff, I mean. I think Andrew knows a little. That day he brought me home, I was pretty hungover, and I have no idea what I told him."

"It's not fair," her sister said softly. "I'm sorry. I thought Andrew did something to you. I wanted to shank him."

Despite the emotion clogging her throat, Kate managed a laugh. "He's actually been really sweet to me since all this happened. I still feel bad about breaking up with him."

"You really can't have a baby?" Miranda asked, taking her hand. "Ever?"

"I can't carry one," she replied, feeling empty. "I feel... I feel like I'm not really... not really a girl anymore. How can I be, when I don't have... everything I'm supposed to have? They had to test my chromosomes. I didn't even know what that meant until I looked it up online."

"That's crazy." Her sister pinched her arm. "Of course you're a girl, stupid, you have boobs. Those doctors are idiots if they had to test you for that. You could have been a model if our whole family wasn't hobbit-sized. And if you can't carry one, then I can. I mean, not right now, but when we're older. People do that, right?"

Kate jerked her head around, shocked. "You'd do that?"

"I'd commit a crime for you," Miranda said, rolling her eyes. "Of course I'd do it. You're my sister."

For a long time Kate just breathed, thinking about it. It wasn't hard to picture, though she didn't know how she would feel about it. Her sister, carrying her baby? Part of her wondered if it might be easier for a stranger to do it, emotionally for her at least. Then after, she'd never have to see them again, and she could forget that she hadn't carried a baby in the first place. She didn't want to feel jealous of Miranda and all that she would get to experience, but how could she not?

"I don't know what to say, Rand."

"Don't be weird," Miranda said, blushing. "You might find someone else. I just wanted you to know I'm here for you."

"Thanks." Kate felt teary again. "Can we not talk about

this again for at least ten years?"

"Deal," her sister said with relief. "Now would you stop worrying so much? The doctors are going to fix you, and I'm going to be your baby-mama. You and Quinn are going to be fine."

Kate let out a breath, her throat tight with emotion. "I can't stop thinking about how selfish I am for wanting to be with him. He's been dealing with Roxie's bullshit for the past three years, and I'm such a mess right now. I told him he should find someone normal."

"Don't be a wuss." Miranda pinched her again. "You've been in love with him forever. If he loves you back, he won't care about that crap."

"Guys who have had rough, dirty sex with their ex-girlfriends probably care that they can't have sex if they date a girl like me. He might not be able to have kids with me. Not to mention all the crazy going on in my head right now."

"I think Roxie lied about the rough sex," Miranda said quietly. "I mean, you're a Goody Two-shoes. She probably did it to scare you off. Quinn doesn't seem like the kind of person that would hit someone else for fun."

"Maybe," Kate said softly. "Or maybe he really is Christian Grey on steroids."

"Well, that might be hot once you get... you know... everything taken care of."

She couldn't help but snicker. Her fourteen-year-old sister was telling her getting spanked might be hot. "God, you're going to be a handful someday. No wonder Mom and Dad are worried about my being a bad influence."

Her sister's face turned red. "Actually, I've thought about this a lot. I'm going to wait."

For what, Kate didn't know, and she didn't want to ask. Miranda was too young to be making any kind of promises, and she didn't want her to say something she might regret or feel guilty about later on.

"Can you help me fix my Facebook page? I want to set up a separate one so I can join a group Mom has been trying to get me in. I don't want anyone to be able to tell it's me though. Not even Quinn."

"I can make it where no one can find you," she replied. "We can change your name if you want and use a doggy profile picture or something."

"I want to reactivate my account too. I hate to get rid of all those pictures and cat memes." Kate sniffed dramatically. "Cat memes are my jam."

"Yeah." Miranda rolled her eyes. "Dogs rule, but okay."

A couple of hours later, Kate was back on Facebook on her laptop while Miranda was setting up a new one from her own. Feeling her stomach flutter, she clicked on Quinn's profile, wondering if he'd ever taken down the pictures of Roxie.

"They're gone," Kate said in relief a few minutes later. He hadn't posted in a while, and apparently he was still as obsessed with cat memes as she was. Most of the posts were tags of Jon and Quinn trading insults back and forth. Quinn had never been big on posting photos of himself. His profile picture was the same one he'd had for a few years— Gollum from *Lord of the Rings*.

"Who's gone?" Miranda mumbled, still intent on her work.

"The pictures of Roxie and Quinn."

"Well, duh. He took those down a long time ago."

"You probably know to the exact day, don't you?" Kate accused lovingly. "You're such a stalker."

"She lives with some dude named Glen. He's a tattoo artist."

Kate raised an eyebrow. "Really?"

"He's not even good-looking." Miranda tapped a few

times on her keyboard, then turned her computer around. "See? Fugly."

Well, she'd certainly downgraded, Kate admitted to herself. The guy was no Quinn Haley, that was for sure. He was scrawny and pale, wearing a wifebeater and a wide-brimmed ball cap. He looked scruffy but not sexy in the way that Quinn did. Just plain scruffy, his chin hair too fine to be considered much more than glorified peach fuzz. Roxie looked happy though, and Kate felt something inside of her ease.

"I don't care what he looks like, as long as she stays away from Quinn," Kate declared. "But you're right. Quinn is way better looking."

Kate's Facebook feed jumped suddenly, and her own face stared back at her. Quinn had changed his relationship status, added her as said person in the relationship with him, and tagged her in a photo of them together with a heart emoji. Then her phone went off.

> **Quinn:** Welcome back. Hope you don't mind.
>
> **Kate:** I don't mind, stalker. I look like a goober though.
>
> **Quinn:** You do look like a goober. My goober.
>
> **Quinn:** That sounded funnier in my brain. Disregard.
>
> **Kate:** I think Mom is okay with me going to Figure Eight. Working on Dad.
>
> **Quinn:** Should I ask Jon to deliver my eulogy?
>
> **Kate:** I think you're safe. We're heading to Atlanta tomorrow morning. Hopefully they'll decide by then.
>
> **Quinn:** Do you want me to come with you? I don't mind… I can drive down tonight. We can snuggle.

Kate felt a bolt of panic. She still didn't want him to know, and she was afraid she was going to be a wreck after the appointment.

> **Kate:** No... I just want to get this over with. I'll see you when we get back.
>
> **Kate:** I scheduled a tour for the campus in Atlanta.
>
> **Quinn:** That's awesome. I miss you. I'm here if you need me, kitten.

She sent him back a cat emoji making a kissing face.

> **Kate:** I had Mom send you a care package for your birthday. I'm sorry I won't get to see you. Don't let Jon get it.
>
> **Quinn:** Cookies?
>
> **Kate:** ALL THE COOKIES.

"What are you smiling about, weirdo?" Miranda asked. "Is that Quinn?"

"Yes." Kate tried to stop smiling and failed. "Yeah."

"You know, I was wondering why Dad hadn't killed him yet." Miranda smirked at her. "Does he know he can use your door? Because he wakes me up every night with that stupid ladder."

Chapter 23

······🙢🙠······

THE HOUSE AT FIGURE EIGHT hadn't changed much since the last time he had broken in. It was one of the smaller houses on the island but still bigger than the McGuire's house by at least a thousand square feet. The three-story exterior was in gray cedar shake, the inside all tile and windows, making everything look sanitized and bright. The first floor was a garage and game room with a home gym. The kitchen and living areas were on the second floor, and the bedrooms on the third floor. After arguing with Jon for half an hour about who got the master bedroom, Quinn told him that it was Kate's room.

"Yeah, like my dad is going to let her stay here," Jon said, rolling his eyes.

Quinn just looked at him.

"You're serious?" His friend groaned. "You are suddenly the coolest friend I have, and you have to drag one of my sisters into this?"

"Actually, I invited both of them."

Shaking his head, Jon dragged his suitcase upstairs. He was about to haul his own up the stairs when his phone rang, and he saw William's name on his screen. He had just seen him the week before at graduation in Durham, and it had shocked the hell out of him that he'd shown up. The day had been a blur of goodbyes for all the friends he had made… some of them he might see in the fall if he stayed the course and went to law school. He'd pulled Kate away from her parents in the crowd and kissed her, and when he looked up, his dad had been standing there watching him with a big smile. It had been uncomfortable for a moment until Kate had given William a hug and thanked him for coming.

"Hello?"

"Hey, kid." His dad cursed. He'd been trying to say his name instead of calling him kid, thanks to Kate giving him the third degree over it. "Sorry. Quinn. Listen, I… uh… I need a favor. Are you in town?"

"I'm out on Figure Eight, actually. Is that okay?"

"Of course," William replied. "If you aren't busy, do you think now would be a good time for me to bring Amelia by? She wants to meet you."

Quinn turned to face a mirror on the wall and studied his rumpled clothes and helmet hair. "You want me to meet you somewhere?"

"I'll just bring her out there, if that's all right."

Feeling his nerves begin to spike, Quinn took a deep breath. "Give me an hour or so to get a shower. I rode my bike in and look like shit."

"We'll see you then. Thanks, Quinn."

Once he had showered and shaved, he studied himself in the mirror again. He'd gotten a haircut in the last week, and with the sides trimmed close and the beard gone, he looked more like his father than usual. They had the same rough build—tall and muscular, the same dark hair that would curl slightly if left too long, and their faces so similar that it kind of punched Quinn in the chest sometimes when he would see his father.

"Got a hot date?" Jon asked when he went downstairs.

Bile rose in his throat. "William is on his way here with his wife."

Jon winced. "Meeting the evil stepmother. You want me to go?"

"No." Quinn felt his chest tighten. He was going to have a heart attack, and he'd just turned twenty-four. He started pressing his hands down over his clothes, as if to banish wrinkles that didn't exist. His palms felt cold and clammy. He had thought he had more time than this and cursed William for springing it on him at the last minute. "Hope you didn't unpack yet. If it doesn't go well, I'm going to back out. I can't deal with this kind of shit, man."

"Didn't you tell me her dad's a politician or something?"

Quinn nodded.

"If she doesn't like you, screw her," Jon said loyally. "If you don't want to do this, no one is forcing you. It's not the end of the world if we don't stay in his damned beach house, you know."

"I'm tired of this crap hanging over me," Quinn said quietly. "Either they accept me or they don't. I doubt William and I are ever going to be BFFs, and if he bails on me again, I'm done."

He went to stand at the window, looking out over the street until he saw his dad's sedan pull in. Quinn felt something lurch inside him. It hit him sometimes, that out of the blue, that his father was letting him into his life.

It was terrifying.

"I used to come up here and break in," Quinn heard himself tell Jon. "In high school. I found out he owned this place and that they were never here, and I'd come out and stay the night sometimes. I'd wear my helmet and raise my visor enough so the guard thought he was me and got a key from under one of the flowerpots... had a spare made."

"Jesus," Jon said quietly. "Why didn't you tell me?"

"Because I knew I didn't belong." He felt his face turn red. "Just get me out of here if this goes south."

"Yeah, man. Anything you need, I'm there. You know that."

He thought Jon looked a little pale and knew his own face had to be turning green. Shoving his feelings down into the pit of his stomach, Quinn walked to the door he'd been on the other side of dozens of times, with Jon trailing behind him.

"Hey, Quinn," he said in a low voice. His gaze flicked past him to Jon. "Brought reinforcements?"

"You remember Jon," Quinn said, turning slightly so they could shake hands. "Are you sure this is still okay?"

"Yeah." His father looked at him for a moment, then gave a weary sigh. "Sorry I didn't have more time. This is probably better though before she thought I had some bimbo up here."

"Just a bimbo's kid," Quinn replied without humor. "Is she coming in?"

William's expression didn't change much, but Quinn was sure he winced a little. "Don't take it out on her," his father said quietly. "If you want to hate me, that's fine, but she didn't do anything to deserve this."

By *this*, of course, he meant Quinn.

"We might look alike, but that's about all we have in common," Quinn replied, feeling a burst of anger. "*I'm* not an asshole."

William blinked at him. "I know. You're better than I ever was, son."

"Will?" A woman's voice called out.

His dad turned, and Quinn met the gaze of his stepmother for the second time in his life.

He'd seen pictures of William's wife. They were

scattered all over the beach house, and he'd seen his sister's Facebook page enough to recognize her on sight. A few times he'd seen her in public with his dad. Wilmington was a small town, but they didn't run in the same circles. Not even close. His impression of her had always been of a stuck-up politician's daughter. In the pictures he'd seen, she never wore jeans or T-shirts, and her short, dark brown hair was always perfectly styled. She always wore the same expression, but he had never really considered it friendly or even warm. So when she stepped into the house behind William and Quinn saw the shock on her face... the dismay... he felt like the biggest asshole in the history of assholes. Her wide hazel-gray eyes were blinking back tears, and it seemed to take every ounce of strength to keep her chin from wobbling.

Feeling like a fraud, Quinn led them into the living room, and he noticed a little dog in her arms as she sat down, which immediately squirmed to get free and disappeared. Wearing a cream pantsuit that was immaculately clean, with a navy blouse beneath, she looked like she'd fit right in at the yacht club. She was so far removed from Vickie Haley that it was hard to believe that they were the same species. He couldn't imagine this woman striking him with her fists or any object she could get her hands on. Couldn't imagine her drunk and passed out in her own vomit. Bringing home an endless parade of men, forcing Quinn to listen to the grunts and groans and squeaks associated with rutting. When he had first learned about Amelia, he'd sometimes imagine that she was his mother. His perception of her had changed over time. He'd become less hopeful of having a relationship with any of them. Until he'd seen her in the store with Kate, he hadn't thought about her in a long time.

"Amelia, this is Quinn and his friend Jon," William said gently. His father hovered between them, unsure of himself, while his wife pressed her fingertips to her mouth and stared at him so hard it felt like he was an exhibit in a zoo. "Quinn, this is my wife, Amelia."

"Hi," he finally managed to say, very awkwardly.

Amelia's gaze flicked to her husband, then back to him. "You are such an idiot."

William cleared his throat. "Yes, I know."

Something touched his leg, and he looked down to see the dog, a little white terrier of some kind, propped against shin. It was about the cutest damned dog he'd ever seen. He leaned down, and a little pink tongue licked his hand.

"That's Artemis," William said. "Little bastard bites. Watch him."

Quinn picked the dog up and cradled him on his back. "Vicious. I can tell," he said quietly, scratching the dog on the stomach. "Hey, little guy. You gonna bite me?"

The dog panted happily, his back legs kicking in ecstasy.

"It's like seeing a ghost," she whispered. "How could you… how could you keep this from me?"

"I'm sorry."

"Look at him, Will." Her voice was shaking. "And when were you planning on telling me he was staying here? When one of our neighbors called to tell me?"

Quinn kept his head down but shot a gaze at them both.

"I don't have to stay if it's a problem," Quinn said quietly.

"It's not a problem," his father replied. "Right, Am?"

"No." She cleared her throat. "It's not… this was just a lot to take in… finding out your husband has been living a lie the past twenty years."

"Twenty-four," William corrected her. "I was faithful to you, Am. I swear."

Her hazel eyes swung over to William, giving him a look so full of anger that Quinn felt like a voyeur watching them.

"You lied to me," she stated evenly. "For twenty-*four*

years. For the past nine, you've been living an even bigger lie."

She meant when his father had started giving him money. When Frank had contacted him and brought them together for the first time, when Quinn was fifteen. That meeting had been about as excruciating as this one. He *hated* this. Hated the pressure and the drama. He would almost rather take a beating by Vickie than this. He felt Jon's presence behind him, lingering in the hallway, and turned his head slightly to look at him. His best friend had his arms crossed over his chest, a look of raw anxiety on his face. He lifted his brow slightly and tilted his head to the door. Quinn shook his head.

"I couldn't tell you." His father closed the distance between them and sank to his knees in front of her. "I…" His words were lost as they pressed their foreheads together, clinging to each other. It was obvious to him in that moment that they still loved each other. That they were in love. Amelia's face was ravaged, tears spilling over her eyes as she shook, her hands clasping William's tightly between them. The dog squirmed in his arms, wanting down, and Quinn let him go.

"I'm going to step outside," he said quietly, wanting to give them privacy.

He strode to the door, Jon following behind him. It was all he could do not to puke in the bushes, but he bent over and put his hands on his knees, struggling for air.

"Jeez, that was intense," Jon whispered. "Are you okay, man?"

"Yeah," Quinn said, gasping. "This was a mistake."

"Do you want to leave?"

He closed his eyes, chuffing a little as his mouth started watering, the urge to throw up getting stronger by the minute. He managed to shake his head slightly.

"I'll puke on Stella, then you'll be pissed," he whispered.

"Wouldn't be the first time she's seen a little puke," Jon replied. "Remember that time I…"

And Jon proceeded to tell him about this time, and that time, when Quinn had pulled him out of bars or frat houses or strip clubs, so drunk he couldn't stand. Quinn had never minded. Jon was the happiest drunk he'd ever met, except after a couple of breakups. Twice he'd thrown up in his own car, and twice Quinn had cleaned it for him because once Jon saw puke, all he did was puke more, and that was a never-ending cycle that neither of them wanted to deal with.

He had calmed down significantly by the time the front door opened again, and William came out, looking like he'd been wrung inside out. He put his hands on his hips and stared up at the sky for a few minutes.

"Sorry," he finally mumbled. "I know this was hard for you, Quinn. It was hard on her too."

He didn't say anything about how it affected him, Quinn noticed. "So what now?"

"She wants to talk to you. Ask you some questions. Just be honest. You don't have to hold back anything," William said. "We brought Artemis to meet you. I thought it would be a good idea if we give it a trial run. Do you mind keeping him for a couple of days? I'm going to take Amelia up to see her sister in New York this week."

"That's fine." He took a breath and let it out.

"And before I forget, your new boss, Mr. DeGraw, wants to meet with you this week. He called and spoke to me yesterday."

"About?"

"I told him you were reconsidering going to law school. I thought it might help to get some perspective from someone aside from Frank or me. As always, it's your decision. He's a nice guy and a hell of an attorney." He handed Quinn a business card. "Give him a call. He'll probably take you out to lunch or something."

Quinn stuck the card in his pocket, then glanced at the house. "Is she... is she okay?"

"Amelia is tough." His dad gave him a pain-filled smile. "She's probably wondering where we are. You ready to go in?"

He lied with a slight nod and followed his dad inside. Quinn sat down across from her, and she handed him a handwritten list of instructions for the dog.

"The neighbors will complain if he gets loose, so try to keep him inside. There's a little doggy door at the back; just make sure the gate to the yard is closed." Artemis was in her lap asleep, and she brushed her fingers through his white coat. She was keeping it together, but Quinn could see heartache in her gaze. "No table scraps. He's on a strict diet because he has stomach issues, so unless you want to spend all day cleaning up after him, I wouldn't give him anything off your plate or leave it unattended. He'll eat *anything*."

"Including shoes, mail, phone cords, and furniture," William added wryly. "I told you he gets anxious when he's left alone. He has a crate, but Am doesn't want him left in there all the time."

"No," she agreed. "Crating at night is fine, or he can sleep on the bed. A couple of hours during the day but no more for the crate. William said he asked you to keep him for us when we go on vacation, but I understand you have a job this summer?"

"Part-time." Quinn felt his cheeks heat. What must this woman think of him, following in the footsteps of a father who hadn't wanted him? "He"—Quinn couldn't bring himself to call William anything in front of her, not even his name—"said I could have guests. Someone will be here if I'm not here, most likely. We'll take care of him."

"William?" Amelia looked at him.

"The kids he grew up with... I told you about the

McGuires," William said, looking embarrassed. "Frank agreed to let the girls come too?"

"He said we'd take it a day at a time. They're in Atlanta until tomorrow." He cleared his throat and looked at Amelia. "Kate is my girlfriend. She's Jon's sister. They have another sister… Miranda. She's fourteen. I don't plan on having any crazy parties or anything like that. Frank and Meredith would kill me. They'll be here some too, I'm sure."

Amelia waved her hand dismissively. "This place has been in Will's family for years. I just don't want to hear complaints from the homeowner's association or any of the neighbors. He said you've never been in trouble."

"No." Quinn squirmed uncomfortably. He'd been in a lot of fights, especially when he was younger, but he'd never gotten caught. "I really don't drink or anything else."

"Where is your mother?"

The question was asked so casually that it didn't really hit him at first. Then he glanced at William and found his dad's expression guarded.

"She lives in Wilmington," he said carefully.

"And what does she do?" Amelia's gaze had dropped to the dog in her lap.

"She's a waitress," Quinn replied.

He didn't know how much, if anything, William had told her, but the way she was looking at him—her hazel eyes regarding him with what might have been maternal longing—made him think that he'd told her enough. He felt an odd connection to her, knowing that if things had gone differently, she might have been more to him than just some painful reminder of his father's sins. "I spoke to my daughter last night," she said softly. "How long have you known about her?"

Quinn shrugged. "Since I was twelve?"

Amelia closed her eyes and turned her face away. "She

didn't want me to meet you. Amanda is… She's angry right now. At her father, mostly, but at you as well."

"I'm not trying to…" Quinn broke off, unsure of what he wanted to say, especially in front of his father, who was just listening with his hands gripping the arms of the chair he was sitting in. "If Frank hadn't pushed, I never would have bothered him. You can tell her… if you want… that I'm not trying to take anything from her. I don't want… I don't want this to…" *Hurt anymore.* He couldn't say it. He just closed down, wrapping an arm around his stomach as his guts twisted and writhed.

"I think that's enough, Am," William said, reaching forward and taking her hand. "We can sit down again after our trip."

Great. Something to look forward to… another torture session. This would be so much easier if he could just hate him. If he didn't still feel the need to prove something to him, to want something from him besides just money. He'd thought those feelings were long behind him until the day his father had shown up with a sob story that had punched him right in the solar plexus. Thankfully, his wife nodded at him, then they left together in William's sedan with William promising to come back to go over the rest of everything and to bring the dog back.

Not before William gave him what almost amounted to a hug, if Quinn had raised his arms and hugged him back, that was. It had caught him off guard and been very brief, but it left him feeling like he was choking on snot for a good ten minutes after they had gone.

"Awkward," Jon finally croaked out after his breathing had returned to normal.

"Christ, you have no idea." His body shuddered as he let out his breath. "What the hell was I thinking?"

Jon glanced casually around the living room. "You have a beach house, dude. Pretty sure I saw a pool in the back.

He can be my daddy if he wants."

Quinn threw a pillow across the room and caught Jon square in the face, letting out a rough laugh. "Don't say that again, you asswipe. That sounded pervy."

Jon just grinned at him. "You have a beach house for the summer," he repeated, "and instead of inviting a horny coed or three, you invited me and my two dorky sisters."

Quinn snorted. "Out of all the McGuire dorks, you are the biggest one, man."

Chapter 24

⸻⸱◦◦⸱⸻

THE EXCRUCIATING EXAM COMPLETE BUT thankfully not painful, Kate sat in Dr. Anderson's office and focused on her words. She didn't want to zone out like she had during her other appointments. A determination had filled her, to fix this *one thing* so she could move on with that part of her life. She was in turmoil but did her best to listen and not get wrapped up inside her own head and think about the ways her body had betrayed her.

"So this *is* MRKH," her mom said after the doctor had been speaking for a few minutes.

"Yes." Dr. Anderson looked down at her notes. "This is a pretty typical case, though it is a little unusual for a girl to not find out until she's Kate's age. Most girls find out much earlier. In my opinion, most girls shouldn't necessarily do anything about it until they are the age Kate is now. She's only behind in that she's had to cope with this in a much shorter time frame." Her dark gaze flicked over to Kate. She was an attractive woman, possibly in her early sixties, with short silver hair and refined features. "I know you have struggled with this. Every girl who has sat in that chair has experienced the same things you are experiencing right now. Every one of them. You do know that there are a lot of girls with this condition?"

"Yes," Kate whispered. "So I'm not a boy then?"

"What?" Dr. Anderson looked at her strangely.

"They tested my chromosomes," she explained, embarrassed.

"That was to rule out another condition," Dr. Anderson said gently. "Turner syndrome. Girls with that condition are girls too, but they might have a missing chromosome or part of one missing. They weren't trying to see if you were a boy, Kate. It's very obvious that you are a girl. You're female. One hundred percent."

Her mom reached over and squeezed her hand. "That's what you thought?"

Kate managed to nod her head.

"That other doctor did not explain things well," her mom said, speaking to Dr. Anderson. "I didn't know about any of this until I read stuff online. The doctor actually told us to go online to do research. What kind of doctor tells his patient to go to the *internet* for more information?"

"Most people don't know about MRKH," she replied. "Even doctors. *Especially* doctors. Unfortunately, there is a lot of ignorance in the world and in the medical field, but the good news is that this condition isn't as unknown as it was ten… or even twenty years ago. Still, I get horror stories from my patients all the time about rude manners, questions, and outright idiocy that they get from doctors and nurses alike."

"One of them wanted to bring in all of their interns from the hospital," her mom said, her voice growing hot. "A bunch of students, barely older than she was, to examine her."

Kate flushed. She'd wanted to kick that one in the face.

"I understand," Dr. Anderson said patiently. "I really do,

and I'm not saying you should have thought about it, especially given Kate's obvious struggle with this."

But if she'd done it, a new generation of doctors would have remembered her condition. *Maybe.* Maybe the men just wanted to look between her legs. Kate shrugged a little.

"No."

"That's all right, Kate," her doctor replied. "You don't have to ever do anything you don't want to do. The positive thing about this is you get to make the decision here. About your treatment. About what you share with anyone. I'm not going to sugarcoat and tell you everything is going to be fine from now on. You're still going to struggle with this. I've had women in here the same age as me who still have the same trouble coping. Who never knew what their condition was called or had botched surgeries that may have never been needed in the first place. Your mom said you joined an online support group but that you haven't reached out yet. I do hope you will eventually. Every girl I've spoken with has said it helps to talk to other girls. They have meetups a couple of times a year, and I know that the mothers are welcome to some of them."

"So is she a good candidate for... for dilation?" her mom asked.

"Yes, I think so. The thing about dilation is you have to be consistent about it. That does discourage many girls from finishing, but if you ever played any kind of sport, it helps to think about it like an exercise. Ten to twenty minutes a day, twice a day if it can be done." Dr. Anderson glanced at her mom briefly. "Do you have your own bedroom?"

"Yeah." Kate raised a brow, wondering where this was going.

"Do you have a lock on your door?"

Kate nodded. "But my sister knows how to break in."

Dr. Anderson smiled. "You might want to warn her or

get another lock. This isn't something to be ashamed of, but you're going to want privacy, and it does make it harder if you don't feel comfortable and relaxed."

She gave her more instructions, such as taking a warm bath first and using lube and what angle to do and how much pressure to use. Kate listened, not looking at her mom the entire time. Then she said it.

"Once you start having sex, you won't need to dilate, but you will need to if you aren't having *regular* sex."

Her mouth flapped open, then closed.

"What would be considered regular?" her mom piped up.

"Once a week, or she will need to dilate. Especially at first," Dr. Anderson said gently. "If you stop dilating and you're not having sex, you will have to start all over again."

She wanted to laugh. Her doctor was basically telling her, *right in front of her mom*, that she better have sex or *else*.

"You're kidding," Kate said.

"I'm not kidding." The doctor gazed at her patiently. "Even girls who have surgery need to dilate most of the time."

"So if I… I'm just going to be a born-again virgin for the rest of my life?" Kate gasped, choking back on a laugh. "Unless I… Jesus."

A sound escaped from her mom that sounded a little like a laugh, but when Kate glanced at her, her expression was poised.

"She still has to be careful, *right*?" Her mom said dramatically.

"Yes, she does. You can still catch any number of diseases, just like any other girl. You should also go to regular gynecologist appointments for a checkup." Dr. Anderson gave her a smile when she winced. "We all hate them. Even me. You find someone you're comfortable with, and it isn't so bad. Some of my patients will take a little MRKH brochure in and leave it for the doctors and nurses. One of the most frequent complaints that I hear is that nurses always ask about the menstrual cycle or ask the patient if they might be pregnant. It's a routine question, but it upsets my patients considerably. If you ever feel comfortable with it, you can give them one of these."

She opened her desk and pulled one out, passing it to Kate, who immediately gave it to her mom to put in her purse.

"Kate had a question a while back, but I would like her to hear it from you," her mom said hesitantly. "She... she wanted to know if men can tell a... difference. And I think I'll step outside a moment and let you answer that and any other questions she might have. Is that all right, Kate?"

She managed a nod, and they waited until her mom was gone before looking at each other again.

"Not for someone fully dilated." Dr. Anderson studied her for a moment. "Some girls rush in too soon... which is fine. There's nothing wrong with that... experimenting with your partner. Just don't have these huge expectations and think you're going to have full penetration the first time. Many girls start using the dilators, then dilate naturally with their partners. Some of them have told me they wished they had waited until they were fully dilated before trying to have sex. Either way is fine, as long as your partner is patient and gentle."

She said this all professionally, but Kate squirmed through her speech.

"How will I know?" Kate whispered.

Christian Grey on steroids.

"You'll come back to see me in a few months, and I'll tell you where you're at."

"A few *months*?"

"It really all depends on you, Kate. The more you do it, the quicker it will go. You're going to be sore for a while after you first start, and you're going to get discouraged. After a month, I think you'll be able to tell a difference. Some girls can do it in as little as three, but I would put it closer to six."

"Can I see the… uh… the… dilator things?"

The doctor went into a storage room next to her office, then came out with a plain white box. She lifted the lid, and Kate's brain started doing a whirly thing until she told it to shut up. There were five white hollow tubes that came to a point, and a gray detachable handle nestled in the box. She couldn't imagine herself doing this… putting these things inside her body. Her only comfort, though it was not much, was that she would have her door locked with a chair in front of it and maybe a dresser too.

"You'll start here," Dr. Anderson explained, pointing at one no longer or wider than her finger. "Each one is designed to follow the other. You just start here, and you work your way up… to here."

She didn't even look at the one on the end. Where the hell was she going to keep these things? Under her bed? She was going to *die* if anyone found them. And she had to take them back to Wilmington with her? In the car? With her dad and her supernosy sister?

"Okay," she said and finally managed to breathe. She turned off the noise in her brain again and met Dr. Anderson's gaze. "Can you show me the angle one more time?"

She told Miranda in the hotel room they shared, later that evening, about what the doctor had said about her needing to have sex and that she had better start knocking before coming in to her room or they would both be traumatized. Her sister laughed her ass off, and Kate laughed with her, explaining the look on their mom's face.

"You have a prescription for penis." Miranda snickered into her pillow.

"An Rx for dick," Kate snorted back.

Because if she couldn't laugh about it, what else was she going to do? This was her reality now. For the rest of her life, she needed the *D*. The thought made her laugh even harder even if it was like a knife still twisting inside her heart.

"Well, you won't have any complaints out of Quinn," her sister said after a while. "Or, I mean, any other guys I guess."

"There aren't going to be any other guys." Kate felt her heart swell up a bit. "I love him, Rand. He's it for me... He always has been."

"So how long before...?"

"I don't know. She said months."

Miranda propped her head up on her hand, her eyes sparkling. "Maybe you can ask him to *give it to you* for Christmas."

"Jesus. I shouldn't be joking around with you like this." Kate buried her face in her hands. "You're already bad enough."

"Don't be a wuss. You should hear how my friends talk. Besides, I'm really glad you told me." Her sister started blinking quickly. "I'm really glad that you're my sister. I'm sorry I went through your stuff all the time and stole your makeup and ratted you out that time you knocked dad's phone in the toilet."

"And I'm sorry I was mean to you when my friends came over and broke your dolls and was such a bitch to you that day in the hallway."

Miranda sniffed. "It was pretty bitchy."

"I know. I meant to apologize a long time ago." Kate closed her eyes. "I stopped taking that medicine, and it feels like I can think for myself again."

"You should just smoke pot like Jon."

"Mom and Dad will kill him if they find out."

"I know. It's fun to mess with him though." Miranda looked like she was in her element. "You can basically get him to do anything for you if you know how to play it."

"I'll keep that in mind. You're terrible, you know? I love you *so much*."

"I love you too, sister. So what did you think about the campus today?" Miranda asked. "You're really going to move all the way down here?"

Kate nodded. "If... if I don't go, I'm always going to associate Atlanta with this doctor visit instead of what I wanted to come here for in the first place. Walking around today, I know college is going to give me something to focus on. I'm going to miss Quinn, but I need to be... I need to feel normal."

"Good luck with that." A pillow sailed across the room and smacked Kate in the face. "You are so weird, and there's no help for you."

Kate threw the pillow back, catching Miranda in the stomach. They were both laughing until someone tapped on the wall of the room, then they clapped their hands over their mouths and muffled it. Miranda left her own bed and lay down beside Kate. They stayed up, talking long into the night, something they usually only did on their vacations out west, where cell phones didn't work and there was nothing to do but stare at the inside of a tent. She didn't think she would have any problem with Miranda at the beach house, despite her mother's misgivings. Her relationship with her sister had changed dramatically in the past few months; her sister had changed too. Miranda was like a guard dog with her, and a friend. She was extremely grateful she'd never told any of her friends about what she was going through. One day, maybe she would open up, but she wasn't there yet. She had heard a rumor that Andrew was dating again, and Miranda had their mom pick up some ice cream just in case it made Kate sad. It had, a little, but she was honestly happy for him. After her diagnosis, Lindsay had stuck by her side, but Brittany had finally grown tired of demanding to know what was wrong with her, and Kate had stopped interacting with her altogether. The last she had heard of Brittany was that she had plans to go to Mexico for the summer, get wasted, and sleep with a bunch of hot guys.

Which wasn't dissimilar to her own plans. She planned on sleeping with Quinn, every night.

She just wasn't going to get drunk, go to Mexico, or have sex.

She texted Quinn when they were an hour outside Wilmington to let him know they were close. Her mom was dozing in the front seat as their dad drove, and Miranda was passed out and drooling in the back by the time they pulled into the garage. She thought about the box stuffed down into her duffel bag, hoping that some crazy accident didn't happen where she tripped and her dilators were strung out all over the house and she was standing there looking like some kind of sex maniac in front of her boyfriend. He was in the kitchen when she breezed past with a "gotta pee" over her shoulder, taking her bag straight upstairs and putting it in the back of her closet as if they were going to come alive like Lumière from *Beauty and the Beast* and start line dancing around her room.

Quinn was grinning though, when she came back downstairs and slung her arms around his waist. He squeezed her so tight she felt something in her spine shift, but that only made her squeeze him back harder.

"Puppy!" Miranda said with overexuberance, popping up between them with a little furry white dog. "Look at the puppy!"

"Ohhhh, who's a good boy?" Kate asked, scratching him on the ear. "He's so cute."

"Mom, we need another dog," Miranda pleaded. "Please? You said we could get one after Daisy. It's been three years."

"Hmmm," her mom replied, giving Quinn a look. "I blame you."

"What's his name?" Kate asked, rubbing him on the chin.

"Artemis."

"It's Artie," Miranda said firmly. "Come on, Artie, want to go to my room? *You do?* Well come on, boy!"

Her sister raced up the stairs, and Kate laughed. "Good luck getting that dog back."

"Is that your dad's dog?" her mom asked.

"Yeah. I… I met his wife yesterday. It was rough."

Something shifted in his gaze that made Kate's heart ache for him. She put her arm around his waist and settled against his side.

"That bad?"

He made a face. "Yeah. She wasn't… she wasn't mean or anything. She was just… hurt."

"Oh, Quinn." Her mom reached over and patted him on the shoulder. "It's going to be fine once she gets to know you."

"Thanks. I hope so." He turned his head to look at Kate. "How did it go in Atlanta?"

"Good," she whispered, looking up at him shyly.

"Yeah?"

"Yeah." She swallowed hard. "It's going to be okay, I think."

Her mom left the room, a wobbly smile crossing her face as she passed them. Kate leaned in to Quinn and embraced him tightly, pressing a kiss to his chin. She wanted to lick it but thought he might find her a little weird. She still couldn't get over the fact that she could touch him any time she wanted to. He was… hers. *Hers.*

"That's good." He relaxed beneath her hands a little. "I'm really glad to hear that."

Her gaze met his for a moment, and she blushed. "I still have to… wait. But only a few months, hopefully."

"Kate." He kissed her on the tip of her nose. "Stop worrying."

"I can't help it."

"I'm not going anywhere. I promise." He nuzzled her hair and pulled her head in to his chest. "So are they going to let you come?"

"Yes," she whispered. "I thought… I thought maybe we could invite them for supper? So they could see everything?"

"As long as you're cooking, McGuire," he said, laughing. "I haven't moved beyond grilled cheese and hamburgers yet."

"We'll have to work on your skills, Haley." She smiled against his chest and snuck her hand under his shirt to touch his back. She snickered a little, thinking about her prescription for penis. It was going to be difficult to keep her hands to herself. She was still going to have to come home to do her *exercises* twice a day, because there was no way she was taking those things with her anywhere. "I think it's time you learned how to grill."

"You gonna teach me?"

"Duh." She pinched his side, the warm, bare skin beneath her fingers without any excess fat. She pinched again, higher up under his arm, and he grunted. "You're ticklish?"

"Yeah." Green eyes locked on her blue ones. "Not as ticklish as you though, so watch it, McGuire."

Her dad came in from the garage then, carrying what

seemed like every suitcase ever under his arm or over his shoulder, and Quinn moved forward to help him, taking most of them off his hands and carrying them upstairs with far less effort.

"Hey, Daddy," she said, following him up the stairs. "I was thinking that tomorrow we could all have supper at Quinn's."

"Sure." He smiled over his shoulder. "Sounds good, honey."

"You haven't changed your mind about my staying?"

"Nope."

Her heart tripped in relief. "Okay. Thanks, Daddy."

He turned around suddenly and gave her a hug, dropping his bags at his feet. His eyes were fierce on her for a moment.

"I'm glad you're back," he said quietly. "Don't go away on me again. Promise?"

"I promise." She swallowed hard. "I do. I promise."

"I'm going to hold you to that," he said sternly. "God help that boy if he makes you cry even one time. Now stay in your room for a bit. I'm going to threaten the life out of both of them if I'm going to let you two stay. Remember the rules?"

Yep. She didn't need him to tell her twice. They still had a curfew. No drinking. No parties. No drugs. Nothing they wouldn't want to tell their gran about. Miranda could stay only one night, and Kate could stay longer only if she came home and did her chores. She scampered into her room, not wanting to witness the conversation between her dad and Quinn.

Chapter 25

·····⁕·····

"QUINN, DO YOU HAVE THOSE ready?" Kate asked, glancing over her shoulder at him as she prepared the steaks. Normally she would just cook them on the stove in a cast-iron skillet, but Quinn was obsessed with this manly idea of learning how to use the grill.

"Uh, almost."

She turned around and saw him stabbing the potatoes like he was trying to kill them.

"What are you doing?" she demanded.

He paused, knife midair. "Getting them ready, like you said."

"You don't have to mutilate them."

"You said to poke them with a knife, and they blow up in the microwave if you don't."

"Not like that." She washed her hands quickly and took the knife from him, then pierced them gently with a fork. "We aren't nuking them."

"But it takes ten minutes."

"No." She nudged him out of the way with her hip. "Go chop veggies for the salad."

"I'm not going to learn if you keep doing it," Quinn grumbled.

"Kate, if a man offers to help in the kitchen, let him," her mom said with a laugh. "Teach him, O Wise One. They all need a little training."

Quinn's blush was cuter than cute, but he gave her a little grin.

"I'm already potty trained. Promise."

"Okay. Don't stab them though." She showed him how to season them, and he rolled them in olive oil and salt, wrapped them in foil, then placed them in the oven.

"Can I help with those?" he asked, stepping up behind her as she was boning out the rib eye roast she'd gotten from Cam's. "That's a lot of meat, McGuire."

"We'll put up the extra steaks… let you get a little practice in this summer," she said, grinning up at him, then winked at her mom. "If he don't poison us tonight, that is."

"Quinn, if you don't rein her in, you won't have a dime to your name," her mom warned. "Kate doesn't have any concept of a grocery budget."

"It's going to taste good though," Quinn replied, grinning. "I won't complain too much."

His dad had been nice enough to fully… even overstock… the entire kitchen, but they had both wanted to make the meal special for her parents. Steaks, potatoes, roasted asparagus, salad, and a dessert. Kate had done her best to stay within reason, though Quinn hadn't complained about anything. The most expensive things had been the steaks, and Bertie had given her a good deal on them from his supplier and tried his best to convince her to come back to work with him.

They worked in silence for a while as she showed him how to separate the meat from the bone, then how to slice the steaks up perfectly. Music drifted from the living room through the house. She could hear Jon and Miranda splashing in the pool and her dad laughing at them. Artie, as her sister kept insisting he was called, was barking in ecstasy as someone threw a ball for him. It startled her to realize that she was... happy. Really, bubbling from the inside... happy.

"You're smiling," Quinn murmured as he finished what he was doing and came to stand beside her.

She smiled at him. "Am I?"

He smiled at her. They both glanced at her mom, finding Meredith smiling down at the magazine she was looking at. He brushed his fingertips down her back, and Kate found herself leaning in to him just a little.

"Want me to start the grill?"

"Not just yet. Can't have you singeing off those eyebrows."

"Are you going to let me do anything?" he complained.

"Eat," she told him with a grin. "All right, you can make the dessert. I have a recipe."

"For?"

"Peach cobbler... but, we're cheating a little. Using Gran's canned peaches. So you don't have to do much, except the crust."

He gazed mournfully toward the steaks. "That's not very manly."

"I'll still let you cook the steaks, Haley," Kate said when her mom started snickering.

Kate walked him through the process, enjoying the sight of him getting his hands dirty with flour. He seemed a little more relaxed than he had been the day before. He hadn't said much more about the meeting with his father and stepmother, but Jon had mentioned it had been worse than rough. It had been brutal. She hated the thought of him ever hurting, so she didn't press him about it, just wanting to be there for him.

"When's the food going to be ready?" Jon asked, poking his head in the door. Artie came bounding through the door, prancing around the kitchen, begging for food.

"When it's ready," Quinn said, grinning. "I'm making peach cobbler."

Jon got a glazed look on his face. "Carry on."

They all laughed when he closed the door. Quinn finished making the cobbler as Kate used Mr. Knight's vacuum sealer to preserve the extra steaks and put them in the freezer. She washed her hands and was wiping down the counters just as Quinn was sliding the cobbler into the oven with the potatoes.

"Grill time?" he asked.

"Yep. Come on, Dorkasaurus. Let's get you initiated."

Her mom had taken one look at the ocean and decided she didn't feel comfortable with Miranda staying after all. They compromised by Kate agreeing to pick her up whenever she wanted and bringing her home and at least one day being allowed to have a couple of friends out as long as they agreed to stay in the pool and not go near the ocean. Kate got up extra early and made Quinn his favorite breakfast… cinnamon pecan pancakes. The coffee was just finishing up when she heard him call her name.

"In here," she called back, turning around as he walked in the kitchen. It felt like her stomach leaped into her rib cage. "Oh my God."

"What?"

He was wearing a dark gray suit. She'd seen him in one maybe once or twice, but it had been a long time, and it had never fit him like *that*. She couldn't stop staring at him. His broad shoulders and wide chest, long limbs and narrow waist. The suit wasn't oversized and uncomfortable-looking like the ones her dad and Jon wore. This suit was made for him. It was a suit that made her very aware that he was a man. A very handsome man. She had almost forgotten that he was going in to the law firm he was interning at to meet with one of the partners.

"Uh, Kate?"

"Yeah?" Her gaze finally made it to his face. He was looking a little amused, she assumed at her ogling.

"You're burning the pancakes."

"Crap! Sorry!" She whirled around and flipped it, then sighed. "Guess Artie can have this one."

"Oh, I forgot to tell you. He's on a diet… they said not to give him anything off the table, or he'll puke everywhere."

"Hmm." She didn't say anything since she'd watched Miranda sneak him several treats already. "Guess it's going in the trash then. Good thing it was the last one."

She turned the burner off and moved the skillet out of the way, jumping a little when his arms came around her waist. He pressed a kiss to the back of her neck, then moved his mouth along to just behind her ear.

"Thank you," he murmured, his breath tickling her ear. "You didn't have to do this."

"I wanted to." She gasped as he slipped a hand beneath her shirt, his fingers grazing the contour of her stomach.

"You shouldn't look at me like you were. I might get the wrong idea."

"Trust me, you didn't get the wrong idea," Kate replied, feeling grumbly. "Is the suit really necessary? You're going to get ogled all day, you know."

"You want me to go naked?" he teased.

She turned around and wrapped her arms around his neck as he brought his mouth down on hers. He kissed the hell out of her for what seemed an eternity, and she'd thought before he didn't hold anything back when kissing, but *this* kiss. Sweet mercy, this kiss wasn't like anything she'd ever had before. Both his hands drifted down to cup her rear, his mouth hard on hers, his tongue sliding in her mouth and teasing her. She felt the soft bite of his teeth and the hiss he gave in return when she did it back. The world tilted when she pressed her hips against his, and he groaned as she felt him against her stomach.

One hand slid up into her hair and the other around her waist, lifting her slightly. His green eyes opened, and he gazed at her with desire threaded in his expression.

"Sorry," he rasped. "I've been wanting to kiss you like that for a long time."

"I like kissing you." She let out a shaky breath, a heavy feeling spreading throughout her limbs, down into her stomach. She wanted to do more than kiss him. She wanted to explore him.

"I didn't scare you?"

"No." She blushed. "We probably shouldn't get this worked up though. You might have a hard time walking around with… that."

He laughed, relief replacing worry on his too-handsome face. "I'll try to remember that… just don't look at me like you want to rip my clothes off next time I wear a suit."

Kate reached up and touched his tie. "You should have given me a warning or something. I never thought lawyers were sexy until now."

"I'm not a lawyer, but thanks," he said dryly.

"What was your backup plan?" she asked, turning to fix his plate as he took a seat at the island bar. "You know… before you decided on law school?"

"I was going to join the Marines."

She just looked at him as she slid the pancakes across the counter. "Better stick with the suit, Quinn. I don't think I could handle you in a uniform. Coffee?"

"Is there a thermos or something?" he asked, taking his

phone out of his pocket and glancing at the screen. "I need to get going soon. I'll probably be there most of today. He said I could go to court with him."

She searched the cabinets and found one, making his coffee the way he liked... black with plenty of sugar. He practically inhaled his pancakes, though he was careful not to get anything on the suit, then gave her another melting, maple-flavored kiss before hurrying out the door. Kate sighed, knowing it was pointless to get anxious or start regretting that they couldn't do anything except kiss. She let Artie outside to do his business, then put him in the garage, then headed home to do her "exercises" and chores.

Miranda was asleep, and her parents had already left by the time she got there, but she checked, then double-and triple-checked every lock in the house before going upstairs, then tested the new lock on her bedroom door that her dad had installed. Her stomach was a ball of nerves as she got the box out of her closet and carried it to her bed. She read the typed instructions that Dr. Anderson had given her, and opened the box, feeling like some kind of deviant even though she knew these were medical grade dilators, not giant dildos. She lay back on her bed, wearing only a long T-shirt, and selected the smallest one, applying lubrication like the instructions stated to. The dilator was no longer than her pinky finger, and she put it about where she thought it would go and...

Holy crap, it still didn't fit.

She'd at least expected the *smallest* one to fit. Even just a little.

It didn't.

Grimacing, she pressed it against the dimple where she'd never fully formed and found absolutely no give. None. Kate closed her eyes and remembered Dr. Anderson's words of encouragement. To not give up the first, second, or even twelfth time. To relax and try to think of something other than what she was actually doing. To remember that there was a reason she was doing this. So that one day, hopefully not too far away, Quinn could kiss her good morning then carry her to his bedroom and do all the things she'd been dreaming about.

It was hard not to think of other girls with this condition. She had spent some time before and after her doctor's appointment reading up about dilation. She learned that there were at least five different surgical procedures she could have undergone, but that dilation was now the preferred method among many doctors, if the patient was willing. She thought for a very long time about girls born a century or more before, who never had any options at all. She pictured some poor farm girl being married off to someone at her father's whim or maybe a young lady who was betrothed to some spoiled lordling who was expected to provide an heir. She'd be a virgin, of course, and taken on her wedding night. How disappointed and horrified the groom would be. How humiliated and confused the bride. She cringed, imagining the pain, because she knew firsthand how wide that path could cut into your heart.

Girls born that long ago would have never had a chance since what was between a woman's legs was so often the only value they had to men. Even today, there were cultures where such practices existed, and her heart hurt for those girls. They might not have a crazy redheaded sister who they could laugh about it with or parents who had been as wonderful as hers. They might never laugh about it at all, and she knew that there was little funny about MRKH. Other girls might be truly shamed by their families and considered a burden, but she knew those girls, wherever they were, were strong and beautiful and brave.

It was, or maybe one day could be, a little liberating to be loved for something else. Right now it still felt like she'd been hit in the heart with a shovel, and she knew that one day not being able to have children was going to hurt as much... probably more... than not being able to have sex. At least this part, she *might* be able to fix.

Though she hadn't been able to give her virginity away, it had been *her* choice to do it with Jacob, however much she regretted it now. She wished she had waited for Quinn, and it was probably a good thing it would be several months before she could do anything, otherwise she might have ripped his suit off at breakfast.

Doing her required twenty-five minutes, she tried not to be discouraged at the progress she had made, which was basically zero. She did the dishes for her mom, then a load of laundry, then headed for her mom's shop around lunch. Her mom had opened the furniture store roughly ten years ago, and all of them had grown up in the shop during the summer except for when Jon had been old enough to stay at home to babysit. In the middle of downtown, touristy Wilmington, it was in one of the old brick buildings close to but not on the water. She greeted her mom's store clerk and went into the office where her mom was staring at a computer screen with a frown.

"Hey," Kate murmured. "You busy?"

Her mom turned, then blinked at her. "Hey, honey. I didn't think I'd see you so soon. You okay?"

"Yeah." Her face burned a little. "I was... uh... I was just at home. I did some dishes and some clothes."

"Oh." Her mom's face was a little too straight. "Where's Miranda?"

"She was still asleep. I'll go back and pick her up later."

"Just make sure that someone is with her at all times," her mom said with a frown. "Everything... go all right?"

She shook her head a little, trying to hold back tears, knowing she was about to whine but unable to help it. "I don't know if I can do this."

"Of course you can, Kate." Her mom stood up and

wrapped her arms around her. "Dr. Anderson said it would be difficult at first. You have to give it a chance."

"But three months?" Kate groaned. "Twice a day, three months minimum? And I have to drive back and forth to the house twice a day to do it."

"There's no reason why you can't take it with you, Kate."

"Every time I think about it, I picture that little dog running around the house with it in his mouth like it's a prize."

A laugh bubbled out of her mom, and she slapped a hand over her mouth. "I'm sorry. I didn't mean to laugh."

"It's okay." Kate cracked a smile. "Miranda's been making fun of me since we got back from Atlanta. Not in a bad way. But it helps to laugh about it sometimes."

"Your dad and I heard you girls laughing through the wall at the hotel." Her mom blinked quickly, her eyes beginning to water. "It was the prettiest sound I've ever heard, my daughters laughing like that. I love you so much, honey. You felt so good after your appointment the other day. Don't give up just yet. Is there anything I can do to make it easier?"

Kate shook her head. "No. I just need to stop freaking out about it so much."

"Why haven't you told Quinn yet? Do you think he won't accept you?"

"He had a girlfriend for three years." Kate felt her cheeks heat. "Roxie told me some… personal stuff about him at Christmas, and I don't know if I'll ever be… anyway. I know he cares about me, but he's a guy. They all want one thing eventually, right?"

"Love is different than what you're talking about, Kate. I think Quinn is more mature than anyone you've ever dated. And yes, he might be experienced, but I know he's been through a lot in his life and I don't think he would deliberately hurt you. You just have to remember to take it a day at a time, and remember there's a... a reward at the end."

"If I do everything right, I might not have to tell him everything," Kate mumbled. "He just knows we have to wait."

"Honey, you have nothing to be ashamed of." Her mom squeezed her tightly. "You were perfect on the day you were born, and you are now. There's nothing wrong with you."

"Except I can't have kids. Or have sex. Or donate a kidney or make you a grandmother. I'll never pass down recipes to my daughter, never do all the things you did with me. If Quinn marries me, he'll lose all those things too." Her voice began to break, but she kept going. All the things she would miss out on that other women took for granted pelted her day after day, and she was tired of living in this new reality. She just wanted to be normal, but the uncertainty never seemed to stop. "Who will take care of me when I'm old? When I'm in a nursing home and everyone else is gone? What if I become so bitter I drive everyone away? I am so angry, Mom. I'm so, so angry, and I don't want to be. I just can't help it sometimes."

"Ah, baby." Her mom kissed her forehead and pulled away to look at her, settling back against the edge of her desk. "I'm so sorry. I know you are, but you don't know what life will bring you. There are so many ways to be a mother or live a fulfilling life without children. You don't know that you won't have kids yet. You're going to have a wonderful, beautiful life, Kate, and whoever is lucky enough to have you... you're going to love each other so much that nothing else will ever matter. You're going to have nieces and nephews even if you decide not to adopt or go through a surrogate. I wish you would talk to some of the girls who are like you."

"I've been thinking about it a little," she confessed.

She didn't know why it was so hard to open up about it,

but maybe she was ready to reach out… almost… maybe. She had just been lurking in the support group, reading everyone else's stories, and many of them sounded similar to her own.

"You know, if you wanted to go to one of those MRKH conferences, I'd take you," her mom said gently. "I know you're still trying to get your legs under you again. It's just something to think about."

"I might… I might just introduce myself for now. On the Facebook group, I mean. I joined. I just… I still don't want to deal with it."

"I'm so proud of you, Kate. Your dad and I have been so worried." Her mom let out a shaky breath. "You're done with your last prescription now?"

"Yeah."

"I should have never let them talk me into putting you on that stuff. Are you… are you really doing better? You're not still thinking that way?"

"No." Kate swallowed hard. "I'm really sorry."

"I want you to keep going to therapy. And I don't want you to take this the wrong way… I love Quinn like he's one of my own children, but *you're* my daughter. I don't think he would ever hurt you. I just need you to be okay on your own. You know I've always told you girls not to depend on a boy to make you happy. I don't want you to lean on him so much that if something happens, you lose yourself like that again."

"I know." Kate's face burned. "I tried to tell him I was a hot mess right now. He wouldn't listen."

"They never do," her mom said, her eyes flashing with mischief. "So tell me, is he a better kisser than Andrew?"

"Mom," Kate groaned, burying her face in her hands. "Oh my God."

Her mom laughed. "I'll take that as a yes then. Come on, I'll take you to lunch."

Chapter 26

"DO YOU KNOW WHO ANY of these people are?" Kate asked, looking over the framed pictures on the shelves surrounding the television. "This guy looks a lot like you and your dad."

"I think that's his brother, Jackson," Quinn said, watching her from the couch. "There's an album around here somewhere with a ton of pictures, and they're all labeled."

Kate trailed her fingers over a few DVDs, then moved over to the music section. It was a mix of eighties and nineties rock, some country, and a few bands she had never heard of before. A few of them didn't have a cover, they were just labeled Will's band. She snagged one off the shelf, then held it up.

"Have you seen this?"

"No. What is it?"

"I think it might be a video of your dad playing in his band," Kate said, eyeing him carefully. "Do you want to watch it?"

Quinn stood and walked over to the shelf, looked at the

other titles, then he took the one from her hand and slid it into the DVD player. He grabbed her hand and led her back to the couch. She had expected it to be bad cell phone footage, but instead it was a live concert in a bar, and the video quality was pretty good. The music started, and she felt Quinn tense beside her.

"I've heard this song before," he said quietly. "Vickie used to listen to this when I was a kid."

"This must be from when he played in Wilmington then," Kate said. She studied the lead singer, a guy in his twenties with long, frizzy blond hair. A few brief glimpses of his face were all that she caught, but he was good-looking. Then the camera moved to the lead guitarist, and she gasped. She grabbed the remote from him and paused it, the frame capturing a young William Knight who looked almost identical to Quinn. "Oh my God."

She turned her head, looking at Quinn, then back at the television.

"Kind of weird, isn't it?" he asked, looking uncomfortable. "Your dad and Jon don't really look alike. I've seen pictures of your gran when she was young, and you look more like her than your mom. Miranda doesn't look like any of you except she has your dad's red hair."

"Dad jokes that she's the milkman's baby, but his side of the family all have red hair and freckles." She reached over and grabbed a family photo off the coffee table showing William, his wife, and his daughter. It hurt her heart, seeing all these pictures and none of them with Quinn. She didn't understand how a father could let his child be raised by a monster. "Does it bother you?"

He shrugged. "It used to."

"Why aren't you angry with him? Quinn, I'm angry for you." She studied the video still of William. He'd been a little heavier than Quinn in the face, probably bloated from alcohol and drugs. The photo in her hands, he was clear-eyed and smiling with his perfect family. His hair was gray at the temples, green eyes maybe just a shade lighter than Quinn's. The same face… same smile. The differences were subtle, but they were there. They were both so very handsome, though she was partial to the younger version. "What he did to you was wrong. What he let her do to you, by doing nothing. I'm glad he's trying to make things right, but still… you act like it doesn't bother you."

"I know." He took the picture from her, then set it back on the coffee table. "Believe me, I used to be angry. I hated his guts. I hated her guts. I got in fights because I was so pissed at the world. I did a lot of stupid things… and eventually I realized I was going to end up just like her if I didn't stop. Luther was a good influence on me there. Nothing ever gets to him. I guess I want to forgive him more than I want to hate him." He glanced at her, his lips moving to a smile but his eyes sad. "Or maybe I'm just afraid that if I let myself get angry, he'll decide I'm not worth the effort."

"Oh," she breathed, a shard of pain nailing her right in the gut. She took his hand and pressed a kiss to his knuckles. "Quinn, of course you're worth it. He doesn't deserve you. Neither one of them do. You're amazing and sweet. Funny and smart. You're always trying to help everyone else, and you don't take care of yourself enough. If you're angry with him, it's okay to let him know. I hope that he's really changing and wants you in his life, not because it's been a burden on him to keep you a secret. I know it's what you want too. I hope that they see how wonderful you are. I can't stand the thought of them hurting you."

Kate wrapped her arms around his neck and kissed him gently, gazing into his eyes. She had loved him for a very long time, but she hadn't had the courage to say it. The words were lodged in her throat, unable to emerge.

"I wasn't ready to meet his wife," he said softly, his fingers tangling in her hair as he brought her face closer to his. "I thought I had a little while to prepare myself, and he just caught me off guard. It feels strange, knowing that they all know, and I'm here in this house, surrounded by all their things, but I don't have any of their memories. I don't know anything about them. Not really. I don't know what to do."

"About what?"

He shook his head slightly. "I feel like his wife is going to think that I'm just sticking around for more money or that I'm trying to be like him because I decided to go to law school. That his daughter will think that. Or that I'm trying to make him choose or take her daddy away from her. His wife said she's angry with me. Amanda, my... sister... is angry with me, and I've never even met her. She probably hates me."

"How old is she?"

"Fifteen."

"She's a fifteen-year-old girl, Quinn," Kate said gently. "She's going to have all sorts of irrational fears and anger issues. Don't let the attitude of a teenage girl determine the rest of your relationship with her."

"You're a teenage girl, McGuire. You never went through all that drama bullshit."

"Are you kidding?" Kate laughed. "You were in college when I was that age. You didn't hear the fights that Miranda and I got in every single day. Mom wanted to strangle us half the time. I tried to be all mature and cool when you were around, you know. I didn't want you thinking I was a spoiled brat."

"You *are* a spoiled brat," Jon said, coming into the room. He froze when he saw the screen. "Whoa. Is that your dad? Or you?"

"It's William," Quinn replied. "Kate found some DVDs of him playing concerts."

"He looks drunk."

"According to him, he probably was."

Quinn found the remote and pressed play, and Jon took a seat across from them. For a while they just sat and listened, watching as the band played. The music wasn't too bad… it was alt rock, just shy of blues, and the lead singer had a pretty good voice. William did backup vocals and sang in a rough baritone. She watched Quinn's face as he watched his father sing, and the longing in his gaze tugged at her heart.

"Thank you, thank you," the lead vocalist said as they ended the song. He did a shout-out to Wilmington, encouraged them all to drink a lot of beer, then announced that Victoria Haley was going to join him on stage. "My future wife, everyone."

Quinn sat forward, his gaze locked onto the screen as his mother joined the band. She was young and really, really pretty. Her blond hair came down to her waist, she wore skintight jeans and a leather jacket over a white shirt. She kissed the vocalist and looked sober and happy, and when she started singing, Kate felt gooseflesh rise along her arms.

"She's really good," Jon said in surprise.

"Yeah." Quinn was frowning. "I remember she used to sing."

His mom had a smoky, sexy voice with a strong southern twang. One of those voices that men noticed and women wished they could emulate. Was it really that simple that she'd been ruined by drugs? Had Quinn's father been the one to get her addicted? Or had she been heartbroken at losing the guy who wanted to marry her, because she'd made a mistake with a handsome guitarist? Quinn had told her a little more about his childhood. What had started as neglect had turned to abuse, and she knew that those scars made up a huge part of who he was. It made sense that he wanted a relationship with his father, but she couldn't help but detest William Knight for abandoning Quinn to his mother like that. It hurt all the more, because she knew that what happened to Quinn happened to hundreds... thousands of children on a daily basis. Women who had no business being mothers and women like her who wanted a baby so badly and couldn't conceive.

"I can't watch any more of this." He stopped the video, his expression tense as he got to his feet, heading toward the kitchen. "Sorry. I just need a minute."

Kate let him go, looking at her brother helplessly. "What should I do?"

"Leave him alone for a little while. He'll be fine." Jon shrugged. "Anything Vickie related gets him worked up."

She put the disc away and ignored Jon's advice, going to check on him, only to find the kitchen empty.

He was gone.

⸻⸻

It felt like a nest of wasps had taken residence in his brain after he watched the video, but by the time he rolled his bike to a stop in front of his mom's house, he'd calmed down enough to wonder if he was making a mistake. There was something wrong with a woman who treated her child the way that she had treated him... and yet, he could remember a few... very few... sober moments with her. She had never been motherly or loving, but before they had lost the house in the fire, he could remember her giving an effort sometimes. Could remember her singing. Signing his homework. One parent-teacher conference that had been a disaster, but she had gone, and that had meant something to him at the time. More than anything, he could remember his mom crying at night when she was alone. He remembered comforting her, but she'd never returned the gesture.

Her same nicotine-roughened voice called out when he

knocked on the side door, and he pushed it open a little, finding her sitting at the kitchen counter writing something. She never called him—she didn't own a cell phone to text and had no idea what social media was—but she was always on his mind, as much as he didn't want her to be.

"Hey," he said, stepping up into the house and pulling the door closed behind him. She was wearing her work uniform. She looked tired but again was surprisingly sober, though he could see beer bottles had accumulated on the counters and the trash was full. "Did you just get off work?"

"Yeah." She peered at him for a moment. "You need something?"

"No." He crossed his arms over his chest and leaned against the wall. "Just thought I would come by and see how you were doing."

"I'm fine," she said, dismissing him as she returned to her writing.

"I saw a video of you."

That got her attention. She looked up at him, frowning. Her hazel eyes studied him for so long it nearly made him uncomfortable.

"Where?" Vickie finally asked, her tone wary. "Doing what?"

"Singing." Quinn moved farther into the room, pressure inside his chest intensifying. "I forgot how pretty your voice was."

Her mouth fell open for a moment. He didn't think he had ever seen her flustered. She almost looked embarrassed. "I... uh... who showed it to you?"

"I found some old DVDs," he said carefully. "William has videos from when he was in a band."

The familiar scowl returned to her expression whenever he mentioned his father.

"I figured you'd suck up to him one day," she sneered. "Going off to be a lawyer, just like your daddy. I suppose it was his money that paid for this house."

"How much money do you think you blew, over the years?" Quinn asked, careful to keep his voice even. "Drugs. Booze. Gambling. He paid for your habits pretty well, don't you think?"

"You don't know anything." She was fuming now. "Get the hell out of here. Don't come back this time."

"I don't know anything because you wouldn't tell me," he replied sharply. "I thought the only reason all this time that you could hate me the way you did was because he did something horrible to you. But he didn't, did he? *Did he?*"

"Yes," she snapped. "He stuck me with you."

Quinn snorted. "You could have gotten rid of me any time you wanted. Left me at a hospital. A fire station. How about a Dumpster? Some homeless person could have probably taken care of me better than you."

She finally flinched at that, and he wondered if the thought hadn't crossed her mind.

"If you came here to start a fight, you got one. Now get out."

"I never wanted to fight with you. I wanted to grow up and take care of you. I wanted to choose you instead of him, but you never gave me a choice. I wanted to buy you a house, not leave you in a shitty trailer the rest of your life." He tried to turn his voice into ice, cold and remote, but knew he was about to desperately fail. "You are my mother. You will *always* be my mother. If you don't want me to come back, I won't. I'm sorry I ruined your life. Sorry you got mixed up in drugs and anything else that anyone did to make you this way. I don't know anything about you. Nothing about your family. I don't even know if you've ever been married or not. Who I was named after. Nothing. I know you're not the person I saw on the video singing today. The only thing I know about you is what you've shown me over the years, and there was never anything kind or gentle about that."

She stared at him for a moment, her features set in an expressionless arrangement though her eyes flung statements of resentment toward him still.

"Well you shouldn't have to worry about me much longer," she said finally.

"What does that mean?"

"What do you think it means? You aren't blind, and last I remember you can read. I'm sure you noticed all the bills from the hospital." She reached for her pack of cigarettes, took one out, and then set it down. "Karma's a bitch. That's what it means."

She didn't look sick, but she didn't look like herself either. Her eyes were clear. Her skin was clear. Yet he caught a dragging tone with her voice at times, as if certain words were hard to pronounce. When he saw her before, he thought it was a slur, but now he wasn't sure. He remembered the names of the tests on the doctor bills. They had all seemed to center around one thing, and she'd done enough drugs to make Mick Jagger proud.

"Your heart?" he guessed.

"Ticking away like a broken clock." She got up from her barstool and went to the fridge, getting out a beer. "I gave up the hard stuff over a year ago. It doesn't matter. It's irreversible."

Quinn processed what she was telling him for a moment, then shoved his feelings away to deal with later. His interactions with his mother had gone from frightened child to belligerent teenager almost overnight. He couldn't remember ever reaching out to her before. There had never been an in-between with them. He knew he didn't want her to die unhappy and alone. That had always been his fear, especially since he had turned his back on her at eighteen.

He approached her carefully, setting his hand on her shoulder, then pulled her into a hug. His entire life, she had never hugged him or kissed away his tears as he had seen Meredith do with her kids. He had observed their family for years. They were always touching and hugging and telling each other how they felt. Kate had always been especially gifted at diffusing situations between Miranda and their mom. He knew, or at least strongly suspected, that Vickie had raised him the only way she knew how. Without love or affection. He had sometimes thought her inherently evil and cruel, but the way she had been on that video had been like a grenade going off in his vision. Yet it was only a moment in time, a split second of her life from before, and she was performing in front of a crowd at that. He still didn't know what to make of her, but he knew that beneath her anger and addiction, she was still human. She was still, despite everything, his mother, and as far as he knew, she didn't have anyone else.

"You don't have to be alone unless you want to be," he said quietly, pleading silently for her to respond in some way. To hug him back. To tell him how she felt… to know if she was scared. He knew from seeing her driver's license how old she was. Only forty-two. He didn't even know for certain if she was lying. It wouldn't be the first time she'd lied to get money out of him. "The money came from his brother. The only reason I agreed to it was so I could get you this house."

Sensing he wasn't going to get a response from her, Quinn dropped his hands and stepped back, feeling the sting of rejection that he should have expected but hadn't allowed himself to consider. Maybe it was enough that he'd made the offer. He couldn't force her to be in his life, any more than he could force William or anyone else.

"I'll, uh… I'll check on you next week," he said gruffly. "Sorry to come by and start a fight. That wasn't what I wanted."

He started to turn, but Vickie caught his arm. Quinn

froze, his gaze jerking down to hers.

"After you left… I was going to meetings," she offered, her voice tentative. "Narcotics Anonymous. I was doing pretty well, then this hit me. I don't see the point in being sober, but the doctor says I might have a year. I might have longer, but only if I stay clean." She shrugged, her hazel eyes growing bright. "I wasn't cut out for this shit. That's not going to change."

No, she wasn't cut out for it, but yet here he stood. A son looking at his mother. She was probably going to let him down at some point. When she died, it was going to break his heart, but he wasn't a scared little boy anymore. He didn't need anything from her, but he needed to give something of himself to her. His strength, which he never would have found without Jon and his family. He knew that miracles would not happen overnight and not to get his hopes up. Vickie didn't like to do anything the easy way… but his relationship with his parents had always left a hole inside him, and the only way he knew how to fix it was to open himself back up and fill it with whatever he could.

"I know. Do you want me to come back?"

"Yeah," she replied, her voice gravelly.

"Then I will."

Chapter 27

K ATE WAS SITTING IN ON one of the beach loungers in the backyard when he returned, lazily throwing the ball for Artie, when he returned. Her movements stilled when he came out the back door, and he crossed over the patio to sit beside her, taking the ball from Artie and tossing it.

"I shouldn't have left like that. I'm sorry."

She laced her fingers with his, squeezing his hand. "I was worried about you. Where did you go? To see her?"

"Yeah." Quinn pinched the bridge of his nose with his thumb and forefinger, trying to stop pressure from building there. He wasn't ready to feel anything for Vickie. Not yet. "She has a bad heart, after taking all those drugs. She said she's dying."

"I'm sorry, Quinn. Do you believe her?" Kate asked, her voice tentative.

"I think she's telling the truth. It's hard to tell with her sometimes." Quinn slipped his arm around her waist and laid his head on her shoulder. "Did you go anywhere today?"

"I went out for a bit. Artie kept me company in the kitchen. I made you a pie and tacos."

"You made me a pie? *And* tacos?" He smiled. Those were two of his favorite food groups. "What kind of pie?"

"Caramel pecan. It's a new recipe," she replied, studying him for a moment. "Are you okay, Quinn?"

"She's only forty-two." He gathered Artie onto his lap when the dog came up to him and for a moment just scratched him under the chin. "It was always hard to watch her when she was high. I left her. I gave up on her. I always thought I'd be able to fix things later, at the same time wondering why I would bother. *If* I should bother. I know you probably think I'm crazy. Jon does. Your dad has been warning me away from her for as long as I can remember… but this might be the only chance I have now."

"You don't have to explain yourself to me. I get it. She's family. I just don't want to see you get hurt."

Too late. He wanted to get on his motorcycle and ride until his head was clear, but he didn't want to leave Kate alone again. He wanted the mind-numbing oblivion that drugs or alcohol or sex could offer, but he'd never given in to those desires before and he wasn't about to start now.

"Want to go see a movie or something? I need a distraction."

"I think there's a concert at Greenfield Lake later," she offered, then winced. "Sorry. You probably aren't in the mood for music right now."

"Actually that sounds good. I doubt I could pay attention to a movie right now anyway."

"Well come on then. I need to get ready."

Kate stood and held her hand out to him, then led him into the house. He hesitated only a moment when she pulled him into her bedroom and closed the door. Artie whined from the other side, then they heard him give a disgruntled sigh and plop down in the hallway. Quinn leaned back against the door, pressing his hands behind the small of his back. His heart kicked up as she slipped her arms around his neck and rose on her toes to kiss him, and she was such a sweet temptress, her mouth slanting across his in hot, openmouthed kisses. He went from unsuspecting to unbearably hard in a flash, his emotions already raw and all over the place. Quinn's hands whipped around from behind his back and lifted her, turned her so her back was against the door and he was the one kissing instead of being kissed, and for a few blessed moments he forgot about everything but her.

Kate arched against him, her legs wrapping around his waist. Her head fell back against the door, and he moved his mouth to her neck, then all rational thought ceased when she grabbed one of his hands and placed it over her breast. He stilled completely, his breathing rough and heart pounding. Her eyes half opened, and she stared at him, her blue eyes hazy with desire.

"You are so beautiful," he whispered. Her body slipped down slightly, giving him more of her weight, and he groaned as she nestled against him. "I could kiss you forever."

"You're pretty hot yourself," Kate whispered back. "You don't have to stop yet."

Yes. He had to stop. Their make-out sessions were unbelievably hot, but he'd taken enough dips in the ocean, pool, and cold showers the past week to know that he should limit these types of encounters. It wasn't that he didn't want her. He did. He wanted every part of her… but he knew that they couldn't have sex even if he didn't know why, and he didn't know how to approach the subject without hurting her.

"I have to stop," he confirmed, trying for a rueful tone. "I'll embarrass myself if I don't."

"Oh." Her face turned red, and she released the tight leg

grip she had on his waist, pushing away from him awkwardly. "I'm sorry. I'm not... I'm not trying to be a tease."

"Hey." He gathered her face in his hands, hating the way shame filled her gaze. "I don't think that."

"Maybe not, but that's all I can do for you," she replied, her tone bitter. "I'm sorry."

"Stop apologizing. I shouldn't have taken it so far." He smoothed her hair back from her face, his blood finally beginning to cool. She was withdrawing from him, receding into her insecurity, though he knew that she'd put on a brave smile and pretend that she was okay. Sometimes she would start crying for no apparent reason, and as far as he could remember, she had never done that before. "I still want to take things slow, Kate. I don't want to screw this up."

"Me either." She let out a shaky breath. "It's just really hard."

He cracked a smile, unable to resist. "It is, but not as hard as it was a minute ago."

"You did not just make a penis joke right now," she said, her cheeks turning pink.

"Is it a joke if it's the truth?" he teased. "You'd better get dressed, or we'll be stuck in line all night."

Quinn leaned down and kissed her again, keeping it gentle this time, but the chemistry between them was instantaneous. Every time he kissed her, it was the same. His mind leaped from kissing to other things, as if he'd spent so much time suppressing thoughts of her being desirable that it was all he could think about now. She was addictively sweet and responded enthusiastically, which in turn made him lose his freaking mind.

Reluctantly he ended the kiss, searching within himself for a smile but failing. Especially when he saw the expression on her face, like she was struggling for courage to say something.

"Do you want to, um…?" Her face turned red, and she reached for his waistband with visibly shaking hands. "I can—"

"No," he said, his voice rough, his pulse hammering, because he knew what she was about to say and he wanted it. Wanted her mouth all over that part of him and wanted to do the same to her, and right now he was barely strong enough to say no. He cursed as she touched him, his head falling back. He let her explore even though he knew he had to stop her. He moved his hands on either side of her and met her intense gaze. She was biting her lip, and it made him want to bite it too. He grabbed her hands and linked their fingers, then kissed her again. He was going to have to take another cold shower, but he'd take a thousand of them if it meant he got more of her. He didn't miss the uncertainty in her gaze or the anguish that flashed in her eyes when he stepped away and let her go.

"Quinn—"

She started to reach for him again, but if she touched him again he wouldn't be able to stop her. He traced the shape of her face and tried to think of whatever he could to sober his thoughts, but all he could think about was what she felt like under his hands and how much he wanted her. If he said that he wanted her, he worried that it might hurt her somehow, but if he didn't say it then she would continue having the doubt that even now he could see swirling in her eyes.

"I promised I'd wait for you, and I meant it. I don't want you to do something you aren't ready for, Kate."

"I never said I wasn't ready. I just…" She squeezed her eyes shut, frustration limning her face. "God, this is so *annoying*."

He couldn't help but laugh, because she looked so cute when she was angry. "Okay, I have an actual penis joke for you. Are you ready?"

"What?" Her face did this thing where it looked mortified and curious at the same time. She gave a squeaky laugh and scrunched her nose at him. "Really?"

"Really. You ready?"

"Yep. Yes. Proceed with your penis joke."

"Okay. What do you call a ghost's erection?"

A thoughtful expression crossed her face, then she shrugged. "I don't know. What do you call a ghost's erection?"

He tried to keep a straight face and ultimately failed. "A boooooner."

She started laughing so hard she snorted, and he knew that as long as he could make her smile and laugh, then whatever secrets she kept wouldn't matter.

Airlie Gardens was a Wilmington landmark… a place that Kate loved more than pretty much any other in the world. It was where their family had taken all of their portraits and where she had always secretly hoped to get married. The gardens were one hundred years old and, like most of Wilmington, had completely embraced the azalea madness. If you set foot in Airlie during the azalea-blooming season, it was like walking into a beautiful dream. Occasionally one of her mother's friends hosted a painting workshop in the gardens, and Kate had pleaded with Lindsay to join her for this one. Not having a job during the summer had been fun for all of two weeks, then it was just her stuck in that house by herself while Quinn was at work during the day.

Ah, but the nights he was home were worth it.

So worth everything.

She sighed, trying to focus on her painting instead of thinking about Quinn.

"How can you decorate a wedding cake and paint a landscape, but decorating your face is anathema?" Lindsay asked.

"Decorating my face?" Kate glanced over at Lindsay's painting and laughed. The tree her friend was supposed to be recreating looked more like a giant phallus, which was probably intentional. "Maybe I like my face. You're going to get us kicked out of here. Put some leaves on that thing."

"You mean like this?" Lindsay's brush swooped down to the base of the tree and she began painting what was, presumably, two azalea bushes near the bottom. "Now it has testicles."

"I can't take you anywhere," Kate replied, rolling her eyes. "Thank you for coming, even if you had to give up face-sucking time with Mitch."

Lindsay waggled her brows. "It's a nice face to suck. Speaking of…" Lindsay glanced around the garden at the other painters. "I noticed you're actually wearing makeup today. Do you know why I noticed? Because you have a hickey on your neck, and you did a horrible job of covering it up."

"I do not!" Kate pulled her hair around her neck self-consciously.

"Girl, if that ain't a hickey, this penis isn't a tree."

Kate tried glaring Lindsay into silence but knew it was pointless. Her friend was incorrigible. The memory of Quinn backing her up against her bedroom door, kissing her like he was burning for her, and the way she had burned in return… She had wanted to do more. It had been agony to back away from the ledge. To not split her chest open and lay her heart at his feet, hoping he would pick it up. She trusted Quinn… she did… but there were so many doubts and feelings that she couldn't move past, and that alone was more frustrating than anything.

What if she never moved past it?

What if she stayed like this the rest of her life?

It physically hurt not to be able to be normal with him, but he didn't ask her any questions, and she tried to put the rest of it from her mind until those moments when she was alone and was able to make progress, a little every day. That progress wasn't much. She'd only moved on to the second dilator. It was hard, frustrating, and uncomfortable. After the first two weeks, at least she had stopped crying every time she did it, but it was more of a push-it-down-in-your-gut-and-stop-being-a-baby kind of thing. Not an it-doesn't-hurt-anymore kind of thing.

"So are you going to tell me or not?" Lindsay asked, setting her brush down and turning to face her. "Are you, or are you not having coitus with him?"

Kate closed her eyes for a minute, trying not to snap at her, because she knew that Lindsay was just being herself. Once upon a time, before Jacob, she had given as good as she got in the teasing-about-sex category. Back when she was living a lie because she wanted to fit in with her friends, but the lie had been safe. The lie had hurt far less than the truth.

"We are not having coitus," Kate replied, deliberately keeping her voice even. "We're going to wait."

She could see Lindsay looking at her curiously from the corner of her eye, but Kate focused on her painting. Her rendition of the five-hundred-year-old Airlie Oak didn't look much like a tree either. At least not traditionally.

It had a trunk. There were branches. But beneath the ground, she'd painted dying roots, and the center of the trunk was hollow and decayed. It might have been the best thing she'd ever painted, though art wasn't really her passion. After cooking, it might have come a close second though.

She felt her phone vibrate and pulled it out of her pocket, trying not to get paint all over her jeans and failing.

changed

Quinn: Where are you? I got off work early.

Kate: I'm still at Airlie.

Quinn: I know. I'm here... Where are you?

Kate: By the Oak.

A few minutes later he was brushing her hair away from her neck and kissing very near the spot that she'd tried to cover with makeup. The spot that she hadn't been able to stop staring at when she saw it for the first time. Quinn had marked her with a love bite, and while it wasn't really in her to like that sort of thing, the fact that Quinn had done it... and the way he had done it... made her ponder the entire love-mark dissension.

On one hand, it was tacky. On the other hand, if Quinn Haley wanted to bite her in less obvious places, she was pretty sure she would have no objections.

"That's... uh... really good."

"That sounded like a question." Kate tilted her head back to look up at him. He had removed his suit jacket and dress shirt and was down to a plain white T-shirt. The summer sun had darkened his skin beautifully while her own overly sunscreened complexion remained as pale as ever. "You don't like it?"

His gaze flicked back to the painting, and he studied it for a long moment. His gaze flicked to Lindsay's, and he glanced away, a hint of a smile at his lips. "Well, it's no giant tree-penis, but it's a tad morbid."

"Morbidity is growing on me," Kate replied.

His expression tightened slightly. "But it doesn't suit you, Kate," he replied softly.

They stared at each other, and a heavy ache settled in her stomach. She knew what he meant. Perpetual sadness had never suited her. It was completely foreign to her, in fact. Still, how could you escape an inherent deformation of your spirit when it was now a permanent part of you? How could she discard this unhappiness even now that she had what she'd always longed for?

"Since you have a ride now, I'm headed out," Lindsay announced, getting to her feet, then handing her brush to Quinn. She kissed Kate on the cheek and pulled her purse over her shoulder. "Quinn can finish my painting."

"Uh… okay." His gaze flicked between the brush and the painting. He glanced back at Lindsay, who gave him a cheeky grin before turning around and leaving. "I don't… I don't want that thing. What am I supposed to do with it?"

"Make it not so phallic?" Kate suggested. She cleaned her brushes off and set them aside so she could watch him work.

"I suck at art," Quinn replied, taking Lindsay's seat. He dipped the brush into green paint and started dabbing frantically at the canvas until the tree had some semblance of leaves, then turned the brush toward the bottom and gave it more than two azalea bushes. "Better?"

"Sure," Kate replied, drawing the word out. "Much better, Haley."

He set the brush aside, then moved his chair closer to hers, reaching out to take her hands. They both had paint splatters across their arms, hers more vivid than his. Kate dipped her finger across the palette and drew a streak of black up his arm. She stuck three fingers in cobalt and dragged her fingers down his shirt. He just sat there, not saying a word as she made him her canvas. When she met his gaze, the desire reflected there gave her all sorts of ideas.

"I wish I could paint you."

His gaze dropped to her lips. "You want to reenact Titanic?"

Kate laughed. "I can't paint people." She pulled his shirt down just a little and trailed a blue-streaked finger to the center of his chest. "I meant I want to get you naked. With body paint."

changed

She'd never noticed before how pupils actually dilated when attraction was felt. She must have been walking around with incessantly dilated pupils in Quinn's presence.

He reached out and placed two fingers in the deep-pink paint she'd been using on the azaleas. He brushed her hair back slightly and moved his fingers down her neck. Past the love bite, across her clavicle, and down toward her bra. He stopped just shy of indecency and pulled his fingers free.

"Now we match," he murmured.

Kate glanced around, wondering if this was what exhibitionism was like. Naughty touches in public places. She glanced back at Quinn and was assailed by the memory of Roxie Rogers telling her all about Quinn's sexual interests. What would Roxie have done with Quinn on the many trails of Airlie Gardens? She wondered if he had ever been here with her.

"I think I'm ready to go now," Kate said, wiping the extra paint off on her jeans. "These should be dry by the time we get to the parking lot."

"You okay?" Quinn touched her chin, making her look at him. "What's wrong?"

Kate shook her head, emotionally cantering as quickly as she could away from feelings. God, she was beginning to get tired of herself. One moment she was so happy. In the next, everything would come back to her in a vicious wave and make her doubt all of it. Her future with Quinn. Her ability to follow her dreams. Even something that should be as simple—at least to most people—as sex.

Kate returned the art supplies to the event host and walked beside Quinn as he carried their paintings. Not paying attention to her surroundings, she was surprised to find he'd taken a detour into the pergola garden. He propped the paintings against a bench and pulled her into an alcove of foliage.

"I don't like your tree."

"I don't like your tree either," Kate said.

"That is the unhappiest tree I've ever seen. That tree isn't you. Your tree is... it's a magnolia in bloom. Or... what is that tree Jon fell out of at your gran's?" Quinn demanded.

"A cherry tree," she replied.

"Your tree is a cherry tree. It's beautiful and pink in the spring, and when I see them I think about you because that is you, Kate. You are not this twisted thing," he said, giving a scathing glance at the paintings, his voice threaded with anger. "Not to me."

Kate looked at him squarely. "What if I am?"

"What if you're what?" he asked, his tone snappy.

"What if I'm defective?" She willed her eyes not to produce tears. She tightened her jaw to keep her lips from trembling. It hurt to breathe. To speak. But she was tired of holding it in all the time. "What if not having kids is just the beginning of what's wrong with me? How do either of us know that this will last, Quinn? Because you might wake up one day and realize that it's not the life you want."

In response, he brushed his lips over hers gently. He gazed into her eyes, and she saw all of the answers that she wanted, and for now, they beat back the plague of uncertainty.

"It's going to last, kitten," Quinn whispered. "It has to. You might wake up one day and realize that I'm not what you wanted. But I'm willing to take the chance and do everything I can to make this work. I want you to tell me everything when you're ready. I already know what I want to say to you. I can tell you those things now if it helps. Nothing you say is going to change my mind. I want you, Kate. I want you no matter what."

The rotten feeling in her chest and stomach went away, abruptly replaced by feelings... this time good ones.

It was time to move forward. To accept this part of herself, because if she let it take any more of her happiness away, she might never get it back. She'd been afraid of Quinn finding out because his perception of her might change. It had already changed, but only because she had allowed an infection to fester inside of her. Because she had closed her heart off to the idea that he might actually, really accept her.

Kate loved him. The way he held her… the way he was looking at her. She thought that he might feel the same, though he hadn't said it. She formed the words in her mind, then moved them to her tongue, but the sound of a group coming down the path interrupted her.

"Let's go home, Haley."

He held her in place, his gaze firm. "Tell me you believe that it's going to last, Kate. Because if you don't, then all of this is pointless."

"It's not us I doubt. It's me. And I'm sorry if my insecurity is inconvenient right now, but that's something I have to work through on my own. It has nothing to do with you."

Quinn tucked her hair behind her ear, leaning toward her. "If you let me, I'll go to therapy with you. I'll go to any doctor's appointment… Whatever you want. And that's what I want, because I know it's hard for you and I don't want you to be alone when you go through that. I'll sit in the waiting room. They don't have to tell me anything. I'm sorry I didn't like your tree. I guess it's just an expression of your feelings, but I don't like seeing you unhappy, Kate. Because it makes me feel like I'm not doing something right. That I'm not enough for you. I want you to paint happy trees."

Kate wrapped her arms around his waist and hugged him tightly. "Quinn, some days I'm going to paint sad trees. Some days they will be happy trees, or angry trees, or just trees. You make me happy. And I am happy, most of the time. I promise that I'm not going to… or at least, I'm going to try not to let it... overwhelm me again. You can't take it personally if I have a bad day every now and then. This wasn't a bad day. This was just me... being me. The new me."

"The new you?" He looked over her head for a moment, and she could see gears moving in his brain. He looked back down at her. "You're going to be a new version of yourself every single day, Kate. Something will happen that will change your perception of the world, or of a person, or a thing. Just like there is a new version of me every day. That night in the kitchen before Christmas... when you found out you were going to Atlanta... my perception of you changed. It had been happening a little bit at a time, but I saw you for the first time that night. I saw what we could be together, and it killed me because I didn't want to hurt you. I didn't want to hurt Roxie. In the end it didn't matter, because I couldn't go back to the old me if I'd wanted to. Just promise me you won't change so much that you aren't my Kate anymore. Because she's pretty damn awesome, and I want her in my life."

His words warmed her heart. She rose onto her toes and pulled him down for a kiss, not caring that there was another couple a few feet away or about anything else. If what he said was true... if you were a new version of yourself every single day... then today she was Brave Kate.

And perhaps tomorrow she might become Bold Kate, or Adventuress Kate. Or even, someday, Sexy Kate.

She would be every fearless edition of herself that she could possibly be and make damn sure that when she painted trees, the happy trees outweighed the sad ones.

·····ༀ·····

Quinn woke up halfway through their movie when he felt Kate's fingers tickling his sides. She was curled against him chest to chest, at some point having slipped onto the couch beside him. Jon was at Topsail Beach with some friends, and Miranda was at home with Frank and Meredith. His eyes flickered open at the second brush of her fingers against his side, and he found her expression mischievous.

"You're disturbing my nap," he grumbled, but he pulled her closer. "Your movie put me to sleep."

"I didn't like it either. Want to go for a midnight swim?"

His eyes opened wider as he came fully awake. Ever since the park they had been touching more and more, but he let her take the lead. If she wanted his hand somewhere, he let her put it there, and so far none of that had been below the waist. When she started touching him, it was pure torture, but he loved every minute of it.

"Anytime I see you in a bikini is all right with me."

She arched a brow at him, a little glint in her eye that made his pulse race. "Maybe the suits can be optional this time?"

His heart stuttered, choked, and felt like it stopped. "What?"

Her face was turning pink. "You heard me," she muttered. "But you have to keep your hands to yourself."

He placed a kiss on her nose.

"Cross my heart, McGuire," he murmured. "I'll keep my eyes closed and hands to myself."

"I don't care if you look." She bit her lip and looked at him, a coy expression in her gaze. "As long as I get to look."

"Then I'm damn well going to look." He kissed her, hard, and got to his feet. Pulled her up into his arms and kissed her again. "You're full of surprises sometimes, Kate."

"Come on then." She led him outside, and he turned off the outside lights, though there were strip lights in the pool along the edge. The house didn't face the Atlantic, it faced the marshland, and there was terracing with thick landscaping separating them from the neighbors along with white fencing around a section of yard for Artie.

Her gaze locked on him as he stripped off his shirt, then pulled off his shorts and boxers. It seemed like an eternity that she stood there, staring at his chest. Her interest drifted down, and she glanced away quickly. Even in the dark, he could tell she was blushing.

"You aren't going shy on me are you?" he asked.

Kate shook her head, then drew a breath, crossing her arms to peel her shirt off, revealing a lacy pink bra. His body reacted as she kicked off her shorts, revealing matching underwear. She held his gaze, unsmiling, as she unhooked the clasp on her bra and pulled it away. Her hands rested nervously at her sides, and he saw her features flicker with insecurity, then she shoved her bottoms down and stood before him with absolutely nothing on.

He looked, and looked, and felt like an idiot for making any promises.

"Come here, beautiful," he said, his voice rougher than he meant to sound.

"You promised," she reminded him.

"I'll keep it, just get in the pool before I have a stroke."

She looked down at herself for a moment, then smiled at him.

"They aren't beach ball size," Kate whispered. "I hope they'll do."

"Every inch of you is perfect." He swallowed hard, his gaze lowering to her breasts. "Especially those."

Quinn reached for her hand and led her into the water, unable to take his eyes off her. She was petite and elegant. She had gained some of her weight back but still had shadows under her eyes that made the blue in them look like two bruises in the dark. Her skin was pale and flawless in the reflection of the water, her breasts small but perfect, tipped by the same raspberry color as her lips. She was pure and sweet and unbelievably sexy. He wanted her... but he wanted more than sex. He wanted her innocent enjoyment of life, her wonder and kindness. She made him forget all the bad shit that had happened in the past. He was more than naked—he was exposed, unable to make a joke or touch her to relieve the tension. Instead, he turned, pretending an interest in the house with its many windows looking out over the water.

"I used to come here all the time in high school," he said, willing his voice to sound normal, wanting to set her at ease. "The first time, I wanted to break everything in there. Every picture. I never hated anyone the way I hated him."

He closed his eyes as her arms slipped around him from behind, her breasts pressing into his back. Her chin dug gently into his shoulder, and he could feel her cheek against his ear.

"I'm sorry, Quinn."

"I could never understand how he could be such a loving father to his daughter but not me. His son." He took a deep breath, all too aware of Kate tracing a path on his chest with her fingertip. "I don't know if I'd want to have kids after all the shit I've gone through."

Her movement stopped. "What?"

"I've been thinking about what you told me." Quinn turned around to face her but kept his hands floating on top of the water. "I just wanted you to know, in case you were wondering how I felt about it."

"You say that now," Kate replied, her voice growing thick, "but you don't know what you would be giving up. Not until you don't have a choice."

"I know it takes a giant asshole to walk away from his own responsibility. I know it would make me an even bigger asshole to walk away from someone because they couldn't have kids. I didn't exactly have the best example of good parenting, and I'm pretty sure I'd suck at it. I just didn't want you to feel like I'd be giving up anything. We don't have to talk about it right now. I know it's too soon for that. There are so many things that you are going to do with your life, Kate. Don't let this one thing hold you back. You are beautiful, just the way you are. And God, I promised I wouldn't touch you, but I want to. So much."

"You promised," she whispered, moving closer. Her legs brushed against him, and he groaned. "Are you going to break it?"

"No." His hands turned into fists on top of the water. "But if you move any closer, it isn't my hands you'll have to worry about."

"Are you going to lose it if I kiss you?" she whispered.

"You're trying to kill me, aren't you?"

"It's a test, Haley. Try to keep up."

Kate kissed him, and if there was one thing Kate McGuire could do better than cook, it was kiss. She pressed herself full length against him and took his mouth, teasing him with sensual softness, then hard and hungry. Her hands squeezed and stroked everywhere but the place he wanted them to. His back, his ass, sliding back up into his hair and pulling, skating back down his side, her nails trailing from navel to nipple in a sweet torment that made him groan. His warning to her unheeded, he couldn't do anything as his erection prodded her. It ended as abruptly as it began when she spun around and dived beneath the surface of the water, leaving him gasping for air. He could have easily caught her but thought it best if there was plenty of distance between them. She swam lazily for a while, and he enjoyed the brief flashes of her body that broke above the surface. He got out of the water as she swam, drying himself off with a shirt and then pulling on his clothes. He went into the house and grabbed a towel for her, leaving it at the edge of the pool. He lay back beneath one of the big umbrellas on a beach lounger and watched her as she came out of the water the same way she'd gone in. She seemed to want him to look, and he didn't mind in the least either.

Kate wrapped herself in a towel and joined him on the beach lounger. Her eyes were red, and he didn't think it was from the chlorine.

"Talk to me," he said softly.

She shook her head and lowered her face against his neck. Her towel covered her torso but left those gorgeous slim legs exposed. It rolled through him like a train that she was in his lap, naked but for one damned towel.

"Just hold me, Quinn. Please."

He was never more relieved to have use of his hands. He wrapped his arms around her and pulled her close, smelling chlorine on her skin. They stayed like that for a long time, not talking or kissing, just him holding her down like an anchor.

Quinn thought she was asleep, then he felt her hand slide beneath his shirt.

"I really want to do something for you," she whispered. "Will you let me?"

He lifted her chin with the tip of his finger, studying her expression for a moment. "You don't have to do anything for me, Kate. I want everything with you, when you're ready."

A breath shuddered through her, and misery etched itself on her face. "I'm really trying, Quinn. I just don't know if I can… I don't know if *I* can wait. If I can ask *you* to keep waiting for me. I'm ready. I am. I… God, you don't know the things I want to do with you. To you. I'm afraid when I go to Atlanta you're going to find someone else. Someone who can—"

"I'm not going to find someone else," he cut in, his voice fierce. "I wouldn't do that to you."

"How long has it been?" she demanded. "Since you had sex?"

"Kate." He sighed, closing his eyes. "It doesn't matter."

"How long?"

"Since I broke up with her. In December. I told you, she's the only one I've ever been with."

"It might *be* December before we can be together like that. It might be longer. Are you sure you want to go an entire year without sex?"

"I have a hand, Kate. I can take care of myself."

Her face turned tomato red, and her gaze dropped from his. "TMI, Haley."

"Would you rather I go out and hook up with someone?" he asked, exasperated.

"I'd rather take your pants off and let you show me how to give you a blow job."

He brought her mouth around for a kiss, her words going straight to his groin. "Only if I can do something for you."

"You can't."

"Then you can't either," he murmured. "I can't do the one-sided thing, Kate. But I can wait for you."

She groaned and buried her face in his chest, mumbling words that suspiciously sounded like *I'm horny.* Surely he heard wrong. He frowned, glancing down at her. Surely she'd said *I'm hungry.*

"Do you want a sandwich or something?" he asked cautiously.

"What?" Kate looked up at him, confusion in her gaze.

"A sandwich," Quinn repeated. "If you're hungry I can grab you something."

She just stared at him. "I'm not hungry."

He blinked at her.

Kate blinked back.

Okay. So she *had* said it.

"How... how far have you gone?" Quinn asked.

She winced a little. "A onetime epic failure. The worst

possible moment of all time. I have less than zero experience because that one was so bad it didn't count and I haven't done anything else with anyone."

"That bad?"

"That bad," she confirmed. "It's the worst mistake I ever made."

"Was it Andrew?" he asked, not sure if he wanted to know but needing to.

She shook her head, but a strange expression crossed her face for a moment. "It was Jacob. Last summer. I... couldn't go through with it. And there was no... foreplay. He just... went for it like he was in a jousting tournament, and it freaking hurt, and I bailed."

"A jousting tournament?" He raised a brow.

"Pretty much."

"Fucker. Where does he live? I'll drive over right now and beat his face in."

She chuckled. "You don't have to be jealous. I think half the reason I did it was because I had to watch you suck Roxie's face last summer."

Quinn grimaced. Last summer seemed a lifetime ago. He had stayed away from the McGuires most of that time because Roxie was flailing, clinging to him desperately. They had crashed at her friend Lauren's house most of the summer. A few times he'd met Jon at the beach, and they had all hung out together, then Kate had started bringing a boyfriend along.

"I watched you suck his face too," he pointed out. "And Andrew's."

"Yeah, but you didn't have a soul-crushing crush on me," Kate replied, blushing. "Probably the worst secret ever, right?"

"I might have caught you ogling me a few times. Even saw a glare or two last summer," he admitted, smiling. "I wanted to punch Jacob in the face every time he touched you, and I hated Andrew on sight. And it might not have been a soul-crushing crush, but I've always thought you were beautiful and way too innocent and good for me."

"I don't want to be innocent. I want to do… stuff."

"Stuff?" He grinned. "What kind of stuff?"

"Don't make fun of me," she grumbled. "You know what stuff."

"I want to do stuff too, McGuire." He traced the shell of her ear gently. For the millionth time, he doubted his vague theory about her being like Shelby from *Steel Magnolias*, but he had nothing else to go off of. He'd started typing words into his phone's search feature several times but always stopped himself. He wasn't even sure what to look *for*. "When are you planning on telling me this big secret of yours? You know, there's nothing you could tell me that would make me change my mind about you."

"I think I know that. I just… I don't want you to…"

"To what?"

"Think of me differently," she whispered, her voice cracking. "Or pity me. Quinn?"

"Yeah, kitten?"

"Do you… do you have a thing?" Kate asked.

Quinn raised his eyebrows. "If you didn't see it earlier, I'm going to cry."

"Not that, you ass." She poked him in the stomach. "I mean… do you have a sex thing? Like… a… fetish?"

"Uh… where is this coming from?" Quinn rooted through his brain for a moment, wondering if he had done something to imply he was some kind of sex freak, but couldn't think of anything.

"Just tell me. It's okay if you like weird stuff. I'd just like to know."

"Weird stuff?" He stared at her. "I wouldn't call it weird. I mean, I like lingerie. I don't wear it, obviously, but you in that pink bra earlier was almost as good as when you took it off. I think Megan Fox is pretty hot, but you look kind of like her, so you can't get mad."

She laughed. "I do not look like her."

"Pre-Hollywood Megan Fox, before the fake tan," he amended. "And for the record, I think she was prettier then."

"Oh, when she was twelve?" Kate rolled her eyes. "Thanks for that."

"Shh." He put his hand over her mouth. "You're killing my dream, McGuire. Let's see… when I was fourteen, I had a pretty big thing for Mrs. Warren in English."

"You did not!" She gasped. "She's older than my mom!"

"Yeah, but she liked to lean over our desks, and she didn't wear a bra sometimes," he murmured, waggling his eyebrows at her until she started laughing.

"What about handcuffs?"

His brain quit working for a minute. "Sure, they can be… fun. I don't particularly care to be the one cuffed."

"Toys?" she squeaked.

He frowned at her. She looked like it was killing her to ask. "Why do you want to know?"

"So that's a yes?"

"You really want to know about this?" he asked, exasperated. "Why would you want to know the details?"

"Just forget about it, Quinn." She sat up, adjusting her towel. "Sorry."

"Hey…" He set his hand on her shoulder. "I just don't think it's a good idea to talk about it like this. We're going to make our own memories, Kate. I don't know what you think Roxie and I had, but I promise you it wasn't a wild romance. We shared some really deep shit. She was… she has issues. With sex, I mean. I made mistakes with her… and I think that everything I did at first made her worse instead of better. I thought if I could get her to trust me, with this one thing, then the next thing, that I would heal her somehow. I was such an idiot. She... she freaked out the first time, even though she told me she was ready... that she wanted it. She had a panic attack. We didn't try again for a long time. And when she came to Duke with me, she was like a different person. I let her do whatever she wanted, because it was what she needed, but I don't need it. I don't want to make the same mistake with you, Kate. I don't want you to think that sex is going to fix everything. I promise you, it doesn't."

She blew out a breath, then turned around to look at him, a wobbly smile on her face. "So that's a negative on spankings?"

He scooped her up into his arms and growled against her neck until she squealed, trying to hold her towel together.

"Okay, okay," she cried, laughing. "I give up."

He turned her slightly, and brought his hand down on her ass, grinning when she squeaked. God, he loved it when she squeaked. "There's more where that came from if you don't behave."

She batted her eyes at him. "Yes, Mr. Grey," she breathed.

Quinn rolled his eyes at her. "Not hardly. Definitely not my *thing*."

"Really?"

"Really, really." He kissed her slowly, doing his best not to think about the fact that he knew her struggle with the towel had failed and there wasn't anything between them now but his clothes since it was only covering her ass. "You ready for bed, squeaker?"

"You going to grope me?" She smiled up at him, like she was kind of hoping he would.

"Can't make any promises, but you can slap me if I get too frisky." He waggled his eyebrows at her. "And if you feel frisky, you can feel me and I won't mind."

Chapter 28

·····❦·····

WAKING UP NEXT TO KATE had to be about one of the best things in the world. She was fused against him, chest to knee as they lay on their sides, legs tangled together as if she couldn't get close enough. He'd worn shorts and a T-shirt to bed but sometime in the night had discarded the shirt like he always did when it started bunching up around his arms. Kate had worn shorts too and a white tank top that probably revealed more than she realized, though he wasn't about to let her know that. She'd been awake for a while apparently, her hands roving down the length of his spine and teasing at the edge of his waistband. The sheet and comforter were kicked to the end of the bed, but they radiated enough warmth that they didn't need it. They had fallen asleep with him lying on his back with her nestled against his side. He considered this a vast improvement other than that brief time he'd woken hours ago to her spooning him.

Quinn lifted one hand from its place on her hip and pushed her hair back to kiss her forehead. Kate raised her eyes to his, and he'd expected shyness from her, but the look she was giving him wasn't shy at all. He slid his hand down to rest behind her knee, then brought her leg up over his. Her eyes closed when he settled his erection against her body. He moved his hand to her ass and brought her all the way in until he was nestled against the apex of her legs.

"Good morning," he murmured, smiling down at her beautiful, blushing face.

She made some noise that might have been "good morning" or could have been "Mufasa." It was hard to tell since it mostly sounded like a moan. She shifted suddenly, one arm sliding beneath his neck, the other she pushed down between them and closed over the hard length inside his shorts, stroking him. Quinn sucked in a breath, not sure if he should stop her. Not sure if he could.

"Kate," he groaned. "God, kitten. You're killing me."

"You think you're frustrated," she bit out, doing it again. "You have no idea, baby."

"This won't... hurt you?" he asked cautiously.

"As long as you aren't into jousting," Kate whispered.

He laughed even if that made him want to find Jacob and kick his ass. Quinn rolled onto his back and pulled her on top of him.

"How about this? You just do... whatever you want," he said. "I'll just lay here and pretend I'm your cabana boy."

"Maybe that's your thing," she murmured. "Letting women have their way with you."

It probably was, if he was honest with himself. He'd always given others control over his life. His mother. Roxie. His father. Even this house had held something over him for the longest time. He'd looked at it as a symbol of his place in his father's life. An empty, unwanted shell. He only hoped that the control he gave up for Kate was worth it. That she understood how much he trusted her. How much he loved her.

Love.

The word and the feeling both held such a complicated

place in his heart. He loved her. He'd always loved her... as a friend. Those feelings had changed for him so quickly. They were deeper. She was hooked into his heart, the strings of hers entwined so tightly within his own that it was hard to believe he hadn't always felt this way for her. He needed to tell her how he felt, but now wasn't the time. He didn't want her to think that this was the only reason he said it.

He slid his hands up her side, against the outside of her ribs to tease the edge of her breasts, then brought her down to feather kisses across her cheek to her ear, then her neck.

"Sit," he whispered, pushing on her hip with one hand until she was pressed against him again.

"You going to tell me to stay next?" she murmured.

He pushed his pelvis up against hers, then did it again when she made a little sound of encouragement. "I might. Do you want more?"

"Yes. Please..."

"Can I touch you, Kate?"

She hesitated for a moment, pulling back so he could see her face. "I..."

"Waist up," he suggested, sliding his hand beneath the edge of her shirt. "Promise."

"Yes," she groaned.

"Take your shirt off." He smiled at her. "It isn't hiding much anyway."

"Just these little mosquito bites," Kate grumbled, but she pulled it off anyway, placing one arm across her breasts in a sudden fit of modesty.

"I like your little mosquito bites, but they aren't that little. Don't hide from me." He pulled her down again, bucking his hips beneath her, raising up to trace her neck and clavicle with greedy kisses, down to those perfect, beautiful breasts, keeping rhythm with his pelvis. She let out a cry when his mouth closed around a pretty pink nipple, her hands going into his hair as he sucked.

"Quinn."

"Mmm?"

She didn't answer, just let out a moan when he moved his mouth over to the other one. She wrapped both arms around his neck and pulled him in tighter, arching against him. He felt explosions of desire and need, unable to get enough of her soft, soft skin.

"On top of me… please…"

"Whatever you want, Kate," he whispered against her skin, switching places with her quickly. "Tell me if you want to stop."

She just made some sort of whimper, squirming to get closer to him. He rocked against her, lifted her legs up around him, and rocked again. He leaned down to kiss her, but she twisted her head away.

"Morning breath," she mumbled, looking embarrassed.

"Mine or yours?" he asked, amused.

"Mine."

"Then I don't care," Quinn said roughly. He was beyond caring about anything except how much he wanted her.

He kissed her, slanting his mouth over hers, teasing her with his tongue to mimic the rhythm of his hips. The rough fabric of his shorts only made him more sensitive, and the scent of her arousal was intoxicating. Kate's legs wrapped around him tighter, and she matched him movement for movement, her hands sliding down and grabbing to pull him closer. She lifted her legs up higher, her eyes locked on his. She was so beautiful, and in that moment he knew she wasn't thinking about anything but him. He was so close, but he wanted to see her. Wanted to give her pleasure instead of pain.

He adjusted the angle slightly, and that was it for her. She bucked under him, her eyes going wide as she cried out his name, and he felt his own orgasm slam into him, his entire body going taut as he jerked against her in answer. She grabbed two handfuls of hair and brought his mouth down against hers, undulating beneath him, their frenzy slowing into shallow thrusts until he stilled against her.

"Oh my God," Kate gasped. "What the hell?"

Quinn froze. "Did I hurt you?"

"No."

Her eyes were wild though, as if she couldn't believe what they'd done. He panicked, wondering if maybe there was something wrong with her heart. Her chest was flushed red, her cheeks pink, but he could see her struggling for breath.

"Are you okay, Kate?" he demanded.

"I'm... wonderful," she said, exhaling hard. Her eyes closed. "I didn't know that's what it was like."

He relaxed marginally, though his heart was still racing from sex and a full moment of terror that he'd done something he shouldn't have.

"You've never made yourself come?"

"Oh my God." She covered her face with her hands. "You can't ask me that kind of stuff."

"There's nothing wrong with it." He pulled her hands down away from her face and grinned at her, enjoying her blush. "Everyone does it."

"Not me." Her gaze slid over everything in the room except his face. "Did you... go?"

"Yes."

She made some weird humming noise in the back of her throat, almost like she was choking. "Huh. Um. Okay."

"Am I crushing you?"

"Don't go just yet." She finally looked at him, her expression uncertain. "I didn't mean to start... anything."

"It's all right, Kate." He propped himself up on one elbow and kissed her gently. "I enjoyed every moment."

A shuddering breath went through her, and tears leaked out of the corners of her eyes, sliding into her temple.

"This doesn't…" She drew a deep, shuddering breath and stopped looking at him again. "This doesn't change anything. I still can't… we still can't…"

"Don't worry about anything. This was wonderful." He reached up to brush away her tears, worry blooming in his chest. She regretted it. He could see it in her eyes, stark embarrassment and doubts growing that her confidence had left a vacuum for. "Kate, it's all right."

"Yes, but it's not normal." She started squirming, so he let her wiggle out from under him. "And now I wish I had told you everything before we did… that. God, I'm so stupid."

"You are not stupid, and you don't have to tell me anything," he replied gently. "I just don't want to do anything that will hurt you. I was worried you were having a heart attack or an anxiety attack."

For a moment a wry smile crossed her face. "It felt like a heart attack. A good one though."

They both almost had a heart attack when Artie jumped out from under the bed and began barking like crazy. Quinn's eyes grew wide as Kate scrambled off the bed looking for her shirt. He grabbed his off the floor and tossed it at her.

"Put this on," he said.

"Go see if someone's here."

"I can't." He felt his face burn with embarrassment. He glanced down at his shorts, then back up at her.

She mumbled something when she glanced at his crotch and shoved his shirt over her head then went to his bedroom door and opened it a crack. They both listened and could hear voices from downstairs.

"Sounds like Jon and Rand." She paused a moment, then she groaned. "And Mom."

Well, that made sense. The first time they'd done anything together, her mom showed up. Kate ran into the Jack-and-Jill bathroom and closed the door behind her quietly. Quinn closed his door and changed quickly, then went downstairs, freeing Artie to run downstairs and bark his head off at everyone until Miranda greeted him with a squeal.

Jon was raiding the fridge when he walked into the kitchen, and Meredith was making coffee. He caught a glimpse of Miranda as she took Artie out into the yard.

"Hey," he said, hoping his face wasn't as red as it felt. "I thought you were gone for the weekend."

"I changed my mind," Jon replied, smirking at him. "Where's Kate?"

"I think I heard her shower going." At least that was the truth. He slid a glance at their mom and found her gaze on his. "Everything all right?"

Meredith covered his arm with her hand for a moment. "Of course, honey. Kate has therapy today, and I thought I'd spend some time with her."

Quinn frowned. He'd almost forgotten about her counseling sessions. She didn't talk about them much, except to say the therapist wanted to know all about her feelings and that she didn't like going. He glanced at Meredith, then away. "Did they tell you anything about her being here with me? If it was a good idea?"

"Kate is eighteen," Meredith replied softly. "They can't tell me anything unless Kate gives them permission. But you make her happy, so that's all I care about right now."

She opened her mouth like she was going to say something but closed it at the sound of Kate coming downstairs.

"Morning," Kate mumbled as she walked in, her hair damp from the shower and looking fresh-faced and beautiful with no makeup on, still wearing his T-shirt with a pair of yoga pants. She poked Jon in the back as she walked past him. "Thought you were staying at Topsail."

"I got back around three this morning," Jon replied, giving her a look out of the corner of his eyes. "Late night? Ouch." He rubbed his side where she pinched him, glaring at her as she moved around the bar and gave her mom a hug and kiss on the cheek.

Meredith reached up and tugged the ends of Kate's hair. "You want to go get your hair cut today after your session? They said they could squeeze us both in."

"Yeah. That sounds fun."

"Miranda didn't want to go. Said she missed her Artie," Meredith said with a smile. "Run upstairs and get dressed. I'll meet you in the car."

After they left, Jon gave him a look.

"What?"

"You need to ask Miranda about Roxie," Jon said quietly.

Quinn blinked at him. "What about her?"

"Roxie said some stuff to Kate at Christmas. Miranda told me she was messing with Kate's head about your sex life."

Quinn walked to the back door and knocked, getting Miranda's attention, then grilled her as soon as she came inside.

"What did Roxie say to Kate?" he demanded.

Miranda sighed, giving Jon a look. "Roxie told us you were some kind of kinky sex freak that liked it rough. She said you were her little slut. Did you really do it in a club bathroom? Because that is *so* gross."

He was floored. All her questions from the night before... were all because Roxie had put that bullshit in her head.

"She told you what?" he exploded, slamming his hand

down on the bar.

Miranda just raised one red eyebrow. "She said you made Christian Grey look like a p—"

"Are you freaking kidding?"

He felt a sharp pinch in his chest, along with a deep flood of anger. Kate hadn't said anything, not because it hadn't hurt her. He knew that it had. She hadn't told him the truth about what was going on with him because she didn't trust him.

As if Jon could read his thoughts, he glanced at him. "There goes your *Steel Magnolias* theory."

"So everything that she's gone through this year… was because of me?" Quinn whispered. It felt like his chest was caving in. "She… she… all of it? Was because of me?"

"No. It wasn't because of you. It wasn't because of the crap Roxie pulled either. It's because of all this stuff she has going on with the doctors," Miranda said, patting his arm. "What do you mean, *Steel Magnolias* theory?"

"Quinn thinks Kate is like Julia Roberts in that movie. Bad kidney means she can't get pregnant or she could die."

"And the juice thing," Quinn added.

"Juice?" Miranda repeated, blinking at him.

"She was having an anxiety attack or something. I got her some juice, and it seemed like it made her feel better." It sounded stupid when he said it out loud, and Miranda was giving him a look that confirmed that he was, in fact, stupid.

"You are so… so far off. Please tell me you haven't said anything to her about that."

"No. Of course not."

"Just tell us then," Jon said quietly.

"No way." Miranda shook her head. "It took her forever to tell me. Just don't say that crap to her."

"Then tell me what I can say. Or what else I can't say,"

Quinn demanded. "I know she can't have kids. I just don't know why."

Miranda sighed. "Just don't say the *B* word. You know… baby. Or even joke about getting pregnant or knocking her up or whatever. She can't have kids because she can't get pregnant or carry her own baby. She would have to get someone to do it for her."

"So…" He glanced at Jon. "Why is she still freaking out about the other thing?"

"You mean sex?" Miranda asked.

Quinn's face burned. "Yeah."

"I can't tell you that. If you want to know, you already know enough to Google it." Miranda gave him a guilty look. "You didn't hear that from me though."

He thought for a moment. "One kidney."

"Yep," she replied.

"No kids."

"Basically, yeah."

"And no… sex." He didn't look at Jon when he said it, and it was all he could do to meet Miranda's gaze.

She gave him a thumbs-up, blushing for the first time. "The last part is fixable. She's working on it, stud muffin. Don't hurt her or I'll shank you."

"Rand?" Jon, who had been quiet the whole time, handed her his phone. "Is this it?"

She studied his phone, then nodded. "That's it."

Jon tried to hand the phone to Quinn, but he shook his head. Kate already didn't trust him. He wasn't going to do anything to break what little faith she had in him. They had made progress last night. Surely that meant something. Did it hurt a little that she hadn't told him yet? Yes… but he understood that it was something enormous for her to put into words. Something she struggled with very hard. There were things in his past he had never told anyone… not even

Jon. Things too painful to ever talk about.

"I promised her I'd wait until she was ready to talk about it. It helps to know what I can say and what I can't."

"You sure?" Jon murmured.

"Yeah." He felt relief roll through him. "It doesn't matter anyway. I love her. Nothing is going to change that."

Miranda cocked her head at him. "So did you have a sex dungeon or something? And I get the whips. I mean, obviously. But what do you do with the chains?"

Quinn looked at Jon. "Make her stop."

"Rand," Jon warned. "Knock it off, or you're going home."

"You two are such prudes. Fine." Miranda rolled her eyes and scooped Artie up, backing out of the kitchen. "I'll ask Google. It doesn't judge me for being curious."

Chapter 29

QUINN WAS ALONE WHEN SHE got back, the lights turned down low with music playing. He was asleep on the couch in the living room, one arm thrown over his eyes and snoring softly.

"Hey," she whispered.

He woke as soon as she touched him, blinking sleepily up at her, then gave her a smile that went straight from her stomach to her toes. God, he was so handsome. Even with his hair mussed—maybe especially with his hair mussed—and the shadow of a beard coming in, he was beautiful. She leaned over and gave him a kiss.

"Mmm. Back so soon?"

"What are you doing, lazybones?"

"Waiting for you." He reached up and touched her hair, which had been cut just above her shoulders. "I like it."

"Thanks. Where are Jon and Rand?"

"Jon took her home. He's staying with someone tonight. It's just us again." He tugged on her hand. "Lie down with me."

"Sure."

She stretched out on the couch beside him, her stomach a ball of nerves. She still couldn't believe what she had done with him that morning. What they had done with each other. The entire day with her mom, she would suddenly remember how he'd felt pressed against her and she'd start feeling hot all over again, followed by that same overwhelming insecurity because she couldn't have sex. She could only mimic it… imitate it like he hadn't been having the real thing for years and now had to go back to dry humping… if he'd ever done that to begin with. That wasn't what she had wanted. She'd never wanted to do things halfway. Not with him. Not with anyone.

"I want to tell you something," he murmured, his lips pressing against her temple. "Just listen. Please."

"Okay," she whispered.

"Only one person in all my life has ever… *ever* told me that they loved me." His arms tightened around her when she tried to move, and he pressed her face into his chest. "Let me finish. I know how you feel about me, Kate. Some part of me has always known. And I know, I guess, that your family loves me. That if I died tomorrow I'd *probably* be missed. I know those things. But I've never been *told* those things, except from her. She broke my heart, but I forgive her… I *have* to forgive her, because that's not the girl I knew. She was so… so broken. And I was too, and for a little while we had each other. If I had never met her, I don't think I would have understood how badly I needed to change if I wanted to get away from that life. The things she said to you, I know she said them out of fear of losing me."

"Quinn." Her arms tightened around him, and she felt her eyes fill with tears. Her heart broke for him. He was the sweetest person… her favorite person in the entire world. No one had ever said it? Not even his mom… not even once? "I do love you. So much that it h-hurts me."

"I know." He let her up enough so that she could look in his eyes, and it felt like she'd been punched. In all the years she had known him, she had never seen him cry, but his green eyes were suspiciously bright. "I love you. I should have said it a long time ago. I of all people should know that it needs to be heard. So I love you, Kate. For the rest of my life, from the bottom of my heart as long as I live forever and ever. You're mine. I'm yours, as long as you will have me."

"I'll have you, Quinn." She pressed her mouth to his, tasting him, just barely brushing her lips over his. He responded with soft, teasing kisses, then the mood changed, becoming heavy and sexual. His hands slid into her hair, and he angled her face, kissing her deeper until she felt the hard length of him against her stomach. Kate stopped, gasping, and uncertain if she wanted to take things any further. Then she realized something he'd said. "Someone told you? About Roxie?"

"I made Miranda tell me. Don't be mad at her."

"What else did she tell you?" Kate whispered.

"Nothing. I swear. I wouldn't have gone behind your back." His eyes flashed with hurt, and she regretted, again, that she hadn't told him everything. Everything about Roxie. About herself. "I get why you didn't tell me, but you…"

She stroked his cheek gently. "I'm sorry. I didn't want to hurt you, Quinn. I tried to stop… having feelings for you. I just couldn't. And Andrew… I really hurt him, and that's just added to all this crap that's weighing on me. I was just using him, and I hate that about myself. The fact that I was too afraid to tell you how I felt. And I'm still terrified, because you're you and I don't want to lose you one day."

"Did Andrew know… everything?"

"I don't know what I told him. I was too drunk to remember." She closed her eyes and laid her head back on his chest and told him everything she could remember about the night she'd spent with Andrew.

He squeezed her tight. "We've all done things we regret, Kate. I'm sorry for everything you've gone through. I'm sorry for anything that I've done to make things worse."

"You haven't done anything. You've been wonderful."

"But you were thinking about suicide, Kate." His voice cracked. "I feel like that was my fault, because I knew as soon as I got back to Durham that I wanted you. I should have been there for you through all of it. I had no idea you were going through this stuff, and knowing you thought about killing yourself… my God, I can't even think about it because it hurts too much."

Kate pushed away the sob that rose in her throat. "It was that medicine I was on. It… it changed me."

"Do you have any idea what that would have done to me?" Quinn shifted so that she was lying beside him, face-to-face. "I called to ask you to go out with me that day."

"I know." She brushed the tears off her cheeks, her heart feeling so swollen that it hurt to speak. "It had nothing to do with you. I had already been thinking about it. And I didn't actually do anything. I was just thinking, and I haven't had thoughts like that in a long time."

"I want you to be okay on your own," he said softly. "I need to know you aren't going to give up on me. I want you to trust me."

"I do." He just looked at her, and she knew what he was really saying. She couldn't say that she trusted him unless she trusted him with the truth. "I trust you, Quinn. It's just… so embarrassing. And it makes me feel like I'm not complete. The doctor I went to in January confused me so much… they said they had to test my chromosomes. Until I went to Atlanta, I thought… I thought I was…"

"Was?" he prompted, when her tongue had been tied for a while.

"A boy," she mumbled, her face flushing. *"I'm not."*

"Kate." He tilted her chin up, his eyes patient. "I know you're not."

"But *I* didn't know. When you start Googling things, you find all kinds of conditions out there that you didn't know about before. And those comments people post online under the articles… they hurt me so much. I think reading those words more than anything else that has happened to me, made me think about… about suicide."

She felt his hands tangle gently in the ends of her hair, his expression hardening. It looked like he was struggling not to speak, and she knew if he said anything, then she would lose courage. She touched the edge of his chin with her fingers, pressing her thumb over his lips to stop him.

"I prayed so hard that it was something else. Anything else. But I had to pray that whatever it was wouldn't be worse, because I know in my heart that there are things that are worse. They told me what they thought was wrong with me, but I wasn't *sure* until Atlanta. I've had six doctor appointments since last fall. I've known since I tried to… since Jacob… that there was something wrong. It wasn't just that he couldn't penetrate. He said I felt different than girls he'd been with before."

"Kate—" She stopped him again, but he took her hand and kissed the back of it. His gaze was intense. "I love you. Nothing you say is going to change that."

She let out a breath, her eyes filling with tears again. "I have a birth defect. You can't tell… from the outside. That's why I never knew anything was wrong until then. I've never had a period, and I never will. Besides my kidney, I'm missing a uterus, fallopian tubes, and the cervix. I have ovaries, so I could have kids if I had a surrogate. Obviously, from this morning, you know I can…" Kate broke off, completely embarrassed now and unable to stop her voice from shaking or look him in the eye anymore. "There's nothing wrong with me… there."

"There's nothing wrong with you at *all*." Quinn touched her cheek, his hand warm against her skin, which felt cold. His other arm tightened around her, and she felt little spasms of tension rolling through him. "I just wish you didn't have to go through this."

"That's not all," she whispered. "I don't have… an opening. They could have corrected it with surgery, but there was another option. I have to do these exercises to… stretch." Her discomfort level and embarrassment was nearly overwhelming. "The condition is called MRKH. There's a longer name for it, but I can't pronounce it." It felt like such a relief to finally get it out even if she was about to ugly cry right in his face.

"I'm so sorry, sweetheart," he said gently. "I wish I could take away all the pain you feel. I love you so much, and it hurts me to see how much you've been hurting. Nothing you could have said was going to change how I feel. Nothing ever will. You're perfect in every way, Kate. Every part of you."

"But you'd be giving up everything to be with me."

"Don't you understand?" Quinn wrapped his arms around her. "I'm not giving up anything. You are my home, because the only thing I feel when I'm with you is happiness. I love you. Do you trust me?"

"Always."

"Then trust me. I love you, and I know one day we're going to talk about having kids. I know that part of this hurts you so much, and… my heart is open to whatever you want… but if there was anything in my life I could do to take in a kid who had a home like mine, then I'd do it in a heartbeat." He cupped her cheeks with both hands. "Being able to give birth doesn't make someone a mom, Kate. I spent my entire childhood wishing for a mom like yours. Maybe your life… our life… isn't supposed to be easy.

Maybe we are supposed to bless someone else. Someone who needs us just as much as we need them."

She hadn't really broken down and cried in a while, but she did then, huge gulping sobs that hurt her lungs because she wasn't getting enough air. He just held her, one arm tight around her and his other hand stroking down her hair to her back, then repeating the motion. It seemed like she cried forever, but it wasn't just the loss she felt this time. It felt like part of her had healed. That part afraid of her future. Of being rejected. Those thoughts were still there… she suspected they would always be part of her. She couldn't ever imagine feeling like a real woman… but for the first time she really knew she was going to be okay. After she had calmed down, she felt him reach over her and search for something beneath the couch.

"I picked something up for you today," he murmured.

"I hope it's a snot rag," she joked, trying to wipe her face and sniffling.

"It's not a snot rag," Quinn said, chuckling.

He turned her over so that she was on her back, pulling her legs up over his bent knees, then settled a dark velvet box on her chest. Her eyes widened as she looked up at him.

"It's not an engagement ring," he said, smiling. "I know neither of us is ready for that. I wanted you to have something to remember me by. A promise that I'm not going to forget you and that I will always love you."

"Quinn." Her voice was barely audible, and it felt like her heart was going to burst. Her hands shook as she opened it and found a ring. A beautiful, small silver ring with two princess cut birthstones, one in emerald for Quinn's birthday in May, and a sapphire for September. Their names were engraved on either side. Her hand was shaking as she pulled it free.

"Put it on me," she whispered.

He slid it onto her finger, his green eyes studying her as

she admired it for a moment before turning and wrapping her arms around him tightly.

"I love you, my sweet Kate. My K. rex, my beautiful, wonderful girl. My future chef. My soul mate. I love you forever, kitten."

"Forever." She kissed him softly. "It's perfect, Quinn. Thank you."

"I'm sorry that Roxie said those things to you. I mean… *really* sorry." His green gaze on hers was intense. "I would do anything in the world to keep you from hurting, Kate. I would do anything for you. Promise me that you're never going to think about that again."

"I won't. I'm still sad… mostly I'm angry, but after I stopped taking those pills, it was like I'd come out of a fog and could think again. I've never had feelings like this before. I really have changed, Quinn. I'm… I'm lost, and I know it's not going to get better overnight. My therapist said it's probably going to get worse before it gets better."

"I was scared this morning that I took things too far. I don't ever want you to feel like you have to do anything for me."

"I just want to be normal, and I don't know how to do that anymore. Especially… that. But I want you, so much, and it's killing me, Quinn, because I can't do anything about it right now. I don't want you to treat me like I'm different. If you want something, then I want it too. I want all of it. All of you. I'm not afraid to try things. I'm just afraid it's not going to be good enough." She felt that hollowness inside, even now. "You know there are girls younger than me dealing with this? I never talked to mom about… that thing girls get every month. She just assumed I'd been taking care of it, all this time, after we had *the talk*. Some girls carry around a pack of condoms in their purse. Since I was thirteen, I've been carrying this stupid pad around, thinking that any day was going to be the day. A few times a year some random person or a friend or even... even *Miranda*... would ask to borrow one, and I'd just give it to them and wonder what was wrong with me. The look on her face when I told Mom I hadn't got my period. I thought she was going to strangle me."

He cracked a cautious smile. "I bet that conversation was awkward."

"Probably not as awkward as this one," she admitted with a small laugh. "Close though."

"At least you don't have to worry about that stuff, right?"

She knew he didn't mean anything by it, but it stung. "I would rather go through it and be normal and have b-babies," she whispered hoarsely. "I can't even think about that part right now. I've been shutting it out, but I know it's going to hit me one day, and it's going to hurt."

"I know." Quinn pressed his lips to her brow. "William told me that it was one of the reasons he didn't tell Amelia about me. She couldn't have any more after Amanda. She was devastated. I just want you to know that whatever you want to do, it doesn't matter to me."

She had known him forever. She knew he wasn't someone who changed their mind very often—he was the most constant person in her life besides her family—but so much had happened to her the past year. If something happened to him, she didn't know if she would survive a blow like that.

His stomach growled then, and she was grateful for the distraction.

"Hungry?" she teased, running her hand beneath his shirt to touch his flat stomach. "I can make something real quick."

"I have a better idea. Why don't you get dressed, and we'll go out?"

"Finally going to use Daddy Warbucks's yacht club tab?"

She snickered at the face he made. "Or you can find us a greasy burger joint and take me ice skating."

"Ice skating." His face lit up. "I haven't done that in a long time. Is the rink still open?"

"Last I heard." Kate wiggled off the couch and tugged on his arm. "Come on. Hurry up, Haley. I'm starving."

"You're always rushing me, McGuire," he said, laughing.

"Cause you're too slow," she shot back, then immediately regretted it when he gave her a wicked look. "Don't you dare."

"I'll give you a head start."

"Quinn…"

"One…"

She yelped and took off, knowing he was going to catch her because his legs were freakishly long compared to hers. She made it to the top of the stairs when she heard him start up them and hadn't even made it to her room before he was there, his hands grabbing at her hips and pulling her against him, his green eyes alive with mischief.

"You cheated. You never said two," she said.

"I said I'd give you a head start. Not a count of three," he murmured. "I caught you. What's my prize?"

She swallowed hard, her heart pounding. "Maybe you'll find out tonight. I want to try. Just don't… expect a lot. It's probably not going to be… normal."

"I won't hurt you."

She felt breathless at the way he was looking at her. Like she could open her heart and he would love every single facet of it that he could see, and she wanted to peer into his heart because she already knew she loved every facet of his. He made her feel strong and brave, and she hoped that part of herself would get bigger and braver again. She didn't want to hurt anymore, and she knew that Quinn would never do anything to deliberately hurt her.

"I know." She gave him a mischievous smile. "You already told me spankings weren't your thing."

"Did I say that?" His hands moved down and squeezed her rear. "I'm pretty sure I could be persuaded."

She slapped his butt as hard as she could, and his eyes widened. She couldn't help but laugh at the shock on his face.

"Maybe I'm the one who likes them." She wrapped her arms around him and pulled him down for a kiss. "Do you know what I want to try right now?"

"I'll do anything," he whispered. "Try anything. Say anything. All you have to do is ask me. Write it down. Send me an email, a text, a letter. Fly a banner in the sky. What do you want?"

"Take a shower with me."

His eyes slid closed, and he nodded. "Yes. Yes, I will take a shower with you."

Kate yanked her clothes off while he stood there, his eyes squeezed shut. "Hurry up, Haley," she whispered. "I promise I won't rush you this time."

......⁊⟡⟜......

The Wilmington Ice House was just a few minutes away from Figure Eight. When they left the rink, both of them were complaining about sore legs and Quinn was whining about a bruised tailbone, but Kate felt free and happy even if she was going to have some serious regrets in the morning. She had chickened out in the shower earlier when his hands had moved down too far, and the hardest thing she had ever done was stop him. He had been *so close*, but her mind had suddenly become overwhelmed with doubts. She knew she hadn't made nearly enough progress dilating, but she wanted him to make her feel the way she had that morning. She wanted to make him feel that way too. It felt like every inch of her skin was alive and aware of him, her heart so full of love that nothing else in the world could ever matter. Even though they hadn't done more than touch and get incredibly clean, it had been the most wonderful shower of her entire showering experiences.

"You hungry?" he asked, before they got in the car.

"We just ate three hours ago," she replied with a laugh. "But go ahead. I know you are."

"Worked up an appetite," Quinn said, smiling, then giving her a wink. "If you're going to make me do sexual Olympics later, I figure I might need nourishment."

She choked, her face turning red. "Sexual Olympics? God, don't get your hopes that high."

"I'm teasing." He brought her hand up and kissed her knuckles. "We don't need to do anything, you know. I don't want to hurt you."

Kate sighed. "I just don't want to disappoint you, Quinn. The doctor said it was okay for me to try things, and I really want to try things."

"Do stuff?" he murmured, squeezing her hand.

"Lots of stuff," she confirmed, blushing.

"I promise, no jousting."

"You're never going to let me forget that are you?" she said ruefully. "Maybe one day you'll get to joust, Haley. Don't retire your lance just yet."

He laughed, big, deep laughs that burst out of him all at once, and she couldn't help but laugh with him. She had never imagined being able to joke about this, and she knew that she wouldn't be able to do it with just anyone. Probably never her mom or Jon. Definitely not her dad. She felt comfortable enough with Miranda, and now Quinn, though Miranda liked to push things. He had always been able to make her laugh, and she'd always been able to make him laugh. That was one of the reasons she loved him. Not just for his looks, though those hadn't hurt a thing.

"You're a nut, you know that?" Quinn said, his laughs

subsiding to chuckles, his expression wry with amusement. "I can't wait to joust with you, McGuire."

She couldn't help but look down at the ring on her hand for what had to be the thousandth loving gaze. "My parents are going to freak out when they see this."

"I already told your dad what I was doing. He did freak out." Quinn glanced at her. "Then he gave me his blessing but said that if I really proposed to you, he'd kill me."

Kate laughed. "If shotgun weddings were still a thing, there's no way you'd get out of this, you know. We're keeping you forever, Quinn."

He covered her mouth with his, kissing her possessively. Hungrily. When he finally broke away, his green gaze told her how much he really wanted to joust, and she wanted that too… or whatever was in between until she was whole.

"That's a good thing, kitten. Because I'm keeping you forever too."

Epilogue

Six months later

ATLANTA WAS ON FIRE.

Not literally, but Kate felt like she was melting as she dashed around the kitchen with a fresh bottle of raspberry sauce, trying not to attract the attention of her instructor, Chef Corbin. He critiqued everything from the way students chopped vegetables to how their tuna steaks were seared, but Kate loved the challenge and energy of his class. Today they were plating cheesecakes. She endured much good-natured teasing from the other students for positioning so hard as a teacher's pet, but overall she loved her classes. It was a good thing, because the other half of her heart was currently in Durham, getting his MBA. Quinn had agreed to take a position with Knight Developers but only if he had enough experience to back up getting the job. After a lot of conversations about it and more waffling than was probably normal, Kate had moved to Atlanta in the fall. She was full-time adulting with an off-campus job, a full load of classes, and her own apartment with her very own roommate.

"Time!" Chef Corbin yelled.

Everyone stopped what they were doing and moved away from their workstations. Kate fidgeted nervously at the bare cheesecake she had been about to decorate before realizing the sauce they had was empty.

"Put it on," her partner Sam hissed.

Waiting until the instructor's back was turned, Kate hurriedly drizzled the sauce over the cheesecake, then placed a raspberry and mint delicately on the side of the plate. A few of the students glared at her, but most of them were doing the same thing when he wasn't looking.

Sam's fingers twitched as the raspberry rolled down the plate and landed in a glob of sauce, but Kate slapped his hand back as it began to move.

Chef Corbin moved down the line, inspecting their plates. He passed by theirs, his brow twitching when he glanced at Kate. They both breathed a sigh of relief as he moved on.

"Next time make sure the bottle is full," Sam whispered.

"Just because you're a guy doesn't mean you aren't capable of getting the supplies," Kate whispered back. "I was supposed to be doing the cheesecake. You were in charge of plating."

He grinned. "Was I? Guess I got distracted by those baby blues again."

"Ha ha." Kate had never encouraged Sam to flirt, but he did it anyway. She cleaned their workstation, because he always ditched her for cleanup, then headed out to the parking lot and immediately began fantasizing about someone throwing a gallon of ice water over her head. The heat in Wilmington was tempered by Atlantic breezes. In Atlanta, the breeze only brought more heat and humidity. Sitting in traffic was even worse. By the time she made it to her apartment, the air in her car had brought the temperature down from hell to purgatory. Her parents had given her multiple lectures about being safe in the big city, so when someone knocked on her window as she was trying to get her backpack, she screamed until she saw who it was.

Quinn.

She was out of the car in seconds, ignoring the heat and sweat as she wrapped her legs and arms around him, scaling him like he was a tree and she was a chimpanzee. He laughed and hugged her back as she covered his face in kisses, not even getting close to his mouth.

"God, I missed you," he groaned.

"What are you even doing here?" she asked. "It's the middle of the week."

"I told you. I missed you." He gazed down at her, a huge smile on his face. "I had midterms, so I'm done the rest of the week."

She realized his shirt was damp with sweat, and she stepped back, making a face. "How long have you been here?"

"Three hours."

"Ugh. In this heat? You should have called me," Kate said, wiping the sweat off her face. "I should have picked a school in New York."

"I got to see you. Totally worth it."

"Well, come on before we both melt." Kate grabbed his hand and tugged him upstairs, where thankfully her roommate Sara had turned the air conditioner down low. They had recently hung blackout drapes that helped reduce some of the heat that poured through the windows. The only downside was it made the entire apartment incredibly dark.

"Sorry," she said as she fumbled to find the wall switch. "I usually leave one of these on."

Quinn blinked as he took in the apartment. "You guys redecorated."

"You like it? We call it vampire with a side of necromancer."

"Very emo. You mind if I take a shower? Back sweat and swamp ass... ya know?"

"And... that is gross. Yes, you may take a shower. I need one too, but I'll let you and your swamp ass enjoy this one alone. You want some lunch?"

"Please. I'm starving." He kissed her, then she watched as he pulled his shirt off and headed toward the bathroom. "Sandwich would be great. If I eat anything hot, I'll probably puke right now."

She made him a sandwich, which he promptly devoured when he came out. While he ate, she took her own shower, then he told her about his classes and his job working for Knight, which he seemed to actually like. He had finally met his sister, and Kate was sorry she hadn't been there for it. Apparently it hadn't gone well and she still wasn't speaking to William. Then Quinn's gaze fell on her hand, and he frowned.

"Where's your ring?"

Kate tugged a necklace out of her shirt and showed it to him. "We can't wear jewelry in class. I keep it on here until I leave." She slipped the ring on and leaned across the counter, giving him what she hoped were sexy eyes. "You don't have anything to worry about. My lady parts are all yours."

"Damn right they are. But I'm not going to say my man parts are yours, because it just sounds weird," he replied, grinning.

"Seriously. Do you think I would cheat on you?" The smile slipped from his face, and Kate was floored. "Quinn, even if I wanted to, which I don't... it's not like I can. I mean... not without having a really long and awkward discussion about it first, which I'm sure would be such a turn-on."

He reached across the bar and took her hand, his thumb grazing the ring. "It's not that. I guess I just get scared sometimes that we moved too fast. Not for me… but for you. You just turned nineteen. I worry—"

"I love you," Kate said fiercely. "And I love this ring. I'm happy, Quinn. Really. Are you?"

"I miss you." His hand tightened over hers. "This is harder than I thought it would be, staying apart so much. I am happy except for that."

Kate felt pressure build up behind her eyes, and it seemed to emanate from within her chest. "I miss you more, Haley."

"Not possible." He pressed a kiss to her fingers. "Love you, McGuire."

Her heart simply turned to mush when he said those words. "I love you too, Haley."

Quinn smiled, but she could tell that it was only to make her feel better. "So, do you still have this weekend off?"

"Yeah? Why?"

"I was thinking we could go somewhere. Just the two of us."

"Like?"

"How about New Orleans?"

"It's hotter than the hubs of hell in Atlanta, and you want to make it worse by going farther south?" Kate laughed.

"But…," he murmured, moving around the counter. "I want to take my future chef on a food tour, and I have tickets to a culinary thing you mentioned two months ago."

"A culinary thing?" Kate bounced into his arms. "You got us tickets for Wanda Waguespack?"

"You said she was your favorite television chef. And I called to make sure it was okay for you to go in since you aren't twenty-one. They said since you were a student, they would make an exception."

"Best boyfriend ever," Kate whispered. "You're going to love it. Thank you, thank you, thank you. Are we driving down? Because I can totally bail on my life if we need to leave early."

"And stopping to pee every two hours? Hell no. We'll fly out. I already got the tickets."

"Cocky much?"

"Want to find out?" He gave her one of those smiles that affected all her girl parts. All of them. Even the ones she didn't have.

"Uh... about that." Quinn's brows rose. "I want to. You know I do, but... I'd need access once a week, and I don't think we can keep up that much travel."

"W-weekly access?" he sputtered.

Kate's face heated. She began to stumble her way through an explanation. "This is going to sound stupid and... weird... but if I start having... you know... then I stop, I either have to keep doing that... or keep having sex. And dilating is no fun."

Quinn cracked up, then sobered when he saw her humor was just a cover for the awkward information she'd just handed him. At the end of the summer on Figure Eight, he'd put the brakes on the physical stuff when she started crying after their first failed attempt at sex. He hadn't hurt her... not like Jacob... but it had hurt. More than anything it had been frustrating. So they both agreed to wait until she finished dilating until trying again, but it was nerve-racking moving in to a new apartment with a roommate who had no concept of a closed door.

"Penile visits," he repeated with a straight face. "So you need my penis to visit you every week, or you have to keep doing that?"

She nodded. "And it sucks."

"We could incorporate that. I don't mind."

His grin made it impossible for her not to return it, but she knew he was teasing and she loved him for it. "Idiot."

"But you love me enough to *demand* weekly penis visits."

"Omagah." Kate covered her face. "You're impossible."

She sighed as he scooped her up and placed her on top of the counter, and she immediately began touching wherever she could reach, letting him do the same.

"You."

Kiss.

"Are."

Kiss.

"So."

Kiss.

"Adorable."

She pinched him. "I am not!"

"Completely adorable, McGuire. I'm sorry. Facts are facts." He kissed her deeply then, his hands threading through her hair. "And I love you and your adorableness so much that I flew all the way down here to see it."

Kate suddenly wanted to be skin to skin with him in the cool, air-conditioned apartment, under her blankets. She wanted them to smell like him, but right now he smelled like the salon shampoo that Sara used. "Take me to bed, Quinn. Now."

His gaze flared, and he yanked her off the counter, keeping her legs wrapped around him as he walked down the hallway with her, kissing her. He set her down on the floor and helped her tug her clothes off before taking off his own, then they slid beneath the sheets, touching and kissing, each of them greedy and gasping.

"I love you, Kate," Quinn whispered against her skin. "God, I love you so much."

Kate let him take the lead, trusting him to be gentle. To know when to stop. If it didn't work this time, she was going to be crushed again.

I'll do better. I have to do better.

His hands trailed low, and Kate opened for him, meeting his gaze.

"Stop?" he questioned.

She shook her head, then moaned at the light touch he gave. It was always the same with him. He could just kiss her, and it would lead to this nearly uncomfortable arousal. He hadn't touched her there since the first time they tried to make love. He pulled back, gazing into her eyes as his fingers delved gently past her folds, back up to the little swell that made her moan. He didn't try to push himself inside her, but she wanted him to try. She twisted her head side to side, too embarrassed to ask for what she wanted.

"You're so wet," he whispered. "You feel so good, Kate. You're so beautiful. Especially here."

She cried out when he pressed the heel of his palm down, rubbing against her in just the right way. She felt that five times now familiar tingle building in her lower stomach, making her tense all over.

"I want to taste you."

The words immediately evoked an image… a sensory grenade as he continued to graze her body with kisses. She didn't usually speak during these encounters… she wasn't sure dirty talk was sexy when you weren't officially capable of having sex. Just having orgasms. It was only him… only Quinn who could make her feel this free.

"Yes," she moaned. "Please."

Quinn reached over and turned on a small lamp next to her bed, and she almost told him to turn it back off, but she wanted to watch. The light illuminated his wide shoulders as he blazed a path, ever downward. She wanted to close her eyes but found that she didn't want to miss a moment as he explored her, his teeth grazing her occasionally then soothing the sting with his tongue. He wasn't shy with his body the way that she was, and he wasn't shy about making demands of her. He pressed a kiss to the inside of her knee, and Kate gasped, her fingers sliding into his hair as he trailed down, stopped, then switched to the other leg, starting at the same spot. She felt like she was on fire, unable to get close enough. She wanted more of him. All of him. If she could wear his skin, he wouldn't be close enough. Unable to concentrate on everything he was doing… his fingers rolling and flicking against her nipples, his mouth on her legs that he'd slung over his shoulders. Her heart was pounding so loud she felt a pulse inside her head.

"Are you ready, Kate?" he rasped against her, his cheek resting against her leg as he looked up at her.

Looking down at him, she was suddenly afraid. Self-conscious beyond belief.

"Kiss me. Please."

"I'm going to, kitten." His smile nearly melted away all her doubts.

"No, I mean…" She tugged on his hair gently. "Come here. Just for a minute."

He crawled back up her body, his erection bobbing between his legs unashamedly. She stroked him as he kissed the corners of her mouth, enjoying his hiss of pleasure.

"Do… do you like this?" she whispered.

Quinn groaned, pressing his lips to her throat. "I. Love. It. Don't. Stop."

His words crushed the uncertainty she felt, at least momentarily.

"I thought you wanted to taste me."

He froze completely, sucking in his breath as he looked down at her in shock. Without further prompting, he slid down the length of her again and hooked his arms around her thighs, pulling her legs over his shoulders again. One stroke of his tongue and she was on fire. He groaned against her, and it was pure madness. Another, then another, and she couldn't have recited her own name. She moaned, thrashing beneath him as his arms tightened over her legs to hold her in place. Her differences niggled at the back of her mind, but in the moment, she didn't care about anything as long as he didn't stop. One big hand came up to toy with her breast, sensitive and begging for attention. The climax that slammed through her was intense and endless, and she cried out his name.

Her chest was heaving as she finally managed to raise her head to look down to find him watching her, and embarrassment finally cut through the haze of arousal.

"I don't mean to brag," he whispered against her thigh, "but that was the best one so far, wasn't it?"

She linked her fingers through his and tugged him upward. "If it gets better than that, Haley, I don't know if I can take it."

He laughed, moving over her. "At this point you could probably wink at it and I'd be done."

She slipped her arms around him as he settled on top of her, giving her his weight. Her eyes closed as she felt him press against her. She was sensitive, but the blunt head of him felt good against her, so she wrapped her legs around him, cocooning him as he bit out a curse. The sensation of his hot, hard length against her was too delicious to describe.

"I want you." She threaded her hands into his hair, locking gazes with him. "I love you, Quinn. I want you inside me so much."

"Are you... do you want to try...?"

"Yes." She felt like her face was on fire. "I... uh... I asked someone like... me. They said to try it with me on... top..."

"Okay."

He rolled onto his back, pulling her over his body. She was nervous, afraid she was going to do something wrong.

Afraid of disappointing him… again. The girl she had spoken with had said some positions were not comfortable for girls with MRKH, especially at first… the missionary position being the most uncomfortable because of the amount of pressure.

"I watched a video on how to do this, but you may have to help me," she confessed shyly.

His eyes widened. "You watched a what?"

"Shut up, Haley." Kate bit her lip to keep from laughing. "You're going to ruin the mood."

"I don't think there's a chance of that. I'm going to need details later. Website names. We can watch it together. Critique their style." His grin slipped as she leaned forward and reached down to position him.

He closed his eyes as she lowered herself, his breathing roughening. It wasn't perfect. She probably wasn't even halfway dilated, but when she moved he groaned, his gaze meeting hers. He placed his hands on her hips, helping her find a rhythm. Panic set in after a few moments that he wasn't going to be able to come, but then she realized…

She was having sex.

With Quinn.

And he was *enjoying* it, and that was the biggest turn-on and ego boost she could have ever received.

She knew he wasn't thinking about her differences because he'd gone frantic against her, not gentle at all, but it was perfect and beautiful, and she let him take over, holding on tightly until the end. Her heart gave a quiet shout of joy as she watched him climax, loving the expression on Quinn Haley's face more than anything in the world. His heart pounded against hers as she collapsed against him, his mouth meeting hers in a sweet, carnal kiss.

She pushed away the doubts that cropped up, knowing that they had both enjoyed it and that was all that really mattered. Not that she couldn't give him everything the way that Roxie could. She felt his love and returned it. The cool air in the room kissed her skin as he left the bed to get them a washcloth to clean off with. He covered them both with the blanket, then wrapped his arms around her and pulled her close. He pressed his lips against her temple, and they lay quietly for a while, his hands skating over her skin. She wanted him again. She suspected that it would always be like this... her craving him and never getting enough. Never close enough. Never deep enough.

"You're awfully quiet." He shifted so he was slightly above her. Caught the trail of two tears as they skipped down her cheeks. "Did I hurt you?"

"No." Her voice was hoarse. "It was perfect. Thank you."

He smiled gently. "You did all the work, McGuire."

She just looked at him, and began to worry. To hope that it would always be this way... that it would always be enough.

"Two years is a long time," Quinn said. "Tell me you want me to transfer down here, and I'll do it."

Kate blinked at him, wiping away more tears. "What about Knight Developers?"

"My dad said the business isn't going anywhere. I still want to get my MBA, and I can get that anywhere." Quinn dropped back down to his pillow and sighed. "You deserve this time alone to spread your wings if that's what you want, but I just miss you so much and I worry about you all the time."

"I'm okay, Quinn. Really," Kate said. "I've made friends. I even met a couple of girls here in Atlanta who have MRKH, and it's helped me figure some stuff out. I don't need a babysitter."

"Ouch." Hurt flared in his eyes. "Say no more."

Kate placed her arms around his neck when he tried to move. "But I want my boyfriend with me twenty-four hours a day, seven days a week, three hundred and sixty-five days a year if that is what he wants. Not because he's worried I'm going to defenestrate myself if Chef Corbin doesn't like my crab cakes."

"That asshole didn't like your crab cakes?"

"Hated them." Kate smiled. "If you want to move your penis closer to me, I'm totally fine with that."

"Right now?" He wiggled his hips. "I will totally move my penis closer to you, Kate McGuire."

"What if my mouth moved closer to your penis?" She couldn't believe she said that. It had just popped out, but she liked the way his eyelids closed and he groaned. Maybe she would start thinking up things to say to shock him.

"I would support your decision."

Her hand trailed beneath the covers. "I think we have a second to that motion."

Quinn caught her hands and pinned them over her head. "Tell me you love me."

"I love you so much Quinn Liam Haley," Kate whispered.

"Order me to move down here," he murmured, lowering his mouth to the center of her breast. "Tell me you can't live without me like I can't live without you."

She moaned as his lips brushed over the sensitive peak. "Move to A-Atlanta." She gasped. "I want to wake up with you every morning. Sleep by your side every night."

"Tell your roommate to start looking for someone else. I don't want to share you with anyone."

Kate couldn't speak at that point, because his hands were all over her, and she found that her own were now free. She would have agreed to anything as long as he didn't stop.

Yes, she had changed after her MRKH diagnosis. But she had found that Kate in love was capable of changing, again and again and again. She would always want to make herself better for him. To love him the only way that she knew how… with all her heart and hopes and dreams. They didn't talk about the future. About the children they would never have. There was plenty of time and tears for that later.

She only wanted to live in the moment, with the love of her life, and chase every happy ending that she could find with him.

Because in the end, love was all that mattered.

And it was everything she needed.

A Note from the Author

If you felt moved by this story... loved it... hated it... please take the time to leave a review.

This isn't based on a true story. My life is, for the most part, too boring to be recounted in a book. Everything here is made up except for some of the things that happened to the character in her life. And the fact that my husband compares my arm length to that of a Tyrannosaurus rex.

Like Kate, I was diagnosed with MRKH, but I was much younger. I was fifteen when my grandmother found out that I'd never had my period and decided I needed to go see a doctor. From what I remember (I blocked most of this stuff out), he actually diagnosed me that day and wanted to perform the procedure himself. He was genuinely excited to have such an unusual "condition" come into his office, as were all the doctors that followed. My mom ended up taking me to see several specialists. I had my chromosomes tested, and they didn't explain what that meant. Until I was in my twenties, I assumed they were testing to see if I was male or female. All of this was before the internet was widespread, and there was no literature available to us. We were only able to go off the information the doctors gave, which was limited. The exams were extremely painful and embarrassing. I was already an introvert, but that pulled me more into myself than ever before.

A few months before my scheduled surgery, I met the man who would become my husband. I still think to this day that if we hadn't fallen in love, I wouldn't be alive. I was extremely depressed, but he made me feel good about myself. He lifted me up. He made me laugh. I always had doubts in the back of my mind. I was paranoid that one day he was going to find a "real woman" who would give him children. We've been married for eighteen years now, and I still love him just as much now as I did then. The doubts are still there, but not as loud as they once were.

I never did have that surgery. The night before it happened, I freaked out. The doctors only gave the procedure a seventy percent chance of working, and the side effects sounded gruesome. They brought their young medical residents in to see the sixteen-year-old girl who was missing her vagina. I had a breakdown and left the hospital.

I didn't know about dilation then. I wouldn't find out about it until I was nearly thirty years old. After I got married and moved away from home, I went to my local library and stealthily researched what I could on the internet. I cried in the middle of the library as I searched for what was wrong with me. I found a public forum about girls with MRKH, but I didn't want to talk about it with strangers. I buried my feelings, and I tried to move on. Tried to accept myself. I avoided going to the doctor, coming to tears anytime I was asked when my last period was. I had to explain what MRKH was to the doctors and nurses. Every. Single. Time. Most of them thought it was "cool." I think I was twenty-eight when I requested my medical records from OKC and went to see a doctor in Shreveport, Louisiana. He gave me the basics of dilation, which I had already read about online. I bought a dilator set from a website, went home, and figured things out on my own.

The purpose in writing this story wasn't to titillate. The inclusion of sex at all was only because of comments posted by various people online about people like me—one in five thousand women born with this condition—who had no control in how they were born. The comments found in Chapter 12, while not verbatim, are representative of actual things that human beings wrote about women with this birth defect, and reading those words at thirty-five were hard enough. I can't even imagine a newly diagnosed fourteen-year-old (or younger, or older) reading those words. You can't control online trolls, but you can control how you react to them. I was nearly done with the book, waffling on including sex or not. After seeing those comments, I gave those jerks a mental middle finger and went for it.

It was a balancing act, making the character old enough to deal with these issues but to also make a hero who would be mature enough to handle them. I hope I did it justice. I crushed the timeline quite a bit. In real life, I'd never expect for a girl with this condition to come to terms with MRKH so quickly. The truth is, most of us never come to terms with it. I've known for over twenty years now, and I still can't believe it sometimes. I still wish that I was normal.

This story has undergone many changes. It was never originally supposed to be about them as young adults at all. In the original conception, they were much older. They fell in love, then they were driven apart. I sent this off to be edited and categorized it as contemporary romance. I was informed that the story was new adult fiction, which I had never heard of before. So in the middle of edits, I read a few new adult books and realized my editor was exactly right. I attended a workshop a few weeks later, ripped the book apart, and began to stitch it back together.

There are, to my knowledge, three other works of fiction that deal with MRKH: *Rokitansky* by Alice Darwin, *Elizabeth, Just 16* by Cecilia Paul, and *The Girl with No…* by R.J. Knight. I've only read the first one and found it moving and heartbreaking. I wanted to write something uplifting. Something funny (at least I thought my jokes were funny), and with a HEA. I intend to read the others once I finish this book (at the time of this author's note, I'm currently finishing edits).

To all the girls out there dealing with this condition: it does get better. You are strong, and you are not alone. You are one in five thousand.

For more information about MRKH, you can visit the Beautiful You MRKH Foundation online at www.beautifulyoumrkh.org or find them on Facebook at www.facebook.com/BYMRKH/.

And please follow me or feel free to reach out!

Social media:

Facebook: www.facebook.com/tsmurphyauthor/

Instagram: www.instagram.com/tsmurphyauthor/

Twitter: www.twitter.com/tsmurphyauthor

Website: www.tsmurphyauthor.blog/

Acknowledgments

I truly would not have been able to complete this book without the support of my husband. I love you, even though you make short-people jokes and started calling me T. rexy. Thank you for believing in me, and not complaining (too much) when I forgot to make dinner, wash your underwear, and pay the bills. To Mom, for showing me how to be strong, even when it isn't easy. Thank you, Dad, for giving me a warped sense of humor. It has certainly come in handy at times. To Grandma Dorothy, for being sassy as hell, telling me like it is, and teaching me how to play cards.

I would also like to thank my editor, Anne at Victory Editing, and her team. Without them I would probably still be banging fruitlessly at the keyboard and all my commas would be in the wrong spots.

My gorgeous cover was designed by Marisa Wesley of Cover Me, Darling. Thank you so much for answering my endless questions and for the beautiful cover. I loved it so much that I wrote a special scene just for the book!

A final thanks to my high school English teacher, Mrs. Wilkins, for planting a seed. I am so glad that it finally started to grow.

About the Author

T.S. Murphy originally hailed from a tiny town in Oklahoma that most people have never heard of. She now lives in Louisiana with her wonderful husband of many years, a herd of cats, a pack of dogs, and a sweet bunny rabbit named Jim. When she isn't tending to her animals or husband, she's working in her garden or chained to a computer writing. In her spare time, she likes to donate forty hours per week to the anonymity of corporate America in exchange for a paycheck to fund writing-related expenditures.

Printed in Great Britain
by Amazon